Praise for

FINAL JUSTICE

About this Samantha Wright thriller:

"This novel hits the ground running...rushed action and steamy romance...fast-paced story...genuine suspense. Samantha Wright is a sassy and independent heroine."

Publisher's Weekly

"...a remarkably well-written novel. It's tightly plotted, fast paced and keeps moving all the way through to the end. The author has obviously done his homework and is able to deliver an historically accurate novel and plausible speculation of what might be...James Miller has crafted a cast of very real characters...a terrific novel that keeps you going until the very end Whether you are a conspiracy fan or not, you'll get a kick out of this one. The only disappointment is that it's over too soon."

Inscriptions Magazine

"A sensitive and well-written novel. A gripping climax and twists and turns in the plot keep you glued to the story. A highly readable work."

Sharpwriter

"FINAL JUSTICE is a remarkable act of story telling. The characters are vivid, recognizable, and absolutely logical. The plots pulls the reader along, irresistibly, unraveling a complicated storyline with simplicity and intensity... The details are engaging (and impressive), and the over-all concept is compelling. If you love a good storyline, you'll love FINAL JUSTICE. If you love a mystery, you'll love this book. Unforgettable."

Darlene Bridge Lofgren

"A page turning, thought-provoking, action novel from a Washington D.C. insider who really knows his meat–political thrillers. The hidden premise springs from the military and political conspiracy surrounding the assassination of JFK who perpetrators are, it's slowly revealed, still incestuously at work in the tribe of government agencies. The action begins in the present just as the new U.S. President is about to nominate a blustery anti-military senator for Secretary of Defense, a nomination that's suddenly withdrawn in favor of the chilly chief of a multinational corporation deeply involved in the international arms business. Enter Samantha Wright, a marvelous character, a leading expert in the U.S. military budget, a senior assistant to the rough-riding senator who lost the toss, and her sidekick, Daniel Garcia, a passionate, tough reporter. Together they are propelled through the Washington power temples and the nefarious arms trade, grappling with an ever-deepening web of intrigue that reveals the assassins of JFK—conspirators in high places who will stop at nothing in their covert war for profit, prestige and power. A great read."

Mollie Gregory
Author, EQUAL TO PRINCES, PRIVILEGED LIVES, TRIPLETS,
and WOMEN WHO RUN THE SHOW—How a Brilliant and
Creative Generation of Women Stormed Hollywood

"Among contemporary novelists, James Miller has the rare ability to take issues of broad social significance and weave them into compelling page-turners. In Final Justice, we are treated to a plausible scenario in which richly drawn characters must overcome the Machiavellian conspirators behind JFK's assassination. FINAL JUSTICE grips readers from page one and holds us in suspense as it masterfully unwinds to its thrilling conclusion."

Ira Spector
Author, LAST CHANCE,
A MONTH OF SUNDAYS,
and Contributor to CHICKEN SOUP FOR THE SOUL

"Former Securities and Exchange lawyer, James Miller, has written a political-action thriller that examines the corrupting influence of big business, particularly the military-industrial complex, in shaping our national destiny. It reads as if it were ripped from today's headlines."

Loraine Despres
Author, THE SCANDALOUS SUMMER OF SISSY LEBLANC,
THE BAD BEHAVIOR OF BELLE CANTRELL,
and THE SOUTHERN BELLE'S HANDBOOK

Final Justice

A Novel

James Robert Miller

FINAL JUSTICE

For additional copies of this book go to:
www.rp–author.com/miller

Robertson Publishing
59 N. Santa Cruz Avenue, Suite B
Los Gatos, California 95030 USA
(888) 354-5957 • www.RobertsonPublishing.com

For the love of my life, Nancy.

THE BEGINNING
Charleston, West Virginia
May 10, 1960

Senator John F. Kennedy stood ramrod straight, smiling like a schoolboy, waving at the enthusiastic crowd. It had been a grueling primary campaign through the poverty-stricken state. At first he had balked at the demand from his campaign manager and younger brother, Bobby, to get up at four-thirty in the morning to press the flesh of the West Virginia voters one last time.

But now he was pleased that he had fallen for Bobby's subterfuge. On this day of the all-important primary vote, he had not been forced to stand in the predawn darkness to grab the calloused hands of the weary line of hardened men drudging by on the way into another coal mine. No, his brother had arranged a surprise: a final campaign rally of over five thousand ardent supporters, cheering and clapping. They energized him for the hours of waiting and anticipation to follow.

But as the presidential candidate from Massachusetts left the stage with a final salute to the frenzied crowd, suddenly he knew, instinctively, deep in his political gut, this primary had been won. He need not let the day ahead be consumed by election apprehension. Now he could plan with certainty the management of the momentum that would gain him the nomination of his party, and then hopefully carry him on to the White House.

And so he could afford to return to Washington in a few hours as his wife wanted. It would be good to respond to her request for an afternoon and evening away from the campaign.

Elated, Jack Kennedy headed back to the hotel that served as his West Virginia headquarters. He decided the morning would be perfect if he could grab an hour or two with an eager, vigorous young woman. As he passed his beaming brother on the stairs leading down from the platform, Jack leaned over and thanked Bobby for the unexpected pleasure of the exhilarating rally. But Bobby's smile faded instantly when Jack added in a raspy whisper that he was going to take a couple of hours for some "r and r."

"Jack," Bobby pleaded. "Not now! Everybody will be watching, scrutinizing your schedule."

Jack Kennedy smiled the smile that the whole nation would learn to adore and winked. "Tell them I'm resting for the rigors ahead, Bobby. See you when I'm feeling better." With that, the next president of the United States carefully negotiated the last two stairs and eased himself into the back of the waiting limousine for the short ride to his campaign hotel.

The Beginning Of The End
Abilene, Texas
May 12, 1960

The two men marched briskly into the brass-paneled elevator cab. They abruptly turned as one and stared straight ahead, the older one neatly folding his hands before him. The younger man held a thick brown litigation-style briefcase close to his side. The older man's narrow, steely eyes shifted uncomfortably toward a tall black man standing erect in the corner of the elevator cab, his right hand resting on the elevator's control lever.

A wide smile crossed the black man's face, "Where ya'll goin' today, gentlemans?"

"To the top, the fifth floor Board Room," the younger man replied flatly.

His older companion glared at the floor indicators above the doorway and muttered, "Indeed."

In a coordinated move, the elevator operator reached out with his white gloved left hand and pulled the main door closed, then pushed the expandable screen protector back across the opening. With the simultaneous pull of the control lever with his right hand, the elevator slowly, noisily began to rise.

"Quaint," the older passenger observed with no attempt to conceal his contempt. The biting sarcasm was a product of his unconditional belief in his superior intellect, but deep down perhaps also the defensive mechanism developed by a man of slight physical attributes. He was a mere five-foot three, the same as when he was twelve years old and other kids called him puny. He weighed one hundred twenty-five pounds distributed on a slim frame. In his late forties, his once thick jet black hair was rapidly thinning. The close-cropped sides had turned all gray. His nose was square and flat. It looked like it had been pushed in pushed in by a fist, as indeed in had on more than one occasion in his youth.

Standing beside the small man in the cramped elevator, his companion appeared much more substantial. In fact, he was of average build, stood five-foot eight and weighed one hundred and fifty-five. But age made a difference. At twenty-seven he carried himself with youthful assurance and rigid confidence. He constantly reminded himself to stand tall and straight, work at being more imposing. The work paid off. He looked solid. His severe crew cut, popular at the time with the Ivy Leaguers, added to his no-nonsense veneer.

At the fifth floor, the elevator ground to a halt. Before the operator could fully open the old doors and the protective screen, the two businessmen charged out of the cab. They moved so quickly to the entrance to the board room of the First Commerce & Business Bank of Abilene that they were out of hearing distance when the black man said, "Ya'll take care now, ya' hear."

J. Kingston Wittlefield, Chairman of the Board and Chief Executive Officer of the Mid-American Manufacturers Company, stopped abruptly at the open door and glared at the five stacks of documents neatly aligned in the center of the oval rosewood table. "Ovals make no sense," he stated emphatically.

"I beg your pardon?" Wilbur Mullen replied.

"The table, Wilbur," Wittlefield explained, exasperated. "Ovals have less work space than rectangular tables. Remember that. Another example of not paying attention to the details. No wonder we have to bail out these people."

"Yes, sir. I see the point, Mr. Wittlefield."

Wittlefield walked to the table and reached for the first stack of documents. "Everything set..."

"Yes, sir," Mullen interjected.

"...and double checked."

"Absolutely."

"No carbons?" Wittlefield demanded.

"All originals, clean, no erasures, proofed and re-proofed. A set for both companies, both law firms, and one for the Bank," Mullen explained.

"Fine." Wittlefield glanced down at his watch. "They are supposed to be here right…" Wittlefield watched the second hand on his silver plated Longines and silently counted—four, three, two, one. "Now!"

Silence fell over the room as the two men from Mid-American Manufacturers stood together, alone.

Mullen looked at his watch, then compared it to the time on the freestanding grandfather clock in the far corner of the room. The bank's clock was slow by eight minutes. "I advised them of the need for punctuality," Mullen said, a hint of apprehension creeping into his voice.

Wittlefield smiled. "I'm sure you did, Wilbur. You can't be held accountable if others simply won't heed…"

Wittlefield turned at the sound of approaching footsteps in time to see a large, heavyset man stroll through the doorway, hand outstretched, a warm, broad smile filling his face.

"Wilbur! Great to see ya'," the man exclaimed, directing his attention first to the younger man before fixing his sight on the older one. "So I finally get to meet the boss. How the hell are you, Wittlefield? Damn important to put a face with a voice. Can't believe we've put this whopper of a deal together over the phone, 'cept of course for your good man Wilbur here who dragged his ass down here to God's country to work out the details." The large man grabbed for Wittlefield's hand and started to shake, then brought his left hand around, grasped Wittlefield's arm and pumped some more.

J. Kingston Wittlefield stood erect, staring upward at the jovial man. "Most efficient, don't you agree, Mr. Cranston, what with you down here, and me busy running our shop up in Chicago? The telephone was the best way to proceed until we cut the deal."

"Yup," Cranston replied. "Telephone's fine, up to a point. But I'll tell ya, Wittlefield, down here we like to take the measure of a man face to face. Nothin' beats lookin' a man in the eye," he slapped Wittlefield on the back. "Now listen here, I'll have none of that 'Mr. Cranston' stuff. Everyone calls me Jake. Rightly so. I'm just a glorified mechanic."

5

"A mechanic who patented the gear-less rotor bearing assembly that dramatically increased the maximum rotation of the rotors on a helicopter—an invention that for the first time gives helicopters the capability for real speed," Wittlefield allowed a genuine smile to cross his face.

"Got that right!" Jake Cranston agreed. He finally stopped pumping Wittlefield's hand, but kept the much smaller, older man firmly in his grasp by balancing his thick arms on the other man's shoulders. "Had a big chunk of luck with that one. And now we'll both benefit—my copter company with its nice bunch of patents, and your money—hells, bells, ain't nobody gonna beat that combo."

"Then it's all agreed," Wittlefield said casually, diverting his eyes past Cranston to a line of men filing into the room.

Cranston finally released his hold on Wittlefield and swung around to face the twelve men. "Boys," Cranston boomed, "this here is the financial wizard, Mr. J. Kingston Wittlefield. And Wittlefield," Cranston went on, waving his arms and around the room, "these here are the boys who really make Cranston Helicopter go. Hell, I'd be nowhere without 'em."

Wittlefield gazed upon the sullen assemblage standing along the walls of the room. No smiles emanated from the top management of Cranston Helicopter, save the solitary broad grin that remained fixed on the face of the founder, President and majority shareholder, Jake Cranston.

"Welcome, gentlemen," Wittlefield addressed the group. "Welcome to the growing family of companies of the Mid American Manufacturers Company. By coming together in this acquisition, er, merger, we are building the crucial financial strength and industrial diversity that is going to put us ahead of the competition in the challenging days ahead."

"Well said," Cranston responded, firmly slapping the older man on the back. Then Cranston's smile disappeared. "But there is one point the boys here wanted me to bring up before we sign off on all this damn paperwork."

Wilbur Mullen looked over at Wittlefield and silently communicated by raising his eyebrows. Wittlefield showed no sign of recognition. He calmly asked Cranston, "And what is that?"

"Well," Cranston began, "it's just that some of the boys here don't understand why you can't put down in writing what you've told me time and again over the phone—that their jobs are secure. Ya' understand. They need to know they can count on the new company the way they counted on me. You know, just set it down in writing that we're gonna be sure the management team of Cranston Helicopter stays together."

Wittlefield smiled, fixed his steely eyes squarely on the first man nearest the door, and then in succession looked at each man as he went down the line gathered around the oval table. When he spoke, it was with apparent conviction. "I would like to do nothing more, Jake, but unfortunately, the legal eagles say we simply cannot be quite that formal. Is that not so, Mr. Mullen?" Wittlefield asked, pointing toward his junior associate.

"That is correct, sir," Mullen said, weighing in with own hard stare. "Mr. Wittlefield asked our law firm if there was any way, and we reached the conclusion that it cannot be done. You have to understand, Mid-American Manufacturers is an old and venerable firm, steeped in tradition. The original corporate by-laws proscribe employment contracts. My research into the history of the company shows that the founders thought that the way to keep your job is by doing your job. It was as simple as that."

"Can't you just change the by-laws?" one of the helicopter men spoke up.

Wittlefield shot a glance at Mullen, and Mullen took the lead. "As a matter of fact, the by-laws could be changed. It has never come up before, because the management employees of Mid-American have always been satisfied with the way they have been treated. But the by-laws could be changed by a two-thirds vote of the shareholders. That would take six, maybe eight months before the proxies could be cleared through the Securities and Exchange Commission, and the votes tallied."

"Whoa now!" Cranston exclaimed. "We can't...ah don't want to wait that long for this here deal to go down."

"And there is no reason to wait," Wittlefield answered. He turned to Cranston, looked him in the eye, and spoke reassuringly. "Jake, you know my position. We want to keep your management team together and see that your company becomes our best, most profitable subsidiary. All your people have to do is keep doing their jobs, and we'll all gain. All our jobs will be safer than ever, as part of the stronger, bigger, more profitable Mid-American Manufacturers family." Wittlefield looked over the unsmiling members of Cranston's management team, and smiled again. "And later, if somebody wants to change the by-laws, we can take a stab at it then. After all, you and your share-holders are going to own twelve percent of the stock of Mid-American. That's a fine start on a shareholders vote."

"Damn straight," Cranston replied.

"Good." Wittlefield reached over and extended his hand to Cranston. "Let's have at it then, shall we?"

The men from Cranston Helicopter leaned in around the oval table and watched solemnly as their President, Jake Cranston, signed the first original of the "Agreement of Exchange of Securities and Merger, by and between The Mid-American Manufacturers Company, a Delaware Corporation, and the Cranston Helicopter Corporation of Texas." As one complete set of documents was signed by Cranston, he shoved the four-inch thick pile over to Wittlefield, who in turn started signing where required, while Jake Cranston began signing the next duplicate set of documents. The process was a lengthy one, for not only were signatures required at the end of the Agreement, but also the initials of the signers had to be placed at numerous points within the over six hundred pages of documents.

At the conclusion of the fifty-minute process, Cranston stood and again grabbed Wittlefield's hand and pumped it heartily. Wittlefield, in turn, appearing small and almost child size in the grasp of the large Texan, congratulated Cranston and his colleagues on the solid business arrangement. Cranston asked all the men present to be his guests at the Lone Star Country Club for a celebration lunch.

Wittlefield motioned to his attorney to gather their copies of the Agreements. He looked down at his watch, then up at Cranston. "No, thank you," he said curtly. "It's time to get back to work."

Wittlefield and Mullen first headed toward the elevator, then with Wittlefield leading the way, detoured to the down stairway. "Stairs," Wittlefield said, "are more efficient than that antique elevator. As they left the lobby of the First Commerce & Business Bank Building onto State Street, Wittlefield glanced at his watch, then looked up and down the lightly traveled street.

In a moment he spotted the shiny black Cadillac limousine racing down the wide boulevard. The car pulled up to the curb. The driver catapulted out of the car to hold the rear passenger door for the two men.

Wittlefield got in first, followed by Mullen and his cumbersome briefcase. As he entered the plush rear compartment, Mullen waved away the driver's offer to put the briefcase in the trunk. Struggling to sit and hold on to the bag, Mullen lost his balance and fell first to his knees, and then collapsed flat on his face into the thick royal blue carpet.

"Shit, I thought you said he was a smart young fuck," Wilbur Mullen heard the thick south Texas accent as he struggled to right himself.

Wittlefield laughed. "That is not exactly how I said it, Lyndon. I described Wilbur F. Mullen here, attorney at law with the prominent Chicago firm of Carlton, Smith & Mills, as our rising star."

"Dammit, son. Then rise off the fuckin' floor and let's see if you can shine like a star," demanded Lyndon Baines Johnson, Majority Leader of the United States Senate.

Mullen pushed himself up with both arms and slid onto the jump seat facing the rear of the limousine. He pulled the briefcase to his side, took a quick breath, then reached out to shake the hand of the powerful Texan. Johnson kept his hands stuffed in his pants pockets and leaned back, his cold steely eyes examining the man before him.

"In fact, Lyndon, Wilbur here is a rising star from your own Lone Star state. You might not guess it, now that he's been Yale educated, but he was a poor boy, a scholarship boy, from Beaumont. Poor as dirt, as I believe you say so charmingly down here."

A massive, Texas-size smile lit up Lyndon Johnson's face. "You got that right," he said. "Beaumont's the home of dirt poor in Texas. Shit almighty! Hottest fuckin' swamp in the state. At least your boy Wilbur here was smart enough to get the fuck outta there," Johnson said, lifting one hand out of a pocket and loudly slapping his knee.

Mullen started to speak, but Johnson cut him off. "Nothing wrong with a Yale education so long as you remember where ya' came from and always remember why you left. Beaumont! Maybe we can do some bidness."

"No doubt in my mind, Lyndon," Wittlefield said firmly. "Mullen here did a solid job on the Cranston Helicopter acquisition. It is exactly what we needed—a huge foot in the door to the aerospace and defense business."

"Got that right, Wittlefield," Johnson exclaimed. "That's where the money's gonna be made. We gonna start spending what we should, get the country strong agin'. And Wittlefield, you aren't gonna be sorry ya' took my advice—those little fuckin' heliocopters you just bought are gonna be perfect for fighting this war that's coming. Everybody's gonna make money at it, just so long as..."

"So long as what, Lyndon?" Wittlefield interjected.

"So long as we win this next damn election," Johnson replied. "And we sure as shit should, with my help, even if it's for that rich Harvard boy who just kicked ass in the West Virginia primary. Of course, I'm gonna make 'em sweat a bit at the convention, but I can count votes better'n anybody, and unless he steps on his pecker in broad daylight in the middle of Times Square, it sure looks like we're gonna nominate Kennedy in Los Angeles in a few weeks."

"Now, Lyndon," Wittlefield interrupted, "don't you worry about Kennedy. I know old Joe, and Joe's son is going to do just fine. I got Joe's word on that before I threw my money his way."

Lyndon stared coldly into Wittlefield's eyes and spoke slowly. "Covering all your bets, Kingston?"

"The only smart thing to do, Lyndon."

Silence fell over the car as Johnson turned and gazed out at the bleak countryside racing by. Suddenly he turned back to his passengers and smiled warmly. "One more thing, my friends. Best be sure Texas gets the lion's share of your bidness."

"Understood," Wittlefield said. "And to be sure it's done right, I'm bringing some young, loyal and very energetic new talent into the company, and into, make that back into, Texas."

Mullen looked at the two men. "Wondering what's up, Wilbur?" Wittlefield asked.

"Always interested in your next move," Mullen replied.

"Simple." The tycoon turned to Johnson. "Lyndon, I am going to save this young man from a life of drudgery at his Chicago law firm. Meet the new President of the Cranston Helicopter subsidiary of Mid-American Manufacturers." Wittlefield smiled at Mullen. "Wilbur, I think it is all too apparent that our Jake Cranston is tired and wants to have more time to enjoy his country club."

The guests in the back of the limousine remained silent for the drive to the airport as their host spoke, uninterrupted, about the coming prosperity for the nation, and most important, for Texas. Nothing could, nothing would, stop it now. Lyndon Baines Johnson was now too powerful for anyone to get in the way of his plans for Texas.

At the airport, as Wittlefield and Mullen got out of the limousine, Johnson reached over and pulled Mullen forcefully back into the car. "What kind of pissant name is Wilbur, son?"

"I'm not exactly sure where it came from..."

"You got a another name, Mullen? A middle name?" the Senator demanded.

"Yes I do," Mullen answered. "It's Franklin."

"Franklin! Outta Beaumont, I'd expect a Franklin to be a colored boy. But what the hell? Just shorten it up. Frank. That's a man's name."

The most powerful man in the United States Senate virtually pushed Frank Mullen out of the car. As the door slammed shut, Lyndon Johnson grabbed the bottle of sour mash bourbon from the fully stocked bar, half filled a crystal goblet, and took a long drink. As his car pulled away from the airport, he looked out at the barren plains and envisioned new factories, assembly plants, highways and overpasses. He knew with certainty that just as nothing had interfered with the dreams of this dirt-poor boy from Texas for unbridled power, now nothing could cut into his dreams for the other crucial part of his personal equation for success—big money, serious money. Big-time wealth, that was what Lyndon Johnson had set his sights on, and the time had arrived to fulfill those dreams.

THE PENTAGON
Arlington, Virginia
July 9, 1961

Lt. Colonel Harry Howard, United States Army, marched crisply down the side aisle of the two-hundred-seat auditorium, pivoted left, and took command of the podium positioned squarely at center stage. He gently tapped the microphone to confirm it was live. Subconsciously, he rapidly moved his right hand to his throat insuring that the tight Windsor knot held the muted black tie rigidly straight. From there his hand passed quickly down over the front of his olive green uniform jacket, feeling the row upon row of brightly colored service ribbons, each carrying its own story of heroic times past. Times past, he thought, but not all that much time. Just ten years in the hot spots of the world, defending freedom, holding the line wherever, whenever, duty called: Inchon,'50; Lebanon '56; Indochina,'60. Without looking, he knew the feel of every medal and ribbon, each a reminder of a good fight fought. The quick touch assured him that all was in order.

His penetrating green eyes stared coldly out at the audience. "Gentlemen, welcome to the concluding meeting of the Army Contract Board for Tactical Air Ops—Rotor Ascendancy/Counterinsurgency Equipment. The Contract Board wishes to thank each bidding company for adherence to the 'time is of the essence' directive issued with the Request for Proposals and for having submitted thorough and comprehensive materials. The Army has concluded that there is no higher priority in the furtherance of its assigned counterinsurgency tactical responsibilities than the rapid completion of the design and development phase for the combined close air-to-ground combat attack and ground troop support helicopter. This must be followed immediately with the commencement of full scale production and delivery to the possible fields of operations."

Frank Mullen looked up from the thick three ring binder resting on his lap and nodded ever so slightly. His information had been correct.

Lt. Colonel Howard paused. His eyes darted away from the prepared text. He thought about talking to the men assembled before him—man to man. He could emphasize how vital their work would be in providing the equipment necessary to defend the bulwarks of liberty. Defense against the constant, growing menace—the threat always from the damn Russians, and now from the Chinese and their sinister Oriental cousins, of every type and from every corner of that vast continent. He wanted to shout to the audience of businessmen that their duty was important—to provide the fighters with the essential tools for combat. He looked about and noticed the old men, the flabby men, the soft men sitting before him. He had observed them as they shuffled into the basement auditorium in the bowels of the Pentagon. Dull men, he feared, the corporate equivalent of the contemptible government bureaucrats now filling some of the key slots in the military hierarchy. But one stood out—young, solid, a "can do" man. That was the report on him, and having readily picked him out of the crowd, Lt. Colonel Howard could see that Frank Mullen was the right man. He sensed these things. Mullen was short, but with a taut frame and a sturdy face. His hair was cut short on the side, military style. Mullen looked reliable. Howard liked what he saw. As for the rest, he was wasting his breath.

The Lt. Colonel returned to the text before him, and quickly read the directive. "Accordingly, the Contract Board requires a final summary statement from each of the seven bidding companies. The statement must address the issue of the bidder's capability from a financial, technical, and facilities perspective, to commence large-scale production immediately upon completion of the design and development phase. The Board requires that each statement last no more than five minutes. We shall begin in reverse alphabetical order with U.S. Aero, Inc."

As the Lt. Colonel took his seat alongside five other uniformed officers sitting in the center of the front row, four men rose from the second row of seats, and jointly approached the podium. One moved cautiously to the microphone. His three heavyset companions stood behind, one man nonchalantly stuffing his hands in his pants pockets; the other two casually turned pages.

"As I understand the question," the President of U.S. Aero, Inc. began, "you want us to discuss how quickly we can complete the design and development of our prototype, and then begin the actual manufacture." He hesitated. "The answer to that is, ah, somewhat complicated by not knowing at this point the findings that will arise from the testing of the design." He glanced behind him. "I think what I'd like to do is have our Vice President for Research discuss the issue from his perspective..."

Frank Mullen slowly moved his right hand to his mouth and discretely covered a slight yawn. He glanced over at the six army men in the front row. He could not help but smile when he noticed that Lt. Colonel Howard had similarly moved his hand to his face in a gesture Mullen interpreted as an attempt to hide his boredom.

After five minutes, thirty-five seconds, Lt. Colonel Howard rose and advised the representatives from U.S. Aero that their time was up, and that despite their pleas for additional time to augment their arguments, in the interest of fairness to all bidding parties, strict adherence to the five minute time limit would be required.

Accordingly, thirty-six minutes later, the Contract Board called on the seventh and last bidder to be invited to address them. Frank Mullen, President of the American Helicopter Corporation, strode confidently to the podium, leaving behind on his seat the thick binder. He adjusted the microphone and spoke directly to the Army officers.

"An award of the Air Tact Ops Contracts 61—Design, Develop and Deploy—to the American Helicopter Corporation would be fortunate indeed for our company and for our growing and deserving community in Texas." Mullen paused, not wanting to move too quickly past the emphasis on the state where the vast economic impact of the contract would be felt. "But the award would also be most responsive to the Army's own requirement for 'time is of the essence' capability. American Helicopter will not stand alone in its commitment to rapid performance. As everyone in this room is aware, we are a part of the multi-industry, multi-resource family of AMERIPRO companies. Yes, building upon our long history of manufacturing excellence as Mid-American Manufacturers, we have now combined that unparalleled know-how and 'can do' determination, with the most advanced technical capabilities and financial strength. As our new modern name implies, we at AMERIPRO act pro-actively for American progress. We do not wait for events to come to us. We boldly go forward, planning and building for the future, and by such conduct, make our own future. That is why," he said, pausing for emphasis, "with AMERIPRO's growing financial resources, we have been able to prepare for this moment. We have state of the art design and testing facilities for our helicopters at the Abilene testing grounds—" Mullen quickly nodded to the row of uniforms—"which each of you has had the opportunity to inspect. But American Helicopter, with the vast resources of AMERIPRO, has also completed the largest, most technologically superior helicopter manufacturing facility in the world. Encompassing over one hundred and twenty-eight acres, it simply has no rival in the world," Mullen stated confidently, looking about the room at his would-be competitors. "Through the AMERIPRO worldwide network, we have insured a totally reliable supply of all necessary raw materials, machined parts, and tool and die equipment–anything and everything required to move swiftly, efficiently, and massively into supplying all the needs for America's military might."

Mullen made eye contact with each of the officers of the Army Contract Board. By his estimate he had spoken only two minutes. The rehearsal time, knowing the specific final question to be addressed and that there would be a strict five minute limit for the responses, had proven to be a valuable advantage. Now, after the almost forty minutes of unrehearsed remarks preceding him, Mullen knew it was time to conclude on terms the military men would appreciate.

"American Helicopter and AMERIPRO stand ready to meet the call of duty, and to meet, or beat," he said emphatically, "all schedules for performance as ordered by the Army." Mullen had used his student deferment to successfully avoid military service and go right from college to law school. He thought about saluting, but then instinctively decided that would be overdoing it. He pushed his shoulders back, nodded to the row of officers, and marched back to his seat.

Lt. Colonel Harry Howard quickly returned to the podium and advised the representatives of the seven bidding companies that the Board would convene in closed session, and would announce it's decision within the hour. Participants were invited to wait, or to receive the decision by telegram later in the day. As the Army officers left the auditorium, each group of helicopter company executives broke into quiet discussion. The President of American Helicopter sat silently, alone.

Twenty-two minutes after departing, the Army Contract Board re-entered the auditorium. Lt. Colonel Harry Howard returned to the microphone and announced the winning bid. Frank Mullen showed no emotion as his company received its first contract in excess of one hundred million dollars. He rose from his seat and went over to shake the hand of each officer of the Contract Board. He asked to whom he should direct his comptroller so that the proper invoicing and billing procedures could be established for the Army's payments under the contract.

Frank Mullen ignored the line of limousines waiting to transport the losing corporate executives to National Airport. Mullen simply walked to the first waiting taxi and directed the driver to head to the airport, but stop at the first available public telephone.

J. Kingston Wittlefield, as usual, answered his own phone at the Spartan corporate offices of AMERIPRO in downtown Chicago. He did not react to the news of the contract award but noted, "of course, you did a solid job, Frank." Then Wittlefield moved on to the balance of his agenda. "Two more things as long as you're down in Washington."

"Yes, Kingston?" Mullen asked.

"The Vice President would like you to see him."

"When?" Mullen responded.

"Now. He's in his office."

"His office?" Mullen asked. "At the White House?"

Uncharacteristically, Wittlefield laughed, almost heartily. "No, Frank. Not The White House. I'm afraid our friend Lyndon doesn't like the atmosphere around there all that much. He's much happier away from the Kennedys and up on the Hill—up with his old Senate cronies. You'll find him at his office on the Senate side of the Capitol."

"Very well, Kingston," Mullen responded.

"And Frank?"

"Yes?"

"After Lyndon is through with you, line up an office for AMERIPRO in the city. Make it near The White House—walking distance. Small, private. Things are going to be active down there, and I want us to have a presence in D.C. It will be more efficient that way. Line up a corporate rate at the Hay-Adams, too. It's an efficient, small hotel across from Lafayette Park."

The conversation ended, as usual, with the click of the phone. Mullen had learned that talk beyond the immediate business at hand was not efficient.

Midday traffic along Constitution Avenue was light and moved along easily until the usual congestion caused by tourists at the White House. Mullen had spent little time in the Washington area, and most of that in the Virginia suburbs at the Pentagon. As he headed up this wide, historic boulevard, with the Capitol dome looming high on the hill in the distance, he liked what he saw. Wittlefield, as always, was right. This place was where things were happening and money would be made. He remembered his last meeting with then Senator Lyndon Johnson and he remembered how far he had come from the dirt poor days in Beaumont.

———— ∞∞ ————

Johnson sat on the sofa, his long, thick legs propped up on a massive marble coffee table, a telephone pressed tightly to his large, fleshy ear. Mullen entered and stood quietly, until Johnson motioned for him to sit at the side chair less than an arm's length away.

"I know, darlin'. That is terrible. Mr. Hoover simply does not have the proper respect for our Attorney General. J. Edgar is just one incorrigible rascal." Johnson paused, intently listening to the voice on the other end of the telephone. "Yes, darlin'. That is exactly what I'm gonna do–give this the benefit of some of my best thinking, see if I can help work this out–be a peacemaker. See ya tonight. Bye now." He hung up the phone.

"Well fuck me!" he exclaimed, giving out a hearty laugh. "That's the best one I've heard all week." He reached over and grabbed Mullen by the arm. "Absolutely nothing better to lighten up a day, ah... ah..."

"Frank, Mr. Vice President."

"That's right. Frank. Got rid of that Wilbur crap. Took some good advice there, didn't ya?"

"Pleased to do so, Mr. Vice President."

The Vice President held up his left hand, while continuing to hold Mullen firmly in his grasp with his other hand. "No. I tell ya' what I want from you, Frank. You're just gonna call me Lyndon—same as old Wittlefield does. I don't much take to the vice president label. Jack Gardner was right—ain't worth a bucket of warm piss. And don't buy that bullcrap story that Gardner said bucket of spit. I was fuckin' there when he said it, son, and he said piss, and he meant it. But goddamn, that was a good one I was just hearin'. Nothing like yet another story 'bout that pissant Bobby shooting himself in the dick agin'. Just because his brother makes him Attorney General, Bobby thinks he can take on ol' J. Edgar. Well, fuck me!" Lyndon Johnson roared, first slapping Frank Mullen hard on the knee, then gripping the knee in a vice-like hold.

"All right. Enough fun," Johnson said, his expression turning serious. "We got ourselves two pieces of bidness. First," he lowered his voice, and looked carefully around the spacious corner office. He pulled a small, plain note card from his pocket, and handed it to Mullen. Mullen quickly glanced down, seeing a line of numbers, some single digit, some double, each interspersed with dashes, twelve numbers in all.

"You deliver that to Wittlefield in person. Next time you see him. In person, you understand?" Lyndon asked in a manner leaving room for only one answer.

"Certainly, Mr. Vice…"

Lyndon Johnson painfully tightened his grip on Mullen's knee.

"Er, Lyndon…" Mullen corrected.

"That's more like it, Frank ol' buddy," Lyndon said, leaning back in his chair and finally releasing Mullen from his grasp.

"And second. Your heliocopter company down there in Abilene needs some more help—that is if it's gonna punch out the number of units we all are gonna need to chase down the slant eyes out there in the Asian jungles."

"Of course…" Mullen started to respond.

"You need a good man. Kingston will find him one hundred percent reliable. Guy's gotta take early retirement. Such a goddamn straight shooter he tells anybody what's what. Diplomacy's not his style. Not his fault some of those starch shirt Pentagon bigwigs don't like the sound of the truth. Anyway, best for him to move on."

"We pay pretty fair…"

Johnson's glare fixed on Frank Mullen. "He'll pull down a flat fifty-five grand—Kingston may have to up that later," Johnson said. "But fifty-five's the number for now. You all gonna find him to be a very valuable asset. Rough around the edges, that's for sure, but he's exceptional, tough, and he's accomplished more in a short period of time than just about anybody—'cept maybe you. In fact, that's what you two have in common–real wonderkids.

Both you pissants gotta be 'bout the same age. You both started with nothing—dirt poor. But now look at ya'—Wittlefield took you under his wing, and you've gotten to be a big shot in bidness real fast. The guy I'm talking about," Johnson beamed, "he's been the fastest promoted guy in the Army since crazy ol' Doug MacArthur."

Johnson laughed heartily for a moment, then stopped. "And about as popular with his superiors." He leaned in real close to Mullen. "But he's a true patriot, Frank, That's what this country's gonna need more than ever now—tough, true patriots." Johnson looked Mullen up and down. "I know we can count on you, Frank—Wittlefield guaranteed it."

Mullen didn't hesitate. "Absolutely," he replied enthusiastically.

Johnson smiled. "Of course, money still makes the world go 'round, Frank. And big challenges require lots of money. That's what you and Kingston are good for." Johnson leaned back in the sofa, reached up with one hand and slowly pulled on one of his enormous earlobes. "So now this fella's gonna expand beyond the strict confines of the military bureaucracy. Know what I mean, Frank?" Johnson stared coldly at Mullen, leaving the corporate executive with the clear feeling an answer was not called for.

"Ya see," Johnson explained, "he's mustering out in thirty days. Colonel Harry Howard."

Frank Mullen felt something he hadn't felt in a long time. He had learned from Wittlefield, "never let them see you sweat. Let them think you have ice water in your veins. That's the way to do business." Mullen thought ice water, but the thoughts could not stop the beads of perspiration from forming at the edge of his hairline.

Johnson stared hard. Mullen thought the man was reading his mind, penetrating his inner thoughts, seeing him sweat. He had to shake it. He had to say something. Slowly, the words formed.

"Thirty days? That would not be very subtle..."

A slight smirk crossed Johnson's thin lips. He spoke, but the lips hardly moved. "Son, I don't fuck with subtle. I play the power game. Harry Howard is your newest man on the payroll down there in Abilene, and I don't give a shit if that ain't too subtle. The only thing I give a shit about, son, and I do believe the only thing our friend Wittlefield gives a shit about, is that you understand one thing."

Mullen hesitated, thinking ice water, willing the droplets of sweat on his forehead to go away. "Yes?" he said more calmly now, "what is that, Lyndon?"

"There are places worse than Beaumont."

The Vice President of the United States softly patted Mullen on the knee, then with a wave of his hand he dismissed Mullen and picked up the telephone. At the door, Frank Mullen put his hand to his forehead to dab away the sweat.

WASHINGTON, D.C.
The White House
August, 1963

The Attorney General of the United States entered the Oval Office through the concealed doorway in the west wall, taking a vigorous bite from the lemon eclair he had grabbed from the President's private kitchen. He glanced back to make sure that the door had fully retreated into the wall, then looked around for his brother. The lone figure at the far end of the room leaned backwards against his desk, facing one of the elongated bay windows looking out onto the White House grounds. Only someone extremely close to the President would know the significance of the arms placed behind his back, the hands meeting at the base of his spine, pressing inward, then relaxing, then pressing again.

Robert Kennedy had learned to avoid commenting directly on his brother's debilitating back pain, even when they were alone. The President did not want anyone to draw attention to the disability, and besides, the pain was one of the few things the two could not share.

"Good morning, Jack," Bobby Kennedy greeted his older brother.

President Kennedy turned very slowly, attempted a smile, but the pain forced him to wince instead.

"Anything I can do?"

"Sure, Bobby. Sneak Judith in here to give me a back rub."

This time it was Bobby's turn to wince.

Then, a real smile crossed the President's face, followed by a laugh. "Only kidding, Bobby. I've learned my lesson. The last time with that broad was the last time. Period. No more." He paused, gazing straight ahead. "Besides, maybe I'm getting old.

Some of the excitement has worn off. It sure isn't like the old days out on the campaign trail."

Bobby nodded. "Jack, it's a smart move. We've got enough problems around here without making more for ourselves."

"Or without letting your friend Mr. Hoover make problems for us, isn't that what you mean?" Jack asked.

Bobby Kennedy's face turned a light shade of red, his expression contorted. "Fuck the old fairie," he spit out.

"Now that is an unpleasant image to conjure up on this otherwise fine morning." The President laughed again, walking slowly toward his brother and the rocking chair next to the sofa in the sitting area of the room. As he came within reach, Jack Kennedy grabbed his brother by the shoulder, and patted gently. "Get over it. We're stuck with Hoover, and he's stuck with us."

"Until after the reelection," Bobby replied.

The President sighed. "We'll see, Bobby. That's all I can say. But I've got more important items on the agenda than J. Edgar." The President clung to Bobby's arm and moved slowly, carefully, to the rocking chair. He held on to him as he painstakingly eased himself down, collapsed into the chair, tears of pain momentarily filling his eyes until a quick brush of his hand swept them away. "I'm moving about as well as the old man," he joked.

"I don't know about that," Bobby retorted as he relaxed into the couch. "Dad's getting around okay in the wheelchair since the stroke. Maybe you should try one," he added, attempting, unsuccessfully, to match the lighthearted note in his brother's voice.

"No," the President replied with a genuine laugh. "I'm not ready for the wheelchair quite yet." He paused. "I miss being able to run things by the old man." The thought lingered between the two brothers until Jack went on. "Got a few more things to handle, including this festering mess in Vietnam."

Bobby frowned, and reflexively looked about the Oval Office. He lowered his voice. "Jack, you have got to stop this thing, before it's too damn late."

Jack held up his hand. "Hold on, Bobby. I didn't ask you to come over to rehash Vietnam. It's all right. I've made up my mind."

Bobby softly pounded his fist on the arm of the sofa, waiting for his brother to continue.

"I'm going to pull our men out," Jack said firmly, "all the way out. We'll give the Vietnamese supplies, we'll give them whatever weapons they might be able to use, but we're going to get American boys the hell out of there. You're right, Bobby. It would be a bloody quagmire."

Bobby leaned forward, and clasped his hands, holding them together like a prayer. "Great, Jack. We can't fight this war for them. They're going to have to do it themselves. How are you going to deliver the message to McNamara and the Joint Chiefs?"

President Kennedy smiled. "Timing, Bobby. Timing is everything. Not right now."

"Jack, you've got to. You've got to turn this thing around."

"If it's going to stick, if we're really going to get our guys out once and for all, then I have got to be reelected. Our good friend Mr. Goldwater may not look so strong today, but if I announce we're changing course before the election, he'll have a field day. I can hear it now. 'Kennedy's soft on communism. Kennedy's going to let the dominos fall all the way to Waikiki.' I'd be handing the Republicans just what they want. It could well be a winner for them."

"I don't think so," Bobby replied. "You're popular out there. The people will be with you on this one, if you explain it to them."

"You might be right, Bobby, you might be wrong. This country is conservative–scared to death of communists. It wasn't that long ago that our old man's pal Joe McCarthy had every one looking under their beds for commies. It's too much of a risk. What I need to do is stabilize the situation, hold it together, make it look like we're staying the course for a year and a couple of months and get through the campaign."

Bobby shook his head. "I don't like it. We can't control what goes on over there. It could blow up, get out of control at any time. Some of our own damn people seem to want as big a war as they can get."

"Well, they're not going to get one! I'm not making the same mistake I made with the Cuban fiasco. I know I can't believe everything the military brass is telling me. Maybe they think I'm the one who's stupid. 'Body Counts'. Can you believe that they're trying to fool me with body counts," he said with a vehemence that his own brother had not heard before. "I just need a little more time to quietly retire more of those gung ho, nuke 'em types and move in some rational thinkers I can trust."

That pleased Bobby Kennedy. The Bay of Pigs and the near calamity of the missile crisis had taught that the escalation in Vietnam was a terrible mistake. He'd spent a year of analyzing and thinking privately, then he had started to speak up. Finally, his arguments had sunk in. He had changed his brother's mind by pointing out there were limits to the nation's commitments abroad, that they had to choose their battles very carefully, and that the jungles of Southeast Asia were the wrong place at the wrong time. Just as he was silently congratulating himself for having won over Jack, he realized that perhaps his own arguments had not carried the day. What had Jack just said? That he'd concluded some in the military were playing him for a fool. That you did not do to Jack Kennedy!

"I still think you're strong enough to go forward now," the Attorney General advised. "Announce it. Get it over with."

"No, Bobby. Not now. The politics don't work." The President rocked the chair fully forward to reach the table and grab the slim, unlighted cigar resting in the royal blue ash tray stamped with the gold Presidential Seal. Kennedy rolled the cigar between his fingers, turned it sideways and raised it to his nostrils, and inhaled. "Fine Cuban tobacco. At least that island does something worth fighting over," he laughed and leaned back in the rocker. "I need time. Maybe I can move sooner before the election. We'll have to see, Bobby. It's been a while since I've ventured out. Really pressed the flesh…gotten a feel firsthand of what's going on out there. If I'm as popular as you say, I'll feel it, and maybe then…

His thoughts were interrupted by a gentle knock on the north door leading to the adjacent office of his personal secretary. Mrs. Evelyn Lincoln entered and closed the door behind her.

"Yes, Mrs. Lincoln?" he asked.

"The Vice President is here to see you," she replied.

Bobby scowled.

"Thank you," the President said. "Tell Lyndon I'll be with him in just a minute."

"Of course, Mr. President."

When she had left the room, Bobby blurted out. "Worrying about Barry Goldwater? Worry about Johnson on this Vietnam change. He's the one who's gung ho to take on–as he so charmingly puts it–the 'slant eyed commies.'" He made no attempt to conceal his irritation.

The President sighed. "Enough about Lyndon, Bobby. Like Hoover, you're going to have to get over it." He let a hint of exasperation creep into his voice. "Lyndon is what he is. He'll toe the line on this one, like on everything else."

"But not without a fight, Jack."

"No, Bobby. Not without talk, and more talk, and more talk. Heaven knows that's what Lyndon does best. But when it comes right down to it, Bobby, that's all he is—talk. And Bobby?"

"Yes, Jack?"

"That is precisely what I'm going to let our friend Lyndon do—right up to our triumphant reelection. Let him talk like we're going to keep fighting the VC out in the jungle. The rightwingers will believe him, and he might even be able to deliver some of their votes. I don't want anyone to know what I'm going to do until I'm good and ready, and until we're safely back in this old house for another term. And then, Bobby, four years after that..."

"What, Jack?"

"Then you can fight it out with Lyndon for this precious job."

Bobby smiled. "And to what do we owe the pleasure of Lyndon's visit this morning?"

"Oh, he's here to talk about one of your favorite subjects— my reelection. Getting me back out there, pressing the flesh. I'm not thrilled with the idea, but I committed to Lyndon and John Connally last June when I was down in El Paso that I'd make another trip to Texas. If you can believe it, Lyndon wanted me to come down there this month for his birthday," the President let out a hearty laugh, and his brother rolled his eyes. "Well, I escaped August in Texas on his goddamn ranch, but I've agreed to make up for it by adding a day to a trip in November. Lyndon says we can fit Dallas in the schedule. So now, you and I are about to have a real friendly chat with my Vice President about me going down to Texas and getting an early start on the campaign. And Bobby? I want you to be real nice to Lyndon, for a change. I need his help to lock up Texas for '64."

Bobby Kennedy gave his brother a mock salute, and got up to greet the Vice President of the United States.

THE DEPARTMENT OF JUSTICE
August, 1963

As usual, the lights on the third floor burned brightly at the Department of Justice at 10:00 p.m. as the inner circle of tough, savvy, and idealistic lawyers met with the Attorney General. Most of them were veterans beyond their years of legal battles and political campaigns. All knew that legal rights were only as strong as the political will to fight for them, and so the coming political campaign was never far from the center of discussion with the President's brother and campaign director-in-waiting.

The roundtable expressions of the lawyers' fervently held opinions included one argument delivered with absolute certainty by a brilliant legal scholar only two years out of the Boalt School of Law at the University of California in Berkeley. She stood at the far end of the conference table leaning forward against the back of an empty chair. "The Vietnamese people, north and south, are no different from the Negroes in our South. They have been systematically oppressed by the western colonialist powers." One of the first female editors of the Boalt Law Review knew that the Attorney General of the United States agreed with her—any other opinion would run counter to all the fundamental principles of human rights and humanitarian goals he espoused at Justice. She did not worry about openly denouncing the current policy of the Administration. Her instincts told her she was saying what the Attorney General wanted to hear. "We must pull out of that war," she argued vehemently.

Robert Kennedy removed his already loosened tie and casually started to wind it around his hand. He smiled at the tall athletic brunette with the sharp, straight nose and full lips. Beauty and brains, he thought, and driven. He was no stranger to ambition, and yet seldom had he seen anyone so dedicated to getting

ahead and being known. He recalled how she'd challenged anyone in the Department to beat her at the fifty mile walk he had
personally led, and damn if she hadn't set the pace the whole
way through the Virginia countryside.

"Your convictions are, as usual, forcefully presented," Bobby
Kennedy reacted.

He looked around the room, and noticed that several of his
lawyers were nodding their heads in agreement. "You seem to
have captured the room," he observed, "just like the Department's physical fitness award." He glanced at his watch, then
stood up. "Just remember, you have to get elected, or reelected,
if you're going to be able to do what is right. Timing is everything in politics." Staring directly at the young firebrand, Kennedy broke into a broad smile. "I would not be the least bit surprised if the President agrees with you."

With that, the Attorney General of the United States decided
to call it a day fifteen hours after first entering his office. As he
left the room, he calculated that he had devoted roughly twelve
hours to enforcing the nation's laws and the other three on politics. In the coming months, he looked forward to reversing his
priorities.

Promptly at 11:15 p.m., the young lawyer stepped out from
the Ninth Street side door of the DOJ, and walked three quarters of a block back to Pennsylvania Avenue. The warm Washington summer night felt soothing and exhilarating at the same
time. She did not need sleep in this city at the center of power,
where all things were possible. She crossed Pennsylvania Avenue, walked a few more paces past the streetlight, waited only a
moment until she saw the familiar black limousine make a right
turn onto Ninth Street, following its usual course back from
Capitol Hill.

The car stopped and she got in. No disloyalty lodged in her
heart or in her head as she excitedly told the second most powerful man in Washington about her day. She had dismissed the
rumors about friction within the Administration. She knew the
Vice President to be a loyal member of the President's team. He
had assured that it was so. And, in his earthy way, he had been

very kind and helpful to her. She concluded her summary of her day with a verbatim recital of the last meeting with "Bobby's troops."

That night Lyndon Johnson seemed unusually attentive and charming, in his powerful way as he made passionate but quick love with the young Justice Department lawyer in the back seat of official limousine of the Vice President of the United States.

THE END

Abilene, Texas
November 22, 1963

Frank Mullen heard the distinctive high-pitched whine emanating from the helipad, looked up from the stack of production reports piled on his desk at the wall mounted clock. "Nine a.m. already," he thought. He had been at it for three hours, but had not made as much progress as he needed to justify taking the rest of the day off for the meetings in Dallas. Still, the business was nothing but government contracts, and the government, for all intents and purposes, was coming to Texas that day. He should hardly begrudge one day devoted to lobbying on his own Texas turf. It would be more efficient than another trip north to the Pentagon.

A firm rap on his door was followed by the entry of American Helicopter's senior test pilot, dressed in his crisp khaki aviator overalls. "Ready to fly, chief!" the pilot announced with authority. "Been some early morning showers, but it's clearing fast. Going to be a perfect day—perfect for flying and for presidential parades. And we're taking the newest model AMH-3 off the assembly line. I bet we beat our last time to Love Field by a full ten minutes."

"All clearances set for Love, Charlie?" Mullen asked. "They do have some special traffic coming in there this morning, you know. They're going to be pretty persnickety as to who flies in, and when."

"All set, Chief. President Kennedy's due at Love at 11:30, so as long as we get going now, we'll be okay. Colonel Howard made all the arrangements. Seems that when the Colonel speaks, the feds still salute. I think he's over in Dallas already."

Mullen looked down at the piles of paper on his desk. "Well, I guess I'm ready. But I could use another eight hours in this day..."

"So what makes this any different than any other day?" the pilot said with a smile.

"Only that I have to make time for the President and the Vice President of the United States." Frank Mullen looked down one last time at the reports showing the ever-improving capability of the American Helicopter division of AMERI-PRO to churn out very expensive and profitable helicopters. He smiled, stood up, grabbed his suit coat in one hand, and a slim, black briefcase in the other, and headed for the helipad. He looked forward to setting a new speed record for the flight from Abilene to Love Field.

The President of American Helicopter had no sooner fastened his seat belt than the whine of the tilted rotor blades above the cockpit intensified. The vibrations increased as the sound that had become so familiar reached the point that he knew the liftoff would follow momentarily. He had grown to truly love that instant when the ground fell away and his stomach prepared for the thrill of flight.

This day the feeling never came. Just as the AMH-3 was about to spin upward, the pilot eased ever so slightly off on the rotor controls, and pressed his hand to his earphones. He spoke loudly into the microphone dangling from his flight helmet, "Repeat again!"

The pilot turned and yelled above the whirling engines. "You've got a call, boss. Mr. Wittlefield."

Frank glanced at the clock on the instrument panel. "We're short on time, Charlie. See if they can patch him in on the radio."

Charlie passed the question on to the control tower. In a moment he turned back to face his passenger. "That's a negative, boss. He wants you on the phone."

"Duty calls, Charlie," Frank yelled. "Keep her warm. It probably won't take long." He unfastened his belt, unlocked the door, and jumped down, crouching low as he moved quickly under the rotating blades and away from the aircraft. When he got back to his office, the light on his private line was blinking.

"The trip to Dallas is canceled," Wittlefield announced firmly. "You stay there and go back to work. See you at the Washington office as planned next Monday. We have a lot to discuss. We must be sure you are prepared for the avalanche of business we are sending your way." The receiver went dead before Frank Mullen could respond.

Mullen stared out the window and down at the newest unit off the Abilene assembly plant, its rotors moving at idle speed. He buzzed on the intercom to his secretary, and instructed her to call the helipad and cancel the flight.

"Oh," his secretary responded. "You're not going to see the President?"

"No, Mrs. Jackson," Mullen replied flatly. "I've got too much paperwork to do right here today. Bring me in the test flight data report on the AMH-4 from yesterday." Mullen returned to work on the papers piled high on his desk.

DALLAS
12:25 p.m.

The motorcade moved along Main Street, passing the densely packed, smiling and waving crowds lining the route through downtown Dallas. As the line of cars approached Dealey Plaza, the lead car filled with Secret Service agents slowed for the right turn onto Houston Street. The slower speed made it easier for those in the President's open-air limousine and the Vice President's car two vehicles behind to enjoy the enthusiastic applause and cheers. As the lead car turned left from Houston Street on to Elm Street, the procession slowed even further, passing the Texas School Book Depository building at the pace of a walking man.

The wife of Texas Governor John Connally swiveled slightly in her limousine jump seat just forward of the First Lady and smiled a deep Texas smile. The Governor's wife gushed with enthusiasm matching the crowds' as she spoke to the passenger sitting behind her husband. "Mr. President, you can't say that Dallas doesn't love you," she said.

Jack Kennedy smiled back at her. "That is very obvious."

At slightly past 12:29, the President's car slowed for its turn left onto Elm Street, following the lead car and heading slowly down the curving avenue toward a railway underpass.

Less than one minute later, rifle shots rang out. At first the President reflexively grabbed for his throat. In time increments that would forever be analyzed in terms of individual motion picture frames, and the speed that one could move the dead bolt of a cheap Italian Mannlicher-Carcano rifle, fatal events transpired so rapidly that no one could, ultimately, provide truly definitive analysis to the difference between one second and the next. In time not much more than the blink of an eye, or a few beats of a human heart, President John Kennedy's skull exploded, blasting his head violently backwards. In another moment his torso slumped forward, and his body fell to the left.

Frank Mullen was interrupted by his secretary, Mrs. Jackson, at 12:48 Central Standard Time. She did not knock, as she customarily did. She opened the door and screamed out, "The President is dead. I don't know about Jackie."

Mullen sat, silently, staring at the hysterical woman. He sighed, then spoke calmly. "Now, now, Mrs. Jackson. I'm sure it's just some mistake, some sick joke. No one would want to shoot President Kennedy. And for sure, no one would want to hurt Mrs. Kennedy," he said to his hysterical secretary.

A New Beginning
White Plains, New York
November 22, 1963
3:05 p.m Eastern Standard Time

Samantha Wright waited for the school bus to come to a complete stop, and only then did she rise from her fourth row seat and walk down the aisle. The vibrant, sandy-blonde haired little girl stepped down to the sidewalk in front of a two story red brick duplex, then pirouetted, and smiled back at the bus driver. "Thank you, Mrs. Knight. See you Monday morning."

The bus driver smiled down at her youngest passenger. "Yes, Samantha. You have a nice weekend. And Samantha? Are you sure you're only three?"

"I'm three and a half, Mrs. Knight," the child proudly responded. "I started kindergarten early, so I get to go to first grade next year when I'm only four. Bye now!" Samantha said, carefully holding her lunch box as she skipped up the walkway to the front door.

Mrs. Knight laughed heartily. Then, having dropped off her last passenger, she reached down on the floor next to her seat, and turned on her transistor radio. It was a long, long time until she laughed again.

Inside the Wright home, Samantha ran to the kitchen, and placed her lunch box down on the dinette table. "Mommy it's me. I'm home," she called happily.

Samantha heard no reply. "Mommy? Where are you?" There was still no audible response. Samantha cupped her hand to her ear. She heard the faint murmur in the background. She listened for a moment, then yelled. "Yea! The television's on."

She raced up the stairs, and turned right to the little den. She entered the darkened room, looked at the black and white screen, and the solemn sounding newsman staring back from the television. Her mother was scrunched deep into the corner pillows of the old worn sofa, a white handkerchief pressed to her mouth. Tears were streaming down her mother's face.

"Mommy, Mommy," she called. "What is it? What's wrong?"

Mary Anne Wright looked at her daughter, and opened her arms. The child ran to her. In a minute, Samantha felt the tears falling on her head. She held on tightly as her mother softly sobbed, "Why? Why? Why?"

CHAPTER ONE

Four Decades Later
Washington, D.C.
The Russell Senate Office Building

Samantha Wright groaned, then leaned back in her chair and stretched her long legs straight ahead under the desk. She stared up at the ornate wood paneling on the fourteen-foot ceiling, clinched her fists, and started pounding on both armrests. "Aargh…" was the first sound through her tight lips, quickly followed by her shout, "That two-faced bastard!"

The matronly white-haired woman in the reception area ten feet away looked up from her computer screen, and back through the doorway. Samantha glanced down from the ceiling and froze under Mrs. Frederick's stare. Samantha attempted a smile, then slowly stood up and walked to the door. Her smile broadened as she reached out for the brass handle and began closing the door.

"Ah, sorry about that, Gertie. I'm a little stressed out today," she said.

"Do take care of yourself, Sam," Gertrude Fredericks replied. "I will. Don't worry," Samantha said, easing the heavy, solid door all the way shut. Samantha turned and leaped toward the telephone on the corner of her desk. She punched in the number, and paced back and forth, trailing the old-fashioned spiral telephone cord behind her. "*Washington Post* political desk," a voice answered.

Samantha snarled, "Get me Daniel Garcia!"

"Let me check," the voice said. "There's a staff meeting going…"

"Listen to me. I don't care about any staff meeting. You just get Danny boy on this line, and I mean right now!" Samantha demanded.

The voice hesitated, then asked calmly. "And who may I say is calling?"

"You tell Mr. Garcia one pissed off senior assistant to the Chairman of the Senate Armed Services Committee."

"I... I understand, Ms. Wright," the calm voice giving way to concerned recognition.

"Do it!" she said as the phone clicked once and was filled with the irritating chatter from Washington's number one rated all news/all talk radio station. Samantha caught only a few words before realizing the early morning talk show was devoted to the same story as the lead article on that morning's front page of the *Washington Post*—the impending announcement by the newly elected President of his choice for Secretary of Defense. The host seemed to be confirming the same rumor as the *Post*, that the President-Elect would nominate her boss, Senator Lou D'Angelo, for the top position at Defense. "That's just great," she muttered.

"Hey there, Sam," Daniel Garcia's chipper voice came on the line.

"Don't you 'hey there' me you conniving bastard," Samantha yelled into the phone. "How dare you? You... you... slimy reporter. You're just like the rest of the lot. Can't trust any of you."

"Samantha! Chill out, babe. What's got you so riled up?"

"I am not riled up, I'm pissed off! And don't you try that innocent boy bullshit on me. What do you think's got me pissed off? Your goddamn story, that's what!" Samantha took a breath, wanting to make certain that her genuine anger was also making the important factual point. "You used what I told you in direct violation of our agreement. No use, ever, of our pillow talk. I'll tell you one thing, Daniel, that's the last talk we'll have on a pillow, or anywhere else, for that matter."

Samantha turned back toward the desk and started to slam down the phone, but Daniel Garcia, enjoying his first front page article in the all-important *Post* was not about to let the rush fade away. "Sam! Stop! I plead not guilty. Read it!"

Samantha heard it, but could not believe he would keep up the pretense. "Read it?" she mimicked, bringing the telephone back to her ear. "I have looked at the goddamn article," she said, grabbing the front page from her desk. "It's right in front of me. 'D'Angelo Tapped For Defense.' All the stuff about how the President-Elect is ready to prove he's the champion of his 'new politics'—been conferring with the Senator about his dramatic plans for cutting the bloated Pentagon budget. Dammit, I told you that in strictest confidence."

"Sam, that's why I didn't use your information at all. Nada!"

"Come off it, Daniel. I'm all over the article, by implication."

"No, you're not," Garcia said flatly. "Not only are you not implicated, every one of my sources is identified, if not by name, by description. Read carefully. Hell, eighty percent of it came from the President-Elect's camp, and the rest from the Pentagon."

Samantha Wright spread out the entire front page of the newspaper and started reading again, holding the phone loosely to her ear.

"Every place I quote someone or attribute anything to anyone, I describe that person. The whole story came together without any need for any info from you, babe. In fact, I didn't need anyone at all from the Senate, other than your good Senator's obligatory 'no comment.' I quoted him at the end."

As Daniel kept talking, Samantha listened, leaned over, grabbed a marker, and continued to read, circling in yellow every reference to every source. Quickly she turned from the front page to the balance of the story on the inside. Her yellow marker kept going, and every time it circled a name, or a "person close to the President-Elect on the staff of the transition," or "a reliable source within the office of the Chairman of the Joint Chiefs."

"Samantha, are you still there?" the *Post* staff writer asked.

"Yes," Samantha replied, the distraction in her voice clearly recognizable. "I'm here, and reading. Hold a sec…"

A moment later the Senior Assistant to the Chairman of the Senate Armed Services Committee completed a more careful reading of the offending article. She stood up straight and tossed the marker onto the newspaper.

"It appears you may have a point," she observed reluctantly.

"May have a point?" Daniel shot back. "There is no 'may have' about it. You know I wouldn't violate your trust. But a deal's a deal. I'm free to piece together anything I want from other sources. That's all I did."

"Okay," Samantha acknowledged, the inflection in her voice instantly registering with him.

"Now wait a damn minute," Daniel Garcia teased. "Don't you go off in the other direction on me. I can put an important story together without you. You're *not* the only source in this town for high-level political comings and goings."

Samantha Wright laughed out loud. "Oh, if I wasn't sure of that before, I am now. Thanks for reminding me," she said, almost sweetly.

"You're welcome. Now, do you mind if I haul ass back to my staff meeting?"

"Go right ahead."

"And tonight?" Daniel asked.

She was about to respond when the door to her office opened, and the dark, still handsome face of Senator Lou D'Angelo intruded. Samantha noticed that the puffy bags under his eyes had all but disappeared. He had finally gotten some sleep. Samantha whispered into the phone, "Check me later, gotta go," and promptly hung up, and smiled, "Good morning, Senator."

She knew from six year's experience with him that she could determine the mercurial mood of the senior Senator from New York from his first greeting in the morning. The mood of the morning typically stayed all day, but it could be replaced by a wildly different attitude toward the world and the people in it the very next day. Please, she thought, if only he's waited to read the *Post* it'll be okay—give her a chance to explain what had actually happened. He hated leakers, unless, of course, the leaks were planted on his direct instructions.

"Good morning to you, Sam," the Senator exclaimed jovially. "Looks like it's gonna be a great one. Grab your coat. Winter has definitely descended on our nation's capital."

"Where we headed?"

"Down in the vicinity of the White House to the Hay-Adams," he said, breaking into a wide, beaming smile.

Samantha smiled too. "To the President-Elect's headquarters?"

"Precisely. The man personally placed the call to the house first thing this morning."

"The story in the *Post* is true?" she blurted out, instantly regretting it.

He laughed. "Looks that way. Hell, all the sources were from the transition team and the Pentagon. Sure am glad it wasn't one of us, puffing me up, floating trial balloons. I understand our new President doesn't care for end-runners any more than I do." He winked. "Come on now, let's go!"

"Am I invited, Senator? This is the kind of meeting I'm sure the President-Elect will want to decide who attends."

D'Angelo grabbed Samantha lightly by the arm, and squeezed gently. "Of course he'll want to talk to me in private first. But then I want you there to immediately start working with his people on the press conference, and start planning the move to Defense. We'll have to act fast, Sam. It's only fifteen days to the Inaugural. The man wants his cabinet in place pronto." The Senator released his friendly grip, and held his hands out in front of him in the talking-with-his-hands stance she knew so well. He leaned in close. "I'll grant you, he shouldn't have waited on his decision, but we all know my position on cutting waste and fat is controversial. Appears we do have a new thinker moving into the White House after all."

He stared down at his ever-moving hands. "At any rate, I need to catch up to the rest of the cabinet nominees and get my Senate hearings right away. No reason I can't be sworn in on Inauguration Day with the rest of 'em." With that, Senator Lou D'Angelo charged through the reception area, announcing to Mrs. Fredericks as he passed, "We'll call when it's official."

Samantha grabbed her overcoat, navy blue attaché case and small shoulder strap purse, and started to follow. Mrs. Fredericks placed her hand over the mouthpiece of the telephone she was holding and said, "Sam, it's for you. The assisted care facility, in New York, about your mother."

Samantha grimaced, and peered down the hall at her Senator racing toward the elevators. "Gertie, I… ah. Ask them what it is. Is it urgent?"

Mrs. Fredericks removed her hand from the instrument and spoke calmly. "May I inquire as to the nature of the call to Ms. Wright? Is it an emergency?" She listened, then repeated, "So it is only a billing matter. I see. Well, Ms. Wright is tied up all morning on very important Senate business. Perhaps you could leave a message. Yes, I can assure you it is all right. I frequently take confidential messages for Ms. Wright. I will be certain that she gets it." Mrs. Fredericks looked up at Samantha who was mouthing the words "hurry up" as she glanced down the hall at the disappearing Senator.

Mrs. Fredericks reached for her message pad and scribbled a few words. As she cradled the phone instrument against her neck, she simultaneously tore out the message sheet, handed it to Samantha, and assured the caller, "Yes, she'll get the message."

Samantha grabbed the piece of paper and rushed out of the office and along the shiny marble floor of the wide corridor, trying to catch up with the Senator. He stood in the open doorway to the Senators' private elevator, motioning for her to hurry. "Come on, Sam! This is one appointment I can't be late for."

"Now, that will be a first," she thought but did not say that if the Senator started keeping to a schedule, it would be a very welcome change.

On the short ride down to the garage for the waiting limousine, the Senator's hands kept in motion, animating his lively discussion of the changes he would bring to the Pentagon. Samantha listened, and glanced down at the message she was clutching in her hand. "January check for mother's care. Did not include the increase. Need $200 more."

"Damn," she exclaimed.

"What?" the Senator asked.

"Damn right!" she smiled as she stuffed the paper into her coat pocket.

———— ∞∞∞ ————

Samantha sat quietly in the Presidential suite at the Hay-Adams, staring at the magnificently intricate design on a Chinese vase resting on the gleaming mahogany table under the shaded window. What was it they called these rooms? It was a living room really, but a living room off the main living room in a multiple room suite. A drawing room? A parlor? She had heard both terms used in White Plains by some of her well-off friends, the ones with the big old houses with the porches, or were they verandas? Whatever, it was a good thing she went into law. To stay at home and decorate a house never would have worked for her, no matter how many times she had thought about a calmer, domestic life, particularly when the Senator's mood was the disturbing opposite of the charming self he was displaying this morning. He was behind the closed door to the main room of the suite, meeting with the next President of the United States. And she was a long way from White Plains.

This basically good man, she thought, who was going to be the next Secretary of Defense, had signaled his desire to have her accompany him to the Pentagon. That, of course, made good sense. She had gained invaluable, in-depth knowledge about the military and its complexities during her six years with the Senator. Yes, this would be her chance to help implement some of the good Senator's meaningful reforms. "More bang for the buck," he always said. At the Pentagon, they could accomplish so much more than in the Senate.

Samantha heard a faint knock on the door to the living room. The Secret Service agent standing by the door turned and opened it. Samantha saw the Senator in profile, slowly shaking hands with the other man. Though while only partially visible in profile behind the door, Samantha instantly recognized the other man's distinctive sturdy jaw and thick gray wavy hair. It was Michael Prescott, the next President of the United States. She stood up waiting for her next instructions.

Senator D'Angelo turned and stared directly at her, then began walking toward her. Looking sullen and cold, he muttered, "Come on, Sam, let's get out of here."

She reached down for her coat, grabbed the attaché case, and turned to follow him, but her way was blocked. She looked up into two violet blue, piercing eyes, fixed on her. She almost gasped, but her reaction was cut off by a calming, quiet voice, "So you must be Senator D'Angelo's assistant. I've heard such wonderful things about you."

Samantha felt him firmly grab her arm, and pull her closer to him. She was not prepared for his strength or the fact that despite his gray hair his smooth skin and boyish smile made him look ten year younger than fifty-five. She stammered, "You, ah, have heard of me, Governor, ah. I'm sorry, I mean Mr. President-Elect."

He laughed. "That's quite all right. I'm still used to the Governor label, Samantha, and yes, I've heard about you. Top-notch lawyer with the S.E.C., followed by six years with the Senator. Ambitious, hard working, exceptionally bright." He looked her up and down, assessing. "Now that I've met you in person, I'm definitely keeping my eyes on you. One of the great things I know I'm going to enjoy about Washington—seeing brilliant careers take off. And if we're going to get this country moving forward again—and we are—it's going to be with the help and vigor of committed professionals like you." Prescott's gaze shifted, glancing past the secret service agents out into the hall. He turned back to her, altered his grip to gently push her toward the door, and smiled. "You better move along. Neither one of us should keep the good Senator waiting. Take care now."

"An honor to meet you," she said as she went through the open doorway.

At the elevator, she started to speak, but the Senator held his finger to his lips, motioning for silence. He waited until they were seated in the back of the limousine, and the car was heading toward Pennsylvania Avenue. The Senior Senator from Samantha's home state of New York turned and whispered, "It's not me. He picked Frank Mullen." The Senator hesitated, struggling with his words. "A goddamn big business technocrat.

46

New politics my ass!" The Senator pounded his fist down on the leather seat. "And our President-to-be has asked me to push the confirmation process through as fast as possible. He said it would be the best for all concerned." He stared out through the dark, tinted windows of the limousine.

Samantha heard him mumble, but could not be certain that Lou D'Angelo had said, "devious bastard."

CHAPTER TWO

The shining silver wing of the Gulfstream V mirrored the brilliant January sun as the jet banked left over the Potomac River, then leveled off for the final approach to the main runway at Andrews Air Force Base. Frank Mullen shielded his eyes from the glare, but kept staring down at the city. The dome of the distant Capitol shimmered in the sunlight.

"Get used to the view of coming and going from Andrews," J. Kingston Wittlefield said to the only other passenger seated in the executive compartment of the newest aircraft in the AMERIPRO corporate fleet. "The change from Reagan National is one I know you'll come to appreciate."

The gray-haired President and Chief Executive Officer of AMERIPRO rotated the comfortable leather swivel chair in the direction of the frail-looking old man sitting on the other side of the marble coffee table. Frank Mullen raised his Spode china coffee cup, toasted the aged Chairman Emeritus of AMERIPRO. "Thanks to you, Kingston, I'll have that opportunity."

"I was only doing what had to be done, for all our sakes. Fortunately, as predicted, our President-Elect proved malleable–put all that new politics malarkey aside. He saw that he'd be better off with a more 'traditional' choice than with that idiot who stumbled into the Chairmanship of the Armed Services Committee after the untimely death of our good friend Senator Watson."

"I take it that your source for the President Elect's actual mood…" Mullen stopped as the rear door to the private compartment opened and an attendant came forward.

"Touchdown in one minute, Mr. Wittlefield, Mr. Mullen. Time to buckle up." The attendant reached down and grabbed for Wittlefield's seat belt within the plush cushion of the leather chair.

"Leave me alone, dammit," Wittlefield snarled. "I'm ninety. I'm not dead. I can handle my own seatbelt."

The attendant jumped back. "I'm sorry, Mr. Wittlefield, I didn't..."

"Just leave," Wittlefield commanded, his dark dry eyes stared at the man. The attendant quickly retrieved the coffee cups and retreated to the separate crew compartment behind the executive suite.

Wittlefield reached down, grabbed the two ends of the seatbelt, then fumbled one end as he tried to connect them. Mullen waited, patiently, until Wittlefield said, "Perhaps the next Secretary of Defense could provide a small bit of assistance."

Mullen reached forward and quickly locked the belt, then leaned back and fastened his own.

As the pitch of the plane turned momentarily steeper, Wittlefield asked, "You were saying, Frank?"

"Prescott's true position on my nomination? Does our source advise that he is genuinely enthusiastic? I will have his real support? No lingering doubts about not going with D'Angelo?" Mullen peered toward the back of the plane to be sure he and his mentor were completely alone.

"No doubts," Wittlefield replied, "he knows the score. He was toying with D'Angelo. I told you when we cast our lot with Prescott three years ago that he might entertain substantial cuts in defense. Typical small-minded, parochial thinking. But he was so damn charming and telegenic, I knew he had what it took—with the help of our resources, of course. Fortunately, he was also capable of being educated on important matters."

"Apparently so," Mullen observed.

Wittlefield leaned slightly forward. His cold eyes came to life. "But we should also give credit where credit is due. We put his education in the hands of the right man. A brilliant strategic move to place our friend in the inner circle of that campaign when it was nothing but hopes and prayers."

Frank Mullen started to answer, but Wittlefield jumped in. "Notice that, Frank?"

"What?" Mullen asked.

"No slamming on the brakes, Frank. None of that steep drop, bump onto the short runway, and throw the thrusters into reverse, like at Reagan National. No sir. Nothing but smooth landings when you get to use the long airfield at Andrews."

"It is more pleasant, Kingston."

"And cheaper, Frank. No landing fees for us here. Don't forget that. And once again, thanks to the Colonel. Damn, Frank, as long as I've known him, there has never been a problem he couldn't solve. Like today. I suggest we come into Andrews even though they *never* let private planes in here, but look out that window," Wittlefield pointed through one of the wide glass portals at the towering blue and white jumbo 747 parked on the special space just off the runway. "The AMERIPRO jet is being treated just like Air Force One."

Wittlefield released his safety belt and tried to stand up, but his deteriorating frame made it impossible for him to straighten up all the way. He reached out and placed a hand on the arm of his chair. As the airplane coasted to a complete stop, and the whine of the jet engines slowed, then stopped, Wittlefield walked slowly, haltingly to the exterior door. In a moment, the door swung back, then glided up and out of sight. The old man squinted, trying to adjust his eyes to the bright sunlight of the cloudless Washington morning. First he saw the two airmen in heavy gray winter uniforms moving a short stairwell into place against the fuselage. A man stood behind them. He was dressed in a plain single-breasted navy blue business suit, his sparkling shaved head glistening in the sun. As usual, the Colonel wore neither hat nor overcoat to protect against the winter air. Wittlefield's expression lit up in recognition.

Colonel Harry Howard bounded up the stairs into the Gulfstream. Without exchanging a word he brushed passed Wittlefield and went to the rear crew compartment and opened the door. "Stay put!" he ordered, then closed the door. He repeated the action in the forward compartment, directing the pilot and copilot to remain at their station. Only after this search and re-connaissance mission was completed, did Colonel Howard approach Wittlefield, and heartily shook the old man's weak hand.

Frank Mullen looked on in amazement. He and Howard were almost the same age, as Lyndon Johnson had pointed out so many years before. The intervening years had been extremely good for his fortunes, Mullen thought, but for oh so little else. Mullen self-consciously felt his age, reminded by the slight discomfort from the pressure of his thick mid-section against his pants. But not Howard. Look at him! He appeared to be essentially the same man who had marched to the front of that Pentagon auditorium so long ago and announced the momentous decision, the first in a long line of massive contracts, that had propelled everything forward—American Helicopter, AMERIPRO, and Frank Mullen. Howard hadn't aged and he hadn't softened one bit. Lean, hard, every inch of his six-foot three inch body in the shape of a youthful recruit at his post boot camp prime. And even the hair had been made an ally. When his short-cropped hair had started giving way to baldness, Howard had shaved his head, taking command and denying nature its intended course. Now, towering over Wittlefield, Colonel Howard looked every bit the warrior. He appeared closer to forty than a man well into his late sixties. As Colonel Howard pivoted on his shiny spit-polished black shoes, Mullen had to acknowledge that anyone looking at the two of them would conclude that Howard was many years younger.

Colonel Howard came up to Mullen, a serious, stern expression locked across his face. "May I be the first to address you as Mr. Secretary?" Howard said solemnly, briskly drawing his hand to his forehead in a salute, and then bringing the hand down for a strong, firm handshake.

Mullen felt the iron strength of the army man's grip, and mentally winced. The always "can do" corporate executive fought off a momentary tinge of depression as he realized how sadly accurate had been his analysis of the great disparity in the effects of time on the two of them.

"Thank you, Colonel. But the title is a little premature. We do have the Senate's confirmation to contend with."

"True," Colonel Howard replied flatly. "Let's take these few minutes to brief the matter," he said, motioning for Wittlefield and Mullen to sit down.

"Yes," Wittlefield agreed. "Stop wasting time and get down to business."

"Fine. How long do we have?" Mullen asked, returning to one of the chairs.

Howard glanced at his watch. "Exactly twelve minutes. There has been a change of plans. I..." the Colonel uncharacteristically hesitated, "was unable to get the clearance for the helicopter landing. We are going to have to make it into the city by land transport. That will add thirty minutes to our schedule."

"No helicopter?" Wittlefield exclaimed. "Colonel, I want the AMERIPRO helicopter in the news coverage of Frank's arrival."

"I understand that," the Colonel said. "But the President-Elect thought that would be too, as he put it, 'high profile.'"

"High profile?" Wittlefield shrieked, his right hand rising from an armrest and starting to quiver. He grabbed his right hand with his left, and held tight, trying to control the involuntary shaking. "What the hell does Prescott mean by that?" he demanded, his face flushing red.

"Take it easy, Kingston," Mullen said calmly, reaching for the call button on the arm of his chair. In a moment the attendant entered the cabin. "James, please bring Mr. Wittlefield his prescriptions, and a glass of water."

"Yes, Mr. Mullen," the attendant responded coldly as he turned and entered the galley.

The attendant returned carrying a silver tray with four different capsules aligned on a white linen napkin embroidered with the AMERIPRO logo, accompanied by a crystal goblet filled with water.

"Just set it down!" Wittlefield ordered.

The attendant did as instructed. Colonel Howard anxiously looked at his watch again. "You're dismissed," he said. The attendant silently retreated to the crew compartment. Howard followed to insure that the door was secured.

Upon his return, the Colonel remained standing. "As I was explaining, President-Elect Prescott believes we should maintain a low profile, business as usual approach to the confirmation process for Frank. Avoid displaying the outward symbols of AMERI-PRO as a worldwide defense company. We want to portray Frank as a solid, efficient manager who knows how to run an enormous organization—downplay that the organization he's been with his whole career is also one of the world's biggest defense contractors. Now that we're so diversified, emphasize that the company makes everything, literally, from soup to nuts."

"That's the nuttiest thing I've ever heard," Wittlefield derided. "We are a military and armaments company, Colonel, and I'm damn proud of that fact. I shouldn't have to remind you."

"Of course we are," Colonel Howard replied. "And without AMERIPRO, I hate to think what would have happened to America's defense capabilities."

Frank Mullen listened to the exchange, and the start of what he feared would be a long and familiar speech. "Yes, yes, we understand all that Colonel," he interjected, "but let's stick to the issue. I go in for the meeting with the President-Elect, and then the press conference."

"That's correct, Frank. The message from the President-Elect is clear. The confirmation is assured. The votes in both the Committee and the Senate are all lined up. He's even assured of D'Angelo's support."

"D'Angelo's on board?" Wittlefield asked. "I don't believe it."

"It's true," the Colonel said firmly. "The President-Elect is certain he's persuaded D'Angelo to go along."

"Promised that weak sister something," Wittlefield scoffed. "What did he have to give him, Colonel?"

"I'm not sure," Colonel Howard replied. "But the deal has definitely been cut. That's not to deny that we still have to be careful. I don't trust that pacifist prick. D'Angelo's always been on this unholy crusade to gut the military. As a mere member of the Committee, he couldn't do that much harm. But with Senator Watson's death..."

"Damn fine man, Watson," Wittlefield interjected. "A patriot."

"True," Howard agreed, "but he's no longer Chairman of the Committee, and the dangerous Lou D'Angelo is."

"But he's under control, Colonel?" Mullen asked.

"Yes," he replied. "For now. We have to keep him that way. He's volatile. The President-Elect believes the best course is to make it easy for D'Angelo to stick with their deal, give a graceful way to support the nomination by throwing him a bone, some sincere sounding lip service about economical management. Emphasize your reputation as a frugal, efficiency expert, capable of finding the fat and cutting it out. And as for AMERI-PRO, assume a low profile on the defense side of the business." Howard looked over at Wittlefield. "So we have Frank arrive for the meeting and the press conference by ordinary car, not by helicopter with the AMERIPRO logo on the tail."

"I don't like it one damn bit," Wittlefield muttered. He looked up at Colonel Howard, and said firmly, "I wanted everyone to see the AMERIPRO helicopter today!"

"I understand that," the Colonel responded calmly. "I don't like it either. I don't like pandering to the likes of D'Angelo, but the strategy makes sense in the short run. And, Prescott is calling the shots on this one."

"All right. I'll go along with it," Wittlefield announced reluctantly, "on two conditions. First, I'll stick to the strategy only as long as I can count on Prescott—one hundred percent!"

"So far, so good," the Colonel responded.

"So you tell me," Wittlefield snarled. "But don't either of you forget that once before we had a young man in that office. I had high hopes for him, but…"

"And second?" Frank Mullen interjected.

"We'll play along," Wittlefield ordered, "only as long as nobody gets in our way. If D'Angelo crosses us for even a second, we bring the hammer down on him. Understood?"

"Understood," Colonel Howard replied immediately.

Wittlefield and Howard turned toward Mullen. The old man stared at him and snapped, "Frank!"

"Yes, yes," Mullen replied. "Understood. I'm sure there will be no need for that."

CHAPTER THREE

Samantha picked at the firm pink flesh of the chilled salmon, one of the more reliable dishes served at the Chronicle, the most popular watering hole on the Senate side of Capitol Hill. It sure proved the old adage, she thought: location, location, location. The Chronicle's success wasn't due to its food, but rather its walking, even crawling, distance from the three primary Senate office buildings.

"Not hungry, Sam? Our little disappointment of this morning steal your appetite?" Senator D'Angelo took a substantial sip of his third rye whiskey and soda, grabbing an ice cube in the process with his teeth and loudly crunching it into tiny, melting pieces.

Samantha checked the time, then looked up and gazed around the room. Ten minutes to noon. In less than forty minutes it would be packed, with a line waiting. But now it was still empty, except for a solitary drinker at the bar. She thought they should leave before the crowd arrived. No sense in allowing the Senator's decision to have a liquid lunch feed the vicious Capitol Hill rumor mill. But it was probably too late. At least one of the waiters would find it an irresistible and probably profitable story to pass along.

"The political roller coaster ride of this morning didn't do my stomach any good," Samantha said. "It's a bit early for me."

"Nonsense, Sam," the Senator replied. "It's good to be ahead of the crowd." He took a long last gulp from his drink, then held his glass up and motioned to the waiter to bring another. His eyes followed the waiter who swiftly retrieved the drink from the bar and brought it to the table. The Senator quickly took a sip, and smiled.

"Do you think that's wise, Senator?" Samantha asked. "We've got a lot of work to do on the confirmation hearings."

"All I'll have to do is preside over the coronation. Our new President has made his choice, and now," he said, slurring his words, "I just have to fall in line as a good man of the party." He reached out and took her hand in his. "And that's why I want you to do our job and prepare for the hearings. Go through the motions." The Senator's face flushed with the effects of the liquor. His hand felt warm and moist. "Of course I want to look prepared up there, look good for the television cameras. Right, Samantha?" he pleaded.

"Certainly, Senator."

"Certainly, indeed," he said, squeezing her hand firmly, before letting go and returning to his half-filled drink. He took another long sip, almost emptying the glass. "So I'm counting on you, Sam, to make the show believable. Maybe even a little interesting. But, Sam?"

"Yes, Senator?"

"That's all I want. Enough to make it look like we've done our job. The bottom line is, the United States Senate is going to confirm the asshole as quickly as possible."

Nothing he said surprised Samantha. But it would have been a whole different story six years ago when she'd come to Capitol Hill with most of her illusions intact. After the two year clerking stint for the cantankerous old judge sitting on the Second Circuit Court of Appeals in New York, followed by another six years at the Securities and Exchange Commission, she'd had enough of interpreting and enforcing the laws. She had wanted to take a step up, help make the laws, create the policies, mold the future. That's what coming to the staff of the Senate was all about. But now she knew what really went on—the deal making, the vote trading, the let's-worry-about-today, today, and we'll-get-to-the-future-some-day, maybe. Certainly 'her' Senator was as guilty as the rest at playing the game of politics, the expediency game.

There was a major exception to the rule in his case, one that made his statements ring hollow. Because in one area Senator D'Angelo had held on to his own ideals. It was a principle for which he had always fought, tenaciously and uncompromisingly, seldom winning, but never caving in, even when the votes were all against him. It was, as the media had labeled it long ago, his 'crusade' to cut fat from the military and impose efficiency. His mantra had echoed in the hallways of the Senate, never more so than in the last year when he had assumed through seniority the chairmanship of the powerful committee primarily responsible for defense funding. It had been a presidential election season. Time to debate policy, to set a course for the future, a year to speak out on the great issues of the day. Senator D'Angelo had done so, with all his energy and all his conviction on the one issue that mattered most to him.

But here he was, caving in she thought, ordering her to just go through the motions, when the nominee coming before the committee obviously was going to be all for the status quo.

"Sam? Sam?" the Senator snapped. "What do you say? You understand what I want you to do?"

"Yes, Senator. We're taking it easy on this one."

The Senator frowned, then tilted his head back and emptied the last drops of his drink down his throat. "That's the size of it."

Samantha knew the crowd would be swarming in soon. There was no need to have the Senator displayed to one and all after four drinks. "Shall we get back to work?" Samantha asked, rising from her chair. She stood waiting for him to follow her move.

He slumped for another few seconds, then placed his hands on the table and slowly pushed himself up. "Yeah, let's get the hell out of this dump."

The maitre d' heard only the last word spoken, and rushed over to the departing couple. "Is everything all right, Senator?" he asked solicitously.

"Yeah, sure, everything's aces, Raphael," the Senator said sarcastically. "It'd be a shitload better if you'd stop watering the drinks."

The man stared blankly at his powerful customer, then lost not another second clicking his fingers in the direction of a man in a tuxedo, standing behind the bar, "Roberto!"

"Si?" the bartender replied immediately.

"In the future, Senator D'Angelo's rye whisky is to be, ah, *maxima. Comprende?"*

The bartender smiled and bowed.

"Don't do us any favors," Samantha thought.

As the Senator and his assistant passed through the bar on the way to the door, they glanced up at the television monitor suspended from the ceiling in the corner. They stopped to watch the President-Elect's nominee smiling broadly as the *Post* reporter Samantha knew oh so well asked, "Isn't AMERIPRO a major defense contractor? How do you plan to be impartial as Secretary of Defense in the awarding of military contracts?"

Daniel got right to the point with that one, Samantha thought.

She stared at the man on the screen intently. The somewhat overweight man smiled warmly, his eyes looked straight into the camera. He appeared calm, in control. He had a round face, soft features. He gray hair was thin, parted to one side, neatly combed back. She was surprised. He didn't look particularly powerful, forceful. And his smile was attractive enough. Not exactly the cold corporate type she had anticipated.

"A very fair question," Mullen's image on the small screen observed. "I should save my full answer to that one until my confirmation hearings before Senator D'Angelo's Committee."

"Buttering you up already, boss," Samantha said under her breath.

"Bet your ass," the Senator hissed.

"But simply stated," Mullen went on, "the AMERIPRO of today is a far cry from the company of years ago. We are a multi-industry, consumer-oriented company, providing the American family many of its needs and wants. The defense portion as a percentage of AMERIPRO's overall business has been decreasing for the last decade. As to defense contracts, I will be placing all of my stock holdings in a blind trust should the Senate confirm my nomination."

"Nice of him to agree to abide by the conflicts of interest law we enacted years ago," Senator D'Angelo mumbled.

Samantha's focus shifted to the handsome President-Elect standing beside Mullen. He was smiling confidently. "It looks like my job of just going through the motions will be easy, Senator," Samantha said softly, then realized the Chairman of the Senate Armed Services Committee had already stumbled out the door and into his waiting car.

"How could you have been so far off in your story, Daniel?" Samantha asked quietly, turning her back to the always curious ears of Mrs. Fredericks. She thought about getting up and closing the door, but decided that would only draw attention to the conversation.

"Funny, that's exactly the question I'm having to answer for everyone around here," Daniel Garcia said. "The editors don't appreciate running a headline on the front page that turns out to be wrong before the newsprint is dry."

"They don't seem to be taking it out on you. You got to cover Mullen's press conference."

"Sure," Daniel replied with a cynical laugh. "They told me to get my ass out there and find out what's really going on with Defense. There's all the delays, last cabinet position to be filled, even though its usually one of the first. Then all the sources said it was D'Angelo..."

"I know about the sources," Samantha interjected.

"Then this last minute change. I think Prescott had decided on D'Angelo, and then something or someone changed his mind. But it wasn't just a change in personnel, it's a complete change in the approach to the defense budget, to the defense establishment. Status quo winning out over big changes. There has got to be a great story in what happened behind the scenes, and about who this new President is really listening to."

"Well, whatever or whoever was behind it, it's a fait accompli," Samantha said lazily.

"What's that? The inside word, nomination approved—a done deal?" Daniel asked.

Samantha whispered into the phone. "I can't go into it now. But I will see you tonight, that is if…"

"If what?" he asked.

"If you show me yours, I'll show you mine."

"What I've got on Mullen?" Daniel asked. "I can't do that, Sam. You know, confidential sources and all that."

"No," Samantha answered. "I don't need the confidential stuff, yet. Just what you've already worked up, the background file, anything to get me going. I'm starting out knowing very little about the man who's coming before our Committee in a week. I'd like to get a head start before all the nominee's propaganda arrives, along with the sanitized F.B.I. background check."

"Okay, Sam, nothing confidential, but I'll bring what I can. Your place or mine?"

"My place is clean and neat. As usual, your stuff will be disorganized and rough. So let's go where it's already a mess—your place. Seven o'clock."

Samantha hung up and stared down at that morning's *Post* headline. Was Daniel right? Had something happened to change the President-Elect's decision? Or had the rumors about D'Angelo getting the job been trial balloons, or diversions? In Washington, it was always difficult to get to the straight story.

She had been right. Nothing happened on the nomination that afternoon, other than a flurry of calls from the media, and a promise from the presidential transition office that complete biographical and background documents on Frank Mullen would be delivered early the next day. One call inquired about scheduling the nominee's first courtesy visit with the Chairman of the Committee. Samantha could tell that the caller was a young, extremely aggressive transition team staffer who apparently saw nothing undiplomatic in pushing hard for a meeting with her Senator that afternoon. He seemed oblivious to the delicate nature of a visit by the President-Elect's nominee with the man who thought he was going to be the President-Elect's nominee.

Knowing that her Senator simply wasn't in the right frame after their liquid lunch, Samantha finally had to cut off the pushy aide.

"Look," she said sternly, "there is no way that the Senator's schedule permits a meeting this afternoon. Got that? Now let's look at tomorrow's calendar."

She could hear the air leaking out of his over-eager balloon. Good, she thought. He might as well get a dose of Washington reality early on.

"Ah, all right. I'm sorry, Ms. Wright."

"You can call me Samantha," she replied, "or Sam. I don't particularly like it, but it sooner or later everybody gets lazy with Samantha and I end up plain old Sam."

"Okay, thanks, ah, Samantha," he replied. "I didn't mean to come across as, ah, demanding. It's just that I was told the Senator would be setting everything aside to expedite the confirmation process."

"That's right," Samantha confirmed, "starting tomorrow."

With that, the courtesy visit by Frank Mullen to Senator Lou D'Angelo was scheduled for the next morning at ten o'clock.

Samantha got off the Metro subway car at the Twentieth Street station, and pulled the quilted collar of her wool overcoat high against her neck, bracing for the icy January night. To her surprise, there was no wind, and the night air felt truly refreshing during the two block walk to Daniel's place. She passed the all-night convenience store on the corner, then stopped and looked up at Daniel's bland red brick eight-story apartment building. She knew instinctively that the cupboards would be bare. It had been a long time since her early lunch, and if she was going to work late reviewing volumes on the life of Frank Mullen, she needed some sustenance. She turned back for the basics of penne and Paul Newman's Sockorama pasta sauce in a jar, some salad fixings, inexpensive Chianti, and for Daniel, the always mandatory Pacifico beer.

At the security entrance to the building, she first tried the intercom to his apartment, but getting no answer, she set her briefcase down, moved the bag of groceries to her other arm, and fumbled in her purse for her keys.

"Spare's change, lady?"

Samantha froze, her hand trembling slightly in her purse.

"Fur sum hot soup, lady, on a cold, cold night, please!" The pleading voice was low, calm.

Samantha's mind raced with thoughts of the ever-growing number of vicious street crimes pervading the nation's capital. Could she make it to her keys, and get a key in the door? No. The voice was only a few steps away, down the four entrance steps, somewhere near, on the sidewalk. Her eyes darted up to the surveillance camera in the inner lobby, slowly swinging in an arc. It was in a position at the far end of its cycle, pointing down at the elevator entrance, almost certainly blind to the events transpiring at the front door. Was anybody watching, anyway? Or was it just one of those that recorded the passing events, for what? Evidence, after the fact?

"Anythang would help, maam," the steady voice pleaded.

Samantha turned and looked into the night. The solitary figure leaned, hunched over, against the scrawny, barren oak tree rooted in the no man's land between the sidewalk and the street. He held a filthy canvas bag in one hand, an old wooden cane in the other. As he leaned against the tree for support, he reached out with his hand, the hook of the cane resting on his wrist. She thought for a moment that he was black, but then noticed his long, straight stringy brown hair, and realized she could not be certain. The layers of dirt were disguising almost everything about him. But in the faint street light, one feature was clear—the man was staring at her through clear, brilliant, penetrating green eyes.

Samantha kept her eyes on his, and felt around in her purse, passing over her keys to find her wallet. Her fingers fumbled on the clasp of the wallet, and she glanced down, pulled out a dollar bill. She looked at the man again, then pulled out another. She stood on the top stair, and held out her hand. The man planted his cane in the sidewalk, then lunged for the money, quickly grabbing it and folding it into the dark recesses of his dilapidated trench coat.

He hunched over, steadied the cane on the sidewalk, and started to move his feet slowly down the sidewalk, not turning back.

Samantha felt a chill wind sweep in from the street. She wasn't sure if she heard the wind or the man muttering "thank yous, lady."

Samantha quickly turned as her fingers grasped for her keys. She inserted a key in the front door, then pushed at the door with her shoulder as she picked up her briefcase, and jumped inside. She stuffed the keys in her coat pocket, darted across the lobby to the elevators, and shakily pushed the call button. She started to count to herself, but was mercifully interrupted by the chime announcing the elevator's arrival from the underground parking garage. The doors parted and she charged into the cab.

"Whoa, babe. What set you off?"

Samantha jumped at the sound, then let out a long sigh. "Oh, Daniel, thank God it's you."

"Like you were expecting one of 'da boys from the Hood,'" Daniel Garcia laughed. "Remember, I may be dark and, how are we saying it these days, ah 'ethnic', but the barrio is behind me, and the only weapons I'm packin' these days are my good ol' notebooks and Blackberry."

"Very funny," Samantha said. "No, it's just that I had a bit of a..."

"What?" Daniel asked seriously.

"A street person right at the main door. An uneasy feeling, that's all."

"Shit," Daniel exclaimed. "Did he touch you? Hassle you? Is he still there?"

"No," Samantha replied calmly. "No to all three. I gave him a couple of bucks and he..."

"You did what? A couple of bucks? Sam, that's the worst possible thing to do. It only encourages the scumbags. Now he'll be out there every night. Don't ever give 'em money! Not in this crazy city."

"Come on, Daniel. You know I don't do it very often. I don't like being conned. But sometimes they do seem, oh I don't know, real, sincere. Like tonight. The man had the calmest voice—he wasn't threatening at all. He just pleaded—pleaded for soup money."

"Yeah, sure," Daniel threw up his hands, then looked at the unlit control board, and punched in his floor. "So you're the Good Samaritan for the night. Looks like twice over," he said, reaching over to grab the grocery bag from Samantha's arm. "You took pity on me, too, and decided to fix dinner."

"No, Senor Garcia, I was hungry, and through brilliant deductive reasoning, concluded that you'd have zilch in the kitchen."

"*Muy bueno*," Daniel said. "And you won't even have to rush dinner." The elevator door opened onto the seventh floor. "Because," Daniel gestured, picking up his one slim briefcase, "there's not much to review. Seems Mr. Mullen has led a quiet life."

"A captain of industry leading a quiet life?" Samantha's curiosity was aroused. "I thought these types were real ego trippers, constantly involved in everything, from politics to charities. Names plastered all over their hometown papers for their good deeds."

"Not our Mr. Mullen. It seems he's done only one thing his whole life."

"Yes?" They reached the end of the hall and Daniel's apartment.

"Make money, first millions, now billions."

"He's that rich?"

"No, not personally. Don't get me wrong. He's filthy rich. His holdings in AMERIPRO, which appear to be everything he has, are worth about a hundred million."

"One hundred million! Jesus!"

"Yeah, not bad. But the huge money he's made has been for his company AMERIPRO, and the old geezer who really controls it, Kingston Wittlefield. Now that old fart's a certifiable multibillionaire. On those lists of the world's richest people."

As Daniel struggled to reach into his pocket for the key, Samantha reached into her coat pocket, retrieved her keys, and quickly opened the door. "After you."

Samantha stepped inside and let the door slam shut. "I wonder why Mullen wants to go into government now." She set down her briefcase and stuffed the keys back into her coat pocket.

"Who knows? Could be a lot of the old rationalizations— public service—give some back to the country that's been so good to him, bullshit, bullshit, bullshit. And of course, the power. But in this case, Sam, I wouldn't rule out one other."

"And that would be?"

"He's spent his whole life making money. Maybe this gig is another way to do that."

Samantha felt a piece of paper in her coat pocket. "Dammit," she muttered.

"What's wrong?"

"Oh, nothing," she said unconvincingly. She pulled the paper out and again read the message of that morning.

"*Que pasa*?" Daniel asked.

"No big deal," Samantha sighed. "A reminder. I don't know where my head was at, but when I sent in my monthly payment to my mother's assisted care facility, I forgot about the increase, effective January 1."

"Increase? Another one?"

"That's right. Welcome to the world of health care. The one on September first I finally got covered in the old Samantha Wright can't-believe-I-make-as-much-money-as-I-do-and-have-nothing-to-show-for-it budget. Now this increase."

"How's she doing, Sam?" Daniel asked. "It's a good place, right—'cept for the cost?"

Samantha started to take off her coat, then stopped, and shook her head. "Great euphemism, huh? 'Assisted care facility.' It's a nursing home, you know, Daniel, as in 'I put my mother in a home.' It's just...oh, I don't know. It seems she should be with me, but I can't...And, she's not getting any better, of course. Some days she seems almost all right, and then other days..." She slipped out of her coat and threw it onto the couch.

"It's tough," he said softly as he took her in his arms.

She stood in his arms for what seemed like the longest time. "I have got to remember to mail another check," she said to herself.

Daniel finished his third Pacifico as Samantha took a sip from her still full glass of red wine, then turned to another print out of press clippings. Daniel reached over and scooped a large spoonful of the pasta from Samantha's almost untouched plate.

"Do you mind?" he asked.

"What?" she replied.

"I thought you were hungry. You haven't eaten a thing. And, as usual, it's the best."

"I guess I wasn't so hungry after all," she smiled.

Daniel took another swig from his beer and attacked her pasta.

They sat in silence. Samantha turned pages, and read. Daniel retrieved one more beer from the refrigerator, moved to the couch, grabbed the remote and started to switch on the small table top television.

"You're right," Samantha announced, closing the last folder and setting it on the table. "Not much human interest material here. Just every year, quarter by quarter, AMERIPRO making more money—increased revenues, greater profits."

"The great American success story."

"I guess so," Samantha agreed, "although you don't see them patting themselves on the back in the press. There's that one article in *Fortune* years ago, and they didn't even cooperate with that. The article says 'no corporate representative would comment.' In any event, the article just rehashes the numbers, hardly says anything personal about Wittlefield and Mullen. Mentions Mullen grew up poor in Texas, but says nothing about a family. Describes him as a cold, efficient, business wiz."

"Sounds like he'll be real fun over at the Pentagon."

"Yeah," she said, "although I suppose it's possible that he could turn out okay."

"What the hell are you talking about, Sam? Mullen is big defense business, through and through."

"Probably. But if he really applied his supposed great abilities to run the place efficiently, he could do some good."

"I suppose it could happen. Sounds like he's the type."

"The type?"

"Number cruncher, calculating. It's been tried before. Ah, Robert McNamara, Defense Secretary under Kennedy and Johnson. Touted as a high efficiency, cost-cutting executive, he'd been President of Ford."

"McNamara! Since when did you become such a student of history?" she asked.

"Since I got assigned to cover this nomination. I had to go back and check precedents, trends, that sort of thing."

"Well I hope McNamara isn't the precedent for Mullen. McNamara didn't cut anything," Samantha scowled. "All he did was manage, or better yet, mismanage, the huge military build up in Vietnam. It was a disaster."

"No shit! Although checking out those clippings shows it wasn't a disaster for everyone," Daniel observed, pointing to the files on the table.

"What do you mean?" Samantha.

"No disaster for our nominee Mr. Mullen, and his boss Wittlefield and AMERIPRO. As I read it, AMERIPRO, or what the company was called before, Mid-American Manufacturers, was pretty much a nondescript manufacturing company, with a helicopter operation, and then boom"

"You're right," Samantha broke in. "AMERIPRO started growing by leaps and bounds during the Vietnam war, and a big part of that was its helicopter sales."

Samantha reached for Daniel's file labeled *The Wall Street Journal*. She spread the pages out across the table. She grabbed one, and ran her finger down a column of numbers. "It looks like in 1964, AMERIPRO for the first time had revenues of over a hundred million—one hundred and twenty four million to be exact. Profits that year were twenty-two million. Then in 1968, four years and a lot of helicopters for the war later, the company had grown over twenty times. Revenues were two billion, eight hundred million, with profits of slightly over five hundred million dollars."

"Like I said, the great American success story!" Daniel exclaimed.

"In 1973, revenues were up to five and half billion, and for the first time they had profits of over a billion. From what I see here, most of it came from government contracts tied to Vietnam."

"Super," Daniel observed sarcastically.

"Funny, though," Samantha said, turning back to the various file folders and thumbing through them until she found one and opened it. "Such dramatic growth and success for a company, you would think they'd brag a little. But there's none of that." She picked up several more sheets of paper. "That's why this one photograph stood out. I think it's the only one in the whole file of Mullen." She pulled it out. "From the front page of the *Dallas Tribune*, September 24, 1964. It's Mullen with General Westmoreland—he was the army commander in Vietnam. The caption identifies Mullen as President of American Helicopter of Abilene, a subsidiary of AMERIPRO. Says he was on a civilian inspection tour delivering helicopter number five hundred to the Army in Vietnam."

"Jeez that's a lot of helicopters," Daniel said.

"Sure is. It says the year before there were only eighty helicopters out there. But according to these files, that was only the start. Tens of thousands more were delivered to Vietnam. Every year, more helicopters. What struck me as so incongruous—in the photo Mullen has the biggest smile plastered across his face. I mean, here they are, in the middle of war in a far off jungle, and he looks like he's having the time of his life. Hardly the cold, calculating, efficiency expert type."

"Well, that was still early on in the war," Daniel explained. "Before the shit hit the fan."

"It's just, I don't know, unseemly."

"Ah ha, your idealism is showing again, dear. I would have sworn years working with a politician would have killed that."

"A few nails in the coffin, but not dead and buried yet," Samantha laughed, but turned serious again and held the reproduction of the old newspaper up close to the lamp that hung over the dinette table.

"What?" Daniel asked, getting up from the sofa and coming over to her. He placed his arm on her shoulder, and leaned into the light.

"I'm not sure. It's this man here," she pointed, "standing back by the tail of the helicopter."

Daniel took the photocopy and held it up close. "Can't tell a thing. Too grainy."

Samantha stared at the photograph. "Do newspapers keep the originals of old photographs like this?"

"Yeah, sure, the *Post* does. The *Dallas Tribune*? Who knows?"

Samantha stared at the picture of the long ago war.

Daniel reached down and placed the reproduction from the *Post's* archives back in its folder. Then he leaned around and took Samantha's chin in his hand. "Enough with photos of old dangerous wars."

He kissed her gently on the lips, but soon thrust his tongue into her mouth. She was slow to respond, until his hand dropped gently to her blouse, and slipped inside to the warmth of her firm, petite breast.

"Seems a little dangerous in here tonight, too," she breathed into his ear.

"I hope so," he whispered.

She began to breathe more rapidly, swaying back and forth in rhythm with his gentle, arousing touch. Slowly, he reached for her hand and started to pull her up. She pulled her mouth away from his, and looked up at the strong, rugged man towering above her. He was six-foot two, his shoulders broad. His complexion was dark and his face intriguing. His nose was flat. The scar in the middle of his chin told the story of a troubled youth. He looked more like a fighter than a reporter, she thought. She liked fighters. She felt safe with him, protected.

She also liked how they looked together. He was four inches taller. He was an interesting, clear contrast to her sandy blonde hair, perky, small nose, and all-American good looks. It was good that he wasn't classically handsome. Along the way she'd met plenty of pretty boys. They were a dime a dozen in Washington. But there wasn't time for them anymore. She'd passed the really big 40. Workouts at the gym and running helped, but she wasn't getting any younger. She'd thought she'd settle down by thirty-five, at the latest forty. She didn't want to think about forty-five. Daniel was younger, in his mid-thirties, but he was mature most of the time, genuine, tough, but gentle and kind when she wanted him to be. It was a wonderful combination that made him an exciting, caring lover. He could be the one.

She settled back in the chair, reached out for the waist button on his jeans, and pressed in, unhinging the pants. Then, very slowly, she pulled his zipper down, and down. She reached in, and explored him with her hands, her journey as usual unencumbered by underwear. She loved his aversion to underwear, one of the endearing lingering vestiges of his life in the barrio. He insisted it wasn't a machismo thing, only that he saw no reason to waste hard earned money on underwear. At that moment, she was pleased.

Daniel moaned and grabbed on to the chair. Samantha brushed her hair aside and opened her mouth and teased him gently with her tongue, before taking him all the way in again and again and again, until she felt his whole body shudder.

Samantha woke with a start, the sheets damp from perspiration and strenuous lovemaking. She still felt fully satisfied, but something was bothering her.

She pressed her hand to her forehead. What was it? The images in her dream—a faded photograph, a helicopter, a smiling Frank Mullen—all swirling about, assaulting her sleep. She reached over Daniel, who was gently snoring, and tried to focus on the illuminated numerals of the digital clock. 2:30. She lay back on the bed, staring at the ceiling, thankful that she'd given in to Daniel's rational arguments and had left a few changes of clothes at his apartment.

CHAPTER FOUR

Two uniformed officers waved on the solitary Lincoln Town Car which maneuvered through the break in the line of barricades, and slowly pulled up to the *porte-cochere* on the Senate side of the United States Capitol. Colonel Harry Howard turned to his passenger in the back seat. "0947. Eight minutes to spare."

"Precisely as planned," Frank Mullen replied. "I don't see any media."

"The scavengers pretty much play by the rules up here in perks and prerogatives country. The egotistical Senator D'Angelo proclaimed that their photo op site would be inside, staged at the main door to his number one power perk—the rotunda hideaway office. He couldn't pass up the chance to show off."

"Probably," Mullen agreed affably.

"You know the way," Howard declared. "Somebody from the staff will escort you in the back door, avoiding a solo encounter by you with the gang. You will meet the press only after your meet and greet, and only while in the custody of the Chairman." Howard paused. "I still can't believe it. A buffoon like D'Angelo taking over our committee."

"Two truths of Washington, Colonel," Mullen observed. "The powerful, like all of us, do die, but seniority in the Senate lives forever."

Colonel Howard flashed Mullen a curious look, then said flatly, "The next in line for the Chairmanship of the Committee is Wayne Hauser—not as forceful as I'd like, but a solid patriot."

Mullen raised his eyebrows, then looked down at the papers before him. "Well, I'm as prepared as I'll ever be to meet the undoubtedly disappointed current Chairman."

"Disappointed, yes, but Prescott must have cut him a good deal to get him to play ball. And," the Colonel smiled, "if he steps out of line, we will show him that he has everything to lose."

Mullen looked at the digital clock in the car console.

"You can leave the car in four minutes."

"You're going to play this out as chauffeur? Wait in the car? Some treatment from an incipient special assistant to the President."

"I trust our private briefing time this morning was helpful?"

"Indeed, Colonel. Thank You."

"As for playing chauffeur, no one pays attention to the drivers in Washington. All eyes focus on the back-seaters. So even if a straggler from the press had been out here, my presence would have gone unnoticed, I can assure you." The Colonel's view swept the area confirming it was clear on this frigid January morning. "So I will wait with the car."

"Very well." Mullen stuffed his papers into a black briefcase. "And beyond the Chairman, everything appears lined up with the other Senators?"

"Affirmative!" Howard said with absolute confidence. "The couple of troublemakers have spent their venom on the Attorney General nominee. They're walking wounded and don't have another fight in them this soon. Surprising, actually. I thought they'd pull it off. If they were going to crush any of the cabinet nominees, it should have been that conniving bitch Goodrich."

"Obviously it helps to have been a law professor to the President-Elect. According to the *Post* Prescott pulled out all the stops to get her nomination through."

"It helped to have been a *special* friend to the man," Howard replied sarcastically

"The rumors are true?"

"Not since we got involved at the start of the campaign," Howard replied. "Before that, who knows? What can I say? He craves fresh pussy, but not as much as power. Prescott's kept to the straight and narrow for these last three years. I haven't got a thing on him in that department."

Howard turned and looked back at Mullen. "Remember, you have to be careful around D'Angelo's staff. He's accepted his marching orders, he's told his people to back off. But he has surrounded himself with..." the Colonel hesitated, choosing his words, "ah, malcontents, who eat up that bullshit D'Angelo shovels out. Don't forget, the staff does the work; some get carried away, have to be brought back into line. I don't like the looks of D'Angelo's chief assistant, this broad that goes by a guy's name—Sam. Samantha Wright. She's a lawyer, never worked a day in her life out of the government—bet she's got all sorts of wacko ideas."

"Right, Colonel. Don't give the staff any ammo to go off the track. Wish me luck," Mullen said.

"Luck has nothing to do with this," the Colonel snapped. "Getting you in as Secretary of Defense is vital to our future. We can't rely on anything but a no-lose battle plan."

Frank Mullen got out of the car and walked briskly up the few steps to the revolving door, nodded at the exterior uniformed guards, entered the Capitol. The guards stationed immediately inside recognized him and whisked him through the VIP security detector, then volunteered directions. Mullen declined his help with a curt "I know my way." It had been several years since he'd been on the front line of the helicopter subsidiary's constant lobbying campaigns, but he readily recalled the path to the Chairman's private office in the main Capitol building.

Mullen ducked down one flight of stairs, turned to the right and then right again. At the far end of the central hallway he could see the media assembled with several mini-cams surrounded by numerous photojournalists. Between Mullen and the crowd stood a very attractive women, slightly taller than he was, dressed in a navy blue business jacket, a matching skirt, and a simple white blouse. Her hair was on the darker side of blonde. Natural looking, classy, tied back. He was not a great judge of women's ages, but while she was clearly mature and professional, she also had an unmistakable youthful, trim, fit appearance. He guessed mid to late thirties. At least he wouldn't have to put up with one of the wet behind the ears kids who permeated so many congressional staffs.

She was waiting by the narrow opening to the side hallway. Mullen remembered that the hallway led to the private entrance to the office. The woman waved, then pointed in the direction of the private entrance. As he approached, she said, "Mr. Mullen, this way please." When he reached her, she smiled. "No problem finding us?"

Frank Mullen returned her smile. "I used to visit with Senator Watson here occasionally."

The woman turned around, looked down at the visitor from her height advantage. "Oh, I'm sure more than occasionally, Mr. Mullen," she said cordially, then reached back and turned the shiny brass knob on the dark mahogany door. She pushed the door open and held it, encouraging him to go first.

"I insist," he said cheerfully, and motioned for her to enter.

"No, I insist," she said firmly, continuing to hold the door.

Frank Mullen shrugged, entered the familiar office, and immediately came face to face with a Senator Lou D'Angelo.

"Welcome, Mr. Mullen," Senator D'Angelo said enthusiastically, reaching down with both hands to pump the nominee's hand. "Pleased you could make it by here so quickly after the announcement. Best to get an early start, so we can move this right along."

"Mr. Chairman, thank you for clearing your schedule."

"My pleasure, and my duty, Mr. Mullen. Now let me introduce my top aide on military matters," D'Angelo said, releasing his hold on Mullen. "Samantha Wright. Brightest aide up here on the Hill. My right hand, uh, person."

Frank Mullen turned and extended his hand, smiling. "Ms. Wright, a pleasure to meet you. I look forward to working with you."

"You got that right, Mr. Mullen," the Senator interjected. "Sam—that's what most people around here call her, and you should be no exception, right, Sam?"

"Yes," Samantha responded matter-of-factly. "Samantha, or, as the Senator said, Sam, would be fine."

"And you please call me Frank in these private sessions."

"Very well," the Senator said. "We're agreed. In private, we're all on first name basis. Makes for a good working relationship. Now, Frank," D'Angelo grabbed Mullen by the arm, "take a seat."

The trio moved to a comfortable area before a real fireplace where a wood fire was giving off a homey glow. "We'll put Sam on the couch over there, Frank, and you grab that other captain's chair next to mine. That way it'll be easy for us to square off," the Senator said, adding a half-hearted laugh. "Help yourself to coffee, and those sweet things there," he pointed at the tray on the coffee table. "Direct from the best damn Italian bakery in Brooklyn. Flown in regular so I can brag about 'em. I got rid of the steward, so it would be just the three of us this morning. Strictly private."

Mullen sat down, placing his briefcase on the thick carpet by the side of the deep red leather chair.

"So, as I was saying," D'Angelo began, "Sam here—been with me several years—she's become my number one expert on the defense budget. Quick study, an amazing aptitude for details. She denies it, but I think she has a photographic memory. And, having learned from the master," the Senator smiled, "she can ferret out waste and mismanagement, and plain ol' fat in that gargantuan military budget of ours."

"Good to hear that, Mr. Chairman," Mullen said, purposefully staying with the Senator's formal title. "I must tell you that I am a believer in Mark Twain's advice to 'blow your own horn lest it not be blown.' I enjoy quite a reputation for exactly the same thing. I detest waste and inefficiency. My whole business life has been devoted to managing large, growing enterprises, but being sure at the same time that the enterprises run economically, and that not one cent is wasted that could otherwise be dropped to the bottom line. I've tried to treat every dollar at AMERIPRO as if it were my own. I plan on the same thing at the Pentagon."

"Sounds good, Frank," D'Angelo responded, "but the Defense Department is a unique operation, dwarfing any private business. It has an uncanny ability to suck up money and presto," he said, snapping his fingers, "it disappears. It sure doesn't drop money to anything like what you in business call the 'bottom line'."

"Ah," Mullen replied, "but that's the exciting challenge ahead. We need to be able to demonstrate there is a bottom line to defense expenditures. That bottom line is value. The value that comes out at the end is at least equal to the money going in up front. Efficient management can deliver value without compromising our defense, Mr. Chairman." For the first time Mullen took his eyes off D'Angelo and stared directly at Samantha. "I'm the man who can deliver efficient management. My track record proves it."

Samantha tried to suppress the surprised look on her face. This was something she hadn't expected. The man whose nomination was preordained had come by for his perfunctory meet and greet. All he had to do was say hello and exchange some pleasantries, but here he was, selling himself. She had to admit it was a pleasant turn of events.

"That may be so," D'Angelo observed, "but there is a major distinction between what you've done before and the enormous task ahead at the Pentagon. You referred to it yourself."

Mullen looked quizzically at the Senator. "How so?"

"You said you had managed growing companies, Frank. More revenues, more profits, more employees. That's not what we're going to be facing in the Pentagon. It's time for streamlining, for using our brains to cut out the fat and waste. Oh sure, our military always has to be mean, but it can be lean, too."

Frank Mullen knew well Senator D'Angelo's ferociously articulated opinions on cutting the defense budget. Fortunately, Mullen thought, they had never enjoyed sufficient support in the Congress. But this was the first time he had heard them in person, and he was ready.

"That, Mr. Chairman, is a matter of overriding national policy," Mullen said, concentrating on conveying a level of sincerity to match the Senator's. "It is a policy that will be established by the President and the Congress. My job will be to carry out policy, to the best of my ability. That means," he turned toward Samantha momentarily and smiling, turned back to face D'Angelo.

"I've got to find the mismanagement and inefficiency, and then marshal whatever resources are allocated to defense in the most productive way. And Mr. Chairman?"

"Yes?" D'Angelo responded.

"If the policy decision is made for the type of dramatic changes you want, I'm the man to carry them out. In fact, it won't be much different from my experience in business."

"I don't follow you, Frank," D'Angelo said, intrigued by the course of the conversation.

"At AMERIPRO, we've been undertaking the kind of change you're talking about. The more I think about it, my experience at AMERIPRO, particularly in recent years, is exactly on point for what you would like to see accomplished at the Pentagon. For many years, AMERIPRO's revenues were mostly from defense related businesses."

"Starting with the Vietnam War," Samantha interjected.

Mullen leaned forward in his chair, and poured himself some coffee. "Yes, that's right, Samantha." He lifted the cup to his lips, sipped, set the cup down, and smiled. "There's no question that the business accelerated rapidly during that time."

"Especially the helicopter business," Samantha said flatly.

"Yes, indeed. The American Helicopter subsidiary under my leadeship accounted for a fair portion of AMERIPRO's revenues in the sixties and seventies."

"Sixty-two percent of your revenues, eighty-three percent of your profits, in 1968, for example," she said.

Mullen reached down for his coffee cup again, and this time took a long drink. "Yes, those are about the correct figures. I see you've done your homework, Samantha."

"As the Chairman indicated, that is my job," she smiled.

"Yes, well done, Sam," D'Angelo said. "Now Frank, get on with your point."

"The figures Samantha refers to are helpful," Mullen went on. "AMERIPRO used to realize the majority of its revenues and," he said, looking over at Samantha, "its profits from defense. But that has dramatically changed over the course of the last decade. We've converted our company to much more of a peacetime, consumer-oriented business. Last year, fifty-nine percent of our revenues came from non-defense sources."

"But fifty-eight percent of the profits still came from the defense sector," Samantha said.

Mullen suddenly felt the room grow warmer. He glanced at the fireplace, then pushed his chair away from the fire. "But the trend is unmistakable—it does take time—but the transition is well underway."

"That sounds positive," D'Angelo agreed. "And the overall profits of the company, have they been hurt by the downsizing of your defense business?"

"Not at all, Mr. Chairman," Mullen answered confidently. "Last year was another year of record performance by AMERI-PRO."

"Of course," Samantha added, "there hasn't actually been any downsizing at all, at least as we'd apply the term to the Pentagon. That is, there hasn't been any actual reduction in the revenues AMERIPRO derives from its military contracts. It's true, isn't it," she asked, "that your revenues from the defense side of the business have continued to grow in actual dollars, and the revenues from non-defense businesses have simply grown more? So aren't you really just saying that AMERIPRO's defense business keeps getting bigger, but your other businesses are growing even faster. A nice set of circumstances for AMERIPRO any way you look at it."

Never let them see you sweat, Frank Mullen remembered, as he felt a touch of moisture cross his forehead. It had been a long, long time since he'd had that feeling. But he knew what Kingston Wittlefield would do. Frank Mullen laughed. "That's remarkable. It brings even the most successful among us back down to earth. We cannot control everything, and sometimes we owe our good fortune to things beyond our control. But our fundamental diversity has helped keep AMERIPRO thriving through good times and bad. As we like to say, recessions come and go, but AMERIPRO grows"

"Good for you," D'Angelo said to Mullen, then shot Samantha a sharp look.

She knew that look. The Senator was ordering her to back off.

The Senator smiled at Mullen. "So I'm sure at the hearings you'll want to bring out this, uh, trend at AMERIPRO toward the civilian, consumer side of the business. That's the sort of information that could prove helpful to secure support among those of us seeking a new attitude at the Pentagon."

"Very well," Mullen agreed. "I'll emphasize that point. And," he said, nodding his head toward Samantha, "I think it's been good to have discussed it here. Allows me to focus on how to explain my experience, and respond to questions."

D'Angelo leaned forward. "Well, I know you've got work to do in preparing for the formal hearings, and we have to take a few minutes to meet with the press mob, so I suggest..."

Samantha interrupted the Senator. "We do have that one specific issue to address with Mr. Mullen."

"Oh, yes," the Senator agreed. "A possible bone of contention, Frank. Have to bring it up. You know my overall position on the defense budget–cutting the waste, closing obsolete bases, civilian personnel cutbacks so we can provide better benefits for the uniformed force, and of course weapons and equipment procurement. The biggest new equipment decision coming up is on this goddamn space age jet helicopter-airplane. A combination supersonic stealth fighter and a helicopter–with retractable wings. Supposed to be capable of breaking the sound barrier. MachCopt, for speed exceeding Mach One. Totally experimental. Jesus Christ, how stupid do they think we are? But the Pentagon under this outgoing administration wants to charge ahead, go into production. I don't—it's a forty billion dollar boondoggle."

"Forty-three billion, three hundred million, at last guess," Samantha corrected.

"Right, over forty billion and climbing," D'Angelo stared hard at Mullen. "I am going to kill the son-of-a-bitch, dead in its tracks, or die trying. I don't need to remind you that AMERIPRO considers itself in the lead for the contract, and I'm telling you there isn't going to be any contract."

"MachCopt would sure put AMERIPRO right back into being a mostly defense company," Samantha observed dryly.

Mullen unclasped his hands, and shrugged. "Mr. Chairman, Samantha, I, of course, discussed this matter with the President-Elect before he nominated me." He paused and seemed to gather his thoughts carefully. "Naturally, from my former perspective at AMERIPRO, I see MachCopt as a magnificent technological achievement"

"Listen, Frank, I don't want to hear it," D'Angelo interrupted.

Mullen held up his hand. "I was just about to say, if my nomination is confirmed, I'll have nothing to do with the MachCopt decision. I'll recuse myself. It will be in the hands of the President and the Congress. I have crossed the Rubicon in this process of seeking public service in order to give back to my country for all that it has given me. I have established a blind trust, and directed the trustee to liquidate my holdings in AMERIPRO."

"Very good," D'Angelo approved.

"But beyond that, Mr. Chairman, I have gone ahead and irrevocably resigned from AMERIPRO, effective immediately. No matter what happens with this nomination, I am forever divorced from any interest in the future of AMERIPRO." Frank Mullen sat back. He looked satisfied.

"Shit," Senator D'Angelo exclaimed, and reached over to shake Mullen's hand. "That's a smart move, Frank. While I'm sure we'll have our differences, I do believe we're off on the right track." The Senator turned to his assistant. "Sounds like our Mr. Mullen has made our job a lot easier with his visit this morning, don't you agree, Sam?"

Samantha looked over at the contented Frank Mullen. "Yes," she said, "I think it has been a good first meeting."

"Great," Mullen replied. "Shall we so advise the press?"

"Yes," the senior Senator from New York agreed. "But let me first give you a few tips on handling the bastards." The moment he used the word he regretted it. He looked over at Samantha, and went on, "at least most of them. There is one exception. I suspect he'll be out there today."

"Who's that?" Mullen asked.

"Oh, a Young Turk with the *Post* by the name of Daniel Garcia. He's assigned to cover this appointment, and other defense matters."

"I know who you're talking about," Mullen said. "He was at the press conference yesterday. Asked about how I thought you would respond to my appointment."

"I missed some of it. How'd you answer that one?"

"Only that I was certainly looking forward to working with you, and I would defer any assessment of your attitude until after we had a chance to meet."

"Yes, that's our friend Mr. Garcia. And I do mean our friend," D'Angelo explained. "He and Sam here are, how do we say it these days? Going steady? No, that's old-fashioned."

"If you have to say anything, Senator," Samantha pleaded, "you might put it simply say we're very close friends."

"I see," Mullen said. "If you don't mind, Mr. Chairman, perhaps we could proceed to tell Samantha's 'close friend' that you and I are going to have a good working relationship."

"Perfect Washington-speak, Frank," the Senator agreed. "You're catching on. Might be we can keep our battles civilized, after all."

With substance deferred to the Senate hearings, for twenty minutes the Senator and the Defense Secretary-Designate engaged in generalities and platitudes before the network commentators and working press. In response to the two questions he managed to get in, Daniel Garcia was advised that Senator D'Angelo had never seriously wanted the job at Defense, preferring instead to fight the defense budget battles from the Hill where the appropriations were approved. The Senator emphasized that since he hadn't wanted the job of Defense Secretary, he of course in no way begrudged Mr. Mullen his opportunity.

When he ended the press conference, the Senator strode back to his hideaway office. He reentered the office by the back door, went immediately to the bar, and poured himself a short rye whiskey over ice. He went to his favorite chair, collapsed into it, and took a substantial sip from his glass.

When Samantha returned to his office a few moments later, D'Angelo said, "A little chat with your reporter friend, Sam?"

"Only a hello. He's off to write up his story."

"Shit!" the Senator exclaimed. "I do hope our new President appreciates the gracious way I eat crow. This ain't easy! But I gotta hand it to Mullen—he's smooth and he's smart. Played that perfectly." He hoisted the glass to his lips, finished the drink, and set the glass down. He started to reach for the brass poker standing next to the fireplace, when he spied something next to the chair. "Damn. Maybe our business wizard ain't that smart. He left his briefcase. Sam, do you mind? He's probably not out of the building yet. Grab that and take it back to him. If you leave it here I'll be tempted to open it up and nose around."

"Sure, Senator. I'll see if I can catch him." Samantha grabbed the briefcase and hurried out. She made it up the stairs and in to the corridor that led to the exit from the Capitol. She thought she saw him going through the revolving door and hurried along.

The uniformed guard smiled as she approached. "Good morning. What's the rush?"

"Was that Frank Mullen who just went through, Pete?"

"Yes. Not the friendly sort, I can tell you."

Samantha momentarily thought that was an odd comment from the guard, but then dismissed it as she rushed out into the cold. She saw the back door of a plain black sedan closing, and assumed the outline of a figure she saw through the dark, tinted glass had to be him. Just as the car was starting to move, she knocked on the window. The car slammed to a stop, and the window rolled down. A stern looking Frank Mullen looked out, then broke into a slight smile.

"Samantha!"

"You left this in the office," she said, holding up the briefcase. "The Senator wanted to be sure your weren't delayed in your preparation for the hearings."

He reached out and pulled the briefcase through the opening. "Why, thank you very much. Nice of you to go to all the trouble. I guess I found our conversation so captivating, I overlooked this old appendage."

"You're welcome. See you at the hearings on Monday."

"Yes, at the hearings," Mullen confirmed. "Or perhaps if I have some questions, or want some advice, I could call. I truly enjoyed our discussion in there. Always valuable to test your thoughts on someone as, ah, prepared as you."

Samantha looked at the next Secretary of Defense and wondered. "Certainly," she found herself saying.

"Great," he said. "Now please, go back in. You shouldn't be out here without an overcoat. I'll call."

With that, he pushed the electric switch to roll up the window. As the car pulled away, Samantha glanced in through the diminishing opening of the closing window. The sun light bounced off the driver's rear view mirror and she saw a reflection of cold, brilliant green eyes staring back at her. A chill knifed through her body. She pulled her arms across her chest, slowly turned around, and walked back into the warmth of the United States Capitol.

CHAPTER FIVE

When the eight-passenger Senate subway car eased to a stop on the basement level of the Russell Senate Office Building, Samantha got out and followed the white granite path to the elevator for the ride to the first floor.

A strange, calm ambivalence had come over her. She knew the Senator had been right. Over the last six years of long hours and hard work, she had become a true expert on the Pentagon morass and its gargantuan budget. The system needed fundamental change, reform, the end of the line for the good ol' boys no-bid contract corruption. And while the Senator knew the broad outline of what was needed, she knew the details. They could have made a great team, if the Senator had become the Secretary of Defense. She should be upset, angry at Mullen's nomination because she and Senator D'Angelo had missed the chance of a lifetime.

But this morning the Senator himself had seemed so—what was it?—supportive. That was too strong, but he was certainly reconciled to the situation. She was sure he was still disappointed, but only a short while ago all the Senator seemed to want was to be certain the incoming President appreciated his support of the nominee. The only time Samantha had seen a flash of the Senator's all too typical anger was when she'd pressed her cross-examination of Mullen. He silently but firmly signaled her to drop it, to do what he'd ordered—"take it easy."

Samantha had to admit that Mullen was impressive. The Senator had called him "smooth and smart." AMERIPRO was a huge operation, not on the scale of the Pentagon, but then nothing was. And AMERIPRO was a hell of a lot bigger than a

Senate staff. Yes, she thought that was the strange ambivalence. She knew Senator D'Angelo so well. He absolutely wanted to do the right thing, but could he? He had never really managed anything, other than a campaign and a Senate office. He sure didn't take to the details, and the Pentagon reform was going to be won or lost in the details. Then there was the Senator's drinking, unquestionably getting much worse in the last six months. She'd bet Mullen was too "efficient" to drink.

She reached the elevator and silently walked in, failing to greet the elevator operator with a warm smile and inquiry about how his day was going. Neither of the other two stern-looking Senate aides who joined her in the elevator said anything either, so they all rode in silence until the announcement that they had reached the first floor. Samantha hesitated a moment, and the two men took the opportunity to scurry out, each racing down separate corridors to their respective seats of power.

The elderly elevator operator looked at Samantha and repeated "First Floor." She started to walk out slowly.

"Are you okay, Sam?" he asked. "Upset about the Mullen nomination? The *Post* said Senator D'Angelo was going to get it."

"Oh, hi Charlie," she answered, suddenly focused on her surroundings. "Yes, yes, I'm fine. Just a little preoccupied."

She left the elevator and as she turned right to go down the wide polished marble corridor to the working offices of the Senate Armed Services Committee, she gasped. She picked up her pace to reach Mrs. Fredericks, who was standing in the hallway. "Gertie! What the hell is all of this?" Samantha pointed to row upon row of uniform bankers boxes, each with a broad strip of bright red masking tape sealing the top.

"The Mullen nomination," the secretary answered. "The document dump. I've seen some hefty one, but this one takes the cake? All from AMERIPRO."

"God, I'd never get through all this even if I had a month, and I've only got four days plus the weekend."

"The journey of a thousand miles starts with…"

"I know, Gertie," Samantha sighed.

As they were speaking a portly man wearing clean tan overalls came into the hallway and grabbed a box and returned to the office.

"I assume he's loading them into my office," Samantha concluded glumly.

"It's the only space, Sam."

"Well, let's get inside and get organized."

Samantha was sitting at her desk and staring at the pile of boxes when Mrs. Fredericks interrupted her. "You must have made an impression this morning, Samantha. It's the man of the hour himself on the phone for you."

"Who?"

"Mr. Mullen is on line two for you, dear," Mrs. Fredericks explained, retreating to her own desk. As she sat down, she moved her chair backwards, closer to the door to Samantha's office.

Samantha took a breath and picked up the phone. "Mr. Mullen?"

"It's Frank, remember, Samantha?"

"Yes, Frank. That was certainly quick. Questions already?"

"No," he answered. "I wanted to alert you to the volume of materials we're sending over."

"Oh, I know. I'm staring at piles of boxes everywhere in my office," she said. The man in the overalls came through the door with another box.

"Good," he said. "They've arrived."

"That's an understatement."

Mullen laughed. "I wanted to be thorough. My life is so intertwined with AMERIPRO, I felt that you needed a complete review of the corporate and business records. I'm sure there will be nothing you can't handle, what with your S.E.C. background."

Samantha hesitated. "My S.E.C. background? How did you know about that?"

"I understood you were an attorney with the S.E.C. before going over to the Senate."

"That's true," Samantha said. "But I don't believe the Senator mentioned that this morning."

"No, perhaps not," he said calmly. "I must have picked that up from one of the transition people. At any rate, I know you know about these things, so I wanted to see if I could be helpful."

"How so?" Samantha asked. He intrigued her.

"I wanted to deliver to the Committee everything I thought might be relevant. We've carefully indexed it for you. We've provided an extensive table of contents, with footnotes, and a cross-referenced index. You have everything in hard copy and on disc. Personally, I still like to work with paper."

Samantha flipped to the list of enclosures. "Yes, I see."

"Good," he replied. "It should help you find whatever you need. But, Samantha, AMERIPRO really has been well-managed. I'm very proud of our track record—with one regrettable exception."

"What?" she asked.

"There was one unfortunate chapter, and I wanted to direct you to it so you'd have plenty of time to review it and be prepared."

"Really. You're telling me about a skeleton in the closet? That's refreshing," she said.

"Yes, ah, well, we're both under some extreme time constraints. It's not that it's really in the closet. I'm sure there was some publicity about it. But it might not have come out if I hadn't brought it to your attention."

"Go on," Samantha encouraged him.

"Back in the early 1970's, AMERIPRO started to do a lot of business in the Middle East."

"Helicopters, I assume."

"Sure, but other things too—anti-aircraft weapon guidance systems, for defense purposes, medical equipment, for civilian and military hospitals. It was at the same time that AMERIPRO had really begun its move into non-defense, consumer-oriented businesses. That was my assignment. Broaden the company's base, diversify. Don't be so dependent on military spending."

"Sounds like smart business."

"It was. Our country's Vietnam defense strategy had been emasculated, and that war was winding down. It was time to change our direction. I devoted myself to the assignment. We acquired a fair number of companies, and built some others from scratch. I was completely preoccupied, and I have to plead guilty to not keeping a close tab on some other aspects of the business. Some of our overseas sales people got carried away. They started spreading around secret commissions where they had no business doing it. Even set up a special bank account overseas just to funnel these payments. They call it 'bachsheesh' over there—in the Arab world, and Iran."

"Bribes," Samantha interjected.

"Absolutely. Bribes to send business to AMERIPRO. And the money for it unaccounted for, maintained by the culprits in—"

"Switzerland?"

"Yes. That was really the problem. I suppose all big companies have to contend with some misconduct by the underlings. You can't keep track of everybody all the time. But a bank account, a big one, off the books, feeding this rather organized and completely unauthorized scheme, that was too much."

"So what happened?" Samantha asked smoothly.

"Fortunately for all concerned, your old agency, the S.E.C. stepped in. Funny how things work out. An Iranian, working for his government, but honest, got wind of what was going on. One of the recipient's of this improper largess let slip where some of his new found wealth had come from, and the honest government employee had relatives in Washington, and they tipped off the S.E.C."

"Violations of the Foreign Corrupt Practices Act," Samantha concluded.

"Correct. It was the company's employees, and the company's off-books account. While top management didn't know what was going on, we should have had better accounting controls—checks and balances—to prevent such things."

"What was the outcome?" she asked.

"A blessing in disguise," Mullen explained. "I stepped right in and worked with the S.E.C. We cleaned up the mess and we took our medicine."

"Which was?"

"Because we immediately admitted the problem, the agency didn't sue the company. We entered into some form of agreement, as I recall, in what was called an administrative hearing. AMERIPRO punished the perpetrators—immediately fired them—established new rules and accounting and audit procedures for all our overseas sales. So there you have it, Samantha. I thought you'd better know right up front."

The work man walked into Samantha's office again carrying two boxes. He set them on top of two other boxes, then motioned to her that he was finished.

"Well, they've delivered the last of your files," Samantha said. "I suppose I should go right to this matter and take a look."

"The appropriate documents are in the boxes marked 'F.C.P.A.'—Foreign Corrupt Practices Act. Three boxes altogether."

"Thank you," Samantha replied. "This has been helpful. That's where I'll start, although it doesn't sound so bad to me. The S.E.C. brought a lot of cases back then. If AMERIPRO had been really responsible, I'm sure the S.E.C. would have thrown the book at you, sued, even pressed the Justice Department to seek criminal indictments. That would have been the typical response."

"That's right. I think the files will show the S.E.C. concluded that those of us at the top were completely exonerated."

"Okay, I'll check that out," she said, "and thank you for volunteering the information."

"You're welcome, Samantha. We're on the same side—just wanting to get through this process as expeditiously as possible. Now you can do me a favor?"

Samantha noticed Mrs. Fredericks leaning back, far out of reach of her computer console, resting with the back of her chair against the open door. Samantha turned and cupped her hand over the phone.

"Yes, Mr. Mullen?"

"Have dinner with me tonight," he asked.

"I don't think…" she started to respond.

"Don't say no," he pleaded. "I've begged off all other engagements to prepare for the hearings, but I have to eat. So do you. And I know I'll have questions for you."

"I'm not sure that would be appropriate," she explained.

"Why not? We're both on the same side. Besides, maybe I could help you some more. You might have some questions about what we just discussed. What do you say?"

"I say that if you are half as convincing before the Committee and the Senate, you'll be confirmed on Inauguration Day."

"Great. I'm sure you enjoy the new hip places around the District, but perhaps you could indulge an old man like me, and meet me at Harvey's Restaurant. It's an aging relic but a favorite of mine."

"I've heard it's still exceptional."

"Indeed," Mullen replied. "See you there at eight."

Samantha hung up, and turned back toward her desk as Mrs. Fredericks came around the corner. "Mr. Garcia is on line three for you, Sam. He's been waiting a few minutes—insisted on holding."

Samantha picked up the phone. "Hi," she said. "Finished your story?"

"Yeah, that one's in the can. Pabulum about the 'everything's routine and fine' bullshit press conference. Now to get to the real story. How 'bout a late lunch, let me in on the fireworks behind closed doors?"

Samantha sighed. "No on both counts," she said. "I can't make lunch today. I'm over my head in documents to review for the Mullen hearings. And as to fireworks, there's nothing to tell, on or off the record."

"Come on, Sam? D'Angelo, the anti-establishment poor Italian super-ego from New York, and Mullen, the rich Texan defense industry guy. Complete opposites. They had to hate each other's guts."

"Come on yourself. They're grown men. From what I've seen, they can work together."

"It doesn't make sense. You're not leveling with me."

"Yes I am, Daniel. Sometimes things are as they seem, even in Washington. But if you're so fired up to check on something, you could do me a favor, or two."

"Wonderful. I get a 'no comment' cold shoulder from my main squeeze on the real inside story of Washington's latest soap opera, and then she sends me off on some errands. What's wrong with this picture?"

"'Main' squeeze, Daniel?" Samantha shot back.

"Oh shit," Daniel replied instantly. "Did I say 'main?' Come on Sam, just an old saying. You know I meant *only*."

"You had better, as promised. No screwing around on me," she said firmly, "or..."

"Oh no, not that!" he exclaimed.

"Yes sir. Back on with the baggie for you. You'll have to wrap that little monster up in latex again."

"'Little'," he screamed into the phone.

"Touche'," Samantha laughed, then added, "Not that it would matter to me again because one more slip, a reversion to your old ways, Danny boy, and as much fun as it is, I'd never see it again, with or without protection. That's the deal. You've been tested, I've been tested. It's monogamy, or nothing. Right?"

"Right!" he quickly agreed.

"Good," she said, "because you know I won't tolerate a player. Now get to work. First, double check your files. AMERI-PRO had a problem with the S.E.C. in the 1970's. Foreign Corrupt Practices Act."

"What kind of problem?" Daniel leaped on the tip.

"Probably not much, but Mullen said there was some adverse publicity. I don't remember a word about it in print outs we studied last night."

"No problem. I've got the paper's files and the NEXUS/ LEXUS and Google searches. I'll recheck by linking 'AMERIPRO' with 'S.E.C.' and Foreign Corrupt Practices Act."

"Great. Thanks. And then see what you can find out about somebody."

"Shoot."

"He was in the Prescott campaign–referred to as an advisor on military affairs."

"Colonel Harry Howard?" Daniel asked.

"Yes, that's him. I think he's been mentioned as part of the transition team too."

"Yeah. He's one strange dude. Wound tight, even for a military man. Never laid any info on me, or any of the other guys as far as I know. Strictly a behind the scenes operator, which is definitely rare in this transition team—everybody keeps stepping on one another to get into the camera shots."

"Anything you can come up with," Samantha said. "Don't go to any trouble. Just whatever you have."

"Why?" he asked.

"Just... curiosity."

"Curiosity? Come on, Sam. What are you getting at?"

"I know I've seen him in some campaign footage, close to the President-Elect. And then I saw him again today."

"Where?"

"Driving our Secretary of Defense nominee. I' pretty sure it was him I caught a glimpse of as they were pulling away."

"So he's an insider, who moonlights as a chauffeur?" Daniel concluded. "Strange, but sounds about right for this disorganized gang. I'll see what I can dig up," he assured her. "I'll be seeing you tonight, right, babe?"

Samantha winced at Daniel's all too common choice of words, but decided against reminding him that he wasn't in the barrio any more and she wasn't a "babe". "No, not tonight. I've got way too much work. We'll talk tomorrow."

"God," Daniel mocked a groan. "I need to see you tonight, and I mean bad."

"Not tonight, darling," she purred, then whispered into the phone, "and remember, if you can't control that hot Latin blood of yours for one night, it's back to the baggy, <u>big</u> boy." She laughed, and hung up the phone, wondering why she hadn't mentioned the dinner with Frank Mullen.

CHAPTER SIX

Frank Mullen climbed out of the backseat of the Lincoln Town Car, then reached around to grab his overcoat. Colonel Howard caught him by the wrist and pulled him back into the privacy of the car.

"Are you certain you can't give her this memento of your dinner," he said, holding out the small ornamental lapel pin. "The sound sensor and transmitter are intertwined into the wire matrix of the design. Weak signal, but undetectable."

"Colonel," Mullen explained, exasperation creeping into his voice. "It's a bad idea. Trust me on this. Samantha Wright is a smart lady. She's not about to accept some trinket from me. Don't underestimate her."

The Colonel's normally piercing green eyes seemed to glaze over. "If you say so," he responded coldly. "I'll be back at twenty-two hundred hours."

Mullen looked at his watch. "Fine, two hours it is."

"Affirmative," Colonel Howard replied. He jammed his foot down on the accelerator. The car jolted away from the curb as Mullen slammed the passenger door.

Mullen walked down the five steps to the main door of the restaurant, stopping a moment for the inside doorman to see his image on the security monitor and open the door. "Good evening, Mr. Mullen. It is a pleasure to see you again."

"Yes, indeed," he replied, handing him his overcoat and cashmere scarf and walking briskly toward the maitre d's station.

"Monsieur Mullen, it is our honor! Congratulations on your magnificent appointment. We do hope you will make Harvey's your home away from home."

"I will, Pierre," Mullen replied, "if you maintain your standards."

The thin smile crossed the maitre d's face. "But of course, Monsieur." He glanced past Mullen, then turned back. "There are two in your party tonight, Monsieur Mullen?"

"Yes. Ms. Samantha Wright will be joining me. Give us booth number four, and keep number three empty."

The maitre d' winced slightly, then bowed again, and came up smiling. "But of course, Monsieur Mullen."

The door behind them opened again, and Samantha walked in, looking decidedly different from the morning. As the doorman took her plain black cloth coat, Mullen noted that the daytime business suit had been replaced with a black crepe evening dress, adorned at the neck with simple string of tiny white pearls. Her sandy colored hair was no longer tied back, but flowed down to her shoulders in a gentle wave. As Mullen looked up, he realized she had replaced her flat shoes with high heels. She towered over him.

"Samantha," he greeted her warmly. "Welcome to Harvey's. Thank you for not foregoing a boring evening with an old man."

"Not to worry, Mr. ah, Frank. When I make a commitment, I keep it."

"Why yes, of course," he said. "In any event, this is such a rare treat. The company of a beautiful woman. I'm afraid I'm inexperienced in such matters. Too much work, never enough time."

"Never?" she smiled.

He leaned toward her and sighed. "I've been married to AMERIPRO all my adult life."

"Too bad," Samantha replied.

He stared at her. She was quite pretty, with clear, sparkling blue eyes. She was wearing makeup, but so naturally that he didn't take notice of it. Her hair flowing freely down to her shoulders made her look younger than that morning. Her body was slim and fit. Maybe he was wrong about her age. She could be in her early thirties. But then he quickly calculated she had too many years work experience.

"Well no more," he said. "The marriage is over and I'm on to bigger and better things. Shall we?" he said, motioning to the maitre d' to escort them to their table.

As they took their seats in the large booth in the corner of the elegant room, the maitre d' said flatly, "The usual for Monsieur, and for the lady?"

Samantha said, "I'll have a glass of champagne, please." The moment she spoke she regretted it. Too fancy. But before she could change the order, Mullen joined in.

"A splendid idea! Pierre, I'll pass on my usual, and join the lady. Bring us a fine bottle of your own selection."

The maitre d' hesitated, then smiled broadly. "Excellent."

As he walked away, Samantha observed, "He seems surprised you're having champagne."

"Yes, well, they do know me here. I'm not much of a drinker. That special I mentioned is tomato juice, with lots of Tabasco. But what the hell? No need for just a briefing session. This gives us a chance," he said, "to let our hair down, ah, so to speak. I don't know about you, but I've had a rather arduous day."

"Not me," she laughed. "All I've done is spend the day listening to you, then reading about you or AMERIPRO."

"Oh my. And now here you are stuck with me for the evening as well."

"Quite the opposite. I found your story inspiring. You started so poor, orphaned, but look at all you've achieved."

"Well," he said, motioning for the sommelier to proceed to pour the champagne. "It was a challenge. The way I grew up I wouldn't wish upon anyone. But then you move on, make the most of it, grab what opportunities you can."

"You've certainly done that," Samantha said with genuine admiration. "Yale on scholarship, a prestigious Chicago law firm, then on to AMERIPRO."

"Yes. Those days were much different. Young lawyers didn't make much money. Chicago was expensive even then, and it was hard to make ends meet on a starting salary. But then my big break came, when Kingston Wittlefield took me under his wing. The company wasn't even called AMERIPRO then."

"I know."

"Of course you do, from all your reading today. No, it was a straightforward manufacturing company—auto parts, machinery, farm equipment—basic stuff. Wittlefield took control of the company through a tender offer for the stock, years before Wall Street caught on to that as a tactic. He had ambitious plans to expand the company through acquisitions. I was fortunate that he included me in those plans. He promised to train me, give me the opportunity of a lifetime. And he was a man of his word."

"And now you're going to leave him and AMERIPRO?"

"Yes," he paused, "it's time to do something else with my life. I figure I've got another ten, fifteen years to be truly productive." He stared into the room for a moment, unfocused, then seemed to snap back. "Wittlefield also taught me that you never rest on your laurels. He's been very encouraging about this move to public service, that it's a great opportunity to apply my business aptitude. So here," he said, raising his champagne glass. "Let's toast to new opportunities, new challenges, new friends."

The two clinked glasses, and Samantha took first a short sip, then enjoyed a longer drink. "Wonderful champagne," she said approvingly.

Mullen set down his glass. "You see, I knew you'd like this place. But you've spent all day with the story of Frank Mullen. Let's order dinner and change the subject."

Samantha went along with the waiter's recommendations, starting with escargot Provencal. As the waiter departed, she said, "I'm certainly not complaining, but lawyers working for the government these days, even for the Senate, really don't make much money—not like our counterparts in private practice. I probably live like you did in Chicago. I scrimp and try to save—I make do somehow, but I don't dine at Harvey's Restaurant. I didn't grow up in poverty, but we—my mother and I—didn't have much money either. She was a single mother trying to raise a child alone when that was quite unusual."

"Tell me about it, Samantha." He held his glass up again, encouraging her to take another long drink. When she put hers down, the sommelier refilled it, and then stood aside as the waiter delivered the first course. Samantha looked at the plate before her. "A lovely presentation."

She eagerly extracted an escargot from the shell. She savored the distinctive taste. "You're an orphan. My father died when I was three. A car crash when he was traveling out of town. He was always on the go. We have something in common."

"I'm sorry. Your mother must be a strong woman to raise you alone."

Samantha lifted her eyebrows. "Lots of women do it these days," she snapped.

"Of course," he said, "I know that."

"I suppose as a captain of industry you haven't had much experience with struggling women," she said.

"True."

"But you're right. My mother was strong, once. We were living in my grandmother's house in White Plains and she had to take care of my grandmother too. My mother was independent, self-reliant. That's how she wanted me to be. She's the one who pushed me toward public service. She was ahead of her time. She was well-educated, and very politically involved, a huge Kennedy supporter."

Mullen raised his eyebrows. "Is that so?"

"Oh yes! She met him when she was a student at Radcliffe. She worked on his first campaign for Senate, in 1952, and then later on the presidential campaign. She met my father on the campaign." She leaned back as the dishes were cleared. "God, I still remember, mother had this one ash tray, dumb thing really, cheap trinket, but she said Kennedy had used it for one of his cigars."

"Exciting times. Of course, Samantha, I'm old enough to recall those years first hand," Mullen explained.

The waiter arrived with two enormous bone china plates, smoothly placing the shrimp and crayfish casserole before Samantha, and announcing "the Steak au Poivre for Monsieur, as usual, well done. Bon appetit," he requested, and walked briskly away.

Samantha took another sip of champagne, then eagerly speared a delicate crayfish. "Scrumptious," she announced.

"I am glad you like it," Mullen said. "Ample portions, as real French food is supposed to be. None of this nouvelle for me. But there I go, aging myself again."

"I agree on the nouvelle issue," she said, taking another bite from her superb dish. "But you're hardly aging yourself. I recall Kennedy."

"But," Mullen replied, "I didn't think you were born yet."

"Thanks," she said, "but I was three and a half when he died. I remember clearly the television screen the day Kennedy was assassinated."

He took a bite from his steak. "I suppose everyone remembers certain events. From my generation, people recall exactly where they were, what they were doing, when FDR died, when the war ended, Neil Armstrong on the moon, and of course, as you mentioned, when JFK was killed."

"Where were you, Frank?"

"Well, when FDR died I was just a kid."

"No, no. Kennedy. What were you doing?" She asked, finished the last sip from her glass, which was promptly refilled.

"I was in Abilene, Texas, at our helicopter plant, working at my desk, as usual. It was about quarter to one, a beautiful afternoon. My secretary burst into my office. Hysterical. She said, I recall her words exactly, as if it were yesterday, 'The President is dead." And then for some reason she said 'I don't know about Jackie.' I know it sounds, I guess naive now, but I simply did not believe it."

"What did you do?" Samantha asked.

"Well, I tried to comfort her, that I was sure it was just some sick joke. There were some crazy people in Texas back then, crazy enough I thought to spread such a sick rumor. But I didn't think crazy enough to actually do it. So I said to Mrs. Jackson, 'No one would want to shoot President Kennedy.'"

The waiter noticed that the lady had not taken a bite for some time, and approached. "May I clear the lady's plate?"

Samantha looked up blankly. "Oh, yes, thank you."

Mullen looked over at the expensive dinner. "Are you sure?"

"Yes," she said. "I guess I wasn't as hungry as I thought."

Frank Mullen took a last bite of steak, and motioned for the waiter to take his plate as well. He reached for his still almost full glass of champagne, and sipped. "A few minutes later Mrs. Jackson returned, confirmed the awful news. It was no rumor or sick joke. Kennedy was dead." He paused, and looked into Samantha's eyes. "But that was a long time ago."

Samantha leaned back in the deep cushions of the booth. "Yes," she said sadly. "My mother was devastated. Something left her that day. Something in her spirit. She's in an assisted care facility now, a very nice one," she added quickly. Frank Mullen seemed genuinely interested. Something about him put her at ease. "She's...she's diagnosed with dementia–probable Alzheimer's."

"I'm sorry," Mullen said. "It's sad, a tragic disease."

"The doctors are never one hundred percent sure of the diagnosis until...until they do an autopsy. Her short-term memory is essentially gone, but other than that some days she seems almost normal. Remembers the old days. She still keeps a photograph of President Kennedy in her room, right next to mine. It's from his Inaugural Address," she smiled slightly. "I suppose she thought he could do no wrong. But now we know so much— his secret life, and if you believe the tabloids some really sordid stuff. But still, even with what we've learned, he inspired a whole generation to public service. I'm certainly trying to make a difference, indirectly because of him."

"Your mother?" he interjected.

"Yes, she pounded the thought of public service into me, holding him up as the example."

"And how about making real money, someday?" he asked.

"Believe me, I know. There is nothing like it. After all, Kennedy was rich."

She stared back at him. "Perhaps so," she said. "I can tell you one thing. The bills to take care of my mother aren't getting any cheaper."

"I'm sure."

As the Grand Marnier souffles he had specially ordered were served, she gently pushed hers away. "I can't touch another drop of booze," she explained. "I'm feeling no pain as it is."

"Nonsense," he said. "The liquor all evaporates in the cooking. Enjoy!"

She shrugged lightly and pulled the hot dish back.

"Perhaps I should bring up a little business?" Mullen said. "Do you have any questions from your day's research. Perhaps something on that AMERIPRO problem I mentioned."

"No, not really," Samantha answered, enjoying a bite of the heavenly dessert. "Your files seem complete. I read the S.E.C. administrative decision. It all appears to be in order. They found no evidence of culpability by your top management, and praised the company for cleaning its own house."

"Good," he said.

"Actually," she paused. "The review of the AMERIPRO matter is going to help me on another front. There's been this scandal over at the Pentagon that's somewhat like the AMERIPRO problems. It involves a number of overseas post exchanges and officers' clubs."

"I've read about that. Some form of widespread organized embezzlement. But what could possibly be the connection with AMERIPRO?"

"No connection," she replied. "Analogous. The commanding officers of the bases knew nothing about what their subordinates were up to—but right under their noses there was this clandestine scheme skimming millions from the base exchanges—phony invoices, commissions and kickbacks to foreign sales agents. A whole set of dummy accounting books to conceal the operation. And at the heart of it—a numbered Swiss bank account, just like with AMERIPRO."

Mullen slowly put his fork down. "So?" he said calmly. "I suppose all these bad guys use off-shore bank accounts."

"But I noticed a little wrinkle to it. In the S.E.C. files there was a mention that your AMERIPRO culprits used the Swiss account as what they called a 'clearing account'. That account paid the bribes. But there was another hidden account, a 'holding account', in Liechtenstein."

"That doesn't ring a bell with me," Mullen said, waving to the waiter for the check.

"As I said, the S.E.C. only gives it a passing mention. It didn't appear to be relevant once they'd found the perpetrators, and the company had imposed new safeguards to prevent anything like that happening again. AMERIPRO's accountants certified that they had traced as much of the money as possible."

"Makes sense," he said, reaching for the wallet in the breast pocket of his suit coat.

"But that's exactly what the Pentagon investigation has turned up. It's in a report filed with the Armed Services Committee. Seems these crooks have structured things the same way—an account in Switzerland, and an account in of all places, Liechtenstein."

"Interesting coincidence," he observed, slipping a Platinum American Express card into the leather envelope containing the restaurant bill.

"Maybe," she said casually, "or there could be some specific reason that only people with experience in such things would know."

"Ah, I suppose," he murmured.

"I may find out because of AMERIPRO, or because you helped me by bringing this S.E.C. matter to my attention."

"I don't get it," he said.

"George Willard," she stated.

Mullen stared at her, his eyes narrowing. He shook his head. "I'm sorry, I'm not following you."

"Of course not," she said. "I have an advantage. I'm fresh with the details. George Willard was the ring leader of the AMERIPRO overseas corruption problem."

"Of course," Mullen replied, moving his hand to his forehead and gently patting. "Our number one bad guy. I shouldn't have forgotten that name."

"You may want to review some of these materials yourself. You don't want to appear rusty before the Committee."

"Of course not," he said. "But what about ah, Mr. Willard?"

Samantha smiled. "I'm going to ask him about Liechtenstein and Switzerland. Who would know better? He's got nothing to hide now, and it could help us evaluate the Pentagon investigation."

The waiter returned with the envelope containing the credit card and the receipt.

"My goodness," Mullen exclaimed. "How are you going to do that? I wouldn't be surprised if Willard has departed for parts unknown."

"Might have," she replied. "But I'll know in the morning. I assume AMERIPRO hasn't kept track of him. But I noticed in the S.E.C. file that one of the reasons they didn't proceed against him was that he had served in the Army, with distinction, during Vietnam. He had been badly wounded, heroically saving his platoon. So I figure the Army might know his whereabouts."

Mullen pulled out his reading glasses and looked down at the bill.

Samantha glanced over, wondering what the damage would be for a fine meal at Harvey's. She stiffened. "Frank, I think we have a problem here."

He fumbled with his glasses. "A problem?"

"The card," she said. "It's corporate—AMERIPRO. I can't let..."

Mullen slipped his glasses back on, and looked down. "Oh, so it is. Pretty careless of me. Of course I can't have AMERIPRO entertaining the senior assistant to the Chairman of the Senate Armed Services Committee."

"In fact," Samantha added, "you shouldn't even have that card any more."

"Absolutely," he agreed. "Should have been turned in today. An oversight." He quickly stuffed the corporate card into his coat pocket, then reached again for his wallet and pulled out a personal credit card. He motioned for the waiter to return.

As they rose from the table, Frank Mullen apologized profusely, explaining that as the night was running late, and he still had much work to do, he'd best not detour to drive Samantha to her apartment in the Virginia suburbs. She assured him that it was perfectly all right. The maitre d' called a cab for her.

At the curb, Samantha thanked Frank Mullen for a pleasant dinner, got into the taxi, waved good-bye and gave the driver the address of her apartment building across the Potomac River in Rosslyn.

Mullen spotted the Town Car waiting in the dark across the icy street and down the block. He walked across to it, got in and heaved a heavy sigh.

"Problems?" Colonel Howard asked.

"No," Mullen replied without conviction, looking down at an ordinary brown paper shopping bag on the floor. "What's in the bag, Colonel?"

"Nothing," he said abruptly. "Junk."

The Lincoln pulled away from the curb, and headed back to the Hay-Adams Hotel.

At her apartment, Samantha turned the key in the dead-bolt lock, but there was no motion. Something was wrong. She opened the door and turned on the lights. Astonished, gasping, she quickly slammed the door, ran down the hallway and pounded on Mrs. Turner's door. She heard the soft patter of footsteps, and then saw the telltale blocking of the light indicating the old lady inside was staring through the observation lens.

"It's me, Mrs. Turner. Samantha Wright."

The old lady opened the door. "It's awfully late, Sam."

"My apartment," she stammered. "I've been robbed."

Using her neighbor's telephone, Samantha's first call was to the building security office, who in turn called the Arlington County Sheriff's Department. Then she called Daniel.

CHAPTER SEVEN

Arlington County Deputy Sheriff Carl Callahan looked like a throw back to an era well before fitness centers. His sizable belly spilled over a thick black leather belt that held up his uniform pants. From his red flushed face a wide, handlebar mustache protruded, its long whiskers moving with every breath he heaved in and out.

Callahan moved cautiously around the combined dinette and living room of Samantha's one bedroom apartment, frequently stopping to mark the appropriate boxes on an incident report form. When he came to the second page of the form, he turned to Samantha and Daniel. "Listen here, lady. The way this works—you tell me what's missing, I put it down here, see?" He pointed to a page in the report with two columns of horizontal blank lines. "You tell me how much it's worth. I don't care, understand? You talk, I write. Your insurance company gets the report. The numbers on the report are the numbers on the report. Simple as that." He smiled.

"Aren't you going to test for prints, take some photos of the scene?" Samantha asked.

As the deputy sheriff shook his head, Daniel placed his arm around Samantha's waist, and gave her a gentle hug. "At least you get to see a representative of law enforcement in the flesh and blood," Daniel consoled her. "In my old neighborhood, all you could hope for was a report over the phone."

"Yeah?" the cop asked suspiciously. "Where you from, anyway?"

"Miami," Daniel spoke softly, shifting his eyes about the room, feigning concern that someone might hear.

"Yeah? I wouldn't go out into beaner country jus' to write down some burglary report neither. Hell, it's bad around here, but they're mean and crazy down there. Cut deep slices out of people with razor knives jus' to watch 'em bleed."

"Man, I know what you mean, Deputy," Daniel said, trying to sound sympathetic. "That's why I got the hell out of there and moved to our nation's capital, where I can be safe."

The deputy sheriff smiled. "Oh, I get it," he replied, "kidding around, huh?"

"No," Daniel explained. "We're just wondering how the hell somebody gets in a supposedly high security, high rise in the Virginia suburbs, passes right through a double locked door, and walks away with what he wants, and nobody sees or hears anything, and the cops don't even dust for prints."

"Look here, mister," Callahan replied, puffing, "don't go getting all worked up. You answered your own question. It was a pro, that's all. Somebody who knows what he's doing–bet he's a loner. The front door, the garage door, however he got in the building, a piece of cake for a pro." The deputy looked around the sparsely furnished room. He thought that it had to be a hard up pro to have made the effort for this place. "He'll know where the cameras are," he explained, "and know nobody's looking anyway. Holds a newspaper up like he's reading and hides his face. As for locks on the front door there," he said, pointing, "bet it don't take him all of ten seconds to jimmy 'em. If somebody happens into the hall, he starts knocking on a door, innocent as can be. Sorry to tell you, but it happens, more than these folks tell you when they rent to you. Got the picture?"

Samantha looked at Daniel, and couldn't control a slight shiver. "Yes, I guess so," she answered.

"No need for photos or prints," the deputy concluded. "This mess is what it is, and a pro ain't gonna leave prints. Hey, be thankful," he smiled, the waxed tips on the wings of his mustache curling up. "If it had a been some hopped up punks, they woulda pissed on your sofa here, or all over the walls," the officer said, waving his pencil around the living room.

"Yeck," Samantha responded.

"And if you'd been in the place, well, who knows what..." He let that one hang, unfinished.

"Okay, okay," Daniel held up his hands.

The deputy's radio phone beeped, and he reached down and brought the hand held unit to his ear. "Callahan here."

Daniel strained to hear the other side of the conversation, but only caught muffled sounds."

Ten four. Be there in fifteen. Out," the deputy said. He turned to Samantha and Daniel. "Look folks. I gotta go. Another burglary over in that there other high rise. Probably the same guy. Here," he said, tearing the second sheet from the crime report form. "Ya'll fill this out. You know, how much cash, model of T.V., whatever, and then put the value here," he said, placing the end of his pencil at the second column of blank spaces. "It'll be the official crime report. Your insurance cain't bitch about it. Mail it in to this here address in five days. Your insurance will order a copy of the report, and that's all ya'll need to do."

Samantha looked at Daniel, then back at the deputy. "But that's the point. This 'pro' of yours didn't take much. Nothing of any value, anyway. I didn't leave any cash here. All he took was some costume jewelry."

"Nothin' with real gold in it, maybe silver? Even small stuff?" the deputy asked.

"No. I wish I could say I had some real jewelry," she said, smiling at Daniel. "But it was all costume stuff. Inexpensive."

The deputy gave her a sharp look. "Okay, so he's a dumb pro. What can I tell you? Have a nice night, now."

He handed Samantha the paper and waddled out.

"Not the best of circumstances," Samantha said to Daniel. "You did get to see me tonight after all."

Daniel gave her that "I'm ready" look she knew so well. "Your misfortune is my..." he started to say.

"No way, Romeo," she said emphatically. "All I'm going to do is take some Excedrin and try to get some sleep."

"Okay, okay," he smiled. "I'll check out 'Night Line' and be in later."

She tried to stifle a big yawn. "Thanks for being here, Daniel."

He leaned over and kissed her on the cheek. *"No problemo, Senorita.* Get some sleep." He headed for the couch, then turned back. "Where were you tonight, anyway? That's a nice change of clothes from this morning."

"Oh, a dinner, a very good dinner."

"Where?"

"Harvey's Restaurant."

"Hot damn. Gone way uptown on me, huh. With D'Angelo?"

"No," she said flatly.

"Come on, now. Who's wining and dining my woman at the most expensive place in town?"

Samantha smiled. "The next Secretary of Defense."

"Mullen? Jesus! What did he say?"

"Later, Daniel." She yawned again. "In the morning."

Samantha awoke with a start, haunting images from the television screen, filled with the face of Frank Mullen, first at a press conference, and then in the back seat of a car, with a driver. The driver's face consumed the screen, then everything turned black.

Samantha got up and pulled her heavy terry cloth robe around her, and walked into the living room. Daniel was asleep on the couch, snoring softly, the television still on. She reached for the remote, turned it off, and moved to the aluminum sliding glass doors that led to her tiny balcony. She looked out through the bleak misty morning and across at the other high rise tower only a stone's throw away. She remembered the deputy sheriff's comments about the apartment rental agents' omissions about crime. Not surprising, she thought. Fell into the same category as the sales pitch for the extra seventy-five dollars a month for the balcony with the so-called river view. She stared out into the grayness, unable to see the Potomac through what she had learned the local weathermen euphemistically called "low clouds." As she stared, small white objects started blowing onto the balcony and pressing against the glass doors.

"Damn!" she exclaimed, and turned to Daniel. She shook him once, then again. "Daniel, get up, it's snowing!"

Daniel rolled over on his back. "What? Huh?"

"Snow, Daniel. The city will be a mess. I've got to get going. I can't afford a wasted Washington snow day."

As Samantha showered, Daniel made coffee, and started scrambling some eggs with salsa and the Monterey jack cheese he found hiding in the back of her refrigerator. When he called "breakfast ready" Samantha rushed out of the bedroom.

"I've only got time for coffee."

"Your loss is my gain," he replied, hungrily eyeing the mound of simmering eggs as he sprinkled another handful of cheese over the top and stirred. "Now, tell me about your dinner."

"Can't," she said, taking a quick sip of her coffee. "I've got to go."

"Holding out on me?" he said. "It'll be strictly off the record, not even background."

"No," she smiled. "That's not it. I'll clue you in when I have the time. But I've got to beat the snow into the office and jump on a lead that might kill two birds with one stone."

"How's that?" he asked, scraping the entire four-egg amalgamation from the frying pan onto a solitary plate.

"A guy by the name of Willard. I need to tie up a loose end with him about Frank Mullen. He may be able to help me with the Pentagon overseas PX scandal too."

"Who is this guy? I *needs* to know, Sam. Sounds like he's right up my Pentagon beat."

"Maybe, maybe not. I'll let you know," she said.

"Okay. But I'll only wait a day, then he's free game. Willard, huh."

"But darling," Samantha said.

"Hold it," he interrupted. "I hate it when you say 'darling' that way."

"Oh, come on, Daniel. It's no big deal. It's that guy who was driving Mullen when we came up to Capitol Hill—did you find anything?"

"Not much. He's about the only guy around this new President who won't ever spill the beans. He did seem to have a distinguished military career. A fast mover. Served in all the hot spots—Germany, Korea, early on in Vietnam."

"What do you mean 'early on?'" Samantha asked.

"I mean before the war really got going. He was in Vietnam when Eisenhower was President."

"Sounds like the gung ho type," Samantha observed.

"Yeah, but then a funny thing. He got out of the Army early— bailed as a Lieutenant Colonel. Didn't hang in to be a full bird."

"Burned out?" Samantha suggested.

"Could be. I haven't been able to find out much about him after he quit the Army in 1961. That is, until he came out of nowhere as an advisor on military matters to presidential candidate Governor Prescott. Of course, nobody knew much then about Prescott either. Small state governor, starts traipsing through Iowa, New Hampshire—looks good on T.V., ends up running away with the whole enchilada. Colonel Howard jumped on the winning horse early. Joined the campaign when there was no campaign. Howard slogged around with Prescott. My sources say he was a combo advance man, go'fer, and fund raiser."

"Look, Daniel. I know I said don't go to any big trouble, but..."

"You want me to go to some trouble, Sam?"

She smiled. "Dig some more. Somewhere along the way I'm going to have to work with this Colonel Howard. Find out anything you can."

"Yes, ma'am. The *Post* stands ready to help our loyal friends in government."

"Thanks. Now I'm out of here." She put her coffee cup in the sink and started for her heavy coat.

"You're welcome," Daniel replied. "But put one thing in that great memory bank of yours."

"Yes?" she replied.

"Information is a two-way street. I want the Willard lead, tomorrow."

"A deal," she said.

"One more thing."

She buttoned her coat. She kissed him quickly on the lips.

"That other information you wanted. Checking on AMERI-PRO's problem with the S.E.C. in the 70's?"

"Yes?"

"*Nada!*" He grinned at her.

"Nothing? Not even some blurb, *Wall Street Journal* sort of thing?"

"Not a whisper," he said.

"That's really odd," she said. "Mullen told me, at least he implied that..."

Samantha grabbed her attaché case and walked to the door. She looked back at Daniel. "Lock up, will you?"

As he swallowed a large helping of salsa and eggs, he gave her an affirmative thumbs up.

———⟨≈⟩———

By the time Samantha arrived at the central Metro terminal under Union Station and came up on North Capitol Street, the willowy white flakes had given way to a driving downpour of heavy wet snow. She immediately decided against spending the rest of the day with wet hair and sopping shoes, and grabbed the first cab in the long line waiting at the station. When she announced her destination as the Russell building only a few blocks away, the swarthy cab driver of undetermined foreign origin let out a long string of expletives.

"Look, buddy, just drive, and then you can get right back in the taxi line." She hated that a rude driver could so easily make her feel guilty, but at the end of the short ride Samantha told him to keep the change from the five dollars she handed him for the two dollar ninety cent fare.

Samantha was the first into the office. Realizing that the snow would do its usual job on Washington work schedules, she looked forward to the quiet she'd undoubtedly enjoy for the next couple of hours. Her first stop was the fax machine. She pulled two sheets out of the incoming bin, and quickly glanced at the friendly note on the cover page.

CONFIDENTIAL
USUAL PROCEDURES
DO NOT USE E-MAIL

"Sam. The attached is a one pager summary of info I was able to retrieve fast from the computer files I've been creating from old personnel records. The hard copy of the full service record would be much better, but it would take a week for me to get it. Keep up the good fight. B.U.D."

Good old Buddy—Army Master Sergeant Jim Bhudhorn, assigned to the Bureau of Personnel. Three years before, he'd given forthright answers to straight questions during what were supposed to be mundane Senate subcommittee hearings on manpower projections. But his clear charting of the reductions in personnel that could be made with the technological advances being introduced on the battlefield contrasted sharply with the mumbo jumbo his superiors had tried to force feed the committee. In the political firestorm, he'd won D'Angelo's respect and Sam's friendship, but he'd gotten nothing but grief at the Pentagon. Since the brass could not get rid of him, it killed his promotion chances. He was just hanging in, waiting for retirement. But Samantha had one friend, and a good, hands-on source, at the Pentagon; and that rarity, a military guy willing to admit that the Pentagon would work better if it was leaner.

Samantha started to read the communication from Buddy.

SUMMARY REPORT-SR-2

(FOR COMPLETE DATA SEE SERVICE FILE, DOCKET REPORT SD-1)

GEORGE WILLARD (NO MIDDLE INITIAL)

DATE OF BIRTH: 21 SEPTEMBER, 1931

SERIAL NUMBER: U.S. ARMY (REG) 479-487-39560

INDUCTION DATE: 30 MARCH, 1950.

HIGHEST RANK: E-8–N.C.O.–MASTER SERGEANT

DUTY STATIONS: FORT BENNING, GEORGIA

FIELD OPS, KOREA

STRATEGIC PLANS, PENTAGON

FIELD OPS, LEBANON

STRATEGIC PLANS, PENTAGON

FIELD OPS, REPUBLIC OF VIETNAM

VETERANS HOSPITAL, CORPUS CHRISTI, TEXAS

SEPARATION DATE: 31 DECEMBER, 1968

COMMENDATIONS AND MEDALS: NUMEROUS

LAST REPORTED ADDRESS:

NUMBER 7 SPIRIT OF THE REPUBLIC LANE

WILLOWBROOK, TEXAS

LAST REPORTED TELEPHONE: (214) 555-1776

Samantha glanced at her watch. 8:20. It was early in Texas, but late for her when she noted the calendar date on the dial of her watch. She didn't have any time to spare. George Willard would have to accept a wake-up call.

She returned to her office with the Summary Report, and punched in the numbers on the phone. The phone was answered on the second ring. A man's voice, a distinctive British accent, "Mr. Willard's residence. May I help you?"

"Oh, hello. Good morning. I'm looking for Mr. George Willard."

"May I inquire who wishes to speak with Mr. Willard?" "Yes, of course," she said. "My name is Samantha Wright. I work in the United States Senate."

"Yes?" he said unimpressed.

"I'm the senior assistant to the Chairman of the Senate Armed Services Committee, Senator D'Angelo." Samantha paused for effect. "I am calling Mr. Willard on official government business."

"Indeed," he said in the same tone. "I shall see if Mr. Willard is available. Please hold."

Samantha heard the click of the phone, and then country and western music. The tune was familiar. A song about bulls and blood and sweat and, there it was, the lyric she remembered, that "thang we call rodeo." She waited one minute, and then two, unable to concentrate on the conversation she hoped to have as she found herself humming along with the memorable tale of a cowboy's love of the rodeo. Suddenly, the phone clicked again.

"George Willard here."

"Good morning, Mr. Willard," she said. "I'm Samantha Wright. I work with Senator…"

"I know who you say you are," he interrupted, "from D'Angelo's committee—Mullen's confirmation hearings."

"Yes, that's correct."

"By contacting me, you may have caused me some considerable problems."

"I only want to…"

"If I decide to talk to you, I'll only talk face to face, and only after I'm damn sure who you are."

Samantha started to assure him, but he cut her off again. "Bring your credentials, and a letter signed by D'Angelo confirming you are the Committee investigator. Fax the letter to me this morning, same number. Come alone. It's zero seven thirty hours. I tee off at zero seven fifty—finish in about four hours. I will stop by the bank on the way back, and return here. Meet me here at fourteen hundred, er, two o'clock, Texas time."

"Today?" Samantha exclaimed.

"Today," he replied, "or forget it." He hung up.

Samantha only had a few precious days left before the hearings. She could hardly afford to take a day and travel to Willowbrook, Texas, wherever that was. She had to start him off with a telephone conversation, then see where it led.

Now what? What problem was he talking about that she'd caused just by contacting him? Stick with the plan, she thought. Bone up on the reams of documents, prepare the Senator's questions. Her number one job was to get organized, and make the Senator look organized for the hearings. She needed all the time she could get for that.

She marched into her office. Why hadn't Willard sounded surprised? And he'd mentioned Mullen. But she wanted to talk to him about the PX scandal. She began taking off her coat. Obviously, he thought he had something relevant to say about the confirmation. She put her coat on a chair. He's stopping by the bank, she thought. What did that mean? If only she had more time. She'd just have to work straight through, pull all-nighters like she did in law school. Yes, that's what she would have to do, after she returned from Willowbrook, Texas. She put on her coat.

CHAPTER EIGHT

The Senator glanced at the letter and reached for a pen, and looked up at Samantha. "Sam, I don't know. Running off to Texas to ah…"

"Dot the i's and cross the t's, Senator. This S.E.C. matter appears to be the only blemish on the AMERIPRO record, so the press could focus on it, for lack of anything else to get excited about. If we're still trying to take it easy on this nomination, I had better have all the answers to diffuse any problem."

The Senator rolled his eyes. "Yes, we're still going to take it easy. Some old S.E.C. technical violations change nothing. I committed to the President-Elect, so this deal is done. Good luck getting out of National today."

"I've checked," Samantha replied. "Most flights are still taking off. My flight's running about an hour late, but I should be all right."

"Where do you fly into?"

"Dallas," she answered. "Willowbrook is a suburb."

Daniel Garcia was frustrated. He had never hit such a stone wall with his Pentagon sources before. His last conversation with a navy commander on the staff of the Joint Chiefs of Staff summed it up. "You'll get nothing from me, and I'd be amazed if you get anything from anyone else here in the old puzzle palace. Colonel Howard looks to have the new President's ear on the military. That's power, it affects everything around here, no one wants to cross him, at least not now." He'd gone on to say everyone was waiting to see who ends up calling the shots in the new administration. Garcia could not get anyone to fill in the blanks on Howard's bio. Why? "It always gets back who leaked to you press guys."

Daniel resented the inference, but the commander had a point. Washington was one big sieve, except, it seemed, when it came to information about the post army life and times of Colonel Harry Howard.

Daniel was about to change course and start in on his quest for George Willard when he realized that the outgoing President's political people wouldn't care if they met with Colonel Howard's disapproval. He picked up the phone and called an Assistant Secretary of State he knew particularly well.

"If it isn't the *Post's* rising star," Victoria Merriweather responded warmly. "It's been a long time, Danny. Too busy to call or," she lowered her voice, "visit your old friends."

"It's not that at all, Vicky," Daniel replied.

"Don't tell me you're still with Samantha?"

Daniel paused, wanting to respond honestly, but also to improve his chances for getting what he needed. "Yes, we're still together," he said, then qualified the answer, "pretty steady."

"My, my," she replied. "That Samantha must have something special to tie down Washington's erstwhile Latin lover."

Daniel laughed. "No, Vicky. Once a Latin lover, always a..."

"I wouldn't know," she said. "But if Samantha Wright doesn't take extraordinary care of you, Danny, and you need a special friend, you let me know."

"I'm glad you said that," he replied warmly, suddenly recalling in arousing detail the last time they had made love. He had been working on a story about women reaching the top ranks of midshipmen command at the Naval Academy, and had run into her with some yachting friends at a bar near the Severn Marina. After a few drinks, she'd enticed him back to a friend's cottage on the eastern shore of the Chesapeake Bay. Following a feast of crabs and corn and beer out on the secluded picnic table by the water, they had started in the open air, on the blanket. As the summer night fell, they retreated to the cabin for what turned into a particularly long and passionate session, even by his standards, which consumed all of the Saturday night, and most of a rainy Sunday morning. As he thought about that time, he said, honestly, "I need a special friend right now."

"That's more like it. What can I do for you, Danny?" she asked.

After he explained what he needed, she said softly, "I shouldn't do it."

"Vicky, I'll keep it in complete confidence."

Finally, she agreed, rationalizing that "Lame ducks sometimes quack. I'll call you if and when I get my hands on something, but we have to meet in person, Danny. You'll just have to sneak away from that Samantha if you want any info from me."

The wheels lifted off the runway at National. The 10:15 a.m. flight to Dallas was twenty minutes late, but Samantha could still make it to the Dallas suburb by two o'clock if there were no further delays.

As the plane zoomed into the sunny blue skies above the snow-laden clouds, Samantha fidgeted with her string of faux pearls. Her thoughts raced from Frank Mullen to George Willard, to what kind of jerk would break into an apartment to rip off cheap costume jewelry. Maybe she needed a break from Washington, from the public service she'd always assumed would be her life. Maybe Frank Mullen was right, she should think about making some real money. Get a high paying job in private practice. She could get a townhouse with room for a live-in caregiver. She could bring her mother home.

When the seat belt sign went off she began to re-read her copious notes from her review of the S.E.C. materials on AMERI-PRO.

The Dallas/Fort Worth International Airport is capable of landing two jetliners at a time, each taking one of the two main parallel runways. With the substantial back-up of delayed flights from the snowy east coast, the air traffic controllers stacked the incoming planes in two long lines.

Samantha looked out the starboard window of the aircraft. She glanced back and noticed the forward tip of another jet plane pull into view. At first it seemed to parallel her airliner's course, but it banked right and sped ahead. As it's fuselage moved swiftly past, the large tail section with its two jet engines quickly followed. Samantha caught, for a brief moment, the unmistakable logo, AMERIPRO, emblazoned across the tail assembly.

From her forward seat, Samantha was able to be one of the first off the plane. She lost no time catching the people mover to the main terminal, and from there she easily located the row of counters for the myriad rental car companies. All were busy, so she was glad that the one she had made her reservation with had a separate line for customers with confirmed reservations. She moved up to the counter in no time at all.

As she identified herself to the young woman behind the counter, Samantha handed over her driver's license and credit card, and quickly added that she did not want the insurance coverages offered by the company. The woman turned and looked at the shelf on the wall behind her holding numerous rental car envelopes on which the customers' names were prominently displayed. Samantha automatically followed the clerk's gaze to the section of the shelf near the alphabetical end, and did not see "Wright." The rental agent turned back to face Samantha.

"I'm afraid," she said in a twangy Texas accent, "we can't seem to find your reservation, Ms. Wright."

"You must. I telephoned it in myself, this morning." She pulled out her airline tickets, and pulled off a yellow post-it stuck onto the front of the envelope. "See, here," Samantha directed the girl's attention. "I wrote down my reservation number."

The girl took the yellow paper, and entered those numbers into her computer. She shook her head. "I'm so sorry. It's just not showing up on the computer."

"That doesn't make any sense," Samantha said.

Suddenly, the woman reacted as if a light had gone off in her head. "Shoot," she said. "I know what it was. We had some computer hiccups this morning. Well, I don't really know what the problem was," she said sweetly, "but the technician was out here, all right. Somethin' must've gotten messed up."

The large digital clock on the wall behind the counter read 1:34. "You do have some cars available?"

"Surely we do," the young woman replied, then hesitated. "Ma'am, I'm mighty sorry, but this is the express line. I'd love to help, but you see," she said, motioning to an older man and woman working in front of computers further down the counter, "my computer is different than theirs. I can't start a new rental contract on mine. They'll have to help you over there," she said.

Samantha looked at the line of a dozen people waiting. She turned back to the helpless rental car employee. "How long is the cab ride to Willowbrook?"

"Willowbrook? Mighty nice out there."

"Yes, yes," Samantha said abruptly. "How long?"

The woman turned to the older man working at the next computer and repeated the question. The older man consulted the woman next to him, and the group reached a consensus. Thirty to forty minutes, depending on traffic. An expensive cab ride she was told. It would be much better to wait for a rental car.

Samantha opened her wallet and confirmed what she already knew. Two hundred dollars. That had to be enough. She grabbed the oversized leather litigation case she had checked out from the Senate supply room and followed the signs to the taxi stand.

⸙

The car turned left off the drab state highway and entered a lovely country lane lined with tall, massive willow oak trees with thin narrow branches bowing low, creating a natural tunnel-like effect. Samantha immediately focused on the shiny silver lettering over the approaching gate and guardhouse proclaiming the entrance to Willowbrook. The cab driver first reminded Samantha that he was a man of his word—"no more than thirty minutes," he'd promised, and now delivered. He then asked again whether she was expected, "because if your name ain't at the gate, you don't get in." Samantha assured him she was expected.

As the cab slowed, the uniformed guard started waving frantically, motioning for the taxi to pull over. An instant later they heard it, the pulsating sound of the siren. The cab driver swerved his car to the right, and waved out his window for an ambulance to pass. Up ahead, the gate opened, and the red and white van with the large paramedic symbols sped ahead. The cab driver accelerated again, and pulled up to the guard.

Samantha rolled down her window with the old-fashioned hand crank and announced, "Samantha Wright, to see Mr. Willard."

The guard looked flustered, "Ah, well," he stammered.

"What is it?" Samantha shouted from the back seat.

"I'm not sure," he stuttered. "You ought to hurry," he said, pointing through the open gate. "Follow the paramedics."

Samantha hesitated, then took in the meaning of what he was saying. "Step on it!" she yelled to the cabby.

The eight-cylinder motor sprang to action, and the car passed through the gate in time to glimpse the flashing lights of the ambulance descending down the wide boulevard lined with more bowing willow oaks. As the cab chased the ambulance, Samantha stared out the window, vaguely noting the enormous houses to her left and the sculptured golf course.

The ambulance was parked at the end of a long circular drive, in front of a towering white stone, two-story house. The enormous wooden double front doors were open, and the ambulance attendants were just disappearing into the house, pulling a stretcher behind them. Before the cab had fully come to a stop on the other side of the driveway, Samantha leaped out, and raced to the front doors. The entryway was brightly lighted, with a huge glass chandelier hanging from the vaulted ceiling above

casting brilliant light everywhere. Two matching circular stair-
cases ascended on both sides of the grand entry room. Samantha
looked to the top of the stairs and saw the paramedics quickly
navigating their bulky stretcher up the wide stairs. Where the
stairs met the landing, the paramedics turned and raced down
the open hallway.

Samantha ran up the stairs. At the end of the long corridor, the doors to the room beyond were open, and she could
see him—a heavy set man, lying motionless on his back on the
floor, his shirt torn open, the paramedics kneeling over him. One
medical man filled a syringe and plunged it into the man's arm.
The other man reached back into a aluminum case, and brought
out two flat, round disks, attached to a machine with wires. He
shouted "clear." The man's body suddenly lifted and arched.
She heard it again, and saw the violent physical reaction. As she
came to the doors, she saw one paramedic turn to the other and
shake his head. For the first time, Samantha saw another man in
the room—tall, white-haired, dressed in a blue blazer and char-
coal gray trousers. The paramedics turned to him. One spoke
wearily. "He's gone. There's nothing we can do."

The white-haired butler offered to escort Samantha back to
the cab. As they walked down the hall, he explained that he had
worked for the wonderful Mr. Willard for almost ten years. Samantha learned that Willard had returned from his customary
round of morning golf, carrying an envelope with him. The butler confirmed that Mr. Willard had said he was expecting her at
2:00, and then through tears, told her that he had last seen Mr.
Willard only minutes before in his bedroom, clutching the envelope, and pacing. He had never seen Mr. Willard so "agitated."
Ten minutes later, the butler had heard a loud thud, and rushed
from the downstairs kitchen. It was then that he discovered him,
the apparent victim of a massive heart attack.

"I'm sure the envelope was for me," she said, giving him her
letter of introduction from Senator D'Angelo. Reluctantly, the
butler agreed to return to the bedroom. They searched the pris-
tine room thoroughly but found nothing, except a copy of the
Senator's letter of introduction, laying flat in the fax machine's
receiving tray.

As Samantha slowly returned to the cab, the butler shook his head, mumbling, "A clean bill of health, only three days before."

"What did you say?" Samantha asked.

"Oh," the grieving man looked away, unfocused. "Mr. Willard tried to take good care of himself. Three days ago he had his annual physical. He was pleased with himself. Another year and he'd gained only three pounds. He told me," the butler started to weep again, "that the doctor had given him a clean bill of health. That's what he called it."

Samantha asked for the doctor's name.

As the cab drove out of Willowbrook, Samantha reached into her briefcase and retrieved her government issued cell phone. She entered 411. When the display on the phone repeatedly flashed "roaming" and the call failed to connect, she tried again and again. "Damn," she muttered. She stuffed the phone into her overcoat pocket and asked the driver if she could borrow his phone.

He reached for the phone, glanced at the dial, and reported "Barely one bar. Don't know why these rich folks can't get their own damn tower." He reluctantly started to pass it back when Samantha noticed a 7-11 convenience store just off the highway. She instructed him to pull over. She got out and walked to the pay phone hanging on the exterior wall, She reached information who gave her the number for Doctor Jimmy Charles. She called, but connected only with a voice mail system, which announced that the doctor was away at a two-day medical symposium. The message directed that if the matter was urgent, the caller should contact one of Doctor Charles's associates who was covering for him. Samantha thought, and then decided to leave a voice mail message asking Doctor Charles to call her at the Senate office.

Her next call was to Daniel. His voice mail message at the *Post* said that he was out in the field for most of the afternoon. She punched out of the call in frustration.

When she returned to the cab, the driver asked "Where to now, lady?"

She thought about the last two fast moving days, and the night at Daniel's when she'd first started learning about Frank

Mullen. She looked at the fare meter. Forty-eight dollars already. "How much is the fare to the *Dallas Tribune*?"

"The newspaper?"

"Yes. The main building."

"That's downtown, Dallas, lady. You can see it in the distance there," he said pointing out his windshield. "I guess it's about thirty bucks."

"Then how much back to the airport?"

"From downtown, forty bucks flat rate."

Assistant Secretary of State Victoria Merriweather had called Daniel back to confirm that she "could be of assistance." She insisted on meeting for afternoon tea at the Colonial Club in Old Town Alexandria "for old times sake. They still do such a marvelous job at the club. Besides, nobody's worrying about affairs of state this afternoon because of this delightful snow."

As they sat down before the tiny table, an array of finger sandwiches spread before them, Victoria remembered explaining to Daniel long before how special it made a lady feel when a gentlemen ordered her drink for her. Testing to see if the lesson had taken, she whispered to Daniel that she would have her usual.

Very much on cue, the white-jacketed waiter approached. Daniel ordered a Dubonnet on the rocks with a twist for one of the numerous outgoing Assistant Secretaries of State.

When she had first invited him to "tea," he'd been surprised that in her social circle the only liquid not consumed at these mid-afternoon gatherings was tea. On this snowy afternoon when he ordered a Coke for himself, Victoria reached for his hand. "Now that is not very sociable, Danny. A lady does not drink alone. And besides, we should relax and catch up on old times. Hard to believe we both arrived in Washington only four years ago? Thank God the *Post's* regular reporter for Latin American affairs was down with the flu and they had to send you to the O.A.S. reception. And the rest, as they say," she smiled and squeezed his hand, "is history. Now I only have a few days left in Washington and then it's back to sleepy Newport. Who knows when I'll see you again?"

"We had a great time," he agreed, and motioned for the waiter to return. He changed his order to a beer. After the waiter had left, he explained that he really shouldn't. He had lots of work to do. She said she understood, but that after all, they were working. In reply, he tried to bring up the subject of the meeting, but Victoria would hear nothing of it. She whispered, "Now Danny, you can hardly expect me to discuss confidential information right here in the main parlor of the Colonial Club. We'll get to it soon enough."

By 4:30, Daniel had consumed four beers, and two Patron Tequila Gold shooters. Victoria insisted that she have her driver take them to her city residence at the exclusive Watergate Apartments, where she could discuss "that private matter." Later her driver would bring him back to his car, she promised, after they had some coffee.

When they arrived at her palatial apartment with the sweeping view of the Kennedy Center and the Potomac River beyond, Victoria pushed a button recessed within the marble mantle in the living room, and the warming fireplace instantly came to life. Victoria excused herself to retrieve the information Danny wanted. He sat down on the semi-circle sofa, enjoying the glowing fire, and the view through the large curved bay windows of the snowy winter twilight.

When the Assistant Secretary of State returned, she was holding a thick manila file folder, and was wearing nothing but a smile. "It has been far too long, Danny boy," Victoria Merriweather said convincingly.

⬥

Samantha took the cab driver up on his offer to wait at no extra charge, and entered the old red brick building. She followed the directions of the guard, and took the elevator one floor down to the basement. A frail, homey looking man with thick glasses sat serenely behind the counter marked "Records Desk."

He looked to be in his seventies. He wore a plain, short sleeve shirt, no tie. The man peered out through his glasses. "Howdy! How ya'll doing today, Ma'am? Name's Lester Boggs."

Samantha almost laughed. The typically gregarious Texas greeting seemed so out of character emanating from this diminutive clerk. But she smiled back warmly.

"I'm doing fine," she lied.

"Mighty pleased to hear it. Now what can I do for such a lovely, and…" he paused, looking up at Samantha, "tall as a Texan young lady?"

"I'm looking for an old photograph that was on the front page of the *Tribune* back in 1964."

"Well, darlin'," Lester smiled, "that's simple. You go right upstairs to the microfiche department, they'll pull out any edition you want and throw it up on a computer screen for ya."

"No," Samantha replied calmly. "You see, I've seen a printout of the newspaper. That's a copy of the newspaper reproduction. It's grainy, and not very clear. What I want to see is the original photograph, or the original negative."

"My goodness. What ya want to do that for? You did say 1964, right, Ma'am?"

"Yes."

"So it's not the assassination pictures you want—that's what we get the most of. Lot's of folks like to stare at those. That's why I keep the assassination stuff right here," he said, pointing at a shelf behind the counter. "All organized, ya know. See, here's the section on Kennedy's arrival at Love Field, then here's the motorcade, then Parkland Hospital, and so on and so on."

"Fascinating," Samantha replied, "but no, what I want is a photograph taken in Vietnam."

"Vietnam? Oh, I see. Well now, you hold it right there," the clerk responded. "Ya gots to understand that the only original photographs we have here are the ones our own boys take. Alot of times we run pictures from the wire services, other papers, then we don't have any originals, ya understand."

"Yes, I suppose I do," Samantha replied. "I've seen that credit line under photos in newspapers. The photograph I'm talking about had '*Dallas Tribune*' right under it."

"Bingo," the man exclaimed. "Then it's one of ours. We sent a lot of our own reporters over there, at least when things was going great guns. That changed when the shit hit the fan and the commies got the upper hand."

"So," Samantha interrupted, "you have the original?"

"1964? Surely we do. We started keeping everything after the assassination—and I do mean everything. I was here before that of course, but we didn't pay all that much attention to record keeping. Then the word came down, keep everything, for history's sake."

"Great," Samantha responded. "How long will it take?" she asked looking at her watch.

"1964—now that's gonna be down in the sub-basement lockers. The only old stuff I keep up here is the assassination stuff, cuz there's always somebody…"

"So how long?"

"Well, now, I'd say about two, maybe three days."

"Days?" she asked.

The old man stared at her through the thick lenses of his glasses. "I said we started keeping everything after the assassination. I'm sorry to tell you, we didn't get real organized for a while. It's going to be a bit of a hit or miss proposition for me to find it. Now don't worry. I will, it's jus' gonna take a little time. I'm real sorry, but that's the best I can do."

Samantha sighed. The Senator had been right. She sure could have used her time better than wasting a day in Texas. "Okay," she finally said. "Will you do your best? I'd like it as soon as you can find it."

Lester Boggs smiled. "I surely will. Now tell me the exact date and describe this photograph for me."

Samantha gave him the date, and told him about General Westmoreland and Frank Mullen standing, smiling, in front of the helicopter, with another man standing in the background, by the rear of the helicopter.

He repeated that he'd do his best and call her to come back for it.

"Come back?" she said. "I'm up in Washington. Can't you send it to me?"

"Now I thought you said you wanted the original, Ma'am?"

"I do," she said.

"Well now, don't it stand to reason that I can't let any original out of here? Then we wouldn't have it anymore. I'm sorry, truly I am, but if you want to see it you'll have to look at it right here."

Samantha raced down the stairs to the cab parked on Main Street. "Thanks for waiting," she said, looking around at the congested street. "Do you think I can make the five o'clock flight?"

"I'll guarantee it," he replied. "We just have a few blocks of this traffic, and then we'll hit the Stemmons Freeway and be on our way."

The cab moved slowly down Main Street, then turned left onto Houston Street, and started to wind its way to the freeway. Samantha kept seeing George Willard's lifeless body lying on his bedroom floor. He'd said he was stopping by the bank, and the butler said he had an envelope, but… suddenly, she gasped, and brought her hand to her mouth.

The cab driver turned around. "You okay, lady?"

"We're there," she whispered.

"What, lady?"

The car had stopped at the traffic light, its turn signal flashing for a left turn. She rolled down the window, and stared up at another old brick building in downtown Dallas. "We're here," she said more audibly.

The cab driver looked back through his rear view mirror. "Oh," he said. "Yeah, this is where it happened."

The light changed, and the cab moved, turning left onto Elm Street after the oncoming traffic had passed. He started to accelerate.

"Slow down," she yelled. "Pull over!"

"Lady, I thought you wanted to get to the airport."

"Just pull over," she repeated.

"Hey, lady, I can't. There's no parking, no waiting along here. Hell, everybody would stop and rubberneck."

"Then find a place. I have to get out," Samantha demanded.

The cab passed the entrance ramp to the Stemmons Freeway and went under the railroad underpass. Where Elm Street met its first cross street, the cab driver made an illegal U-turn, and returned to Dealey Plaza.

Samantha walked the entire plaza, from the Main Street intersection to the monument on the grassy knoll. Vague, distant memories from childhood filled her thoughts. As she stood on the sidewalk on Elm Street and looked back at the sixth floor of the building, suddenly the event of years before, when she was only a child, seemed so real and so close. The haunting black and white images on the television screen, the newspapers and magazines spread out across her mother's bed, showing in still motion every angle of the tragedy. And, she remembered, the tears, always, everywhere, for days and days, the tears.

Samantha walked up the street, and lingered at the entrance to the building. Finally, she entered the Texas School Book Depository.

When she came out an hour later, she didn't speak. All she could do was remember what she'd seen this day as images of the present melded in her mind with the memories of images from that fatal day long ago—memories blurred through a veil of tears.

She found the cab driver and silently motioned for him to return her to the airport.

When they reached the terminal, the cab driver told her the fare was one hundred and fifty eight dollars, and claimed he had not charged her for the waiting time at the Tribune building, or at Dealey Plaza. Samantha reached in her wallet and handed him two hundred dollars.

At the ticket counter, the clerk made it sound like she would almost certainly make it from the standby list onto the six fifty-five flight. As she walked into the waiting area for the gate, she decided to call Daniel. She set her briefcase down, but when she reached into her overcoat pocket for the cell, she felt a piece of paper. She pulled it out and reread the message in Mrs. Fredericks handwriting. Dammit, she thought, how could she forget to send the check—the increase—the $200 a month? She did a mental inventory of what she had with her. Her checkbook? Yes. An envelope, stamps? No. It would have to wait until tomorrow. But she could call. It was almost eight o'clock in the east. The business office would be closed, but she could leave a message– let them know she had gotten their message, and the check was, no, would be, in the mail, tomorrow. And she could speak with her mother.

She placed the call. This time it connected. She waited through eight rings for the answer. She left a voice mail message for the executive director, and then entered the three-digit extension for her mother's floor. After another ten rings, a night nurse answered.

"Hi. This is Samantha Wright. I know it's a bit late, but can my mother come to the phone?"

"Well," the nurse replied, "she's all tucked in, but the last time I checked she was still awake. She didn't want no T.V. tonight. She was listening to music on the nifty C.D. player you got her. I'll go see. I can take her one of the portable phones. It'll take a minute or so."

"Great. Thank you," Samantha said. She looked over at the gate and saw the passengers on the flight to Washington lining up. As she waited on the phone, she cupped her other ear to listen for her name to be called.

After what seemed like several minutes, the nurse came back on the line. "She's right here, Ms. Wright, but, ah, she is a bit confused tonight."

"I understand," Samantha responded, then paused until she heard the nurse saying in the background, "It's your daughter, Mrs. Wright. Say hello."

"Hello," her mother said weakly.

"Hi, Mom. How are you feeling tonight?"

"I'm fine."

"Good. That's good. I can't be long, Mom. I'm sorry. I'm waiting to catch a plane, in Dallas, on my way back to Washington."

"Dallas?"

"Yes, a quick business trip. But Mom, I did take a little time off. I went to…, ah, a museum, dedicated to President Kennedy. It was very interesting."

"President Kennedy?"

"Yes, Mom."

"Who is this?"

"Mom, it's Samantha."

"Samantha? Samantha who?"

Just then Samantha heard her name being called over the loud speaker. "Look, Mom, I have to go. I'll see you soon, real soon. I promise. I love you."

"Who is this?" came the reply.

Samantha slowly pressed the off button, then walked to the waiting flight. She could not remember when she had felt so sad.

An hour into the flight, Samantha tried calling Daniel's apartment from the air phone, but there was no answer. She repeated her efforts when they were thirty minutes out from Reagan National, hoping he could pick her up at the airport, and longing for his company on the night after what seemed like the longest day of her life. When he still didn't answer, she resigned herself to stopping at the ATM at the airport for some cash, and then catching the METRO back to Rosslyn.

CHAPTER NINE

Daniel awoke with a piercing headache. His first thought was that he could not handle tequila anymore. He was definitely out of shape. His second thought was that he had just fucked up badly. At least, he had gotten the information for Samantha. But he knew he was rationalizing. When he realized there might be a story in it, he had wanted the information as much, maybe more, than Sam. But he felt disgusted with himself.

Slowly, painfully, he got out of the bed, and reached for the pile of clothes he had so eagerly abandoned hours ago. He groaned as he saw the clock on the night stand. How could he get back to his place, or retrieve his car over in Alexandria, at five o'clock in the morning? As he buttoned his shirt and walked softly out of the bedroom, he remembered that within the complex of Watergate buildings was a hotel. He could get a cab there.

Before closing the front door behind him, he thought about leaving the photocopies she had shown him after their first bout of lovemaking. No matter how many times he asked, she wouldn't let him take them. To shut him up, she'd locked them in her filing cabinet in her study. He couldn't get to them now. He would just have to remember what he saw. He quietly closed the door and went hunting for a taxi.

Samantha tried pounding on the top of the alarm clock, but kept missing the off button. The intermittent buzzing would not go away. She hit it hard, and finally it stopped. She got up, stumbled to the kitchen, put the coffee on, then retired to the bathroom for a long, hot shower.

It was nearly 8:00 a.m. before she was ready. She looked out at another dreary Washington morning, the dark sky laden with moisture. It wasn't snow, it wasn't rain, it was a mess. She looked down at the streets and saw that the snow of the day before was a dingy residue—another commuters' nightmare.

Should she call Daniel? Where had he been? She wanted to tell him about Willard's sudden death, and see if anything had turned up on Colonel Howard.

Daniel had just finished listening to his messages—three from Samantha—when the phone rang. He knew he couldn't avoid it. He picked it up, determined to sound like he had some sleep. "*Buenos dias,*" he said, attempting through a dry mouth to sound upbeat while his head still felt like it was splitting open.

"Daniel, it's me. Where have you been?" she asked calmly.

"Working," he replied, convinced it was only half a lie. "Mostly for you on the Colonel Howard thing."

"So, come up with anything interesting?"

"What was interesting was I couldn't find out anything. I got a complete stonewall at the Pentagon. Either people didn't know, or they weren't talking. Howard hates providing information to the press, and he's made that well known. Nobody wants to take a chance on crossing the guy who looms large in their futures."

"So?" Samantha answered.

"So, babe, because I can't stand to be stonewalled, and because you asked me to see what I could find out, I pulled out all the stops, and came up with some interesting stuff."

Samantha's curiosity was piqued. "Like what?"

"Like I suspect Colonel Howard is tight with Frank Mullen—if how Howard spent a fair amount of his time after he got out of the army is any indication."

"Howard and Mullen are close?"

"Sam, you can never reveal where you got this, or what the source is. Understand?

"Of course, Daniel. Get on with it," she demanded.

"Sam, I'm telling you it's supersensitive, because Colonel Howard is going to be a top aide to the President, but also because no matter who you are, this information is entitled by law to strict privacy."

"By law? What are you talking about?"

"I've had a look-see at Colonel Howard's passport and foreign travel file."

"From the State Department and the American embassies?"

"*Exactamundo*," he replied triumphantly.

"Daniel," she replied seriously. "Those files are sacrosanct. It's at least a heavy duty misdemeanor, maybe a felony to leak that stuff."

"Well..." he started to say.

"So what's in them?"

He lowered his voice. "From his foreign travel record, he seems to have spent the better part of the last forty years traveling abroad in some very interesting places."

"Such as?" she asked.

"Vietnam through the sixties right up to the downfall in 1975."

"Typical military, or even ex-military, I'd say."

"Okay, I'll buy that," Daniel agreed, flashing back to the exact circumstances of the night before and how he had gained the information. "But immediately after Vietnam, Howard started traveling back and forth to Iran, until that regime had its downfall in 1979. Then he switched gears again—Iraq became his favorite foreign destination. Went there at least every month, through the 1980's and right up to the eve of guess what event."

"The Iraq/Kuwait War."

"Right. His passport records show he left Bagdad on August 14, 1990, one day before Iraq invaded Kuwait. He'd been there for a solid month."

"He really takes to the world's hot spots, doesn't he? How's that make him close to Mullen? I thought Mullen's just sat at his desk making money."

"Making money from selling military hardware, particularly helicopters, right?" Daniel observed.

"Yes, that's been a big part of it."

"So you might be interested in what Colonel Howard says on his visa applications and embassy forms to be the reason for his exotic travels."

"Tourist?"

"Just a simple worker bee. He calls himself 'helicopter technician.'"

Samantha let out a whistle. "A helicopter mechanic is our next President's trusted aide on military affairs? I don't believe it!"

"Of course not. It's just a bullshit cover, particularly when you tie in two more tidbits."

"Come on, Daniel. I don't have all morning."

"Number one, he's got some very special travel privileges. He travels with the equivalent of a VIP diplomatic passport."

"What do you mean?"

"A very special perk, reserved for only the highest government officials, while they're in office, or in the Foreign Service. Colonel Howard has the same privileges stamped permanently on his passport. No customs checks, no waiting in line, all thanks to President Johnson."

"Johnson?"

"That's how the Colonel got hooked up. A private presidential order."

"It still stands after all these years?"

"Apparently, unless some President goes to the trouble to issue an order changing it."

"Powerful stuff," Samantha observed. "Quick, Daniel. I have to get to the office. What else?"

"You might like to know the only other places he's visited with constant regularity."

"Where else has AMERIPRO sold a heap of helicopters."

"Wrong turn, Sam. Not thinking places with helicopters, more like what AMERIPRO gets for all these helicopters."

"Daniel! I don't have time for riddles."

"Money, dollars, yen, mucho dinero. The Colonel's other primary destinations all have something big to do with money, as in international finance—Switzerland and Liechtenstein—at least they did when he really frequented them."

"Wow," she said. "What do you mean when he frequented them?"

"He stopped going. He'd been touching down in those places at least every month through the sixties and into the seventies, and then it stopped."

"When was that?"

"Listen, I can't remember everything I saw exactly," he explained, thinking that if only he had kept a clearer head he could be doing better on this interrogation. He held his hand to his forehead. "I had to read and hope to remember as much as I could. With Liechtenstein, it was, ah, January 23, 1973. That was the last time he was there. Switzerland was about the same time. Been going there every month for years, and then quits cold turkey."

"January 23, 1973," Samantha repeated. "You don't have copies of any of this? Did you see the presidential order?"

"No," he said quickly, "on both counts. The order was just referred to in the file, and as for copies, there was no way she'd let me…"

Samantha's stomach suddenly churned like it had when she'd seen the body of George Willard. She wasn't prepared for this topic, but she couldn't avoid it either. "The State Department. Strictly confidential files only available to the top people," she confirmed. "It was Victoria, wasn't it?" she asked, knowing the answer. "A very special source, wasn't it, Daniel? An intimate source."

"Samantha," he answered, hoping a little humor would diffuse the situation, "you know I can't reveal my sources."

"You don't have to, you bastard," she yelled. "You went back to her again, didn't you? Old story, old flame, old excuse—she can't keep her hands off you. I told you the last time—you cheat on me again and…"

He knew he couldn't pull it off. She'd see right through any attempt at denials. The conversation was over, but he desperately wanted to keep it from ending there. "Listen, Samantha. It wasn't like that… it was the only way to…"

"Shut up!"

"We'll talk later," he pleaded. "About everything. About Howard, and that guy Willard. Maybe I can help you with—"

"Willard's dead, Daniel. And so are you." She slammed down the phone.

―――∞∞∞―――

When Samantha finally made it into the office, Mrs. Fredericks stared at her. "Are you all right, Sam? It's 9:30."

"Yes, Gertie," she said. "Tiring trip. I got in late last night."

"Not a good morning to be late. The Senator is waiting for you."

"I'll go right in."

"And here," Mrs. Fredericks grabbed an envelope from her desk. "This fax came in for you yesterday. It says 'Urgent and Confidential' on it."

"What is it, Gertie?"

"I really don't know, dear. I pulled it from the in-tray and put it in the envelope for you. Some numbers or something. No cover sheet. The originating fax number's at the top. I checked the area code. It's from the Dallas area."

Samantha glanced at her office and the AMERIPRO boxes piled all around. She turned and moved toward the closed door to the Senator's office, opening the envelope as she walked.

At the door, she knocked and turned the door handle as she looked down at the solitary plain sheet of paper. Near the top was a handwritten word, almost illegible. It seemed to start with a capital "L", then several letters running together, and at the end, as if the writer realized as he wrote that it wasn't clear, the printed letters "stein." Below that were a series of numbers. She pushed the door open, continuing to look down. "12-3-48-21..."

"Come on in," she heard the Senator order. "I hope that's you, Sam."

Samantha quickly folded the paper, and tucked it into her suit jacket pocket. "Yes, good morning, Senator..."

The Senator interrupted, "We have a visitor, Sam..."

Samantha instantly tried to smile, and opened the door the rest of the way.

"...with an interesting proposition."

As Samantha entered the office, she saw Senator D'Angelo sitting in his favorite chair, and seated next to him on the spacious couch, the nominee for Secretary of Defense.

"Your ears must have been burning, Sam," the Senator exclaimed. "You're the topic of conversation."

For a moment Samantha froze. Frank Mullen stood up, and moved toward her with his hand extended. "Good morning, Samantha. Sorry to drop in unannounced, but I've had some additional thoughts I needed to share with the Chairman first, and then, with his approval, you."

Samantha quickly shook hands, forcing a thin smile. "That's quite all right," she said unconvincingly.

The Senator looked up, concerned. "Are you okay, Sam?"

"Oh, yes, sure," Samantha replied, realizing she wasn't succeeding in her efforts to act normal. She tried again, attempting a warmer smile. "Just a little tired, but I'm fine. So what's up, gentlemen?"

Frank Mullen grabbed her by the arm and directed her to sit down next to him on the couch.

"It looks like one of those good news, bad news situations, Sam," the Senator explained. "Good news for Frank and you, bad news for me."

Samantha looked at them both, puzzled.

"Why don't you lay it out for her, Frank?" the Senator suggested.

Frank Mullen turned to face her and leaned in close. "The Senator and I have had a very candid discussion. He's made it clear to me that you are not only the best assistant he's ever had, but that you are the most knowledgeable person when it comes to understanding and dissecting the Pentagon budget. The good Senator," Mullen said, motioning toward D'Angelo, "let me know that if he had, ah... truly wanted to take on the task of Secretary of Defense, you would have been an invaluable, that's the word he used, 'invaluable,' part of his team."

"That's very kind of the Senator," Samantha nodded at D'Angelo.

"His kindness is only surpassed by his patriotism," Mullen said assuredly, "because he has made it equally clear that he is willing to set ego and personal interest aside for the sake of accomplishing all of our mutual goals, to rein in the defense budget and provide the country with a lean, efficient and fully capable defense."

"It's my passion, as you know, Sam," the Senator added. "And with this new President, we finally have the opportunity to make it happen, to make the break from the past, consistent with his 'new politics' and all."

"If Mr. Mullen is of the same mind," Samantha observed.

"Oh, I am, Samantha. We know that we may not always agree on every issue, or budget matter, but our goals are absolutely the same. As the Chairman has had this passion to reform our defense establishment, I've had the passion all my life for efficient, economical management. But, Samantha?"

"Yes," she replied, wary of the conversation.

"I can't do it alone. I must build an experienced, talented, tough team to manage the Pentagon." He nodded toward the Senator. "Should the Senate deem to confirm me, to put it bluntly, I'm going to need all the help I can get. The Senator and I agree, there is nobody better qualified to provide that help than you. I want you to be one of my three Deputy Secretaries of Defense."

Samantha was stunned.

"You see what I mean about good news, bad news, Sam," D'Angelo blurted out. "It'll be shitty for me, personally, but you could accomplish so much. You'd be invaluable to Frank, and I could count on you to be sure he does the right thing, keep him honest."

The Senator reached over and slapped Mullen on the knee.

Mullen smiled. "It makes sense all around. And I suppose I don't have to tell you that you'd be the first woman in that high a position at the Department. Talk about shaking up the old boy network."

Samantha started to speak, then stopped.

"I know," Mullen interjected. "This has all changed around so fast. We only met two days ago, and I know you and the Senator had every right to suspect...well, to not be sure of me. But now we've had a chance to get to know one another, share our views on the challenges ahead, and it's as clear to me as I hope it is to you, we should be a team."

Samantha stared at the former C.E.O. of one of the country's biggest defense contractors. He sounded so convincing.

"I'm still gonna watch him like a hawk," the Senator added, "and you can sure help on that score, Sam. But our nominee has convinced me. His eagerness to have you join him says it all. I think the President-Elect knew what he was doing on this one."

"Thank you for that vote of confidence, Mr. Chairman," Mullen replied.

Samantha couldn't clear her head. George Willard's dead body, and passport files on Colonel Howard, Daniel and Victoria, and images from long ago, and in her pocket, what was that? Suddenly all her thoughts cleared, giving way to one word—Liechtenstein. She reached in her pocket and felt the paper—the handwritten scrawl—Liechtenstein.

"Samantha?" the Senator commanded.

"Oh, I'm sorry," she replied. "It is rather sudden." She looked at Mullen. "I'm very flattered."

"Flattered, smattered, Sam," D'Angelo jumped in. "It just makes sense."

"Yes, I guess it does," she replied. "And President-Elect Prescott and Colonel Howard, are they in agreement? A deputy position is a major political plum."

She watched Mullen closely, but saw no reaction in his eyes.

"My agreement with the President-Elect is that I will select my own team—the best possible people for the jobs, free of political, ah, considerations. But yes, I've run the idea by him. He's all for it. Says he met you already, and was very impressed."

Samantha looked at him curiously. "Yes, we met, very briefly, just a hello, really. We didn't discuss..."

"Well, you made an excellent first impression, Samantha."

"And Colonel Howard? You've cleared this with him?" she asked.

Mullen's eyes narrowed ever so slightly. He shrugged. "Actually, I have not. No reason to."

"Oh," Samantha replied, hoping her voice was remaining steady. "I assumed you would consult with Colonel Howard."

"No," Mullen interrupted. "I hardly know the man," he said emphatically. "My channel of communication is direct with President-Elect Prescott. So now, Samantha, we're agreed?" Mullen stated.

Samantha felt again in her pocket for the strange paper from Texas, referring to Liechtenstein. It had to have come from George Willard. "It sounds great," she said, "but I do need a little time to think it over."

"Time?" D'Angelo replied. "Sam, it's a tremendous opportunity."

"I know, I know," she replied.

"Well," Mullen said confidently. "Of course it will be hard for you to leave the Senator. Take a deep breath, give it some thought, and then get back to me as soon as you can."

"Thank you," Samantha paused. "I mean, I'm almost sure I will."

"I'm counting on it," the Senator said. "So one more thing, Sam. It wouldn't do to have you continue preparing for the hearings and sitting right behind me at the Committee table. An appearance of a conflict what with you responsible for prepping me on the questions for the man whose gonna be your new boss. Why don't you write up a summary of what you've done to date, and I'll assign Mancuso or maybe Rosselli to the hearings?"

Samantha reflexively frowned with the names of the mental lightweights whose positions on the staff were attributable solely to their fathers' generous campaign contributions to the Senator's political action committee.

As Mullen departed, Samantha rushed to her office, closed the door behind her, and snatched the paper from her pocket. Yes, she could make it out now. It couldn't be anything else. "*Liechtenstein*," in handwriting, and below it, typewritten, twelve numbers. She stared at the paper, then held it up to the light. At the very top of the fax transmission, she saw it. The tell-tale numbers. First the time and date of transmission, and then the sender's fax number. There it was. Yesterday, two minutes after two o'clock in the afternoon, Central Standard Time. On the line after the time, the number that was both George Willard's telephone and fax number.

Samantha stared for a long time. She took a deep breath, and then another, willing her energy to return. Suddenly, her next move became clear. She reached for the phone and entered the direct dial number of her former supervisor and best friend at the Securities and Exchange Commission. Then she went to the photocopy machine.

At 12:00 noon exactly she left the Russell Building, and rushed through the freezing rain to the waiting cab. The windows of the cab were frosted over. She didn't notice the black Lincoln Town Car pull away from the curb and fall into traffic one car behind the taxi.

CHAPTER TEN

The Securities and Exchange Commission is what is called in Washington, D.C., an "independent" regulatory agency. While the President nominates and the Senate confirms those who fill its five positions as S.E.C. commissioners, they do not report to the White House or to any cabinet officer. By law the Commission is to remain bipartisan, no more than three of its members from the same major political party.

Since its creation in 1934 under the New Deal legislation of Franklin Delano Roosevelt, the S.E.C. has remained relatively free undue political influences. But in Washington, all things are relative. In 1972, as Richard Nixon prepared for a no holds barred campaign for reelection to the Presidency, he sought to place in all positions of government people who would use their powers to insure the success of that effort. After that reelection, he sought to repay his supporters, and take retribution on his opponents. Thus it happened that the S.E.C.'s otherwise excellent reputation was tarnished by a brief interlude during Nixon's tenure: the agency was not free to conduct its investigations of corporate wrongdoing without improper influence from outside political forces.

When Samantha Wright was completing her two year clerkship for a federal appellate judge and was casting about for the best place to utilize her fine legal mind and respond to her strong desire and her mother's wishes to engage in worthwhile public service, many whose opinions she respected recommended the S.E.C. She was told the S.E.C. was a dynamic, prestigious place for her to serve, and a good place to learn the ins and outs, the good and the bad of corporate America. Samantha's mother even pointed out that John Kennedy's father had been the first Chairman of the S.E.C.

On this cold January day as she entered the headquarters of the S.E.C., Samantha recalled with pride her time in these offices.

Lionel Lawrence bolted from his old wooden chair and sprang like a schoolboy from behind the cluttered desk, demonstrating that six years and more than a few additional pounds around his tall, thick frame had not slowed him down. "Samantha Wright, it is so good to see you!" The large African-American man opened his arms and smothered her in a loving bear hug. Then he held her shoulders and pushed her back a step. "The brains of the United States Senate," he exclaimed. "You are a sight for an old bureaucrat's sore eyes."

Samantha looked up at the gentle giant whom had taken her under his wing and led her through her first forays into the Washington maze. For the first time since the Frank Mullen nomination had stormed into her life, she felt solid, on balance again. "Lionel, you're the one who's a sight for sore eyes. I can't believe it's been so long."

"Oh, I can," the man roared jovially. "What did I tell you? The move to the Senate would be great for your career, but they'd swallow you up, never let you out to come visit old friends. Hell, on that rare occasion when they get a brainiac to work for them instead of some ass-kissing political wannabe, at least they're smart enough to let 'em do the work."

Samantha smiled, and tossed her wavy hair off her shoulders. "You were right, as always, Lionel. I love it, but the Senator sure piles it on."

"That's because the tiny bit of his brain he hasn't yet pickled still sends out the right message 'Let Samantha do it! Let Samantha do it!'"

"Lionel, that's not fair at all. Senator D'Angelo is ..."

"Now don't give ol' Lionel the party line, Samantha darlin'. You don't come to me for the bullshit or the sugarcoating, and you know it." He reached over to the long wooden meeting table that jutted out perpendicular from his desk, grabbed the aerosol can, and waved it in front of her.

Samantha looked at the gag label on the tattered old can and broke into a wide grin. "You still have it after all these years?"

"Damn right I do," he exclaimed. "Now and again some smart ass grabs it and hides it someplace. Think they're being cute. Whenever it happens, I just start bringing all these wet-be-hind-the-ears so-called lawyers into my office, one by one, and cut 'em new ass holes and send them down to the library for the most boring research projects imaginable. I tell them that they can stay there until my departing gift from the smartest young lawyer to come through these doors is returned. I tell them I'd be better off with two of you than the twenty law school refu-gees I got working here now." He gently returned the can to the table. "And lo' and behold, my can of A number 1 guaranteed to work or your money back 'Bullshit Repellant' mysteriously re-materializes."

"But really, Lionel, Senator D'Angelo isn't..."

"Listen up, Samantha. The fact that your Senator has been hit-ting the sauce extra hard lately is not exactly a state secret. In fact, word is that's what tipped the scales against him on the Defense Department job. Our about to be inaugurated new leader appar-ently doesn't take to tried and true good old Washington habits like getting bombed every night, and at an occasional lunch."

Samantha scowled. "I'll plead 'no comment' on that."

"That is precisely what I would expect of you, darlin," Lio-nel agreed.

"But I will say," Samantha said with little hint of her usual enthusiasm, "that the President's choice seems quite, ah, impres-sive, and persuasive. I was super skeptical, but the more I see of Mullen the more it seems he may be right for the job."

"But?" he asked.

"But what?" she responded.

"Samantha, this is Lionel you're talking to. I know you, re-member! And I know that wonderful mind of yours. You didn't speak it, but I heard the voice of doubt."

"I don't know, Lionel. What I'd really like to do is grab some lunch, tell you about the latest turn of events, and then pick your brain on something."

"What's that?" he asked.

"Liechtenstein bank accounts."

Lionel Lawrence, the Director for Complex Case Prosecutions for the S.E.C., whistled. "In that case, let's go somewhere private."

They drove in Lionel's twelve year old Buick along M Street, past the Washington Navy Yard, and then down to the old waterfront docks along the Anacostia River. "Matty's Place!" Samantha shouted gleefully.

"Where else?" he said.

As he had expected, the simple fish restaurant with its stained concrete floor and white paper place mats spread out on the red linoleum table tops was empty. "Looks like business is pretty bad," she observed.

"Naw," he responded. "Matty's doing fine. Still the best fish in town, although it'll take all these new administration folks some time to get tired of being ripped off by the fancy French places and 'discover' this secret. It's happened with every change of administration I've seen. Takes 'em about six months, then pow!—there's a line out front and Matty is trendy again. But on a wet, cold afternoon as the old administration packs its bags and the new guys haven't found the toilets yet, I knew we'd pretty much have this place to ourselves."

They took the table for six at the far end of the restaurant. Lionel held the chair out for Samantha, then squeezed in across the table from her, his back against the wall. The waiter immediately took their orders.

As Samantha started to tell him about the surprise meeting that morning with Senator D'Angelo and Frank Mullen, Lionel noticed a man in a tattered trench coat wander in, and slowly take a seat at the counter. He kept his coat on, but removed his hat revealing an unkempt head of long, stringy brown hair flowing down to his shoulders. The man ran his hands through the hair, pulling the mess back over his ears. Typical Matty's Place, Lionel thought, open to princes and paupers alike.

Interrupted only by the arrival of the food, Lionel listened intently to Samantha. When she had finished, he took the last large spoonful of the spicy bouillabaisse and rolled it around in his mouth, and swallowed. "Now that's good food," he exclaimed, savoring the juicy morsels of crab and scallops that permeated the broth.

"Are you sure it's all right to eat that at this time of year?" Samantha asked.

"Absolutely," he said. "All that talk of shellfish only in certain months, it's an old wives' tale. At least it is at Matty's."

"So? What do you think?"

Lionel licked his lips. "Well, I think you really have gone uptown on me. Hobnobbing with the new President no less."

"For about sixty seconds," she laughed.

"Doesn't matter. Plenty of time for his roving eye to size you up. Be careful, darlin'."

"Honestly, Lionel, he's going to be the President of the United States. Whatever the rumors about the past, he'd be nuts to fool around under the Washington microscope."

"All I'm saying is watch out. You're breathing in rarified air that swirls around the real powers in this town—ergo this job offer. It's one hell of an opportunity for you. The type that for once is coming to somebody who is truly deserving. The next Secretary of Defense could not find himself with a better deputy than you."

Samantha smiled. "Thanks, Lionel. I think that's exactly what the doctor ordered."

"Now don't go thanking me," he said, patting her on the hand. "I'm telling it like it is, and I'm also saying that because it sure would make me look good to have my finest protégé' go on to such a prestigious job in government."

Samantha laughed. "So I am doing what I'm supposed to do—make you look good."

"Always keep that in mind as you plan your career," he advised her, smiling. "I've got another reaction, too. This highfalutin job offer, even before his own confirmation hearings, could be a diversion, keep you on ice, out of the way."

"I've thought of that. But at the same time with what I've done over the last six years with the Committee, I've earned a shot at a position like this. I can do it, I know I can."

"Got that right."

"But I also know these top jobs don't just fall into your lap, as deserving as you may be. You've got to lobby for them, fight for them. And yet, here I am, only a couple of days after meeting Frank Mullen, he offers me the chance of a lifetime. I'm flattered, but suspicious. But then, my suspicions don't make any sense either."

"How do you figure that?" he asked.

"Basically because there is no reason to maneuver me out of the way. Whatever negative on Frank Mullen is out there, I've already gone into it, thanks to his own help."

Lionel gave her a quizzical look. "His own help?"

"Yeah, it's funny, but Mullen made a special point of volunteering that AMERIPRO had a problem with the S.E.C. back in the 1970's."

"I recall hearing something about it. An early Foreign Corrupt Practices Act case."

"That's right. Turned out to not be a big deal. Ended up in an administrative slap on the wrist for the company and Mullen was cleared. No civil or criminal cases were brought. Mullen told me about it up front. I reviewed the whole S.E.C. file and didn't find anything that would be of any trouble to Mullen at the hearings."

Lionel shook his head. "Well, not exactly."

Samantha looked puzzled. "What do you mean?"

"Only that you didn't review all the S.E.C. files."

"I had to plow through three big boxes of documents."

"I mean," he said, "there's something that should be obvious to you. You've seen the files from the S.E.C.'s administrative hearing. The administrative report and the order of the Commission."

"Yes, that's right," Samantha replied.

"But you haven't seen the S.E.C. investigation files."

Samantha thought quickly. "No, I was told that was everything from the S.E.C."

"I don't care what you were told. It wasn't always so, but now I see all the agendas for Commission meetings and everything that goes before the Commission for approval. It doesn't take any Commission approval to release the administrative files— that's all public records anyway. But only the Commission can authorize release of the underlying files of the private investigation, and they don't do it very often. You know, the investigation files contain confidential stuff like the identities of witnesses, and information about investigative techniques used by the staff. The Commission never wants to release that type of information—says it would compromise future investigations. When the Commission doesn't want to release something, it's easy to fall back on the old 'investigative techniques' excuse. I happen to know the illustrious S.E.C. hasn't even been asked to release the investigation files on AMERIPRO to the Senate Armed Services Committee or anybody else. I would have seen the request. Therefore, my brilliant but still not all knowing in the ways of Washington colleague, you have not seen everything on AMERIPRO."

Samantha blushed. He was right. She had assumed, when she shouldn't have. "I need those files, Lionel."

"Maybe you do, maybe you don't," he said.

The look of determination that had crossed her face only moments before suddenly gave way to bewilderment. "All right. Again I have to ask the master, what do you mean?"

Lionel laughed. "Only that it's probably not a big deal. If the Commission didn't bring any civil law suits, or seek any criminal indictments, and stuck to the administrative order, it means the Commission didn't find any egregious wrongdoing. It decided on a mild slap because that's all the investigation showed was required. Happens all the time, as you know."

"Yes," she agreed, "but does it happen all the time that the corporate bad guy responsible for a company's S.E.C. problems gets canned from his company, but ends up living a life of luxury only to die of an apparent heart attack a few moments before he is to be interviewed by the lawyer for a powerful Senate committee."

"Oh," he sighed with admiration. "You got something, don't you?"

Samantha explained the events in Texas in detail. When she finished, Lionel let out a low whistle. "Now that's interesting. I'm sure the investigative file would have more detail on your George Willard."

The waiter came over and removed Lionel's completely empty bowl, but stopped at the plate before Samantha with the grilled red snapper she had barely touched. Lionel commented that Matty would be offended by her lack of attention to one of his finest dishes, but Samantha instructed the waiter to take the plate away anyway.

When they were alone again, Samantha said. "So I do need those files on the investigation."

"That doesn't sound like you're ready to take the job offer."

Samantha shrugged. "I want to, Lionel, but I think I'd better concentrate on the job I have right now, and that means dotting my i's and crossing my t's. Now where have I heard that before?" she laughed.

"Spoken like a true student of one Lionel Lawrence," Lionel said, pleased. "But it's not that simple. Those files are old. They have to be found, and the Commission has to approve their release. That takes getting it scheduled on the Commission's calendar and preparing a recommendation memorandum." Lionel saw that determined, pleading look in Samantha's eyes. "No you don't, Samantha. You are not an employee of the S.E.C. anymore. You will have to go through all the procedures."

"Lionel. We're all in the same government. I don't have time for procedures. While you're jumping those bureaucratic hurdles, the hearings will be over and Frank Mullen will be solidly ensconced in the big office on the E-ring of the Pentagon. Besides, you know I work fast. Let's not make a mountain out of molehill. I just need a quick once over and see if there's anything there."

"Samantha, the answer is no."

Giving no sign of having heard him, Samantha then pulled a photocopy of the one page fax transmission out of her pocket. "Lionel. I need some information on Liechtenstein bank accounts in general, and I think this one in particular." She handed him the sheet.

"What is this?"

"A fax I received from the dead man, George Willard. He sent it a few minutes before he died. This scribble at the top," she pointed at the paper, "says Liechtenstein."

"You're a better reader of illegible gibberish than I," he responded.

"I'm sure of it," she said. "What Willard got in trouble for was off-books bank accounts used for paying foreign bribes. Apparently an account in Switzerland and one in Liechtenstein. I'm betting this has to do with the Liechtenstein account."

"Okay," he grouched. "I'm not making any promises. I'll check around, see what I can find. This is all before my time, you know. I came in with the clean sweep a couple of years after this AMERIPRO case."

"Clean sweep?" she asked.

"Oh, I don't think we ever talked about it. The S.E.C. did have some problems back in Nixon's day."

"I remember hearing something about Nixon appointees. If it was during the Nixon years, that would coincide with the AMERIPRO investigation."

Lionel smiled. "I've got an idea. There's a senior investigator, been around longer than me. I'll touch base with him. He's a real pro when it comes to foreign money transactions." Lionel folded the photocopy and slipped it into his suit coat pocket. "I'll see what I can do to help you dot your i's and cross your t's, so," he grinned, "you can get on about the important job of straightening out the Pentagon. Promise me one thing, Samantha."

"Anything," she smiled.

"After you've saved fifty or a hundred billion dollars over there, send a little our way. I still need to hire about ten more lawyers to replace you."

As they got up, Samantha turned and saw for the first time the man sitting at the counter. From his tattered old trench coat she thought he might be homeless, stalling for time in the warmth as he cradled a cup of coffee in his hands. Then she noticed his hearing aid, and the glistening black fountain pen resting on the counter top. Lionel pressed his hand against her back, gently pushing her forward. "I've got to move along, Samantha. Weekly staff meeting." They quickly left the restaurant.

CHAPTER ELEVEN

Lionel Lawrence grabbed the telephone with one hand, the S.E.C. staff directory with the other, quickly found the name he was looking for, and confirmed that the office was across town in the S.E.C. Annex building on Buzzards' Point in southwest Washington. Lionel entered the number and waited until a quiet voice answered the phone. "Timmons here."

"Felix, this is Lionel Lawrence."

"Mr. Lawrence, yes?" Felix answered softly.

"Felix. I need a big favor, and I need it fast."

"Certainly, Mr. Lawrence."

"I understand there was an investigation, a little before my time, under the Foreign Corrupt Practices Act, of a company called AMERIPRO."

"Yes," Felix answered.

"Do you remember it?"

"Yes."

"Good. I need the whole investigation file, and need to find out who worked on it."

"I did some of the work," Felix answered.

"You did?"

"It was my first investigation dealing with secret offshore bank accounts. Now that is pretty much all I do."

"That's what I thought, Felix. You're the expert, so that's perfect. I need those AMERIPRO files, and then I need to pick your brains a bit."

"Certainly, Mr. Lawrence. What is the case number and work category so I can fill out my W.D.R.?"

The Work Duty Record, of course, Lionel thought. "Felix, for the moment I just want you to keep track of your time, call it research. But Felix, it's very important research. It may be in response to a congressional inquiry."

"Then I should record my work under that category. The form has a specific code for congressional..."

"Hold off on that," Lionel interrupted. "This is unofficial at the moment. All we're going to do is take a quick look at the file, and then discuss it with Samantha Wright. You remember Samantha? She was on my staff, and left to work with the Senate Armed Services Committee."

"I remember," Felix said flatly. "Should I fill out the CRL form?"

"No," Lionel answered, his exasperation growing. "I'll take care of the Congressional Relations Liaison, at the appropriate time."

"Very well."

"So Felix, when can we get the investigation files, and meet? Time is of the essence."

"Hold one minute, please," he responded.

God save me from the bureaucrats, Lionel thought, as he reached around with his free hand and rubbed the kink that poked a nerve in his neck. A minute passed, and then two, but when Felix came back on, he had good news.

"Our records indicate that the AMERIPRO files were not shipped to the Federal Records Storage Facility when the Commission moved to its new buildings. Peculiar, but helpful."

"Peculiar?" Lionel asked.

"All closed files were to be stored in the central federal facility when the Commission moved. The AMERIPRO files were closed, but for some reason were kept with the Commission files."

"Where?"

"Here at the Annex. I should be able to retrieve them myself in two or three days."

"Felix!" Lionel exclaimed. "I need them sooner."

"Can you authorize overtime?"

The simple fact was that Lionel could not, and Felix knew it, for the S.E.C. was operating under a strict zero growth budget plan, which eliminated overtime pay for the balance of that fiscal quarter. "Felix, I'm sorry. I can't. The budget…"

"I know," Felix responded, "I thought perhaps at the Director level you could provide exceptions to the overtime freeze."

"You give me more credit than I deserve."

"I was only checking. In the past, there were always exceptions."

"Not this time, I'm sorry to say," Lionel replied. "So when can we retrieve the files?"

"Mr. Lawrence, our file control system is arcane. There has never been enough funding to modernize the system."

"Felix, it's an emergency," Lionel finally blurted out.

The S.E.C.'s expert investigator specializing in foreign bank accounts did not respond at once. Lionel could visualize the bureaucrat on the other end of the phone worrying. When he finally replied, Lionel was pleasantly surprised.

"An emergency involving AMERIPRO?" Felix Timmons asked.

"Yes," Lionel replied.

"I'll be ready to meet with you at eight o'clock tomorrow morning," Felix said emphatically.

Lionel next called Samantha at the office, but when he was told by Gertrude Fredericks that Samantha was in conference with the Senator, he left the message that he would have the information first thing in the morning, and that he would call her shortly after eight o'clock. The secretary added the message to the pile of others for Samantha, six of which were from Daniel Garcia.

When Lionel realized that she might not get the message in time to return his call that afternoon, he called her apartment, and left the same message on her answering machine. He would call her after 8:00 the next morning.

———— ∞ ————

While Lionel was negotiating with Felix Timmons, Samantha was doing much the same with Senator D'Angelo. The behind-closed-doors session began as soon as Samantha returned to the office when Samantha was forced to admit that her long lunch had been devoted to continuing to investigate the Frank Mullen matter.

"I don't know why I'm having such a hard time getting the message through to you," D'Angelo said. "I want this nomination approved, and my God, Sam, you should too. Mullen has offered you the career opportunity of a lifetime. And with me here chairing the Committee, and 'Mr. Efficiency' being guided by you in his every move at the Pentagon, it's a perfect combination."

Samantha sat solemnly, unable to rationally explain herself. "I understand all that," she said, "but I'm just not certain."

"Listen to me, Sam. I respect your analytical abilities, your attention to all that detail. But sometimes you can't sweat the small stuff. You've got to look at the big picture. That's what I did when I committed to Prescott that I'd support Mullen's nomination."

"I still don't understand why you did that, Senator, even before we had a chance to prepare..."

Senator D'Angelo's face turned blustery red. "Because it is my goddamn prerogative, that's why! I decide who I'll support and when. Understand that," he shouted, and reached down to the coffee table and retrieved his rye and soda.

"I didn't mean to ..."

"Then don't," he yelled again, taking a long sip from the glass. "And understand another thing. What I did I did for the good of the country. For now that's between the President-Elect and me. You'll see, when the time is right, and it won't be too goddamn long after Mullen is sworn in as our next Secretary of Defense. Then you'll see," he said, slowly slurring the words, "that it's all for the best. Trust me on this, Sam!"

"Of course, Senator. Again, it's just a matter of..."

"It's a matter of nothing. Forget goddamn old farts who keel over with heart attacks, and those bureaucrats over at the S.E.C. They don't mean squat!"

The Senator got up and lumbered over to the large globe of the world standing before the bay windows. He pushed a button and one half of the globe retreated into a recessed pocket, revealing a fully stocked bar. He grabbed the rye whiskey, poured a copious amount of the brown liquid into the glass, and then added a splash of soda. He turned back to Samantha and lifted his index finger from the glass and pointed at her. "Next Monday, I want the hearings on the nomination of Frank Mullen to be our next Secretary of Defense to go off without a hitch. Without a hitch, understand?"

Samantha nodded and walked out in silence. When Mrs. Fredericks handed her the telephone messages, she picked through them with little interest. She discarded all of Daniel's, and put several of the others aside. When she got to the message from Lionel Lawrence, she placed it with her saved messages.

Samantha decided against the two block walk in the dark to the METRO at Union Station. She instead took the Senators' subway from the Russell Building over to the Capitol, and from there caught a cab. When she got to her apartment, he was waiting, standing in the hallway by the door, hands stuffed in his jeans' pockets. At least he had the good sense not to use his key, she thought.

"Daniel, I do not want to see you and I have nothing to say to you," she said wearily, feeling for her keys in her purse.

"You have got to listen to me," he pleaded.

Samantha unlocked the door. "No I do not," she said. She entered the apartment, slamming the door behind her.

Daniel knocked on the door once, then again, and again. "I'm not going away," he called. "You're going to have to talk to me sooner or later."

"Later," she called back, "much later. As in never!"

Samantha put down her purse and large litigation bag and threw off her overcoat. She went to the sliding glass doors looking out onto her postage stamp sized balcony, opened the doors and stepped out. She looked up at the sky, and saw first one, then another brightly sparkling star in the clearing sky. She took in a deep breath of the chilly air, looked over at the matching apartment tower. She wondered if they'd caught the burglar. She gazed at the quiet street below. That's when she saw them— under the streetlight, two men just standing, looking up at her.

Slowly she backed into the apartment, and ran for the door. "Daniel, get in here!"

"I knew you'd see the ..."

"Shut up!" she demanded. "I am not really speaking to you... you macho creep!" She grabbed him by the lapels of his heavy brown leather jacket and pushed him to the balcony. "Look!" she demanded.

"Where?"

"Down there." She pointed at the bright light on the corner. He stared. "I don't see anything," he said.

Samantha pushed him aside. The street was deserted except for a solitary dark Lincoln Town Car driving around the corner, and heading in the direction of Key Bridge, and Washington.

Daniel and Samantha re-entered the apartment. She closed the sliding doors and secured them with the lock she'd always considered superfluous in a high rise.

"Sam," Daniel began, "I think I'd better stay here tonight."

"No," she said flatly. "Not tonight, not ever again. You blew it big time."

"Please, that doesn't make sense, any more than somebody watching you and being so... so visible. A pro wouldn't do that."

"Yeah, and a pro wouldn't break in and steal costume jewelry, but he did. Just ask Arlington's finest!"

"No, he wouldn't," Daniel agreed shaking his head.

"This is crazy," Samantha concluded. "Someone in the restaurant today at lunch. I had a thought—he might have been listening..."

Daniel looked at Samantha and held his finger to his lips. He picked up her coat and held it for her, then moved back to the sliding glass doors and quietly released the lock, and slid the doors open again. He motioned for Samantha to follow. When they had squeezed onto the tiny balcony, he closed the doors behind them, and whispered. "Unless your professional burglar wasn't really taking anything out, but was putting something in."

"What are you talking about?" she asked.

"Watergate."

"Daniel, you've got a hell of a nerve bringing up the apartments where your...your rich bitch lives."

"Shush," Daniel whispered.

"Don't shush me, after what you've done."

"I'm not talking about the Watergate Apartments, well not really. I'm talking about the scandal, the scandal that forced Nixon out."

"That's the second time I've heard Nixon today. Nixon's dead, he's history."

"True, but the Watergate scandal, which started with a break-in at the Watergate Apartments, will always be a major topic around the *Post*. It made Woodward and Bernstein famous, and rich. Every reporter's dream."

"Great. I'm out here in the freezing cold, with a liar, a philanderer, talking about his career. I have had it with you. I no longer give a damn!" She turned and started to open the doors.

He pulled her back and quickly whispered, "This isn't about me. I was just going to point out that the best theory on the reason for the burglary at the Watergate was they were trying to plant listening devices in the Democratic Party Headquarters."

Samantha stopped cold. "Bugged?"

"Let's take a look around," he suggested calmly.

He silently motioned for her to follow, and opened the doors and led her back into her own apartment. They looked around until his eyes focused on the telephone sitting on the kitchen counter next to the answering machine. He walked quietly over to the phone, and turned it upside down. He saw nothing. He picked up the hand instrument and pointed to the four screws holding the assembly together. She nodded, went into the kitchen and rummaged through a drawer, and finding what she wanted, brought him a small Phillips screwdriver. When he unscrewed the back of the plastic unit, a minute metallic and plastic disc fell into his hands. It was no bigger than the head of a pin. He carefully examined it, gently dropped it from one palm to the other, then nodded his conclusion that it was a listening device. He started to put it in his pocket, but Samantha grabbed him and motioned for him to return it to the phone.

"Are you nuts?" he mouthed silently.

She shook her head and grabbed a piece of paper and a pencil from the kitchen counter and wrote out a note. "Let's not let them know we know." Samantha pointed to the telephone and Daniel quietly returned the disc to its original hiding place. As he tightened the last screw, Samantha spoke in her normal voice, "I'm hungry. We can talk this all out over some dinner."

"I'm starving, too. Let's go," Daniel replied.

They quickly exited the apartment and spoke not a word as they took the pedestrian bridge over Arlington Boulevard to the nearby restaurants at Rosslyn Circle. Samantha chose their favorite pizza place but as they sat down, she checked the room carefully. "For the record, you remain the biggest louse in the world, Daniel. I am sitting here with you because extraordinary circumstances seem to require it."

He started to interrupt, but she cut him off. "Shut up. That's the end of that subject. Now, as for being spied on, what do you think they're up to and why so obvious?"

"Don't know." He paused, thinking. "These electronic eavesdropping gadgets they have now are so tiny, but the smaller they are, the less power to transmit. That one is just a speck. Maybe they have to be close to pick up the sound."

Samantha contemplated that. Daniel quickly changed the subject, and started in vain to explain away Victoria Merriweather, and beg forgiveness. Samantha bolted upright in her chair.

"What?" Daniel said.

"If you're right, a derelict at the counter—he had a fancy pen and a hearing aid—if he was listening, he knows about Lionel, and what Lionel was doing for me." She reached for her cell phone and started to input the number she hadn't called in a long time, but still knew. She hesitated. Cell phone? Listening devices? She jumped up from her chair, grabbed her purse, and raced to the pay phone. She inserted some coins and entered the number. On the third ring, Bea Lawrence answered the phone.

The soothing southern voice brought an instant smile to Samantha's face. "Samantha, it is so good to hear your voice. Lordy, we do need to get together and catch up on old times."

"Bea, I can't wait. It's all my fault. Work, work, work."

"That's what Lionel tells me. You're working yourself to the bone. Now what you need is some of Bea's home cooking."

"We'll do it, Bea," Samantha assured the woman. "I'm sorry to call so late," she added, "but I really need to speak to Lionel."

"And I knows he'd love to talk with you, Samantha," Bea Lawrence assured her, "but he had to run out. He ought to stick with my home cooking too. Stubborn old fool told me he devoured the bouillabaisse at his lunch with you today, and now he's got a bad stomach somethin' fierce. He's gone out to the all-night store to get 'em some medicine. He said he needs to get a good night sleep on account of he's got an important meeting tomorrow, and it involves you."

"That's right. He's supposed to call me first thing in the morning. You say he went to the store?"

"Yep. Poor man was hunched over somethin' bad, holding his big belly. I told him I'd go, but he wouldn't hear any of that, not at this time of night."

Samantha thought about passing a message on to Lionel through Bea, but couldn't see how to phrase it without worrying the precious lady. "I really need to talk to him, Bea."

"Well, he can call you at home when he gets back. Shouldn't be long."

"All right," she said automatically. Then she remembered the phone was tapped. "Ah, actually that wouldn't work, Bea. You see I'm out, and won't be home until real late."

"How about your cell, then?"

"Ah, no," she said uncertainly. She didn't know if it was safe, and she didn't want to alarm Bea.

"Looky here then, Samantha, can't it wait until morning? All the big fool is going to do is come back here and take his medicine, maybe upchuck a bit, and then hopefully get a quiet night's sleep. When he gets this bad stomach of his, the best thing for it is sleep. If you're going to be out late, maybe you can just talk first thing in the morning."

"That's all he's doing? Getting some medicine and coming right home to go to bed?" she asked.

"That's all there is to it, honey."

"Okay, Bea," Samantha agreed reluctantly. "Tell him I called and look forward to speaking with him in the morning." She was confident they'd be okay talking on the S.E.C. and Senate phones.

When Samantha returned to the table, Dan wanted to know all about the guy with the pen. She quickly told him she had lunched with Lionel and about the man at the counter.

She reluctantly caved into Daniel's insistence that he stay the night on the couch. They also agreed that when they returned to the apartment, they would announce to any unknown listener that Samantha had indeed decided that Frank Mullen was going to make a terrific Secretary of Defense, and she his deputy.

No one was on the streets in the redevelopment area of southwest Washington only a few miles from the Virginia suburbs. Longtime residents of Washington knew that just as the horrific street crime of the nation's capital dramatically decreased during snow or sleet or freezing rain, the criminals returned with a vengeance the moment the sky cleared.

Lionel Lawrence knew the facts of life in his hometown, and conducted himself accordingly. If the abdominal pain had not been so intense, he would not have ventured out at all. But as he had to go, he did so with caution. He parked immediately in front of the well-lighted all-night store, and locked his car. As he entered through the automatic door, he noted that there was none of the usual loiterers or homeless hanging about. He assumed they had all gone to the shelters to wait out the last few days of ugly weather. He quickly found the family-size Mylanta, made his purchase, and returned to the old Buick. He reached forward, and started the engine.

He backed up in a full semi-circle, and as he applied the brakes to shift gears from reverse to drive, the car came to a stop in the dark shadow of the store. The pain in his stomach struck hard, causing him to gasp and hug the steering wheel. He slumped to his side, and reached for the plain brown paper bag. He grabbed the bottle inside and tore off the protective plastic, leaned back and swallowed an amount he knew exceeded the recommended dosage. But as soon as he did so, he felt better. He brought his head forward, and at that moment Lionel glanced in the rearview mirror. He saw the dingy head of matted brown hair rise from the back of the big sedan, and the brilliant, cold green eyes seeming to flash in the dark. Lionel responded, but it was the sluggish response of a man who was sick. He grabbed for the door, but it was too late.

Lionel's eyes bulged as he helplessly stared at the gruesome image reflected in the mirror, and at the thin piano wire passing down over his face and snapping tight against his throat. He tried to call out with all of his might, but no sound, no air would pass through his garroted throat. Lionel Lawrence's executioner pulled twice more on the wire to be certain, and then let the unconscious body slump forward. The killer reached around and firmly jammed the car's transmission into park. As he brought his arms back around, he patted Lionel's coat with gloved hands, and finding his wallet, lifted it out, and placed it in his own coat pocket. From that same pocket he withdrew a cheap handgun of the type used every night by innumerable thugs who terrorize the Washington night. He affixed a silencer to the barrel, then placed it to within two inches of the barely alive man's skull, and pulled the trigger, twice.

The killer slumped back down in the back seat, and opened the rear door on the side of the car furthest from the store. He lowered himself to the ground, and hunched over, walked slowly away, confident that even the cold-blooded murder of a relatively high level government bureaucrat would be written off as just another unsolvable handgun killing in the city that had earned the title "Murder Capital of America." And, the killer thought, it was good that the man had gone out. It was easier to break into an old car and kill one than to break into a house and kill two.

CHAPTER TWELVE

Samantha had wanted to save time by taking the METRO to the office as usual, arguing that she would be perfectly safe with the crowds of commuters swarming all around. Daniel insisted on driving her. When he flashed her credentials at the guard, he was waved ahead to the security check point, then cleared for the down ramp into the exclusive Senate garage under the Russell Building. He parked his cherry red '66 GTO convertible, and walked her to the office. He insisted he would stay until they decided the next course of action, after she heard from the S.E.C. This time, Samantha overruled his 'macho man syndrome' and sent him on his way, hissing, "I'm still irrevocably pissed at you." Besides, she thought, if she was to learn anything from the S.E.C. files, it certainly would not happen with a *Post* reporter hanging around.

"See if you can find anything more about Colonel Howard," she directed. "I'll call you when and if I need you."

Samantha retrieved *The Washington Post* and *The New York Times* from the reception area's coffee table where she had once learned during an all-night work session that a Senate employee delivered them by five o'clock each morning. She went into the kitchen, microwaved a mug of instant coffee, then returned to her desk. She still preferred the *Times* for the hard news, but this morning decided on the *Post* first, in the hopes of catching up on the latest political gossip revolving around the incoming administration. In the few days since her world turned upside down with the Frank Mullen nomination, she had completely lost track of what else was going on in the world.

The headline heralded the narrow vote in the Senate Judiciary Committee in favor of the nomination of Tracy Goodrich for Attorney General. The *Post* reported that while the final vote in the full Senate would be close, the grueling battle had been won. In the last paragraph on the front page, the story started to analyze the effect on the Senators' votes of the fact that the nominee was, once again, a woman. "Here we go," Samantha thought, turning to the inside page for the rest of the article. To her surprise, the story concluded that Tracy Goodrich's gender had had little effect one way or the other; the Justice Department, with roughly fifty percent of its staff attorneys being female, was now considered to be beyond any gender controversy. "About time," Samantha thought.

She quickly skimmed the balance of the article, until her speed reading habits caught a principal word in the last paragraph. "Defense" with a capital "D" compelled her to stop, and read carefully:

> As to the last remaining bastion of unquestioned male dominance in the hierarchy of the federal government, the new administration appears poised to impose change. The Department of Defense has remained a singular male institution with no woman having served at the top of the military command in the Joint Chiefs of Staff, nor at the pinnacle of the civilian authority as Secretary of Defense or one of the key three Deputy Secretaries. With the nomination of Frank Mullen to be the next Secretary, the number one job remains with a man. But sources close to the President-Elect have confirmed that the leading contender for one of the Deputy positions is a woman, and that both the President-Elect and Mr. Mullen are committed to advancing women to the highest positions within the Department.

Samantha stared at the article, her head filling with Senator D'Angelo's words. "The opportunity of a lifetime," he had repeatedly advised her. And now, the opportunity was being presented as not just her own, but as one of the last remaining breakthroughs for women in government.

As she thought about it, her focus shifted to the photograph on the opposite page. President-Elect Prescott was charging up the stairs to the main north entrance of the Pentagon. Samantha's eyes dropped to the caption explaining that the new leader was paying an informal visit to the building he had served in as a Lieutenant Junior Grade in the Navy twenty-five years before. A welcoming party stood at the top of the stairs. Samantha could make out most of the faces. The Chairman of the Joint Chiefs, the Chief of Naval Operations, the Marine Corps Commandant, and the Chief of the Air Force. Missing or not showing in the photo was the Army Chief of Staff. She looked for crusty old General Emery; he was not there. She thought it odd that the Army would miss being represented at the first meeting with the incoming Commander-in-Chief, even if it was an "informal" visit. Then she saw the tall, bald man, standing at the entrance to the building but behind the others, holding the door, his face in profile. An Army man. Colonel Harry Howard. Samantha stared intensely at the photograph.

Samantha heard the main door open, and put the newspaper aside. Mrs. Fredericks poked her head into the office. "Sorry I'm late," she said.

"Late?" Samantha replied. "What time is it?"

"It's five to nine."

Lionel had not called. That was unlike him. She reached for the phone, and entered the number to Lionel's direct line at the S.E.C. The phone rang and rang. She hung up, and reached for her good old Rolodex, quickly flipping through the cards she had for people and offices in the S.E.C. She found the main number for the Complex Cases Unit. A woman answered with no greeting and no identification of the office, only a solemn "Yes?"

"Good morning, this is Samantha Wright…"

"Samantha. This is Jane. Jane Vellums."

"Jane, of course. I was by there yesterday. Sorry I didn't see you. How are you? How are the kids?"

At first the only answer was silence. Then Samantha heard it, the unmistakable sounds of a sob, from Jane, and from others nearby.

"Jane… Jane! What's wrong?"

"Oh, Samantha," she wept, "it's Lionel. He's… he's dead. Last night. The street scum, they killed Lionel."

Samantha felt the room spin and her head pound. She tried to take a breath, but couldn't. Her hands trembled. And then the tears came—the tears of anguish, confusion, terror.

She slowly got up from her desk, slammed the door to her office, and collapsed back into her chair. She placed her head in her hands, and cried some more.

—————∞∞∞—————

At the Washington D.C. offices of AMERIPRO, J. Kingston Wittlefield sat in a wing chair. Anger welled up in him. He stared at the clock on the wall of his private office. His hands began to shake. The meeting was scheduled to begin ten minutes ago, and he could not tolerate the inefficiency of tardiness. As he reached for the ever-present medicine, the regular business line buzzed. Wittlefield grabbed the phone, not waiting for a secretary to answer it. "AMERIPRO," he exclaimed.

"I could not get to a secure phone, and I have been delayed. The President-Elect scheduled a…"

"I do not tolerate delays. We must meet. I must know if this matter is contained," Wittlefield barked into the phone.

"It is difficult to be certain."

"We must be certain. We must prepare for all contingencies. Remove yourself from any other matter for the rest of the day, and report in."

The old man slammed down the telephone, and popped two large capsules into his mouth. He grabbed for the silver pitcher with his shaking hands, and tried to pour water into a glass. The water splashed all about, and then the pitcher fell, crashing onto the glass and breaking it into pieces. The dry capsules pressed against his throat, cutting off his air. He coughed, and gagged, and with a horrendous retch, sprang the obstacles free, spewing medicine and saliva over his tie and shirt and pants. The Chairman Emeritus of AMERIPRO leaned back in his chair, gasping for breath. Very slowly he started to recover from his latest attack.

The intercom on Samantha's desk buzzed. She ignored it. It buzzed again. Samantha forced her hand to the button, and pressed.

"Hold all my calls, Gertie," she pleaded.

"Sam? Are your all right?" the secretary asked.

"No," she replied simply.

"What is it?"

"I... I can't discuss it," she responded, lifting her finger from the intercom button, and returning to her silence.

In a few moments, the buzzing started again. Samantha got up from her desk and opened her door. Mrs. Fredericks looked up from the telephone console and saw Samantha's swollen red eyes. "Sam," she exclaimed.

"I can't take any calls, Gertie," she said feebly.

"I know," Mrs. Fredericks replied. "But this man is so insistent."

"Take a message," she responded.

"I already have. He's waiting on hold, but he asked me to take this to you," she said, handing Samantha a small piece of notepaper.

Samantha looked down and read. "Felix Timmons. S.E.C. Mr. Lawrence would have wanted me to call."

Samantha muttered, "I'll take it." She turned and went back to her desk, closing the door behind her. She picked up the phone. "This is Samantha Wright."

The caller hesitated. "I could get into a lot of trouble for this."

"For what?"

"I... I, ah, was to meet with Mr. Lawrence first thing this morning, to discuss nonpublic information about an investigation."

"AMERIPRO?" Samantha asked, knowing the answer.

"I can't say right now. We have to meet. Someplace safe."

"Of course. Wherever you'd like."

"They say Mr. Lawrence was mugged. It was terrible. But I don't know," Felix Timmons stammered.

"When do you want to meet?"

"I don't know. Lunchtime, but perhaps it's best not to wait. I have accumulated so much leave. I could take an hour this morning."

Samantha tried not to think of Lionel, to think of someplace safe, someplace secure they could talk. Then it came to her. She told him where they would meet in a half hour.

Impatiently, Samantha paced back and forth in front of the huge wooden doors, the guard smiling each time she turned and passed him. Finally, he asked her, "Do you want to go ahead in and I'll bring your guest when he arrives?"

"No," Samantha insisted. "I'll wait for him here," she said, looking at her watch and wondering. It had been fifty minutes since they'd spoken.

Then she heard the footsteps echoing down the long marble corridor, and she looked back over her shoulder. A slightly built man, with round, tortoise-shell glasses, was walking toward her. He was neatly dressed in a plain dark blue suit, a white button-down shirt, and a red regimental tie. He looked liked an aging preppy. He was carrying nothing. He nervously looked first to one side, then another, and then behind him.

The man stopped in front of her and whispered. "Ms. Wright."

"Yes," she said, "I'm Samantha Wright."

"I know," he replied. "I looked up the Employee Newsletter from when you left the Commission, the one with your picture on the cover. I had to be sure I would recognize you. Are you sure this is the right place? We can talk?"

"Yes, as long as we keep it low. The recess will start any minute—then we'll have fifteen minutes."

"And the television cameras?"

"They don't shoot into the gallery."

"All right," he said, as the guard opened the door and waved Samantha Wright and Felix Timmons into the balcony gallery of the United States Senate.

They sat down quietly and observed a solitary Senator standing at the podium, addressing a television camera. The gallery was empty. Only the presiding Senator sat at the rostrum above the podium, with the sergeant at arms standing idly by.

In a few minutes, the Senator slammed his fist on the podium, and looked straight into the eye of the television camera, and concluded his remarks with a fervent plea that "the new President live up to his campaign promise delivered so eloquently on that hot afternoon in Boise, and not let the fiemettle fish of the Yankee Fork tributary of the Salmon River destroy any more timber and mining jobs of the hard working citizens of the most beautiful state in the union, my glorious Idaho."

The last syllable of Idaho had not fully escaped the distinguished junior Senator's mouth than the presiding Senator crashed down his gavel, declaring a fifteen minute recess.

Samantha turned to Felix Timmons. "What is in the files?"

"Nothing," he replied.

"What do you mean? There has to be something," Samantha exclaimed, then looked about and lowered her voice.

"No," Felix whispered. "You don't understand. There are no files. The investigation files on AMERIPRO are missing."

"That...that can't be," Samantha exclaimed.

"I'm sorry," he said, "but it is. They were supposed to go to the Central Federal Records Center when the Commission moved out of its old headquarters on North Capitol Street and into the two buildings we use now. We were instructed that all closed files were to go to the CFRC. Anything still active would go to the new Annex—where I work—but the space is so limited that we could not take the old files. But for some reason the AMERIPRO files were ordered to be sent to the Annex."

"You're sure?"

"Oh, yes," he whispered. "I verified it with the TF-F."

"The what?"

"The Transmittal Form-Files. No record can move without one."

"So the files went to the Annex."

"No, that's the point, the Annex has no record of receiving them."

"Must be a paperwork screw up," she said. "The files could still be there."

"Unfortunately, no. I worked on the AMERIPRO investigation, and when it was closed, I'm the one who boxed the files and sealed them. That," he explained, "is included in my job description."

"So?" Samantha asked.

"I remember that there were at least a dozen standard storage boxes, 'banker's boxes,' all properly identified with my initials across each seal. I always used bright orange sealing tape. I looked through all the file storage areas at the Annex. I worked most of the night, without," he explained, "receiving any overtime. I would recognize any files I sealed. They are not there."

"Another dead end," Samantha muttered.

For the first time, timid Felix Timmons parted his thin lips and smiled. "Not necessarily," he said. "I worked on the case."

"And you're a foreign bank account expert?"

"Yes," he replied proudly, "I started learning with the AMERIPRO case. My education was cut short on that one."

"Cut short?" Samantha asked.

"I was going to brief Mr. Lawrence on this."

He stopped as he saw the tears well up in Samantha's eyes. She reached across the seat and squeezed his hand.

"Go on, please," she pleaded.

"I must tell you that I am not comfortable discussing this outside of the S.E.C."

"But I was a staffer," Samantha answered.

"I know, and I believe Mr. Lawrence would have shared this with you, so I have concluded that I should too." His glistening blue eyes blinked. "Mr. Lawrence was the best."

She reached into her suit coat pocket for some Kleenex, and dabbed her eyes. "I know," she said softly.

"Whenever I worked with Mr. Lawrence on a case," Felix went on, "he always insisted that we dot every 'i' and cross every 't'. That is what he always wanted."

Samantha nodded, dabbing her eyes with the tissue.

"We were not allowed to do that in the AMERIPRO case," he said.

She looked at him and caught the angry blush on his pale face. "Before we could complete the investigation," he went on, "the company came to the S.E.C. and admitted that there had been offshore bank accounts used for improper purposes, agreed to fire the wrongdoers and set up procedures to prevent it from happening in the future. They said they would account for the money, which after all is the shareholders' money. The Commission agreed, and directed the staff to close the investigation."

"You didn't like that?" Samantha asked.

"It was not my decision. The Commissioners make the decisions. I do as directed."

"It saved you time and effort," Samantha tried.

"I was not interested in that," he said out loud, then lowered his voice again. "I wanted to learn to trace the money through foreign bank accounts. The S.E.C. hadn't done much of that up to that time. I learned a lot later, it became my specialty."

Samantha felt in her coat pocket and pulled out the fax that had been sent to her by a man who was now dead. And she thought about the fact a copy of the fax had been given to another man now dead. "George Willard sent this to me. The AMERIPRO employee who was fired for supposedly masterminding the bribery scheme. Could this be the number of the Liechtenstein bank account used in the scheme?"

Felix examined the numbers printed on the page. "It could be. The numbers sequence fits some of the patterns I've seen before. But I can't be sure this is the account from the AMERIPRO case without the files. Why don't you ask Mr. Willard?"

Samantha looked at the quiet, lifetime bureaucrat sitting beside her. She decided he should know. "Because he's dead," she said, quickly adding "also."

"Oh, my," he sighed. His eyes widened. "How?"

"From an apparent heart attack after faxing this to me, and minutes before we were supposed to meet."

Felix Timmons flinched. "Oh my."

"Is it possible, some how, to find out if this has something to do with the Liechtenstein account? George Willard obviously thought it was important for me to see this."

He examined the paper again. "It was a long time ago," he said, running his fingers over the numbers again. "But with what I know now, and the confidential sources I've developed over the years, it may be possible. I could finish some unfinished business."

"Unfinished business?" she asked.

"The AMERIPRO investigation. The key to what I do in S.E.C. investigations is track the flow of money, particularly when the culprits are sophisticated and are doing all they can to hide the money trail. We're pretty sophisticated ourselves now. But back when AMERIPRO came into the S.E.C. and said it had uncovered the problem and had recovered its money, we weren't that experienced. The Commission decided to end the matter, as far as it was concerned. Right at that point in our investigation, I'd traced the money that flowed out of the Liechtenstein account back to the U.S., but I hadn't gotten as far as verifying that it all went back to AMERIPRO."

"Was there some doubt?"

"All I knew then was that I had not gotten to the point of complete verification. I got as far as confirming that there was a big transfer from the Liechtenstein account back to the U.S., no further."

A buzzer went off, and the Senator who had been presiding slowly walked up the steps to the central rostrum, and reached for the gavel.

"Where? To the AMERIPRO account?" Samantha whispered.

"As best I remember, we received information generally as to where it was transferred, but nothing specific. You see, back then the banking authorities of Liechtenstein were not very co-operative with our investigations. They had various levels of confidentiality of their accounts, and if the account holder paid enough in what they called 'service fees', then information about the account was kept completely confidential, no matter what international agreements on exchange of such information provided. It was funny. Most people thought Switzerland was the best place to hide money, but the Swiss were much better at providing us with information, usually off the record. So because Switzerland had this long history and reputation for stability and numbered bank accounts, that is where your typical criminal preferred to hide money, and that's where you'd expect bribes to be stashed. But for the few truly sophisticated people who really wanted to conceal their transactions, Liechtenstein was actually the best. Despite plenty of pressure, all our investigation found was that the AMERIPRO Liechtenstein account was closed, and the money transferred to an unidentified bank in Dallas, Texas."

"Dallas," she said. "Dallas. How much are we talking about?"

"Again, Ms. Wright. It's been a long time. A number that sticks with me—twenty million."

"In total?"

"I think so," he said. The loud wooden gavel pounded, calling the empty Senate chamber to order.

Samantha turned in her seat and faced Timmons. "Felix, George Willard made sure I had these numbers. It was the last thing he did. There has to be some very important reason. You have got to help me find out."

He waited a moment, then let another thin smile cross his face. "Things have changed now. Liechtenstein found the pressure from international law enforcement too great, and it's more cooperative. An investigator still has to know what he's doing, and the right people to talk to. But on occasion they've needed something from us, so we trade." He straightened his shoulders. "So if these are the numbers of the old AMERIPRO Liechtenstein account, I may be able to go back and retrace what happened, and . . . finish my job."

"You didn't like not being able to finish, did you, Felix?"

"Not after I learned later on during the Watergate scandal that AMERIPRO was a huge contributor to the Nixon reelection campaign, but that somehow large portions of its contributions were 'misplaced' by the campaign."

"Wow!"

"And after the election, the lawyer for Nixon's campaign came to the S.E.C.," he said sadly.

"I remember hearing something about that—I don't remember his name."

"He wasn't there very long, but he was there for the AMERIPRO case."

"Nobody yelled conflict of interest?" she asked incredulously.

"Not back then. The AMERIPRO case got no publicity. The Commission said it wanted to encourage companies with problems like AMERIPRO to report them voluntarily to the S.E.C. It said what AMERIPRO set a perfect example for how a company ought to respond if some of its employees did wrong. So the Commission issued a release and told companies that if they came forward and turned themselves in, the problems could be corrected confidentially, without adverse publicity."

The Senator at the rostrum announced that he recognized the junior Senator from New Mexico. As the petite white-haired lady approached the podium and the television cameras, Samantha grabbed Felix and said, "Let's go."

They walked down the long, wide main corridor of the Capitol heading for the central rotunda. Two large groups of school children converged noisily under the rotunda, with several of the youngsters twirling around and staring up into the enormous dome.

Samantha pulled Felix over to the white marble statue of Thomas Jefferson. "So you're telling me nobody questioned the handling of the AMERIPRO case."

"Yes" he said meekly. "I was pretty new to my job with the S.E.C. and, ah, I didn't think it was my place to ah..."

"No, I understand that," she said reassuringly, "but it sure smelled with the AMERIPRO connection to Nixon."

"To the few of us involved it didn't seem right. But then soon after, the Watergate scandal heated up, and that was such a big event. The AMERIPRO case seemed unimportant in comparison. And then Nixon resigned, so there didn't seem to be any reason to raise it again."

"Until now," she said.

"Until Mr. Lawrence said it was an emergency," Felix replied.

Enough of an emergency, she thought grimly, for someone to kill.

Felix agreed to see what he could find out, and report back to Samantha. He wrote down the numbers from the fax into a small notebook he carried in his coat pocket. He asked where he could reach her. She thought of the bugging of her apartment phone and still wondered if her cell phone was clean. E-mail was out. Nothing confidential about it. She thought of the office, knew those phones were regularly checked and cleared. But if Timmons called there, the Senator could easily find out. The S.E.C. investigator's role as a confidential source would be compromised. She thought of missing files and telephone listening devices, and being followed, of Daniel and Victoria, and mostly of dear Lionel. The idea came to her suddenly. "I need to get away from here and think this through," she said. "And I may as well go where I might do some good. I'll call you from Texas."

"Texas?"

"Yes, Dallas."

Samantha returned to her office and grabbed the overnight bag she'd always kept there for sudden trips with the Senator. It was lunchtime, and the Senator and Gertie were out. She would have liked to have explained in person, but instead left a note for the Senator, telling him that she simply had to make a quick, confidential trip to Texas. The trip would help insure the Mullen nomination would go smoothly. She promised to return to help in any way he wanted with the hearings starting in three days.

Unfortunately, Senator D'Angelo read the note after a lunch at the Chronicle during which he had consumed four rye whiskeys and sodas. The bartender had made certain that the drinks were doubles. As the Senator read the note, his already ruddy complexion turned even redder as he became angrier and angrier.

CHAPTER THIRTEEN

Daniel Garcia panicked when he called Senator D'Angelo's office. Mrs. Fredericks coldly informed him that Samantha had apparently gone on another trip, taking her overnight bag with her. Adding her own interpretation of events, she told Daniel that obviously Samantha was trying to recover from the emotional trauma which had caused the morning of crying, and Gertrude Fredericks made it clear she assumed Daniel was the cause. In response to his pleas, Mrs. Fredericks told Daniel that even if she wanted to tell him where Samantha had gone, she could not, because only the Senator knew, and he was not available to discuss it, particularly with Daniel.

"But Mrs. Fredericks," Daniel argued, "it's urgent. You've got to understand."

"Goodbye, Mr. Garcia." Mrs. Fredericks disconnected the call.

It was at that point that Daniel lost control. He slammed the phone down, and called Samantha's apartment. On the third ring her machine picked up. "Sam, it's me. I don't know where you've run off to, but you've got to call me. We're in this thing together. Call!" It was only after he slammed down the phone again that he realized his mistake. Desperately, he recounted his message over and over again, and then felt somewhat relieved when he concluded that while he had revealed that she was traveling, he had said nothing that could lead the unknown listeners to Samantha's whereabouts, for he did not know himself.

A short time later, Frank Mullen called for Samantha Wright. When Mrs. Fredericks told him that she was not there, and was not expected back for the rest of the day, the nominee for Secretary of Defense asked to speak with Senator D'Angelo. Mrs. Fredericks hesitated, having smelled the now familiar odor of liquor on the Senator's breath after he had returned from lunch. Usually under such circumstances, she would take a message, and allow the Senator to return the call when he was in the proper frame of mind. But Mr. Mullen was persuasively insistent, explaining that it was a matter of utmost importance to his nomination that simply would not wait.

Mullen was able to detect the slight slur in the Senator's voice even from D'Angelo's simple "hello." Mullen explained that he was under some pressure from the press to attach a name to the prospective woman who it had been rumored was under consideration for a top position in the Defense Department. He desperately needed to talk to Samantha.

Senator D'Angelo responded by exclaiming, "Dammit, Frank, I'd like to help, but Sam didn't give me the slightest idea where in hell in Texas she was going." But the Senator assured Mullen that when she touched base, he would insist that she call Mullen immediately.

While Daniel sat by his phone at the *Post*, J. Kingston Wittlefield stared out through the windows of his private office within the AMERIPRO Washington headquarters. His gaze fixed upon the workers laboring across Lafayette Park assembling the reviewing stands for the Inaugural parade. He turned to the lone figure standing behind him. "What do we know about her last trip to Texas?"

"Four stops," came the reply. "Willard's house in Willowbrook, a pay phone, the *Dallas Tribune* building, and," the man paused, "Dealey Plaza, including almost an hour in the Texas School Book Depository."

"The Plaza?" Wittlefield exclaimed. The old man's hands started to shake. "The situation is ominous. It must be controlled—this woman is dangerous."

"Agreed. But..."

"But what?"

"It will not be easy. She is an aide to a Senator. This operation has the potential for a high profile. It could get messy."

"Don't talk to me about messy. Results are what we need. We'll have to divide our forces. You stay here, close to the reporter. She will contact him. I'll go to Dallas. We'll do whatever is necessary."

—— ⚬∞⚬ ——

Samantha waited in her seat until the other passengers filed off the plane. The clarity of her decision of a few hours before to go to Dallas had eroded. When the flight attendant asked her if she needed any assistance, Samantha replied "not really," but then asked for a suggestion for an inexpensive place to stay in downtown Dallas, near the *Tribune* building. The flight attendant recommended the Governors' House Hotel. "It's old but classic," she said, "and it has a great bar." She leaned close. "The rooms are clean. It's a fine place to party, when you're in the mood, honey."

At the airport, Samantha turned on her cell phone but then spotted a line of public phones. Why take a chance? She used the pay phone to call the hotel and made a reservation, then looked through her notes and found the number of George Willard's doctor. He was back from his medical symposium, and because she pleaded that it was urgent, he agreed to meet with her in two hours, at the close of the working day. Next, she phoned the records office of the *Dallas Tribune*. When she asked Lester Boggs if he'd found the photograph she had been looking for, he cheerfully replied that he thought so. She looked at her watch and calculated the traveling distances. There was no way to get to downtown Dallas and see the photo, and still make it out to Willard's doctor by five o'clock. Reluctantly, she postponed going to the newspaper offices until it opened at nine o'clock the next morning.

Lester Boggs did not think to mention that he'd only just called the home number she had given him, and left a message that the photo was available for her to see.

For one of those strange reasons of human habit, Samantha went back to the same rental car counter she'd approached before. This time there was no one in line. The rental car clerk had almost finished keying her information into the computer, when Samantha happened to glance at the computer terminal. She froze for a moment, then grabbed back her credit card and driver's license with an abrupt "never mind." The startled clerk stared after Samantha as she went from car rental company to car rental company, first leaning over the counter and seeming to examine the computers. It was not until the third rental car company that Samantha found a computer that was not emblazoned with the bold lettering and distinctive logo of AMERIPRO. In three minutes she was on the shuttle to her compact car.

Doctor Jimmy Charles was six-foot six, lean to the point of gangly. He adjusted his reading glasses and looked down his long sharp nose at Samantha's credentials. He listened to her assurances that she was working on a very important Senate investigation. His blank expression revealed that he remained unimpressed. "In any event, what do you want from me?"

"I need to know the cause of death of George Willard," she said.

"The cause of death?" he replied. "Now listen here, that's highly unusual. I mean, that's personal to the family."

"But it's vital to my investigation," she explained. "At least to know if it was natural causes, or if there is any possibility of foul play."

"Foul play? I don't know what you're talking about. George Willard?"

"Yes," she explained, recounting the sequence of events of Willard's sudden death just before his scheduled meeting with her, and his holding of an envelope a few minutes before his death, which envelope was nowhere to be found in his room. She told the physician of the butler's recalling that Mr. Willard was pleased with his clean bill of health from his physical of only a few days before. That led her to question the sudden death.

"Oh, now I understand," he said. "Listen, I'm sure you're a very important person in Washington," he said in a way that left no doubt that he did not mean it. "But down here in Texas, we respect a family's right to privacy. I'm not gonna just open up the medical records of one of my patients to someone who comes marching in here with a fancy ID card. Get the family to agree, or get a court order or something."

"Court order?" Samantha exclaimed. "I don't have time. Dr. Charles, I'm not trying to cause any trouble, but I need to know how somebody goes from a clean bill of health to dead in a matter of a few days."

He shook his head. "Listen up. It's real easy. I'm not about to tell you anything confidential, but I sure am gonna make this short, and be done with it. It's nothing that George Willard himself wouldn't have told anybody hanging around the nineteenth hole at the country club."

"What is it?"

"It's true we'd done his annual physical," the doctor confirmed. "The result was a clean bill of health, relative to George's overall condition."

"Overall condition?" she asked.

"Yep. George Willard was diabetic. It was pretty well stabilized, but you never really know what silent damage has been done to the vital organs by the disease. George's heart appeared strong enough for a man his age…"

"So it was a heart attack?" Samantha interrupted.

He thought for a moment, then chose his words carefully. "I'm told that is what the official cause of death will be listed as in the obituary in the newspaper."

"You're told?" she asked.

"Well, yes," he said. "I was away. Besides, I don't usually attend autopsies. I understand massive, sudden cardiac arrest was the conclusion."

"Doctor! This is so important. Can you be sure? Can you review the autopsy, or redo it? I have got to know if there is any doubt as to the cause of death. If someone could have caused it."

The physician shook his head. "I don't see why anyone would..."

"Doctor!" she exclaimed.

He shook his head again. "I'll need the appropriate procedures. Some sort of complaint filed with the police, or subpoena from the Senate."

Samantha looked anguished. "Doctor, you must believe me, there is no time. All I'm asking is that you take a look, personally, and let me know if I'm wasting my time. Let me know if there is any possibility, at all, that his death wasn't from natural causes. Then I can get a subpoena."

Doctor Charles seemed to be considering this.

"I'll follow procedures," Sam said. "I promise, but at least first give me a hint if I've got any reason to do so."

"I'm not promising anything, except I'll think about it," he replied, his reluctance and skepticism clear. He stared into her pleading eyes. "All right. Where can I reach you?"

She started to give him her cell number, then thought about the Governors' House Hotel. She stopped. "I'll call you. When do you think you might have something?"

"Tomorrow," he said brusquely. "Call me midmorning."

Before heading to downtown Dallas, she asked to use the phone in the doctor's waiting room. She called her office. Mrs. Fredericks told Samantha how concerned she was about her, but Samantha assured her there was nothing to worry about. The secretary read Samantha her messages, including the one from Daniel, then told her the Senator really wanted to talk to her. When Mrs. Fredericks said that the Senator was not himself, Samantha understood the office euphemism for "the Senator had been drinking." She could not handle it right then, and convinced Gertie to not let him know that she had called.

She drove into the city, retracing her path of only a few days before and followed the directions to the hotel that the rental car company had given her. Samantha took one look at the old hotel nestled among the city's skyscrapers, and could tell that it had once been a grand place. The old-fashioned elevator ride with a real live elevator operator who talked nonstop as they slowly passed the first and second floors convinced her she had found a charming hideaway.

She gasped as she entered the room, and smiled for the first time in what seemed like ages. The room was almost filled with a huge, dark mahogany four-poster bed, with elaborate wooden carvings at the top of each of the bed posts. Her smile faded, and she sat down on the bed and thought about Lionel's death. She wept uncontrollably for the second time that day. Soon, exhaustion set in, and she gently rolled over and slept on a bed that was almost identical to the one she'd so often cuddled on with her mother in that lifetime long, long ago.

Samantha's sleep was troubled by the ghostly visions of an old photograph, of her mother, Lionel, the body of George Willard, the logo of AMERIPRO, and Frank Mullen. When the telephone rang, her eyes sprang open. She leaped from the bed, stumbling in the darkness. It rang again and again as she desperately tried to expunge an overwhelming feeling that she was lost. She remembered Dallas, the old hotel, the four-poster bed. She found the phone and the light next to it. Her hand touched the thin metal chain hanging down and she pulled. A dim light filled a tiny area of the room. As the telephone kept ringing, she held her watch up to the light. It was a few minutes after eight at night. She was in downtown Dallas.

She shivered. Who would be calling? Who could it be? No one knew where she was. The ringing continued. She thought about running, hiding, but as the phone rang yet again, she reluctantly picked it up.

"Samantha? Are you there? Are you all right?"

The voice was familiar, and yet she couldn't place it.

"Samantha. It's Frank Mullen."

The last vestiges of sleep disappeared as she bolted awake.

"Frank?" she exclaimed. How the hell could anybody find her here? How the hell did he find her?

"Yes. I need to talk with you. I know something is going on. Perhaps I can be of help. But we need to talk."

She took a deep breath. Calm down, she thought. Calm down. "All right," she said slowly. "Ah, what do you want to talk about?"

"Our futures. Yours and mine. It's urgent."

"Okay, talk," she said.

"In person."

"All right," she replied again, biding for time, hoping against hope her voice was sounding steadier over the phone than the shaky resonance she heard fill the room. "As soon as I get back to Washington, I'll call and…"

"No," he insisted. "I told you it was urgent. I'm here in Dallas."

"Dallas?" she gasped. She curled her fingers around one of the four posters. Get a grip, she told herself. "Where?"

"Actually, I'm just downstairs, in the lobby. I love this old hotel. Many fond memories. It's still got the best steaks in Texas, and that's saying something."

Samantha felt the moisture leave her mouth, her face flushing. "Downstairs?" she replied weakly. "I, ah, I'm sure it's very good, but I don't eat meat."

"Oh come on," he said cheerfully, "they always have a couple of great fresh fish dishes." Then his voice deepened and lowered. "Samantha, it won't wait. I'll be in the Cattleman's Dining room. As usual it will be crowded, but they've been kind enough to save us a table. I won't take up all of your evening. Just a dinner conversation, and then I can get out on the last flight back to Washington."

The phone went dead before she recovered enough to demand to know how he had found her.

Samantha sat on the bed and replayed his words. She remembered the elevator operator. She wouldn't be alone, anywhere in the hotel. And he was, after all, the nominee for Secretary of Defense, undoubtedly well known at the hotel.

She washed her face, and lightly applied her makeup. Then she changed into the simple black evening dress she had always kept stored in the overnight bag—the one that clung to her in all the right places. She put on the black heels. The outfit had come in handy many times, and with a look in the full-length mirror she was sure it would do the trick tonight.

Thank God, she thought, the door to the room has a peephole. She peered through it, and seeing no one, walked out into the hall, and took the elevator to the lobby.

Frank Mullen had been right. The restaurant was full, with every table in sight taken. The bar was packed, mostly with men. She noticed they were invariably wearing traditional business suits, with cowboy boots. She lingered by the bar for a few moments, smiling and tossing her hair about her shoulders. After a couple of glances confirmed that she had attracted a fair number of admirers, and witnesses, she approached the maitre d' and asked for Frank Mullen. As he walked her to the table, she felt safe, noticing the many eyes attentively following her progress.

"Samantha, I'm so glad you decided to join me," Mullen said as he stood up and shook her hand.

"My pleasure," she lied.

"What would you like to drink?" he asked.

"I'll have a white wine," she answered.

Mullen snapped his fingers, and a waiter approached. "The lady will have a Chardonnay, Grigich Hills '88 if you have it."

"I do believe so, Mr. Mullen."

"Good. And I'll have another Jack Daniels and branch water," he said, handing his empty glass to the waiter.

Samantha looked at Mullen and smiled. "Drinking tonight, Frank? Hard day?"

"Yeah," he replied. "I've had better. Returning to this old place brings back memories. When the helicopter division of AMERIPRO used to win big contracts, this is where we'd come to celebrate. I'd try to relax a little with a drink or two."

"Are you celebrating tonight?"

"Not unless I get your unqualified agreement to take the Deputy position."

"I thought I had pretty much indicated I would."

"I thought so, too. But the Senator tells me there may be some question, something having to do with your sudden trip down here. And I need to know you're on board. Actually, the President-Elect and I would both like to leak it to the right folks in the press."

"I see," Samantha said. "So Senator D'Angelo told you I was coming to Texas?"

"Yes," he replied. "I told him we absolutely had to wrap this up and I needed to speak with you."

"But how did you find me here?" she asked calmly.

He paused, then smiled. "It's amazing what a nomination to high public office and the attendant publicity can do for you. We had the staff at the transition office call all the airlines flying to Texas at midday, and found out you had flown American into Dallas. I took a chance and jumped on the next flight myself. I guessed you'd rent a car and so I checked all rental car companies until I found yours. A helpful agent behind the counter pulled out your rental agreement and there it was—local address, the Governors' House Hotel."

Samantha mentally kicked herself. How could she be so... so, inexperienced in these things. "So they just give that information out?" she asked.

"That's where the publicity comes in. I guess the young lady wanted to help the next Secretary of Defense, particularly one that is apparently being portrayed in the Dallas press as a bit of a local hero. When I introduced myself, she said she already knew who I was. Said I was all over the local news and on the front page of the *Dallas Tribune* today."

"Congratulations," she said.

Before she had even finished the word, two rugged looking men came over to the table. "Mr. Mullen," the larger of the two said, extending his hand. Mullen started to rise, but the man quickly added, "now don't you get up, ya hear. Me and Jed," he said, pointing a thumb at his companion, "don't want to bother ya. Jus' wanted to stop by and congratulate ya on your appointment. Damn, it's gonna be great to have a man from Texas up there in D.C.—somebody with his head screwed on right.

Between us," he said, lowering his voice and winking at Mullen, "we ain't so sure 'bout some of them folks up there, including this Governor Nobody whose taking ov'r the White House with all his 'new politics,' whatever the hell that means. But you, hell, you're one of us. And we're sure you're gonna give the go ahead to MachCopt. Lots of jobs round here depend on that baby. Me and Jed's, that's for sure."

"You work for the helicopter division of AMERIPRO?" Mullen asked, a hint of pride in his voice.

"Hell," the man replied, "sure as shit wish we did. We'd a been proud to work for your company, Mr. Mullen. You boys' been the backbone of our economy—when the cattle's been down, or the oil in a bust, AMERIPRO has kept this part of Texas going. Course I don't need to tell you that. But hell, to answer your question, me and Jed don't work directly for ya. We've got us a related business. Own a little fabricating plant. Small, but we're the best for a line of precision tools. We ain't but a few blocks from the main helicopter plant over in Abilene. The place where MachCopt is gonna keep us all busy. Yes, sir, hears they's gonna spend over forty billion building the best damn flying machine ever. That's a shit load of a job."

Frank Mullen looked at Samantha as the big man released his firm grip on Mullen's hand. "Well," Mullen said, smiling at the man. "Thanks for coming over, gentlemen. I appreciate your support."

"Damn straight," the one named Jed added to the conversation before the two returned to the bar.

Samantha leaned forward and spoke softly. "It must be hard for you not to be able to participate in the MachCopt decision."

Mullen shrugged. "To tell you the truth," he said, "it isn't. In fact, with every day I'm out of AMERIPRO, the better I feel."

"What?" she asked. "Why, Frank?"

"Other than practicing law for a few years at the start, I've lived, eaten, slept, and breathed AMERIPRO." He leaned forward and lowered his voice. "And between you and me," he said, darting his eyes about the room, "the old man who controls AMERIPRO..."

"Wittlefield?"

"Yes. Well, he's a tyrant, a tough, mean son-of-a-bitch to deal with. Brilliant businessman, a genius at finance, but it's time I got out from under his control, do other things, important things with my life while I still have time, and the good health and drive to do it. Use my talents for something other than just making money. Take those fellas," Mullen said, pointing back by the bar, "their fabrication shop may be small, but if they supply tools to AMERIPRO, I guarantee you they're the best in the business."

"I'm sure," Samantha agreed, finding herself rapidly easing into the conversation.

"And if it is decided by the powers above me that the Mach-Copt program isn't going to go forward," he smiled, "then good businessmen like Jed and his partner, who employ a lot of people, are going to need help to convert their businesses to do something we do need."

"I couldn't agree more," she said. "That's why with every Defense Department budget fight Senator D'Angelo has led, he's always introduced legislation to provide funding for programs to help those affected, like converting obsolete bases to peacetime uses. I bet you didn't know that?"

"Actually, I did. I'm all for it, and I'm the experienced businessman who can make it work," he replied. "That is, if I have the right people around me to help. Samantha, I've got to have you commit to the job."

The waiter came over and took their orders. Over his charred and blackened porterhouse steak and her plain grilled trout, Frank Mullen repeated his arguments for why Samantha Wright had to accept the position as Deputy Secretary of Defense. As the dinner hour passed, and the bar noise escalated, he argued persuasively, and convincingly.

When he asked her to authorize him to notify the President-Elect that she'd be joining the team, she came very close to saying yes. Instead, she told him that she almost certainly would take the job, but she needed to tie up a few personal loose ends first. "Clear some old cobwebs that are hanging around," she explained. As he looked at his watch and announced that he had to go if he was going to make the last flight back to Washington, she promised to call him tomorrow and undoubtedly, and finally, say yes.

"When?" he asked.

"I'm sure I'll finish up early and call you by noon."

She walked with him through the lobby and stood by as he told the bellman he needed a cab to the airport. She waved as he left, and then walked back to the elevator for the ride to the third floor. She opened the door to the room, and after closing it behind her, she locked the deadbolt and the security chain. She sat on the bed and took off her heels. She thought about moving to another hotel. If Frank Mullen could find her...But then she looked around at the lovely old bed, at the locked door, and the need to move faded.

She pulled her old flannel nightgown from the overnight bag, and changed. Before slipping under the warm comforter, she walked to the single window and looked out at the night lights of modern Dallas burning brightly. When she saw the heavy metal surrounding her window and partially blocking her view, she didn't know what it was at first. Then she looked down, and up. She backed away from the window, and checked, and then rechecked, that it was locked securely. She pulled down the antiquated roller window shade, and then the heavy embroidered drapes. She convinced herself that she did not have to worry about the fire escape outside her room.

An AMERIPRO Gulfsteam V landed at Love Field, Dallas at 11:30 that night. J. Kingston Wittlefield walked slowly down the steps, collapsed into the back seat of the waiting limousine, and ordered the driver to take him to AMERIPRO's penthouse apartment on the thirty-eighth floor of a high rise in downtown Dallas.

CHAPTER FOURTEEN

Samantha lay in the four-poster bed, curled up in the comforter, sheltered in her mother's arms. Around the bed were the newspapers and magazines and the photographs, flashing past her eyes in rapid fire, the pictures of the sorrow, and the bloody pink dress, and the faces of the people in mourning. And spinning around her, the face of her mother, crying and angry and grieving, and repeating, "Why? Why?"

Samantha awoke with a start, her heart pounding, her skin clammy. She brought her hands to her face and took a deep breath, and willed her racing heart to slow. She fumbled for the light on the nightstand, and blessed the illumination for chasing away the shadowy visions of the night.

She looked at the clock-radio. An hour and a half before she could see the photograph at the *Tribune*. Time enough to call Daniel, but she decided against it. He could wait.

She couldn't resist a bath in the large, freestanding brass tub, and felt refreshed and better ready for the day ahead for having treated herself to it. With her towel wrapped around her, she crossed the room to the window and pushed back the curtains. She gave the window shade the little pull down it needed to go flying back up onto its roller. Samantha looked out through the metal rails of the fire escape. The January Dallas morning was bright and sunny, but she could see from the jackets and overcoats of pedestrians passing by on the sidewalk of the main street below that the temperature was still cool.

As she dressed in the dark gray three-piece suit that was her sole remaining choice from the overnight bag, she turned on the television, looking for the weather report. She changed the channel from the commercials on NBC to the lead-in to the morning show on ABC just in time to be told, "Good Morning America is brought to you by AMERIPRO's Progress and Profits for a Healthy, Strong and Secure America—AMERIPRO—providing for People Like You."

Samantha quickly changed the channel again, then picked up the hotel telephone. Felix Timmons answered on the first ring.

"Timmons here."

"Felix, it's Samantha."

"Yes. Are you in Dallas?"

"I sure am. How are things going?" she asked.

"Very well. I've been on the phone all night. I can provide a report in three hours. Eleven o'clock your time. Call me at (202) 555-7845. After that, be available to meet with someone after we talk."

Samantha scribbled the number down and read it back to him.

"Correct. At eleven o'clock, Dallas time."

The phone went dead. That sounded very promising, she thought, as she turned the television off and grabbed the large Senate issued briefcase. She would have time for coffee, and perhaps a croissant, before making the two-block walk to the *Tribune*. She looked through the peephole of her door, and finding the hallway empty, walked out and down to the elevator. The same talkative elevator operator of the evening before greeted her cheerfully, and talked of the beautiful, warming Dallas day ahead.

On the way through the lobby she stopped at the newsstand and bought that morning's *Tribune*, then found the small coffee shop. As she sipped the strong, smoky tasting coffee, she quickly thumbed through the first section of the paper, then came to the local news section. Staring back at her was a smiling photograph of Frank Mullen at the center of the page, below a blazing headline **"AMERIPRO CHIEF TO DEFENSE DEPARTMENT— GOOD NEWS FOR TEXAS!"** She quickly read the sub headline. "With over forty billion at stake on MachCopt, Texas stands to reap the economic rewards." She hurriedly completed the article, finding little news and much commentary. She particularly noted the concluding sentence of the story reporting that, "The *Tribune's* sources in the Senate confirm that the Mullen nomination enjoys wide support with no discernible opposition."

Samantha finished her coffee, and took a last bite of the cold dry pastry that was passing for a croissant. She left the newspaper behind as she headed out.

Samantha entered the building at precisely nine o'clock. This time she waved to the guard and announced that she knew where she was going. She took the elevator to the basement, and found the meek-looking Lester Boggs sitting behind the counter.

"I'm back," she proclaimed.

"Well now, so you are, honey," the records clerk replied. "I do believe I found what you're looking for. Reckon it's a pretty big file, but your photo's got to be in it."

"A big file?" Samantha asked. "I was looking for one photo."

"Well I knows that," Lester said. "But our photographers don't just take one photo, you knows." He reached down behind the counter and pulled out a large manila envelope, with black markings on the cover. "This here's all the pictures the photographer took on that trip to Vietnam in '64. Real photos, of course, none of that digital crap back then." He handed her the envelope, and pointed to a card table and folding metal chair in the corner. "Ain't the best accommodations in town, but that's all we got. Sit yourself down and have a gander."

Samantha looked at the table and the dark corner. "It'll be fine," she said. "Except maybe there's a little better light."

"Sakes alive," he replied. "Got me there. Cain't very well expect you to see all that much without light. Here," he said, pulling an electrical plug out of the wall behind the counter. "You take my desk lamp. That outta do the trick."

Samantha plugged it in next to the table and sat down. Then the clerk came over. "Try this, too," he said, handing her a magnifying glass.

She thanked him and started her search. At first she rapidly flipped from one photo to the next, attempting a short cut through the large stack containing hundreds of photographic records of the war that had faded into history. She began to linger, staring at the people and the places. It was so long ago, she thought, but the young faces of the American soldiers looked as fresh as yesterday, as real as today. She peered at the dirty and sullen Asian faces, their bodies weighed down by weapons, marching through jungles and on dirt roads, passing naked children, and old women. And in photo after photo, the bodies, bloodied and still, twisted, mangled, burned—dead.

At times Samantha closed her eyes, seeking respite from the terrible visions of war. Then she returned to the photographs. And as she did so, yet another recurring, overriding presence in the photographs emerged. Helicopters were everywhere, carrying soldiers, firing guns, filling the sky.

And then she saw it. The front page of the Dallas newspaper from a time when the war was raging. General William Westmoreland standing beside a much younger, slimmer Frank Mullen. Yes, she told herself, even without the caption, she probably could have recognized the young Frank Mullen in the forefront of the photo. Then her eyes focused on the man standing behind Westmoreland and Mullen, by the tail rotor of a helicopter, a man not identified in the newspaper caption. Ramrod straight, icy stare, a head with such close cropped hair that he could be bald. She picked up the magnifying glass and focused intently on the unidentified man. Staring back from the clear, original photograph was the face of the special military advisor to the President-Elect of the United States, Colonel Harry Howard. She set the photo down on the table.

Then she started turning rapidly from one photo to the next. There he was, again and again, always in the background, always with helicopters, and always the same cold expression on his face. And wherever Colonel Howard was seen, so was Frank Mullen. The same Frank Mullen who had told her and Senator D'Angelo that he barely knew Colonel Howard.

She separated the photos into two groups. Those with Howard and Mullen, and those without. She stuffed the photos she didn't need back in the envelope, and approached the clerk.

"How can I get copies?" she asked.

"Well, missy, you just turn the photos over and look at the identifying number on the back, and we order them up. Takes about tens days to two weeks."

"Ten days! No," Samantha explained. "I need them now!" She reached down for her purse and pulled out her official Senate credential card. "It's official business of the United States Senate."

"The United States Senate?" he repeated. "Well, now, I'm sure that'll make a difference. Let me see," he said, staring down at the stack of photographs. "When do ya really need them?"

"Now! As soon as possible."

"As soon as possible?" he repeated. "Well, hold on, let me see what I can find out. I'm gonna have to go upstairs to the lab. You wait here. You being with the government and all, I guess I can leave you here. I'll see how fast we can be of service. Modernizing the whole place up there, bringing in those fancy new laser printers, but I don't believe they're hooked up yet. Make yourself comfortable. I'll be back." With that, Boggs double-timed it over to the elevator.

When he'd been gone for over fifteen minutes, Sam got up and looked around the basement archives. Behind the clerk's counter she saw the long row of shelves, packed with binders. She recalled the first time she'd met Lester Boggs, and how proud he was of his organized photographic record of the Kennedy assassination. Samantha spied the labels on the binders—"Arrival-Dove Field"; "Motorcade"; "Parkland Hospital". She walked around the counter and put her hand on the first binder—"Arrival-Dove Field", then moved on to the next. She pulled it out and turned back around, laid it out on the counter top, and opened it. She saw immediately that Lester had done his job. The original photographs from the *Tribune's* own photographers were obviously mixed in with copies of others the newspaper had acquired, and all were arranged in chronological order, carrying the viewer in one continuous montage along the route of the fateful motorcade. She followed the topless Lincoln limousine with its treasured passengers down Main Street, past the cheering, smiling crowds; she stared at the people lining the street, struck by how happy everyone seemed to be.

She stopped at one photo of the rear of the car as it turned right onto Houston Street, holding it up to the light, focusing on the Texas School Book Depository in the background, and remembering how she had just visited the museum inside the building.

As she turned over more photos, she saw clearly that it had been a beautiful and warm day. And then the photos showed the President's car turning again, by the School Book Depository, the sign for Elm Street visible in the background. The President was waving, and Mrs. Kennedy was smiling. Samantha stopped, knowing, remembering what was to come.

Her eyes darted to the pile of Vietnam pictures on the table on the other side of the room, and then up at the wall clock. She hoped the clerk hadn't forgotten her and gone off on some break. She let out a long breath, then returned to the binder filled with photos. She turned over one photo, and then another, and then... There it was! The first photograph showing that something was terribly wrong. The limousine in the foreground, a flashing blur of a car moving fast, desperately trying to gain speed to carry the President out of harm's way, or to emergency medical assistance. But in the background, the images were clearer. People no longer smiling, hands no longer waving. The people were falling, ducking, seeking shelter, their faces frightened, confused. Samantha turned away, but then looked down again. She was about to turn to the next photographic vignette when she noticed, behind the speeding car, up on the hill, leaning against the block wall, at the pinnacle of the infamous grassy knoll—a solitary, shadowy man in a long coat, standing ramrod straight. Samantha held the photograph to the light, and examined it closely. The strange image was there, the lines were there.

Samantha grabbed the binder, came out from behind the counter, and raced over to the table. She sat down, adjusted the light, and stared. She held the photo up to the light again. The photographer's vantage point looking up at the grassy knoll from the Elm Street curbside sprang to life. She grabbed the magnifying glass and examined an original photo from the stack of Vietnam pictures, and brought the two together. Through the thick, clarifying lens of the magnifying glass, she saw it. She saw it, almost clearly. She stared at the man in Vietnam, the third man, standing back by the rotor of the helicopter, and then at the assassination photograph. In spite of the grainy images, in spite of the haze of time, she convinced herself, the only difference between the two figures was that on the grassy knoll above Dealey Plaza on November 22, 1963, Colonel Harry Howard was smiling.

Lester returned. "Ya see," he said, pointing to the binder of Kennedy assassination photographs on the table. "I told you everybody comes in here looking for those. Cain't resist."

Samantha shook her head. "How soon? When can I get my copies? And this one too," she added, pointing to the photograph from the motorcade.

"Well, now, sure nuf that new highfalutin equipment isn't ready yet. Come back next week and it'd be a snap. But I begged and pleaded for ya. The lab's all backed up, but they promised they can have it in jus' two days."

"Two days?"

"Now hold your horses. I said that's the best they could promise. Down here we don't like to promise what we cain't deliver. But they said they'd try to have 'em tomorrow. Come back then, or I can send them to you."

"I'll come back," she replied softly, and then muttered "tomorrow."

When she finally left the *Tribune* building, Samantha spotted a free standing open air public phone across Main Street. She started for it but then saw the driver of a black limousine parked at the curb get out of the car, and go to the phone. She glanced at her watch. She realized it was only four minutes until she was to call Felix Timmons. She looked up the street and saw the hotel. She began walking as fast as she could.

The limousine driver hurriedly got back into the car, and started to drive in the same direction.

"Wait!" the command came from the back seat. "You stay with her. It looks like she's going back to the hotel. I'll call on the cell phone when I'm finished." With that, J. Kingston Wittlefield got out of the back of the car, and walked slowly with the aid of his cane into the *Tribune* building.

Lester Boggs knew it was peculiar that the old man wanted to see whatever the young lady had just seen. His suspicions were quickly alleviated by a fifty dollar bill. Inspired, the clerk advised the old man that the woman had seen a lot of photographs, but suggested that he might save time by simply looking at the form the lady had filled out to order copies. After another fifty dollar bill had changed hands, Wittlefield's review took only a few moments. When he saw the photograph of the grassy knoll, Wittlefield asked the clerk for a glass of water, and popped four capsules into his mouth.

Before leaving, Wittlefield inquired about obtaining copies for himself. When he was told how long it would take and Wittlefield asked why, the clerk explained that the copies had to be done in the newspaper's own photo lab, and work was always backed up there. "So the original photos and the negatives are all right here," he asked, "in this building?"

"Never leave the building," the clerk replied.

Samantha returned to the hotel with no time to go back to her room. She walked directly to the wooden phone booth in the corner of the lobby, and closed the door completely.

Felix Timmons answered the pay phone at a convenience store three blocks from his office. "The numbers you had, they were the account numbers for the AMERIPRO account at the Banque de Savoy in Liechtenstein. The account was opened on July 12, 1961, and closed on January 23, 1973."

"How much money?" Samantha asked.

"My source cannot access the detailed account reports without drawing attention, which he will not do. He was able to come up with the opening deposit—five million dollars—and the balance at closing—twenty million."

"And the twenty million was returned to AMERIPRO?"

"All my Liechtenstein source knows is that the twenty million was wired out of the account on January 23, 1973, to the First Commerce Bank and Trust Company of Dallas."

"So it's a dead end," Samantha sighed.

"No," Felix replied matter-of-factly. "I have other sources. A certain bank officer in Texas who escaped an indictment when all around him were falling—he cooperated with my investigation. He's still appreciative, and is willing to speak with you."

"What can he tell me?" Samantha asked excitedly.

"I'm not sure. He will not talk over the telephone. He will meet you today," Felix paused, "at one o'clock."

"Where?"

"He says it is a pleasant day in Dallas. He'll only meet out of doors where there are people around. At Lone Star Park, in downtown. He says there is a central fountain. You should go there, and wait. He will come to you."

"What's his name, Felix?"

"He does not want you to know. All I can tell you is that he knows that the twenty million did not go where I understood it was to go."

Samantha left the phone booth and approached the registration desk. She grabbed a map of downtown Dallas and found the park in the heart of the financial district. It was six blocks away.

She returned to the phone booth. Her first call was local, her second back to Washington.

The receptionist at Doctor Charles's office at first said that the doctor was unavailable for calls, but when Samantha identified herself, she told Samantha to hold. In a moment, Doctor Charles came on the line.

"Can you help me, Doctor? Can you tell me anything?" she asked anxiously.

"You will follow the proper procedures? You promise you can get formal authorization?"

"I promise."

"The conclusion of the autopsy report was as I was told, a massive cardiac arrest," Doctor Charles said flatly.

"I see," Samantha responded, the disappointment heavy in her voice. "No doubts?"

"No doubt as to the conclusion," he confirmed. "But as to the cause…"

"What?" she asked.

"The autopsy showed George had a healthy heart, and good, relatively clear arteries, with no significant blockage. The diabetes had not taken a toll. I was right about that. As I hoped, we had the disease under control."

"So?" Samantha pleaded.

"It is difficult to be sure. Sometimes the heart goes. But there was a note in the autopsy. A sign of two penetrations, injection marks, one on George's arm."

"Yes," she replied quickly. "I remember the paramedics were injecting something in his arm as they tried to resuscitate him."

"That explains that one. But there was another, on his thigh."

Samantha almost blurted out that had to be it, and then she remembered. "Oh," she said flatly. "That's right. He was diabetic. Insulin injections. Don't diabetics often inject themselves in the thigh?"

The phone line remained silent until the doctor cleared his throat and lowered his voice. "Yes, that is the conclusion that someone might reach, someone who knew of George's diabetes. But you see, George hated needles, hated injections. He told me it went back to his painful recuperation from his injuries in Vietnam. They stuck him with so many needles he told me he couldn't stand another one. That's why I had George on Exubera."

"What's that?"

"It's new, quite expensive. An insulin inhaler. Most important for George, it avoided needles."

"Doctor Charles," Samantha interrupted. "That means there was an unexplained injection mark on Willard's thigh?"

"Yes," he replied. "The autopsy showed the heart had been healthy, but the death was the result of a heart attack. Theoretically, and I do mean theoretically, without the signs of heart disease, or a heart weakened by the diabetes, the cause of the attack could have been an embolism, an obstruction of the blood vessels going to the heart."

"And?" she asked eagerly.

"Again, theoretically, looking for a reason for an embolism—it's caused by a foreign body, an embolus, that occludes a blood vessel. It could have been caused by an injection."

"An injection?"

"An injection of air. It would require real force—force to push the air bubble in—it could be done, not easy, but it would cause the heart to stop, dead."

"Can it be proved?" she asked excitedly.

The doctor was slow to respond. "If that's what it was, it's tricky to prove. Maybe some bruising around the area of the injection . . . but it would mean redoing the autopsy by specifically investigating that possibility."

"Then do it! You've got to. I'll get whatever authorization you need."

"Ms. Wright, I had a patient with diabetes. His heart could have been weakened by the disease, but apparently it wasn't. I would like nothing better than to be certain of my patient's cause of death, but all we have is the inconclusive note in the autopsy about a puncture. That is all we will ever have. While you and I were meeting yesterday, George Willard's body was being cremated."

Daniel Garcia was sitting at his desk at the Post chomping on a micro-waved burrito from the snack bar when her call finally came.

"Samantha, where are you? Are you okay?" he gasped, the thick gooey mass of beef and beans and cheese clinging to the roof of his mouth.

"Listen, Daniel," Samantha spoke rapidly. "I don't have much time. All I can say is things are moving very fast. And while I hate to admit it, I need your help."

"Anything, but where are you?"

"Dallas," she shot back.

"Jesus Christ! What are you doing there?"

"Later, when you get here. Now, you've got to get back to your girlfriend…"

"Sam!" Daniel pleaded. "You're my…"

"Shut up. Get to Victoria. I need to find out if our Colonel Howard did some international travel in November, 1963, particularly anything within a few days of November 22."

"November 22?"

"Find out if he left the country, and if so, from where and to where. Got that? I need something to verify that Colonel Howard was in Dallas."

"Dallas? Right, sure, Sam."

"Get a document out of the bitch this time. And then get down here."

"Got it. Where do we meet?"

"Go to the Governors' House Hotel. Wait in the lobby. It's a busy place. I'll contact you somehow, sometime tonight. And Daniel? Don't waste any time fucking around!" She slammed the phone down, and decided to walk to the Lone Star Park. She needed the fresh air.

<hr />

Daniel called Victoria immediately, and caught her just as she was about to leave for lunch. At first she complained about waking up alone, but Daniel explained that it was he who was the disadvantaged one, having to cover an early morning press conference instead of staying with the wonderful lover he thought about every waking moment since they had parted. With promises of a repeat in the very near future, his plea for more information from the confidential passport file fell on receptive ears. She told him the file was still in her safe because she had not had the chance to return it without someone noticing. He told her the information he needed, and that he had to see the documents to be certain. She agreed to cancel her lunch, and meet him instead.

Daniel pulled out of the underground garage and muscled the GTO convertible into the heavy lunchtime traffic. He darted in and out of lanes, racing for the Theodore Roosevelt Bridge and the George Washington Parkway beyond. He concentrated solely on the traffic ahead, and did not notice he was being followed by a black Lincoln Town Car.

The outgoing Assistant Secretary of State locked the door to her office, then opened the safe. She pulled the file out and started to look for the information Daniel wanted, but there were so many documents. She knew she had to hurry. Frustrated, she grabbed the briefcase she had been issued almost four years before, and started to place the file in it. She caught herself, thinking that really was not very smart. She reached for her purse, stuffed and pushed, and managed to squeeze in the documents. She closed the safe, and called for her driver and car. She laughed as she thought about seeing Daniel again, and about how much she enjoyed leaking information that could damage the new administration.

Daniel arrived first at the scenic turnout off the George Washington Parkway. As agreed, he parked the GTO at the north end of the half-moon shaped lot, in the particularly private space that in the past had served him so well as his own scenic lovers' lane. Looking back for Victoria's car, he could not see the entrance to the lot, or the first few parking spaces. He did not see the black Lincoln Town Car pull up and park. Nor did he see the occupant get out, position himself in the adjoining woods, place an earphone in his ear, and aim what appeared to be an expensive fountain pen at the GTO.

Victoria's stretch sedan with its U.S. government license plates arrived a few minutes later. She instructed the driver to go past the Lincoln and park a few spaces away. She explained that she needed to clear her head and was going to take a short walk. She grabbed her purse, and started walking for the other end of the lot. When she reached the GTO, she got in.

"Still no new car, Daniel?"

"This baby may be old," he replied, "but she's cherry. I never heard you complain when we put the top down on a hot summer night and came out here."

"Daniel," she said sweetly, "I was not complaining."

His smile widened as he leaned over and gave her a quick kiss on the lips. "Now about our Colonel Howard's travel in November, 1963?"

"Daniel, do you love me only for my information?" she said coyly.

"For everything," he replied.

"All right," she said, biting down on her lower lip. "I haven't found what you're looking for…"

"Shit!" he responded.

"Oh calm down," she snapped, opening her purse. "I didn't have time before I left, so I brought the whole file with me."

Daniel started to reach for her.

"No way, Danny boy. This is top secret. I don't want your prints on it. I'll do the looking."

As she opened the file and starting turning over the documents, he kept leaning closer and closer, trying to fix in his memory everything passing before his probing eyes.

"November 1963. Here we go," she said, looking first at one page, then another. "Well, that's easy enough. Your traveling man didn't travel much."

"Not much?"

"Two places. Let's see. Embarked from Dallas, Texas, November 10, 1963, to Liechtenstein. Returned November 12, to Washington, D.C."

"Fast trip," Daniel observed.

"I'll say. But this is interesting," she added. "His next trip wasn't so short. He departed from Dallas again, November 23, 1963."

Daniel whistled. "Dallas! You're sure?"

"It's right here," she said, pointing to the document on her lap.

"Where did he go?"

"A place where a lot of people were going then," she replied. "Vietnam."

Daniel sat quietly for a moment, then muttered, "Not really."

"What?" she asked.

"Victoria, this was 1963. From what I've read there really weren't a lot of our people going over there yet. It was real early in the war. All we were sending were what they called advisors. No real fighting troops. Maybe ten, fifteen thousand Americans at most in '63."

"Well, Colonel Howard..." she paused, then looked again at the papers. "I should say, civilian Colonel Howard. This shows that he was a civilian by then, but he was one of the Americans going there, and for a long time."

Daniel leaned over, straining to see the document on Victoria's lap. "A long time?"

"He was there for almost a year. Returned, let's see," she said, running her finger across the page, "September 30, 1964. Came through customs in Washington. This is interesting," she added. She thumbed back through the pages, then came back to the one on her lap. "Yes. When he went through customs the agent made the first notation in his file of the Presidential Order granting Howard his special privileges."

"What does it say?"

She held the document up. Daniel could see a large red stamp in the upper left hand corner. "Here, on the U.S. Citizen's Disembarkation Report, in handwriting—'Special Note—Party travels under Presidential Order Number 9, issued 11-23-63."

"The day after..." Daniel said, his voice trailing off.

"What have you gotten into?" Victoria mouth opened in a perfect "O." She looked genuinely concerned.

"Not sure," he answered honestly.

"Dammit, Daniel. I've taken a huge risk here. If anybody ever finds out I've shown you this—if they find out I've taken it out of the State Department—I'm in serious trouble. The least you can do is tell me what the hell is going on."

"I know, Victoria. I will, as soon as I know myself." He took her hand in his. "Really I will."

"Promise?" she replied.

"Promise. But, Victoria, I have got to get a copy of that."

"Are you nuts? There's no way I can do that. I'll be lucky to get this back where it belongs without someone finding out."

"I understand. But this is a matter of the highest national importance."

"So is my ability to return to Washington when this fly-by-night administration is out of here in four years, and the good people return. I won't be able to do that if anybody finds out I give secret State Department files to *The Washington Post*."

Daniel smiled when he saw his opening. "That's the point, Victoria. This information is going to be very bad news for this new administration. I see a serious scandal on the near horizon revolving around Colonel Howard and his powerful role as a presidential advisor. It could shake them up real good."

Victoria smiled. "A scandal? Just as they're coming into office? That would serve them right, the bunch of know-it-alls."

"Precisely," he encouraged her.

"I'll tell you what," she said, closing the file in front of her. "You can't take an original from this file."

"Victoria. I only need it long enough to copy it. Then I'll get it back to you, pronto," he pleaded.

"Not on your life. I wasn't born yesterday, Danny boy. An original confidential government document to the *Post*, and the next thing I know I'll be the one on the receiving end of a scandal. No. This file is going back where it belongs. Pronto, as you said. I will," she smiled at him and squeezed his hand, "somehow make a copy of the one page. I don't know how, but I'll think of something."

Daniel started to reply, but she cut him off. "Don't you try any more sweet talk on me, Daniel Garcia. That's the best you are going to get." She stuffed the file back in her purse, and started to open the door. "I'll call you tonight."

"I, uh, I won't be around. I'll call you, okay?" he replied.

"Suit yourself," she answered. "We can plan our next date then too," she added.

Daniel reached for his door handle. "What do you think you're doing?" she asked.

"I'll walk you back to the car," he replied.

"Oh, sure," she responded sarcastically. "Here I am, divulging super secret information to a *Post* reporter and he's going to waltz me right back to my official car and driver. You are nuts. We'll talk tonight." Victoria leaned over and kissed him hard on the lips, then opened her mouth, and moved her tongue into his. She moaned, and reached her hand down to his crotch and gently rubbed. He spread his legs slightly, and pressed himself against her hand. Just as she could feel his quivering response, she pulled away and laughed. "Tonight!" she repeated, jumping out of the car and slamming the door behind her. She walked back along the pavement toward her car, making sure that she exaggerated the swaying of her hips against her thin silk skirt.

Daniel followed her progress until she disappeared around the curve in the scenic lookout. Then he started the powerful V8 and returned to the parkway for the drive to Reagan National Airport.

Victoria wrapped on the driver's window to wake him up, but did not wait for him to get out and open her door. She did that herself, and climbed in back. "Back to Foggy Bottom," she ordered.

She heard the engine start, and the automatic doors lock as was the customary procedure for all official vehicles. She opened her purse and retrieved her compact mirror, and checked to see if her lipstick had been smudged. Then she heard an unfamiliar voice say, "Put that down."

Victoria Merriweather dropped the mirror and looked up into a thin black metal extension protruding from the barrel of a small pistol, held by a steady hand in a leather glove. Her stare fixed on the brilliant cold green eyes of the man holding the gun. "I know you," she said feebly.

"Obviously," he replied calmly. "And you know too much about me. In any event, you know I am serious. Now give me the documents in your purse."

"You can't..." she tried to say, but he cut her off.

"I can," he replied coldly. When she again refused to hand over her purse, he aimed the gun between her knees, and pulled the trigger. While the bullet tore a substantial hole in the leather seat, the silenced gun made only the slightest popping sound, but it was sufficient to cause the Assistant Secretary of State to scream. The scream was barely audible outside the sealed car, and there was no one around to hear her anyway on this dreary afternoon. Soon, her screams turned to whimpers as he quickly reviewed the documents, then threw them onto the front seat. He turned, started the car, and moved it to the even more secluded spot that had been occupied by the GTO only a few minutes before. As she cried, the powerful man got out of the driver's seat, came around, and picked her up in his arms and placed her inside the trunk, alongside the unconscious body of her official driver. She looked up pleadingly. "You've got the file. I'm ruined. Leave me alone."

He slammed the trunk hood shut. Wittlefield was right. This matter had to be controlled, contained, stopped. It was a delicate situation. She was a government official, in a government car, with an official driver. It would be very difficult, maybe impossible, even for them, to control the investigation of two more deaths. But she had examined his file, and talked to the reporter. Obviously, she was too stupid to let the fact that her release of the file was a felony stop her. It was clear. She would talk, no matter what. It would be messy. He would just have to do his best. A time in the past flashed in his mind—a time when he had to act, boldly accepting extraordinary risks. They had succeeded that time, without exposure. He could do it again.

He quickly surveyed the site. They were alone. He reopened the trunk. She didn't have time to translate her terror into a scream before he placed the gun against her temple and pulled the trigger, twice. He leaned past her limp body, and pressed the gun to within two inches of the base of the head of the driver, and again shot twice.

He would have preferred to hide the car and its contents where it would never be found, but he did not have the time. The call he had received from Dallas made it clear that he was needed there immediately. He calculated that he need not remain long in Dallas, and could quickly return to complete the clean-up of this job. Or he could call for assistance. No, he thought, Wittlefield would have fits if he knew he had involved others. It would be better if he finished the job personally. He knew the ways of Washington. On a Friday afternoon as the old administration wound down its affairs, no one would notice a second tier political appointee failing to return to her office. A search would not begin for hours, perhaps even until after the weekend. He should have time to return to do a professional job of disposal. There would be a furor over these two deaths, or disappearances, but it would pass. The most important element in the operation now was to leave no trace linking him to the killing. After verifying that it had no surveillance cameras, he parked the official car in a commercial parking lot on the fringe of Old Town Alexandria. He removed the contents of Victoria's purse and stuffed the papers into the breast pocket of his trench coat, then walked briskly to the nearby METRO station.

At the airport, he walked to the general aviation terminal, stopping at a large trash container to push the empty purse well down into the garbage. Before running to the waiting AMERI-PRO jet, he removed his gloves and telephoned the company's Washington office. He directed that the car he left parked on the turnout on the George Washington Parkway be retrieved and returned at once to the ground transportation fleet. He was about to hang up when he thought of the odds for and against a search being commenced for the State Department car, and the chances the car would be found before he could return. He ordered the

AMERIPRO long range, intercontinental 767 to be moved from its Chicago home base to the test flight airfield outside El Paso, on the border with Mexico. Colonel Howard then hung up the phone. Contingencies—he always planned for contingencies. The hell with Wittlefield and his paranoia. It was his responsibility to be sure things were done, and done right. He didn't need Wittlefield to tell him who he could or could not trust. He placed one more call, and communicated his final plan to cover all conceivable contingencies.

As an expert pilot himself, he closely followed the navigational course of the jet. He was thus able to select the perfect location at which to rid himself of the fragments of his coat and gloves he had carefully torn into shreds using a screwdriver from the plane's tool kit. The biodegradable materials with a few telltale blood stains were jettisoned through the under fuselage portal and fell scattered over several miles of the snowy Great Smoky Mountains.

CHAPTER FIFTEEN

Samantha stood inside the lobby of the Governor's House Hotel, peering out through the tinted glass of the revolving door at the congested traffic traveling slowly along Main Street. Throngs of pedestrians crowded the sidewalks on both sides of the street. She noted the continuous flow of people entering the hotel, and heading into the bar and the Cattlemen's Dining Room for lunch. It had warmed up considerably after the chilly morning. The temperature on the sunny street was almost seventy degrees. The people made her feel secure enough to walk.

She exited the hotel and walked briskly, occasionally stopping to pretend to window shop, glancing back to see any signs of being followed. She crossed Main Street twice, each time looking back, but saw nothing that struck her as out of the ordinary.

She reached Lone Star Park a few minutes early, walked around, observing several couples sitting on blankets, eating from their brown bag lunches, obviously enjoying the spring-like weather. She found a bench near the central circular white marble fountain and sat down. She sized up every person walking through the park, looking for a sign that he was the one. She tried to visualize what an almost indicted banker would look like.

Even if Samantha had not been so focused on the people walking by, it was unlikely that she would have paid any attention to the limousine parked on one of the side streets converging at the park. Only the front portion of the hood and the headlights could be seen from where she sat, and from her distance no one could see the lens of the minute television camera concealed within the car's hood ornament.

J. Kingston Wittlefield sat in the back of the limousine, hidden behind dark tinted windows, admiring the clarity of the picture provided by the camera manufactured in Thailand by a wholly-owned subsidiary of AMERIPRO-INTERNATIONAL. The televised picture of Samantha sitting on the park bench was perfect, until it all turned to yellow.

"What the hell is that?" Wittlefield yelled from the back of the limousine.

Samantha noticed first one couple, then another, and another, fold their blankets and stroll away, to return to their jobs in the office towers surrounding the park. But as the park cleared of office workers, Samantha saw a bright yellow school bus pull up and discharge a rollicking band of small children. Samantha guessed they were second graders.

As she watched the children play, a man approached and circled the fountain. He stopped at the water's edge, and squinted through eyeglasses. Samantha noticed him at once, smiling momentarily at the thought that his glasses were the same style as Felix Timmons'—round and tortoise-shell. His rumpled black suit and blue shirt with a thin solid navy blue tie seemed out of place in the middle of the park that had been turned into a playground. She continued to sit, patiently.

The man walked around the perimeter of the fountain again, as if counting the number of paces it took to make the circle, then hurried over to the bench. He sat down, crossing his legs and turning his back to her, staring at the rambunctious children.

After a minute he said softly, holding a hand up to fully shield his face, "Ms. Wright?"

"Yes, I'm Samantha Wright," she replied.

"Don't look my way. Look at the water. Try not to move your lips."

Samantha glanced at the back of the man's head, his severe crew cut revealing little more than all white stubble. He would not let her see his face, so she tried to freeze into her memory the person she had seen just moments before walking around the fountain. She now knew how important it was to remember a face.

"I don't have much time. The twenty million, January 23, 1973. When it arrived by wire, the bank held it for one day, and then it was disbursed, again by wire."

"To AMERIPRO?" she asked, holding her hand up close to her mouth.

"No," he replied emphatically. "To twenty different accounts at twenty different banks in Texas."

"Twenty?"

"Back then we didn't have branch banks in Texas. Every bank on every corner was an independent bank. Hometown-like. Local banks, subject to local control. The money went to twenty small banks, where that size of money was a big deal."

"To whose accounts?" she asked.

"Different names, all with the word 'trust' in them. Not a one of them the same." The man twisted his head, glancing back and forth, surveying the park, and the traffic circling around it. He looked at the school bus, and detected nothing.

Samantha sighed. "All different. Can they be traced?"

"I doubt it. I know how these independent banks work. They live or die by a few important customers. I'm sure this important customer would not have wanted the records kept for any longer than required by law."

"And?"

"And I'd say those records didn't last longer than seven years."

"Damn," she said.

"It doesn't really matter," he said. "The people who got the money didn't know where it came from. Only my bank's trust department knew its origins, sort of."

"What do you mean, 'sort of'?"

"No one knew how the money got into the Liechtenstein account. Heck, we didn't know about the Liechtenstein account at all, until that day, January 23. Then it was simply a matter for the trust department to do as instructed. Unseal the confidential instructions and proceed. The instructions provided the number for the account in Liechtenstein, and a numerical code word to access the funds in the account. We were instructed to order the wire transfer of all funds, and then disburse the funds to the twenty different accounts. There was no room for questions. The trust instructions were absolute, with no discretion left with the bank. The bank either followed the instructions, or faced being liable for the twenty million."

"Liable?" she asked.

"Ms. Wright, you're a lawyer. When a bank accepts trust instructions, even if they are sealed, it promises unconditionally to follow those instructions to the tee, and confidentially."

"Yes. But there are banking regulators and…"

"Even if there had been questions, I can assure you the banking regulators in Texas had no interest in the matter. Around these parts there's a strong interest in what people down here call 'letting sleeping dogs lie.' Particularly when you're dealing with real power."

"Power?" Samantha said. "AMERIPRO is that…"

The man laughed a thin, snickering laugh, then turned and looked around again, still carefully concealing all but a passing profile of his face from Samantha. He saw something near the school bus, a slow moving car, inching its way past the bus. He followed the movement as he spoke. "Oh, AMERIPRO is plenty powerful," he agreed. "Big then, much bigger now. But it couldn't pull something like this off with all these Texas banks. No, that power was unique."

The man now saw it clearly, the black limousine off to the side of traffic, moving but not making real progress. He studied the car, and the darkened windows.

"I have to go," the man said, an unmistakable trembling entering his voice.

"Go? I need more."

"I'm doing what I can, lady. I'm willing to go out on a limb for Felix Timmons. That's why I'll try to get you more, after the bank closes at five o'clock. Maybe I can get you a copy of something." The man stood up, watching the limousine. "You go back to your hotel. You're at the Governors' House, right?"

"Yes, but I really should move to…"

"Stay there. Always lots of people around. You'll be all right. Be in your room between five and six. I'll call you if I can get it." He stuffed his hands in his pants pockets, and tried to look natural.

"Get what?" she pleaded.

He kept his back to her, and mumbled. "The funny thing is, folks around here wouldn't be surprised at all. It's been whispered about for a long time."

"What?" she yelled.

The sound of her voice jolted him. He turned and faced her, large beads of sweat rolling down his face. "The instructions, to the trust department for the handling of the money–the instructions from Lyndon Johnson."

"Lyndon Johnson! Trust instructions. January 23. Why?" Samantha demanded.

"Instructions for after his death," he answered, turning back to verify the location of the limousine. "LBJ died on January 22, 1973," he said, then walked in the direction of the exit from the park on the opposite side from where the limousine lingered.

Inside the limousine, Wittlefield strained and stared. He was certain they had been talking. But uncharacteristically, he was unsure of the next course of action. The woman had to be dealt with, but he wasn't ready. He did not recognize the man. He ordered the driver to follow the man.

The traffic was much lighter after the lunchtime rush, making it easier to keep up as the man dodged and darted for three blocks. When the man looked all about, he did not specifically notice the car from the park among several other black limousines on the streets of the financial district of Dallas. Hoping not to draw attention to himself, he stuck his hands in his pants pockets, lowered his head, and slowly walked into his building.

The camera on the hood proved invaluable, but when the television screen revealed that the man was entering the headquarters building of the First Commerce Bank and Trust Company of Dallas, Wittlefield slammed his cane into the picture tube, destroying any further surveillance capability for the limousine that day.

Samantha waited in the lobby of the hotel until five minutes to five, hoping that Daniel would walk through the door. She counted back the hours to when they had last talked, and figured in the time change and the flight times. It was possible he could arrive at any moment, if he had gotten what he needed from Victoria, and moved on.

She thought about going to the police, but then recalled the banker's statement, now sounding more like a warning, about people "around here" wanting to let sleeping dogs lie. She contemplated contacting the F.B.I., or the Secret Service, but what did she really have? Nothing concrete, nothing real. But soon! In just minutes, probably no more than an hour, when the banker called, or Daniel arrived. Tomorrow, she would have photographs—not grainy newspaper reproductions, but clear photographs.

She looked at her watch one last time, and then walked to the elevator for the trip back to her room. She listened to the elevator operator's now familiar banter, but interrupted long enough to ask him if he was always on duty. "We're staffed twenty-four-seven," he said. Sam was especially pleased that he didn't mind at all walking her the short distance from the elevator to her room.

Once inside, she repeated her procedures of the night before. She double locked the door, and attached the security chain. She checked the lock on the window, and pulled the shade down. She picked up the phone and made sure that it was working. Then she waited.

Daniel was able to catch the 2:20 p.m. flight only because it departed the gate twenty-five minutes late. He'd arrive at the Dallas/Fort Worth Airport by 5:30, Dallas time. He'd only been to Dallas once, many years before, but had a distinct recollection that the ride into the city from the airport could easily take an hour. He checked with a flight attendant and confirmed that the Governors' House Hotel was in downtown Dallas. But she added that on a good traffic day, the trip might not take more than forty minutes. As the jetliner cruised southwest, Daniel could think of little else than two dates—November 22 and November 23, 1963.

———— ∞ ————

The records clerk of the *Tribune* looked up at the clock on the wall as the minute hand nosily moved from twenty-nine after the hour to the closing time of 5:30. He smiled and reached over and turned off the desk lamp, then pushed away from the counter, and walked to the door. Before he could pull on the door, it opened, and the frail clerk looked up at a tall, bald, stern looking man. "Howdy there," Lester Boggs greeted the stranger. "Like to help ya, but I cain't. It's closing time. Open up agin' tomorrow at nine o'clock, sharp."

The newcomer looked around him, then shoved the small man inside. In one fluid motion he quietly closed the door behind him and dropped an olive green duffle bag to the floor.

"Say, now," the clerk said retaining his naturally friendly demeanor. "Ya see, there's nothing I can do. Rules are the rules."

"Where are the photographs, and the negatives?" the man asked coldly, grabbing the clerk by his collar and lifting him up.

Lester gasped for breath, and stammered. "Everything's here," he said meekly. "Here and in the subbasement right below. What... What can I help ya with?"

The man dropped the clerk to the floor, pushed him, and sent him sprawling against the counter. The little man turned over, and crawled, trying to get behind the counter. He reached up and grabbed the top of the counter, and slowly pulled himself up. Peering over, he saw the man coming at him slowly.

He sprang with all his might for the telephone. As his hand reached the dial on the old black rotary phone, the clerk looked up. The first thing he saw was his assailant's piercing green eyes, staring coldly down at him. Then he saw the pistol, with the silencer protruding from the barrel. The last thing Lester Boggs ever saw was the steady motion of the man's finger pulling calmly on the trigger.

The killer turned away from the body and retrieved his bag. He opened it and methodically went about his business of placing six incendiary devices in what he expertly determined would be strategic spots in the basement and subbasement of the building. The job was completed quickly for the man was working with explosive mechanisms he knew well. They had been manufactured in Taiwan by a subsidiary of AMERIPRO and originally sold to the United States Army for three hundred and thirty-eight dollars each. When fifty thousand of the devices had been declared army surplus, AMERIPRO had bought them back for two dollars and twenty cents each. Most had been resold for one hundred dollars apiece to countries in the Middle East, but a small quantity remained stored at a AMERIPRO warehouse on the outskirts of Dallas.

By 5:45, no call had come. Samantha paced around the room, turned on the television, then turned it off. She walked to the window, and did the trick with the shade. First down, then up. The shade leaped from her hands, springing to the top. She jumped with the sound.

She stared out the window at the nearly dark sky, and the lights of the office towers outlining the modern Dallas skyline. Samantha looked down at the alley, and the street beyond. The crowded streets of the day were now nearly empty. Only a pedestrian or two, and…she strained, trying to focus. A man, a shadow, in a trench coat, at the corner of the alley, hiding from the street light. She rubbed her eyes, and pressed her chin against the window. The glare from the table lamp reflected against the glass. She hurried across the room and turned the light off, then rushed back to her third floor vantage point. She stared out again, and saw nothing. She grabbed for the shade and pulled it down all the way, and sat in the dark, waiting.

At 6:00 she got up to flip on the light by the door. As she felt for the switch, she heard the footsteps, quietly coming down the hall. Instinctively, she went to the door and pressed an eye to the peephole. The concave eyepiece magnified the face, seeming to bring it right into the room. She gasped, and jumped away from the door.

And then the pounding started.

"Samantha. It's me, Frank Mullen."

She felt about the room for the phone and picked it up. No sound. She shook the hand piece and pounded it into the bed, and held it up to her ear again. The phone was dead.

The knocking continued, harder. "Samantha. Come on. I know you're in there. You promised me an answer by midday. Samantha!"

The knocking grew louder and louder, the door handle creaked as it twisted. She grabbed her purse, and leaped for the window. She pulled down on the roller shade, but nothing happened. She pulled again and again. It was jammed. She looked back at the shuddering door, then desperately tore at the shade, throwing the contraption up and behind her as she struggled with the rusty metal latch holding the window shut. The pounding increased and reverberated. She could hear the door straining and weakening. At last the latch turned, and she reached down and pulled the window up with all her strength.

The cold night air rushed in as she jumped out onto the steel encasement, and crawled toward the ladder-like descending stairway. She grabbed the handrail, and held on as she brought her feet underneath her, and felt for the rungs of the steel ladder. Her foot caught the first one, and she started down. Then she looked at the dark alley below, and saw him again. The shadow, the man. The pounding on the door echoed through the room and out the window. In an instant she changed course, and pulled hard on the railings, and reached for the ladder leading up.

Samantha climbed up one flight, peered into the window of a dark room, and pounded on the glass and struggled to open it. It wouldn't budge. From below she heard a crash, and her name being called. She turned and scrambled up the next ladder, looking down only when she reached the next platform. Then she saw him, his face silhouetted against the light pouring from her room. Frank Mullen crawling out onto the fire escape, calling "Samantha!"

She gasped for breath, then sprang for the last ladder, to the top floor, and the roof beyond. There had to be a way down from there—a way to escape.

Samantha kept her focus on the climb ahead, clawing her way up, never looking down at the man chasing her from below. She heard the clanging of shoes against the metal steps coming closer and closer as she propelled her body to the last short ladder to the roof. She climbed straight up into the Dallas sky. In a moment she reached the top and grabbed for the rusty old metal parapet. Holding on with both hands, summoning all of her strength, she catapulted up and over.

She hit the rock roof hard, scraping her knees against the sharp gravel. Stunned for a moment, she slowly stood up, and peered back over the roof. Mullen was coming, and coming fast.

She turned and surveyed the scene, looking for the door or the hatch that had to lead down, down to safety. She saw it in the dark at the far corner. It had to be a door. She took a step and then another. And then her world turned blinding white, with brilliant flashes of light enveloping her. The route to her escape vanished. She could not see the door. She could not see the roof. The light was followed by a deafening roar, and a hurling wind. Her senses failed her, and Samantha collapsed to her knees, driven down by massive forces she could not comprehend. And then she heard it. A sound not unfamiliar, crashing all around. It had a rhythm, a recurring modulation.

She looked up against the driving wind, and as she did so she saw the machine, and the man jumping out of it. Instantly she felt his painful grasp around her arm as she was dragged across the rocks. The man pulled her up and tossed her through the opening onto the carpeted floor. She heard the door slamming shut, and detected the increased pitch in the whining sound as the whirling increased, and they started to rise.

Samantha struggled to sit up against the forces of gravity as she felt the powerful liftoff. She pulled her knees under her, and grasped onto a cushion. Her eyes reached the level of the window, and she looked out and down. Below the roof of the hotel shown in glaring white spotlights, then the light disappeared. In the sudden darkness she thought she saw Mullen falling over onto the roof. But just as quickly the vision out the window turned all around, and her eyes were filled with light again, only this time different. She looked down to see the bright orange flames shooting out from a building two blocks from the hotel. She knew the building—the *Tribune*.

She turned around, and faced a small handgun pointed directly at her eyes. The old man holding the gun with both hands motioned her to move onto the seat across from him.

"Welcome young lady, to the most important achievement in military aviation in our lifetimes. Sit down," he pointed with the barrel of the gun, "fasten your seat belt, and enjoy your ride in the first prototype of MachCopt, the supersonic stealth helicopter of the future," the Chairman Emeritus of AMERIPRO ordered.

Samantha felt behind her, and did as instructed.

"Our flight will not take long," J. Kingston Wittlefield said, raising his voice only slightly to overcome the mild whirling sound barely penetrating the soundproofed cabin.

The pilot in the forward seat placed his hand over an electronic sensor, and MachCopt plunged downward, racing toward the ground. Samantha gasped, and the old man smiled. "Don't worry. We'll fly fairly low to the ground from now on. Our flight pattern will be a little more private that way. But with our revolutionary satellite imagery navigation, MachCopt can discern and identify an object on the ground the size of a raisin, and then," he smiled, "avoid it, or destroy it."

As MachCopt leveled off at twelve feet above the surface, the pilot moved his hand across another sensor panel, and

Samantha heard a new, low whooshing sound coming from below. Her eyes darted back and forth.

"You may want to turn around and look out and down," Wittlefield said jovially. Samantha turned, and saw the small swept back V-shaped wing protruding from somewhere under the helicopter's belly.

"The wings," Wittlefield explained, "are going to their fully extended position. They stabilize our flight at even this relatively slow speed, allowing the pilot to sit back and relax, and let the on-board computer do the work. And, of course, it's those little wings that will let what might otherwise appear to be a helicopter fly at above the speed of sound," Wittlefield explained.

Samantha turned away from the window as the pilot pulled off his radio headset and turned around. Samantha recognized the bald head and stern look from the photographs, and then she saw the violent green eyes, and knew she had encountered this man, face to face, before.

"Colonel Harry Howard," she spat out.

The Colonel barely looked at her. He turned instead to Wittlefield. "We should do away with her now," he said calmly. "I must get back to Washington."

"To clean up the mess you left behind," Wittlefield replied sarcastically.

"I had no choice."

"Just as you had no choice other than to blow up the entire newspaper building. The press will be rabid. The investigation will be furious."

"I had no choice, if we wanted to be sure."

"We had to be sure," Wittlefield agreed reluctantly.

"The evidence is destroyed. Now all we need to do is contain the situation, as we did once before."

The old man's face turned bright red. "We had powerful friends then."

"We have powerful friends now!" the Colonel exclaimed.

Wittlefield slumped back in the seat and cradled the pistol in his lap, and took in a deep breath. "Powerful, yes. Friends? I don't know. If we are to be certain to contain this, we must do it ourselves. We must be sure we know everything she has learned on her disturbing odyssey, and everything that has been passed on to her reporter friend. Zero tolerance for loose ends on this operation, Colonel. Zero tolerance," he repeated to himself.

Chapter Sixteen

Mullen stood on the hard rock roof, legs spread far apart, bending over, his hands braced against his knees. His chest heaved in and out as he inhaled deep, long gasps of air, desperately trying to catch his breath. When at last he started to regain some semblance of control, he looked up just in time to see MachCopt clear the Dallas skyline, and then precipitously plunge toward the ground. Someone else seeing such an abrupt fall might assume the experimental aircraft was crashing, but he knew it was only descending at previously unheard of speed for a helicopter—descending to its ground-hugging flight mode. He knew the extreme aerobatics were a programmed part of the aircraft's detection prevention system.

Slowly he stood up, willing his weary, out of condition body to go forward. He moved as fast as his pained legs would carry him toward the door leading down to the hotel. He knew Mach-Copt could only be going to one place.

—⚬⚬⚬—

When the cab driver said that the leaping flames and billowing black smoke they could see ahead were coming from the direction of the Governors' House Hotel four blocks away, Daniel jumped out of the cab and ran through the grid-locked traffic and dense pack of onlookers. As the hotel sign came into view, he stopped and looked up. The brilliant white light shining down from the rising helicopter illuminated several city blocks around the hotel. He saw that the fire was raging in a building two blocks past the hotel. He breathed a sigh of relief as he pushed his way through the crowd and the lines of police trying with only partial success to impose order.

Daniel made it to the main entrance of the hotel and walked into a deserted lobby. He rushed to the reception counter but found no one. He tapped a bell at the end of the counter, then hit it hard, sending the noisemaker flying across the reception area. Spotting a door identified as "Manager's Office", frantically he placed his hands on the counter top and vaulted over. He pushed the door open, called inside, to a vacant room.

He turned back toward the lobby, spotting a lone man stumble through a doorway marked "stairs" and start running across the lobby. Daniel jumped back over the reception counter, yelling, "Mullen, you bastard. Stop right there!"

Mullen looked up, then put his head down and raced for the exit. As Mullen pushed on the door, Daniel threw himself at the man all Washington assumed would be the next Secretary of Defense. The full weight of Daniel's body plowed into him, knocking the wind from his lungs and forcing him to the ground. After that, there was no struggle. As Mullen lay spreadeagled on the floor, Daniel Garcia shouted, "Tell me where the fuck Samantha is or I'll beat your brains in right here."

Mullen for the second time in five minutes found himself gasping for life sustaining oxygen, unable at first to speak. When he could finally form a few words, he pleaded, "Get off me, I…I can't breathe."

Daniel looked down at the man, and realized that he was telling the truth, and that there was no way the older, smaller, weaker Mullen could escape his grasp. Daniel rolled off, stood up, grabbed Mullen by his coat collar, and pulled him up to his knees. "Talk now and talk fast," he warned.

Mullen got to his knees, then rolled over and sat down on the floor, coughing and gasping for air. He looked at Daniel and knew that the man was deadly serious.

"I," Mullen started, then coughed again. "I think I know," he stammered.

"Don't give me any of that 'think' shit. Where is she?" Daniel demanded, pulling forcefully on Mullen's coat.

Mullen took a deep breath, and then another. "Look," he said, feeling his control slowly returning. "We're on the same side."

Daniel grabbed him again and shook him violently. "Fuck you, Mullen. If you've hurt Samantha, I'll drag your ass down to east Miami and let *mi compadres* slice your balls off!"

Mullen felt the sweat pouring on his face, but he took another breath and silently kicked himself—"never let them see you sweat." He stared up at Daniel and felt the fear passing. In a moment he was in control, the feeling he needed to have–the ice water in his veins. Frank Mullen sneered.

"That is a very colorful description, Mr. Garcia," Mullen replied. "But having me sliced up by your criminal friends wouldn't help anybody." He took another breath, and spoke more calmly. "It doesn't really matter whether you believe me or not, but I'm on Samantha's side. Only a few minutes ago," he said, pointing up toward the roof, "I was trying to save her."

"Save her? Bullshit!" Daniel replied contemptuously. "From who?"

"From Wittlefield and Howard," Mullen answered firmly.

"They're your *compadres*," Daniel responded.

Mullen paused. "They *were* my 'compadres' as you say. But they're crazy now, completely out of control. I can't go on with them—I won't be destroyed by their insanity. *Comprende, Señor Garcia?* They've got Samantha!" Mullen placed his hands on the floor, and started pushing himself up.

"Where the fuck do you think you're going?" Daniel demanded.

Mullen stood all the way up, and said firmly. "I'm going to the only place where they could take her in the MachCopt prototype."

"MachCopt? What the fuck?" Daniel shouted.

"If you just arrived, did you happen to see a helicopter that appeared very different from any you've seen before—a helicopter with wings, taking off from the roof of this hotel?"

"I saw something flying off past the fire."

226

"That was the only prototype of AMERIPRO's supersonic, re-tractable delta wing helicopter. Wittlefield and Howard snatched Samantha from the roof, and fled in MachCopt."

"From the roof? What the fuck was she doing up there?"

"I'm sorry to say, she was running away from me. I guess I was unable to convince her of my bona fides. Understandably so, with what must be going through her mind. But now they've got her and we have no time to spare," he said as he started walking for the door, "if I am going to save her. They won't let her live after they've interrogated her."

"You, asshole," Daniel exclaimed, grabbing his arm, "are going nowhere. We're calling the cops, now!"

"That's like signing her death warrant," Mullen replied. "Don't be so sure about the Dallas police. AMERIPRO has a lot of friends in Dallas and on its police force. More to the point, if the cops start showing up where I'm going, Howard and Wittle-field will know before they get within five miles. They'll just kill her, and take off in MachCopt." Mullen shook his head. "No, the only chance is for me to go directly to them. The sophisticated detection electronics they have guarding the site lets them know any intruder coming their way, and high intensity cameras let them identify anyone, day or night. If they see it's me, they'll let me come in."

"And they'll let you get close?" Daniel said, finding himself reluctantly going along.

"Yes," he replied. "They still believe I'm on their side."

Daniel held on to Mullen's arm.

"It's the only way," Mullen said reassuringly, then motioned to the crowds jamming the streets outside. "Besides, it looks to me like the Dallas authorities have their hands full with what I wouldn't be surprised is the biggest fire in the city's history. By the time we got anybody's attention, Samantha would be dead."

Slowly, Daniel let go of his arm. "You're not going anywhere without me."

Mullen shrugged. "I think we can make that work—make them think I'm bringing you to them."

Daniel swallowed hard, and thought of Samantha. "Let's go!"

———— ⊶⊷⊶ ————

MachCopt hovered ten feet above the roof of the huge corrugated steel building. Colonel Howard touched an illuminated square on the sensory board on the main control panel. The roof of the building slowly retracted, revealing a brightly lighted, sheltered landing area. In a moment, the aircraft gently descended to the floor below. The whirling stopped, and Wittlefield declared, "Safely back to our home base."

Colonel Howard got up from the pilot's seat and climbed back to the rear compartment. He grabbed Samantha roughly by the arm and pushed her toward the door.

"Now, now, Colonel," Wittlefield said as he continued to point his gun at Samantha. "No reason to be brutal."

Colonel Howard looked coldly back at the old man. "Let's get this job over with and get back to business." He jumped out, pulled Samantha from the passenger compartment and held her forcefully by the arm as he stretched out his other hand to assist Wittlefield in making the short step down to the hangar floor. Wittlefield stumbled slightly, then grabbed on to the Colonel's sleeve to steady himself.

"Watch her," the Colonel demanded. He kneeled down and pulled a lever on the undercarriage of MachCopt. Aheavy, six-inch thick flexible cable popped out. He grabbed the end and walked it over to a shiny, stainless steel service pylon at the edge of the landing pad. He inserted the cable end into an opening portal at the base of the pylon, then stood up and ran his hand over the bank of sensor pads on its top. "All operating systems will be checked and verified within twenty-two minutes," Howard advised Wittlefield. "Then we'll refuel."

Howard walked back from the service area and extended an arm for Wittlefield to hold, and with his other hand grabbed Samantha in a vice-like grip. He walked toward a room at the far end of the hangar, shoved Samantha ahead, ordering her to "Move it!"

Inside, the room was filled with television monitors, computer consoles, and row upon row of flashing electronic lights. "This control room is state of the art," Wittlefield explained as he slowly pulled himself up onto a gleaming white laboratory stool. Then he opened his suit coat, and carefully placed the gun in the breast pocket. "I'm sure we won't need this now," he said, smiling at Samantha. He waved his hands around the room. "Yes, sir, the best money can buy, and the best the combined genius of the AMERIPRO team can create."

"Too bad it's all for nothing," Samantha spat out as the Colonel pushed her into a straight-backed steel armchair. He pulled from his pockets two pairs of plastic composite handcuffs and quickly pinned Samantha's arms to the chair.

"She does talk," Wittlefield responded cheerfully. "Feisty, but I'm afraid your comments are all for naught. You see, MachCopt is going to go forward. It must. There is too much at stake. Once again the future of the country depends on us. MachCopt is vital, and I am positive our next President, and," Wittlefield pointed at Colonel Howard, "his top military advisors, will see it that way." Wittlefield laughed heartily. "Don't you agree, Colonel?"

Howard stood over Samantha, glaring down through his icy, flashing green eyes. "Of course," he replied.

"You mean the future of AMERIPRO depends on it," Samantha said. "That's what all this is about." She looked around, inspecting the room. "Always has been, hasn't it? Billions and billions of public money spent on AMERIPRO this and AMERIPRO that."

Wittlefield smiled again as his right hand started to shake ever so slightly. "Colonel," he said, reaching into his coat pocket, "could I have some water?" He held out four large capsules in his hand. Turning back to Samantha, he said, "But of course. That is the free enterprise system. We at AMERIPRO are entitled to make a profit on what we produce." He took a cup of water from the Colonel and popped the capsules into his mouth, sipped and swallowed hard. Wittlefield shook his head backwards, grimaced, and then looked back at Samantha. "You cannot have people like me, and Colonel Howard…"

"And Frank Mullen," Samantha interjected.

"Yes, and Frank Mullen. People like us who had to claw our way up from nothing. You cannot deny us our rights, our…" He paused, took another drink of water "…our mandate to make money. You see, you must have enormous funds to be certain that the government does what is good for it. We need the power, the influence, or the idiot politicians might not do what is right."

"No," Samantha yelled. "I don't see any such thing."

"But of course you do," Wittlefield replied. "You must! You're a smart lady. You know we cannot entrust this great republic to the vagaries of weak and immoral politicians. You work for that damn drunk D'Angelo. He can't be trusted with the defense of our country."

"He is not a drunk," she shouted. "He's a fine man, a great Senator."

Howard laughed. "Fine Senator my ass. He's a drunk, and a mean one at that. Ask that seventeen year old girl he beat up so bad she had to have her jaw wired back together."

Samantha's face turned red. "You bastards! The Senator would never…"

Howard formed a fist with one of his hands, and pounded it into his open palm. "Shut up!" he yelled.

"Colonel, control yourself!" Wittlefield ordered. He looked back at Samantha. "You see, young lady, what the Colonel is referring to is true. A little control device we created some years ago to use at the appropriate time if we needed to keep your Senator in line. Now while it is also true that the teenager in question was paid a tidy little sum by Colonel Howard to put herself at risk in the compromising situation with the Senator, it is also the simple fact that your Senator took the bait, got himself drunk—no one forced him to empty the contents of the bar in that luxury hotel suite—and then let his temper get the best of him. The video and the girl's sworn affidavit make a compelling case."

"Enough talk," Howard demanded.

"No, Colonel. We have an intelligent woman here. A savvy lawyer, a person who thinks she knows the ways of Washington. I believe there are benefits in sharing some of our experiences. Perhaps she will then do the same for us, and we will learn what we need to know."

"Go to hell!" Samantha sneered. "You're nothing but traitors."

A cold stare crossed Wittlefield's face. "That," he yelled back, "is blasphemy you... you, bitch! *We* are the patriots! You should say a prayer every day, giving thanks that we have been here, insuring the safety of our country against its enemies... its enemies, foreign and domestic!" Wittlefield's hands began to shake again. He grabbed for the water and took a quick drink. "Oh yes," he yelled, "without us, we never would have won the Cold War. Someone had to protect the country, protect the future. That is why we had to compromise your precious Senator D'Angelo so many years ago. We gazed into the future and knew that we had to be able to control him to protect the country."

"And you had to kill a president," she screamed, pulling and twisting at the handcuffs restraining her. "You bastards are crazy!"

Howard approached her and swung his hand far back over his shoulder and propelled a vicious return swing, landing a powerful blow against Samantha's cheek. Her head flew to the side as a deep red trickle of blood flowed from the corner of her mouth.

"Colonel! Please!" Wittlefield exclaimed. "There is no need for that. In the last few days we have had sufficient violence." He stared at the Colonel. "Out-of-control violence, creating out-of-control situations. But we'll address that later." He looked back at Samantha, hesitating, searching for his words. "You don't seem to understand. We had no choice. I want you to know that I had high hopes for Mr. Kennedy. His father was a fine man."

"Joe Kennedy?" Samantha exclaimed. "He was a scoundrel," Samantha said more softly. "Everybody knows that."

Wittlefield sighed. "As I was saying, I hoped Jack Kennedy was a man of the world, would do what was right, protect and defend the country from its enemies. But when we learned from my good friend Lyndon that Jack was going to retreat…"

"Your friend Lyndon who was on your payroll to the tune of twenty million dollars," Samantha said disgustingly.

Wittlefield raised his eyebrows, and smiled at Howard. "You see, Colonel. I told you if we chatted with her, our Miss Wright would let us know what she knows." He turned back to Samantha. "So you figured that out, did you? Congratulations. That is quite some detective work after all these years. I must admit we thought that trail was very cold. Too bad Lyndon never really got a chance to enjoy the money himself. You know the old story— fly first class or your heirs will. But I must tell you that we were in fact relieved when Lyndon passed on. His death should have terminated any ability to trace such things."

"Tough shit," Samantha said, running her tongue out of her mouth and licking away some of the blood.

"Well, yes, that is quite surprising, and unfortunate," Wittlefield replied.

"Yes," Howard agreed, raising his hand again.

"Colonel!" Wittlefield called out sternly. Howard returned his hand to his side.

"Well," Wittlefield went on calmly, "as I was saying, Jack Kennedy was going to turn tail and run away from our responsibilities to support the freedom fighters in Vietnam. America, retreating! Can you imagine that? We could not accept such a thing. Thank God Lyndon learned of it when he did. Funny how these things happen. You know, the Kennedy boys didn't care for Lyndon…"

"They were smart," Samantha put in.

"Yes," Wittlefield agreed. "Smart like you're smart. But look where it got them, and now you," he added sarcastically. "They should have listened to Lyndon. But no, they froze him out. Hell, Lyndon learned of Jack's treachery by pure luck. Came from a gal he was…ah, a gal whose company he was enjoying. Of all things, she worked for Bobby Kennedy in the Justice Department. Passed on what she had heard."

Samantha glared at the old man. "So to keep the bloody billions flowing into the AMERIPRO war making machine, you just sent Colonel Howard here out onto the grassy knoll at Dealey Plaza to shoot the President."

"I did not shoot him," the Colonel said flatly.

"Yes, well," Wittlefield sighed. "It was a little more complicated than that, although," he hesitated, "not very much more. Lyndon told me about the motorcade route. Actually invited me to join him in his limo. I declined—I told him I wanted to personally coordinate getting all our employees to turn out to lead the cheering crowds—and lo' and behold, the route provided a perfect opportunity. But successfully killing a President takes more than one person, that is if you want to be absolutely certain of the outcome, and at the same time be certain that you maintain control of the situation. Got to keep things from getting out of hand, you know, getting messy. I cannot tolerate that. Killing a President—he's just a man, really, but still, it's a momentous event, no two ways about it."

Samantha's stomach churned and her head spun. She thought this could not be happening. She was tied down in a hangar in the middle of nowhere, listening to two insane men cold-bloodily discuss their infamous murder. A chilling terror gripped her. She fought for composure. The face of her mother, weeping, flashed before her and she felt the tears welling in her eyes. She fought them furiously. She swore to herself—do not let these bastards have the satisfaction.

"We should not be discussing this," Howard said emphatically.

"Nonsense, Colonel. Unfortunately, the lady seems to have figured most of this out. We have already learned that she knows you were on the grassy knoll. That is important if we are going to contain these recent events. But, yes, Miss Wright, the Colonel devised a simple but foolproof plan that needed only two more people. It was important to apply enough force, but limit the numbers involved to only those absolutely necessary. The more people, the more difficult to control, the more chance for leaks later on. That would not be acceptable. So the Colonel recruited two shooters—young, reliable men, true patriots who had served under him in Vietnam, absolutely loyal to the Colonel—right-thinking Americans who knew how important it was to stop the Commies in their tracks. The Colonel agreed to take the greatest risk, to be the spotter, to briefly stand out in the open, risking exposure to give the command to fire. A classic ambush. Crossfire and all that."

"Oswald?" Samantha demanded.

Wittlefield nodded. "There, you see again, Colonel. From our open discussion here we have learned that Miss Wright has not figured that part out." Wittlefield smiled at Samantha. "That is good. We didn't see any way anyone could penetrate that one. People could speculate all they wanted, but they would never know for sure. You see Miss Wright, Oswald was just what he said he was the one time he made it before the vultures of the press. He was a patsy. I dare say he would probably have been convicted by any court of law if good fortune had not gratuitously smiled on our little enterprise and sent that nut case Ruby to do our bidding. In any event, our brave shooters—Sergeant Kanesellers and Corporal Sawyer—and Colonel Howard here, safely made it away."

"Where?" Samantha demanded.

"Oh, that's right. You don't know that yet. But again, fortunately, Colonel Howard's close tab on what you and your reporter friend have been ferreting out has revealed to us that you would know it as soon as you had the opportunity to speak with Mr. Garcia. Regrettably, someone at the State Department violated every rule in the book and leaked that Colonel Howard departed Dallas on the day after the, ah, event, for the Republic of Vietnam. Stayed away until the Commission Lyndon appointed finished its little investigation. As it turned out, I decided that there could always be a potential problem if our two other colleagues in the venture were still around. Colonel Howard balked at my orders at first."

"Top notch men," the Colonel spit out. "Loyal men, damn it!"

"Of course they were," Wittlefield readily agreed. "I've acknowledged their heroic duty. But to keep control, that was the important thing. As usual, the Colonel saw the wisdom of my approach. He accepted his orders and handled the situation. Right, Colonel?"

The Colonel did not reply. He just fixed his icy stare on Wittlefield.

"Sadly," Wittlefield smiled, "those two brave soldiers gave all for the cause. A special operations endeavor in the North of Vietnam, wasn't it, Colonel? An impossible mission, a tragic loss—the first MIAs of the war, actually."

Colonel Howard grimaced. "We should *not* be going into this," he retorted angrily.

"I have decided we will," Wittlefield replied matter-of-factly. He turned to Samantha. "Then the Warren Commission Report was issued with that fanciful little explanation of a lone gunman shooting a magic bullet that first supposedly hit Mr. Kennedy, and then roamed around in his body for almost two seconds before altering course to go on to hit Mr. Connally. I'm still not sure how that bizarre theory got into the final report. Lyndon and his cohort Mr. Hoover were so damn determined to put the matter to rest with Oswald, I suspect they must have planted that tall tale with someone working with the committee most anxious to curry favor with the new power structure in Washington."

"Are you saying Johnson didn't know you assassinated the President?" Samantha demanded.

"The simple answer is no. Don't get me wrong. Lyndon was a ball-buster all right, but cutting to the chase, he was, after all just a politician. He was a talker, not a doer. Not like me. I certainly could not take a chance on letting him in on our scheme. Who knows how he might have reacted? We had financial arrangements, but that was strictly "bidness" as he liked to say. Eliminating Mr. Kennedy, I seriously doubt Lyndon would have gone along with that. I don't think he would have accepted that as necessary bidness. I already explained, tight control, only on a need-to-know basis. That's how we were successful. After the fact, Lyndon never asked, that's for damn sure. What he suspected, who he suspected, I have no idea. In any event, he never once mentioned anything about the assassination to me. He didn't question me when I asked for a special presidential travel order for Colonel Howard. If I may be so bold, even when he ascended to that office they call the most powerful in the world, he didn't want to cross me. Might be dangerous. Might have feared for his own life for all I know. At any rate, the dust settled, except for all the crackpots and theorists. Oswald was the designated assassin, and Colonel Howard's assistants had been lost in Vietnam, so the Colonel was free after a while to return to America, and continue to serve."

"Selling your war toys."

Wittlefield stood up, walked over to Samantha, and stared down through his aged dry eyes. "I must say I am disappointed in you, Miss Wright. You keep denigrating the vital role our products played in the defense of liberty. Why, Lyndon simply could not have conducted that war without them."

Samantha peered up at her demented captor. "Exactly."

Colonel Howard cocked his head, and walked over to the bank of security monitors. "Someone is coming," he said calmly, staring at one screen showing a distant car driving along a narrow two-lane road. He pressed his fingers down on a succession of color-coded bands, and the picture on the central television monitor suddenly zoomed into focus. Two faces inside the car came into view.

"Ah, that would have to be Frank," Wittlefield observed.

The Colonel pressed again and the images on the television screen magnified into life size clarity. "Yes, it's Mullen, and he's got the reporter with him."

"Thank God," Wittlefield replied. "I was growing concerned as to how we were going to retrieve Miss Wright's pesky friend."

Samantha strained at the cuffs binding her, trying desperately to see the screen.

—⬦⬦⬦—

Daniel pushed his foot down further on the accelerator and the big Lincoln V-8 responded instantly as the digital reading on the speedometer topped ninety-six miles per hour.

"It won't do her any good if we crash," Frank Mullen observed from the passenger seat.

"How much further?" Daniel demanded.

"You can see it up ahead," Mullen pointed slightly off to the left. "There, where the floodlights surround the large hangar. We're approaching the surveillance perimeter, at which point they will be able to see us, up close and personal," he added, reaching into his coat pocket and pulling out a snub-nosed pistol. Mullen held the gun up, and pointed it at Daniel.

Daniel caught the motion out of the corner of his eye, then turned his attention off the road, and squarely on Mullen. "So that's it, you son-of-a-bitch!" Daniel yelled.

Mullen brought his hand up to his nose, obscuring his mouth. "Calm down, and keep your eyes on the road. I told you, I'm on your side. This," he said, moving the gun up closer against Daniel's head, "is necessary if they are going to believe that I'm still with them. I guarantee you Colonel Howard is watching us through the surveillance cameras. If they think anything other than I'm bringing you to them, they will take off in MachCopt and that will be the last you see of Samantha."

Daniel glanced nervously at the gun, then returned his eyes to the road, and started to speak. Mullen cut him off. "If you have to say anything, cover your mouth. Look natural—scratch your nose. We don't need any lip reading."

Daniel did as instructed, then asked, "Where the hell could they go?"

"Wise up, Garcia. Wittlefield's a multi-billionaire. He has many friends, some who are not friends of the United States. Some very big foreign customers. There's lots of places in the world that would be perfectly happy to shelter him, for a price."

"He'd still have to get there."

Mullen stretched out his arm, bringing the gun even closer to Daniel's head, but blocking even more of his own face. "Howard will have come up with a contingency plan, in case things got beyond their control, in case they face exposure. MachCopt is still experimental, so it can't stray very far from this home base. It's the only facility that can provide the specialized maintenance it requires. That's how I knew they'd come here. They had to. But it's probably refueled and ready to go. I'm sure it could get them well into Mexico for a rendezvous with one of the long-range jets in the AMERIPRO fleet. But I doubt they think they'll have to do that. I'm sure the plan remains the same—eliminate this threat, go on with business."

"And having you as Secretary of Defense would be good for business," Daniel sneered.

"Not any more. I'm finished doing business with that old monster and his deranged cohort," Mullen replied. "Slow down, turn left, and pull in over there," Mullen directed.

Howard followed the progress of the car on the monitor, and as he saw it pull up to the MachCopt hangar, he reached inside his pocket for a silver handgun. He retrieved the dull black silencer from his other pocket and slowly twisted it on to the barrel of the gun. "Your boyfriend is here," he announced like a hangman to Samantha.

"Is MachCopt ready, if necessary?" Wittlefield asked. Howard moved his hand down a long line of dials and blinking lights. "All systems A-OK.," he reported.

Daniel hated the plan, but saw no alternative. Mullen insisted they walk straight in, with Mullen's gun pointed squarely at Daniel. When Wittlefield and Howard relaxed, he would get the drop on them.

Mullen followed Daniel into the bright lights of the interior of the hangar, and called out. "Kingston, Colonel Howard. I have him." Then he raised his hand, and brought the heavy metal handle of the pistol crashing into the side of Daniel's head.

Daniel yelped, and fell to the floor, holding his hand to the side of his bleeding temple.

The door to the control room at the far end of the hangar opened. Colonel Howard came out first, pulling Samantha by her arm. Wittlefield followed closely behind. As the threesome approached, Wittlefield jumped ahead, smiling broadly at Mullen, then sneering down at Daniel's prostrate body. He came up to Mullen and extended his hand. "Solid job, Frank," Wittlefield exclaimed. "With the lady and her reporter friend here," Wittlefield said, pointing at Daniel, "the situation is back under control."

Mullen glanced at Daniel and noticed a thin stream of blood oozing down the side of his face. At that exact moment, Mullen felt the moisture beading on his forehead. He quickly lifted his hand to his head, and tried to wipe away the perspiration. He looked at Wittlefield and recalled again so vividly the old man's admonition to "never let them see you sweat."

"Yes, back to business," Mullen agreed, reaching his hand out to shake Wittlefield's. Wittlefield came in close, and the two shook hands. Wittlefield held on to Mullen's arm, steadying himself, turning back toward Howard.

"It's a good thing, Colonel, that Frank stayed on top of the situation, as usual. I told you we would need our entire team to handle this. It would only have gotten messier if we still had to launch an operation to silence the reporter. As it is, the investigation of your arson of the *Tribune* building will be intense, but ultimately will lead nowhere. And there should be time to get back to Washington to clean up your, ah, other problem there."

"If not, I could call in reinforcements," the Colonel replied.

"Reinforcements!" Wittlefield yelled. "Are you crazy Colonel? Never! We handle these matters ourselves—the three of us. No one else can be trusted."

The Colonel glared, then looked down at his watch. "I'm sure it will not be necessary." Turning to Mullen, he added, "You were right to insist on coming down here."

Daniel moaned, and then stared up at Mullen, now hoping against hope for some sign from him. Instead, Mullen smiled, then laughed. "Yes, Colonel. For once you concurred in my logistical plans."

The Colonel nodded. "For someone who never served his country in uniform, you did all right tonight."

Samantha pulled against the grasp of her captor, and for a brief moment pushed him off balance. But Howard recovered swiftly and swung his arm crashing against her face, sending her to the ground.

Samantha shook her head, dazed. "You're crazed," she panted. "You might have gotten away with Willard, or Lionel, or even burning down an old newspaper building, but you'll never cover up killing a *Post* reporter and an aide to a United States senator."

Wittlefield stared blankly at first, and then shouted in response, "You stupid woman! You and your boyfriend are nothing! We killed a President and got away with it! And we just got another one elected. Colonel!" he ordered, "get on with it."

Colonel Howard started to raise his fist again, when suddenly Mullen clenched down on the frail old hand holding on to his arm, and pulled and twisted, forcing Wittlefield off balance and spinning him around. Before the old man could respond in any way, he was securely in Mullen's grasp, with the pistol pressed against his back.

Mullen's motion was fluid and swift, but as the Colonel had just reminded him, Mullen was a civilian. Howard on the other hand had maintained the sharp reflexes of a field operator. While Mullen thought he was moving quickly, Howard reacted instantly to the first sign of unexpected action. He crouched down and grabbed Samantha, and ruthlessly bent her arm behind her to the point where further motion would break it. She cried out in pain, and as Daniel and Mullen responded to her cries, they saw the looming figure of Colonel Howard pulling Samantha to her feet, and pressing the silencer on the barrel of the pistol against her temple.

"Do not flinch, do not move!" the Colonel commanded. "Or," he smiled, "she's dead, right here, right now!"

Mullen pressed his gun again Wittlefield's back and the old man squirmed.

"Mullen," the Colonel shouted in a loud but steady voice, "you don't know what you're doing. There are only certain spots on the body you hit to drop a man instantly. Your gun isn't on one of them."

Mullen started to move.

"Don't even think about it," the Colonel commanded. "You chose your target. It was a bad choice—what you'd expect from an amateur. Wittlefield can survive a small hole in the back. If you try to change your target, she's done!"

Daniel's eyes darted from Samantha to Mullen, and back to Samantha. She struggled. Howard pressed her arm a little more. The pain became excruciating. Tears filled her eyes and flowed down her cheeks.

"Mullen you fool," Wittlefield exclaimed. "You'll ruin everything."

"No," Mullen screamed. "You're the one ruining things—ruining my chance—my last chance—to do something right. Your madness—it can't go on. It's over!

"Shut up!" the Colonel demanded. "Nothing is over unless I say so. I say you are going to back off. I'm taking the lady here over to MachCopt. I'm going to tuck her inside safe and sound. You are going to release Wittlefield and then he's going to join us. If he doesn't make it to MachCopt, the lady dies. If he does, we fly away."

"No!" Daniel yelled. "They'll just kill her then."

"No, we won't," Howard shouted back. "Your lady here is going to become a little insurance policy. Nobody is ever going to say anything about any of this, and she'll live. In fact, she'll live in luxury. If we kill her, we know you would talk. There would be nothing stopping you. So, lady and gentlemen, it's a Mexican standoff. Hell, Mullen, you can still be Secretary of Defense—we can still do business."

"Nobody will buy that Samantha just flew away," Daniel screamed.

"Sure they will," the Colonel argued. "You're a newspaper reporter. You'll make up some story like you assholes always do."

Before another word could be spoken, the Colonel pulled back on his captive, and steadily marched backwards toward the supersonic helicopter. He kept his gun firmly pressed to Samantha's head as he stopped at the control pylon and released his grip to free his hand to work the controls. As he did, the cable automatically disengaged from the pylon and retracted into the undercarriage of the aircraft. He pressed a button and the wide doorway to MachCopt slid open. He grabbed Samantha again and backed into the cabin, then pulled her in after him.

In a minute the rotor blades started to spin slowly. Then the voice of the Colonel boomed out from the loudspeakers on the side of the aircraft. "Let Wittlefield go, now!"

Daniel stumbled to his feet. Mullen looked at him. "I don't see any choice," Mullen said meekly.

"Let the bastard go!" Daniel ordered.

Mullen released his grip. Wittlefield slowly moved toward the open door of the aircraft. A few paces from the door, he looked back. Daniel saw his face turning red and his hands wobbling up and down. "Traitor!" Wittlefield yelled, then turned around and slowly climbed into the crowning technological achievement of AMERIPRO.

As soon as Wittlefield was in, the compartment door slid shut, and the overhead rotors began spinning faster and faster. Over the sound of the whirling rotors, Daniel and Mullen heard a grinding sound coming from above, and looked up to see the roof of the hangar sliding away.

Inside MachCopt, Colonel Howard reached around from his position in the pilot's seat and handed the gun to Wittlefield. "Tightly, against her temple," he instructed. "Be sure they see the gun ready to blow her brains out."

Wittlefield took the gun, moved next to Samantha, and forced her to look out the window at her would-be rescuers. The whine of the rotors intensified, and then Samantha felt the pull in her stomach as the liftoff began. She stared straight ahead, through the window in the door, and to Daniel standing, despondently, on the floor of the hangar. In a moment, she saw the floor fall away, and Daniel disappeared from sight.

At that same moment, she felt the cold steel of the gun's silencer moving, wavering, bouncing from above her ear, and then around and below it. She rolled her eyes to her right and saw the Colonel moving his hands across the controls, and his feet pressing against electronic sensors on the cockpit floor. She shifted to her left, and there was Wittlefield. His face had turned bright red, his eyes swollen with moisture. She focused on the hand holding the gun. It was shaking, jerking up and down. Out of the corner of her eyes she saw the helicopter passing through the opening in the roof, and continuing straight up into the night sky.

She knew if anything was going to happen, it had to be instantly. Samantha shoved her shoulder into the old man, then swung her elbow up and punched his shaking hand. He let out a yelp. The pistol went flying. She pushed Wittlefield and grabbed for the gun. Her hand reached it at the same time as the old man's. She twisted and turned it. The old man caught his finger in the trigger guard, and squeezed the trigger. The bullet exploded through the barrel and silencer, creating a mere popping sound. But as the projectile tore into the control panel in front of the Colonel, the loud crashing of glass and splintering of composites resonated throughout the compartment. Sparks flew and danced onto the Colonel's bare hands.

"Shit!" the Colonel shouted as MachCopt stopped its upward climb and hovered above the roofline. Then suddenly the roof loomed close below them. MachCopt plunged downward, crashing down hard on the hangar floor, bounced back up five feet, then down again.

The two passengers were thrown about the compartment, arms and legs flailing. The old man groaned in pain, and fell limp against the rear bulwark, releasing his grip on the gun. At the edge of her peripheral vision, Samantha saw Daniel and Mullen, standing against the far hangar wall, their eyes riveted on the bizarre spectacle. She seized her chance. In one movement she scooped up the gun into her jacket pocket, leaped for the door and slammed her hand against the locking handle. The door started to slide, and she hurled her body out through the opening. The Colonel spun around from the pilot's seat and sprang toward her. He grabbed the edge of her coat.

MachCopt rose off the floor, three, then four feet, with Samantha dangling below it, held over the struts by the Colonel's fierce
grip. Samantha struggled and pulled. As the helicopter hovered,
the seams on her coat sleeve gave way, releasing her. Samantha
dropped to the floor, out of the clutches of Colonel Howard.

Samantha rolled over twice, then righted herself and desperately crawled away from under the whirling machine. She
leaped to her feet and ran toward Daniel. He smothered her in
his arms, and in unison they turned and watched MachCopt
crash down on the floor on the exact spot from which she had
just escaped. The aircraft rose again, slowly, but steadily. It
passed through the opening in the roof, and hovered. Then the
small delta wings extended from under the aircraft, and the nose
tilted downward. MachCopt banked to the left, then swiftly flew
off into the southern night. In a moment, the only trace of Mach-
Copt was a lingering foul burning odor and traces of smoke.

Samantha reached over and touched Daniel's bleeding head.

Daniel raised his hand to his head, and forced a smile. "I'll
be okay. How 'bout you?" he asked, pressing a finger to the
blood trickling from the corner of her mouth.

"I'll live."

Daniel turned and grabbed Mullen by his collar and moved
in close to his face. "No thanks to you, asshole. Forgot to mention your plan to try to lay me away."

Mullen shrugged. "Had to make it look realistic. Now that
we're even for that tackle at the hotel, may I suggest that we get
the hell out of here?"

The trio raced to the car. Mullen held the doors and motioned for Daniel to drive, and Samantha to get in beside him.
Mullen jumped into the back seat.

They drove in speeding silence along the dark, wide expanse
of Texas prairie.

"They told me everything," Samantha said quietly. "It was
Colonel Howard who led the plan for the assassination, with
two accomplices who did the shooting. The three of them left for
Vietnam the next day."

"That squares with what I found out from Victoria today," Daniel said. "Howard left from Dallas on November 23, 1963, for Vietnam. And he traveled on a private presidential order issued the same day, by President Lyndon Johnson."

"Amazing," Mullen said quietly.

"Yes," Samantha agreed. "They hid out in Vietnam until the Warren Commission Report was released. By that time, the two shooters were dead—Wittlefield ordered Howard to be sure they never came back. Their whole plan was to use enough people to assure success, but as few as possible, as Wittlefield said, 'to control the situation.' With two fewer men alive with knowledge of what happened, and the official investigation completed, Howard was free to come back to the States. Wittlefield figured they were safe."

"Amazing," Mullen repeated.

"So you didn't have much contact with Howard?" Samantha asked.

"No, didn't know the guy until recently," Mullen answered.

Samantha turned in her seat and smiled at Daniel. "Thanks for coming," she said.

"*De nada*," he replied.

Then she turned all the way around, and faced Mullen. "It's hard to comprehend. This all started with your nomination only a week ago, and now here we are with the answers to the assassination that changed history."

"Indeed," Mullen replied.

"Yes," Samantha shook her head. "It's an event that everyone from that generation remembers—where they were, what they did, what they said, when they heard the news. Where were you again, Frank, when you heard the news?"

Mullen shrugged. "At my desk at American Helicopter, in Abilene."

"That's right," Samantha said, snapping her fingers in recognition. "You told me at dinner."

Daniel glanced over and gave Samantha a quizzical look.

"Yes," Mullen sighed. "I didn't believe it when I heard it."

"That's right," Samantha said. "You remembered exactly what you said. You told your hysterical secretary that it was a sick joke."

"Precisely," he agreed.

Samantha looked deep in his eyes, and recalled what she had heard at dinner. "And then you said, that 'no one would want to shoot President Kennedy.' That's exactly what you said."

"Yes," Mullen said, looking curiously at Samantha.

Samantha leaned over the back of the seat and stared into Mullen's blue eyes. "How did you know the President had been shot, Frank?"

Frank Mullen stared back, perspiration accumulating on his forehead. "What do you mean, Samantha?" he said, his voice rising. "My God, my secretary burst into my office saying someone had shot the President."

"No, Frank," Samantha said, calmly, confidently. "You told me you remembered everything as if it was yesterday. She said 'the President is dead.' She was worried about Mrs. Kennedy but she didn't say why. But you reassured her. You said 'No one would want to shoot President Kennedy' and then you said that 'For sure, no one would want to hurt Mrs. Kennedy.'"

Mullen hesitated. "Well, I don't recall. She said 'shot' or 'dead.' What's your point, Samantha?"

Samantha sighed. "You knew, Frank. You knew the President had been assassinated, you knew how—they were going to shoot him. And you knew Mrs. Kennedy wasn't going to be hurt. All Mrs. Jackson had told you was that the President had died. She didn't say he'd been assassinated, and she didn't say how. But you knew it all."

Mullen sat quietly for only a moment, and then reached inside his coat pocket and pulled out a gun. He aimed it at Samantha and this time it was his turn to heave a heavy sigh. "I had so hoped you would let it rest, Samantha. You can't actually prove anything against me, of course, but I can't very well have you and Daniel going around spreading such stories about me."

Mullen saw the reflection of Daniel looking at him in the rearview mirror, and pointed the pistol at his head. "Don't try anything, Daniel," he ordered. "It's time to slow down."

Samantha stared at Mullen. "Why, Frank?" she asked quietly.

Mullen stared back at her. "Wittlefield ran the show, Samantha. Controlling everything. I just got in too deep. Before I knew it, I was rich and powerful, and I couldn't get out."

"To kill the President?" she asked softly.

"There was no choice," he said flatly.

Samantha looked at him in disbelief. "And the AMERIPRO problem with the S.E.C.? Why did you tell me about it, Frank?"

He glanced out the window, then back at Samantha. "I really did want to serve my country," he explained. "I don't know. I thought I could make up for…for what we'd done. I knew you and D'Angelo would be opposed to me, unless I could convince you. I wanted to demonstrate that I was being straight with you—that I deserved the job." He hesitated, then smiled. "It was the same reason I came for you tonight at the hotel."

"Why was that?" she asked.

"Not to hurt you, not to force you into their hands. Believe me. I wanted to give you one last chance to turn things around, take the deputy position, forget the insanity, do something worthwhile with your life. Nothing was going to bring anybody back from the dead. I was offering you the easy way, but…"

She looked at him, then broke into a cold, sneering smile. "There's no easy way out, you traitorous bastard."

Samantha looked over at Daniel, then started to reach for the door.

"Freeze!" Mullen demanded, aiming the pistol squarely at the side of Samantha's head. "Pull over," he demanded forcefully, moving his finger nervously across the trigger. "Now!" he yelled.

A strange, stunned look crossed Mullen's face. His head lowered for a moment, and he muttered, "You could have had money, power, everything…"

"Yeah," she replied, "like you."

Daniel pulled the car over to the side of the deserted country road. Mullen got out of the car, opened Samantha's door, and motioned with the gun for Daniel and Samantha to get out. He pointed them to the steep embankment running along the road and down to an open, empty field.

"This is crazy, Mullen," Daniel yelled. "It won't do you any good."

"Maybe so," Mullen answered coldly, "but now that you know everything, you leave me no choice. Control the situation, as Wittlefield always says. He's gone, along with that prick Howard. They'll never talk. And neither will you." He motioned again with the gun. "Get down there, now!"

Daniel grabbed Samantha by the arm and stepped onto the loose soil. They stumbled down, half crawling, half sliding, until they hit the hard Texas clay. At the bottom of the embankment, Samantha and Daniel turned, and looked back up at Mullen fifteen feet away. "Turn around," Mullen ordered.

"Fuck you, you coward," Daniel replied as out of the corner of his eye he caught a slow hand movement by Samantha reaching into her pocket. "You want to shoot us in the back, just like you bastards did with Kennedy."

Mullen frowned. "Actually, Colonel Howard tells me there is no question but that the forward shooter delivered the fatal shot," Mullen pointed the gun directly at Daniel. "But suit yourself."

Suddenly, the Texas prairie was all-consumed—blinding, flashing white light, followed by a powerful roar, sweeping down from above, engulfing them. From experience, Samantha instantly knew what was happening, and reacted. She pushed at Daniel and yelled, "Run!" Then she leaped to the side of the embankment, and ran and dodged, grabbing for the gun in her pocket. As she freed the gun with its silencer still attached she spun around and dropped to one knee, and examined the pistol.

Mullen stood at the top of the embankment, frozen in the intense spotlights, holding his arms above his head, desperately trying to fend off the onslaught of blinding light and deafening noise and pulsating wind.

Samantha shielded her eyes with her hand, and looked up at MachCopt, circling over its prey like a hungry vulture. She saw the deep blue smoke spewing from the helicopter's underside, and smelled the foul odor of burning plastic and rubber. Samantha brought her hand down from her eyes and clasped her hands together, steadying her hold on the gun. Squinting into the light, she aimed as best she could, pointing up, in the direction of the hovering monster. She squeezed the trigger.

Inside the cockpit, J. Kingston Wittlefield stared out through the window, saw Samantha kneeling, then aiming and firing the small pistol. Wittlefield laughed, and reached for the microphone to the exterior loudspeakers, and shouted, "you can't hurt MachCopt with that pea shooter, you stupid bitch!"

Howard frantically wrestled with the controls of the already wounded machine, his feet desperately punching back and forth across the electronic stabilizer sensors. He whirled around and grabbed Wittlefield by his throat, and yanked him forward, pulling the wrinkled old face up to his. "I told you the prototype needed the full armor protective shield," he yelled. "You idiot, just to save money, you cut the…"

Blindly, instinctively, Samantha pulled the trigger again, and again, and again. The silencer concealed the noise of exploding gunpowder propelling the bullets toward their target, but the effect was the same. In rapid order, the bullets penetrated the unprotected underbelly of the prototype flying machine.

MachCopt tilted on its side, then swerved, and reeled. Dense black smoke billowed out from the cockpit, and streams of red and orange flame burst through the windshield. Samantha pulled the trigger again. A moment later a deafening crack exploded from the prototype. The rotors slowed, and MachCopt shuddered and moaned. One moment, it lingered in the air, in the next instant the supersonic helicopter crashed straight down toward the earth and a terrified Frank Mullen cowering directly beneath the main fuselage.

Samantha saw Daniel running to escape the crash. Reflexively, she dropped the gun, jumped to her feet and ran in the opposite direction, desperately seeking the outside boundary of the crash zone. As she ran, the ancient raspy voice screamed out through the loudspeakers. As MachCopt crashed onto Mullen and the car, the ugly voice reverberated around the desolate Texas plains, "Traitors! Traitors! Traitors!"

The scream was silenced forever by the massive explosion as MachCopt's volatile jet fuel mixed with ordinary gasoline from the Lincoln incinerated everything for a hundred yards. The flames shot through the night sky of Texas like the celebration of the Fourth of July.

Chapter Seventeen

Samantha and Daniel did not trust the local authorities investigating the crash of the experimental helicopter. For his part, the sheriff clearly did not believe that they had simply stumbled on the accident, but after detaining them for one day as material witnesses, he had no choice but to let them return to Washington.

When they arrived at Reagan National Airport late Saturday night, Samantha told Daniel that she simply wanted to get a good night's sleep. The tone in her voice made it clear that she planned to sleep alone that night, and for the foreseeable nights to come. She promised she would call him in the morning so they could discuss the next course of action.

Samantha got up early on Sunday morning. She was sore and had several bruises, and a throbbing headache, but she needed to get out and get some exercise. She jogged across the Teddy Roosevelt Bridge and along the running path paralleling the Potomac. She had hoped the run would work its usual magic, but as she ran along the portion of the path that passed under the west wing of the Kennedy Center for the Performing Arts, she slowed, then stopped and stared back out across the river, to the hills of Arlington National Cemetery. When one of the early morning joggers stopped to see if the woman who was standing with tears rolling down her cheeks was going to be all right, she simply waved him away.

Around noon on Sunday, Samantha called Daniel to tell him how she was sorting things out in her own mind.

"The bastards killed Victoria too," he cried out.

Samantha understood that he felt responsible for her death. She knew how she felt. She felt responsible in some way for the deaths of dear, sweet Lionel, and George Willard, and gentle

251

Lester Boggs at the *Tribune*. Fortunately, the initial indications from the investigation in Dallas were that no one else had been trapped in the fire.

In their telephone conversation, Daniel said he would have to be alone for a little while, and then he was going to start on the most comprehensive story the *Post* had ever printed. Samantha didn't invite him to her meeting with Senator D'Angelo. She knew the Senator would not want to talk with a reporter present.

Samantha caught a cab to the Senator's house in the Great Falls suburb in Virginia. The housekeeper showed her to the living room. As she waited, she gazed out the expansive bay windows to the tranquil Potomac below, and to the unique Washington skyline beyond. On this sunny Sunday, the view of the nation's capital that had so often inspired her in the past made her want to return to New York.

Wearing a navy blue sweatshirt and matching draw string velour pants, Senator D'Angelo came down the stairs from the second floor. As he greeted Samantha in a soft, weary voice, she could see in his eyes the effects of another hard night of drinking. He gently touched her swollen jaw, and the gash on the corner of her mouth that she had been unable to cover completely with makeup. "Are you all right?" he asked.

"I'm fine," she lied.

They sat together and she told him everything she had learned. When she got to Wittlefield paying the underage girl to bait the Senator so they could blackmail him later, Samantha said, "They set you up, Senator. It could happen to anyone."

"No, Samantha," he said, sad and exhausted. "It wouldn't have worked with most people. There's no excuse for what I did. I checked my street smarts at the door that day, and I let the demons take over."

"I understand," she said softly. "And now I understand why you cut the deal with the President-Elect and agreed to support Mullen's nomination."

Senator D'Angelo shook his head again and again. "No, Samantha! No!" he pleaded. "You can't believe that," he said emphatically. "I've always worried about that, ah, incident coming to light, but it didn't have anything to do with agreeing to support Mullen's nomination. No, I accepted the deal from Prescott for the good of the country, not to protect my ass. And when it came right down do it, I wasn't so sure I was right for the job. The Senate, well, it can excuse some of my problems. But Secretary of Defense? Directly in the chain of command for the armed forces? No. And when I put down what I really wanted to accomplish at Defense, the most important priority was killing that damn boondoggle MachCopt."

"You won't have to worry about that anymore," she said confidently.

"But I didn't have to worry about it anyway. That's what Prescott gave me."

"What?" she asked, perplexed.

"Oh, that's right," he said. "I kept that to myself, didn't I? For once I didn't go blabbing my mouth off. Yes, my agreement to support Mullen had nothing to do with that underage girl. Prescott offered a deal I couldn't refuse. If I bowed out gracefully and supported Mullen, Prescott agreed to kill the MachCopt project. He didn't really want it and with the former C.E.O. of AMERIPRO as his Secretary of Defense, he figured he could kill it without the right wing super patriots claiming he didn't know what was good for the country."

Samantha smiled, and then looked back out at the Washington skyline, and for the first time in days let out a hearty laugh. "And when Mullen came in for that first meeting with you," she asked, "and you made such a big point of telling him that you were not going to rest until MachCopt was killed?"

"Playing with him. Besides, he would have been suspicious if we hadn't brought it up. That's why I insisted you raise it."

Senator D'Angelo picked up the telephone and, when he informed the aide that his call had to do with the circumstances surrounding the deaths of Colonel Howard, Frank Mullen and Kingston Wittlefield, he was immediately put through to the

President-Elect. When he heard the basic nature of the call that the crash was not some simple accident, President-Elect Prescott professed shock and dismay. But the Senator also detected serious consternation in the President-Elect's voice. As an old Washington veteran, D'Angelo knew that an explosive story linking one of his would-be cabinet members, his advisor on military affairs and a major campaign contributor to the assassination of President Kennedy would raise fundamental questions about the new President's judgment. Prescott's inauguration was a week away. He needed an overwhelmingly successful honeymoon with Congress and the people. The honeymoon period was crucial if the new administration was going to have any chance to move the country forward again.

President-Elect Prescott was blunt. He told Senator D'Angelo that he saw no purpose in reporting the matter to the political hack who would in a very few days no longer be the top law enforcement official of the United States. Rather, he concluded that the proper course would be to direct that Samantha meet immediately with the person who would in those same few days become the new Attorney General. The appointment was set for the next morning.

Samantha met with Tracy Goodrich on Monday morning at the transition offices in the Hay-Adams Hotel. Because the new President had not been sworn in and taken office, Goodrich proposed they discuss the matter alone. When she formally took over at Justice, she assured Samantha, she would bring in the appropriate additional law enforcement personnel.

At first, Samantha could not help but feel intimidated in the presence of the most forceful woman she had ever met. Goodrich was in her sixties, but her well-known dedication to physical fitness, which included annual runs in the Boston marathon, had paid off. She looked at least ten years younger, and her slim, taut, five-foot eleven frame carried a woman who exuded energy and confidence. The Washington rumor mill whispered that this woman would be the closest advisor to the new President. Physical and political access to the President–a powerful combination, Samantha was thinking when the Attorney General-Designate interrupted with a brusque reminder that she was running a very tight schedule.

Samantha recounted the events of the prior week, striving to be specific to recall conversations precisely. She broke down only once, when she explained how Lionel had died because electronic surveillance at the restaurant and on her telephone had revealed his role in assisting her.

Samantha had no doubt that the next Attorney General was totally focused on her detailed recitation of the facts. If Samantha had not been feeling the residual effects of stress and loss of sleep, she might have noticed a subtle change in Tracy Goodrich's demeanor at the point in the briefing when Samantha recalled Wittlefield's explanation of how he had come to learn of John Kennedy's decision to withdraw from Vietnam. When Samantha mentioned Lyndon Johnson, Tracy Goodrich's eyes opened wide. When Samantha said that Johnson had learned of Kennedy's private decision not through formal channels, but from a woman with whom the Vice President was having an affair, Tracy Goodrich paled, and her demeanor became solemn and distant.

At this point, Samantha noticed that the incoming Attorney General was visibly reacting to the story. "I apologize. I'm talking on and on, and I know your time is short."

Goodrich smiled faintly. "I believe you, Samantha, but I have to point out that unfortunately all of the direct and perhaps most of the forensic evidence has been destroyed with the death of the culprits."

"Yes," Samantha said, "but I still hoped that the banker in Texas could provide a copy of the trust instructions from Lyndon Johnson linking him to the twenty million dollar payment from AMERIPRO." But Samantha sighed deeply and told Goodrich of her conversation with the S.E.C.'s Felix Timmons. He had informed her that the Texas banker had left a cryptic message with Timmons over the weekend. The banker said he had not been able to locate any such document and could only assume that it had been destroyed. The banker remained quite concerned for his own personal safety, however, and apologetically informed Timmons that he had fled the country to go into hiding. Samantha could not help but laugh slightly when she told the Attorney General-Designate that the mild mannered S.E.C. bureaucrat was furious that the banker had apparently continued in his wrongful ways. The recorded message from the banker had advised Timmons that he had managed to set aside a million and a half dollars from the First Commerce Bank and Trust Company of Dallas for his personal contingency escape plan.

At the end of the meeting, Samantha explained that she was going to New York to visit her mother. On the way, she said she would visit the offices of the New York Times and determine if a clean copy of one of their newspapers from years before might have a reproduction of a photograph that would be clear enough to be able to discern the features of Colonel Howard's face peering down from the grassy knoll at Dealey Plaza. Goodrich wished Samantha luck, but went on to say what they both as lawyers knew to be the case. Photographs, particularly old newspaper copies of photographs, involve very tricky evidentiary issues when presented in court. The incoming Attorney General advised that blurry, grainy pictures are subject to varying interpretations and differing opinions as to what, or who, they actually depict. "Even with the modern technological advances of digitally enhanced imaging," the Attorney General-Designate explained, "you can't be sure. You know how it works," she said to Samantha. "For every expert who says he can give an unequivocal identification, there is another who will dispute it. You can believe it with all your heart, but I doubt you'll get any consensus that the figure you see standing on that knoll in Dallas was Colonel Howard."

Samantha left the Hay-Adams pleased with her complete and accurate description of the events, but unsure what the official response from the new administration would be.

───── ∞∞ ─────

Early the next morning, Samantha called Daniel to see how he was doing.

"Better," he said. "I'm writing at a feverish pace, trying to finish the story today."

Samantha said she would call him when she returned.

Samantha caught the shuttle to New York's JFK Airport, and rented a car for the drive into the city, and then out to the nursing home in White Plains.

Her stop at the *New York Times* took very little time. Even with the help of a magnifying glass, Samantha could tell that while she knew it was Colonel Howard standing on the hill, smiling, others would simply conclude that it was a bald or short-haired man, of undeterminable height, in a coat. The next Attorney General was probably correct that no positive, non-controvertible identification could me made.

Driving to the suburbs gave her time to think. But as she pulled into the snow-lined driveway of the converted old country estate, the only thing she had decided was that she needed to see her mother more often.

Samantha checked in at the executive director's office, and wrote out a check for the January increase in the charges, and prepaid the correct amount for the month of February. She noted the paltry balance in her checking account. She realized that the Senate payday was still a week away. She made a mental note to go online and transfer funds from her savings account to cover the check.

She went to the nursing station and chatted for several minutes with the head nurse about her mother's condition. "As you know, Ms. Wright, she has her good days, and her not-so-good days."

"How is she today?" Samantha asked.

"She was so excited to hear you were coming, dear," the kindly woman replied, "that I think she's trying her very best to make this one of the good days."

Samantha smiled and crossed her fingers.

Mary Anne Wright sat up straight in the old rocking chair, staring out the window at the snow-covered lawn. Samantha came into the room quietly, and stood by the door, watching her mother rock back and forth. Samantha smiled when she saw that her mother was wearing make-up and her pure white hair was neatly combed back. Samantha was pleased when she saw the single red rose pinned to the front of the cheerful floral dress she had given her mother at Christmas only a few weeks ago. It seemed like a lifetime ago.

Samantha took her mother's hand, bent down, kissed her and held her tight. "Oh, Mom, it's so good to see you. I love you," she cried.

Samantha's mother pulled her only child closer to her, and hugged her with all her strength.

"How are you, Mom?" Samantha finally asked. "You look wonderful today," she said truthfully.

Mary Anne Wright squeezed her daughter's hand and smiled.

"Don't you feel like talking?" Samantha asked as she sat down on the bed, still holding her mother's hand.

Her mother just smiled, and stared at Samantha.

"Well, that's fine," Samantha said cheerfully. "You don't have to talk if you don't want to. I'll just sit here and chat away."

Samantha told her mother about the weather, and about how she was thinking of getting a job with a private law firm, and about all the excitement in Washington around the new dynamic President who would take office next week. Samantha almost dropped her mother's hand for a moment as she reached over to the nightstand by the bed to pick up the photograph of her and her mother when Samantha was only three. But as Samantha reached for it, her mother pulled her back, and held onto her firmly.

"It's okay," Samantha assured her mother. "I'm staying right here." Samantha stared at the old photograph, and smiled when she realized it reminded her that she was very much her mother's daughter. Then she glanced at the other photo, the one behind in the simple gold frame, of John F. Kennedy delivering his Inaugural Address.

Samantha looked back at her mother and started talking. She was not sure if she had come to tell her mother the story, and she worried that it might be too much for her, but once she had begun, Samantha could not stop. Somewhere along the way, her mother stopped rocking, and her gaze fell squarely on the nightstand. As Samantha described the unbridled greed and insanity that had led to the despicable crime, tears welled up in her mother's eyes.

When Samantha had told it all, she reached behind her for some tissue, then leaned in toward her mother to dab away the tears rolling down her mother's cheeks. As she did, Mary Anne Wright stared intently into her daughter's eyes, then tightly grasped Samantha's hand and pulled her in close against her breast. She brought her arm around Samantha and hugged her tight. The old woman tried to speak, but no words came out. She took a deep breath, then tried again, and slowly the whispered words flowed.

"I'm...we're so proud of you," she said softly.

Samantha heard the words without understanding. She pulled away slightly, and stared into her mother's eyes. Those eyes glanced away, fixed on the nightstand, and filled with tears again. But at the same time, her mother's face broke into a wide, gleeful smile. Samantha watched, fascinated, for she had not seen her mother smile like that in long, long time.

The moment Daniel opened the door, Samantha could tell he had been drinking. Once in the apartment, the empty Pacifico bottles and solitary shot glass confirmed it.

"Daniel!" she said, disgusted. "This is hardly going to help you write the story. When's the deadline for the first morning edition of the *Post*?"

"I'd say when hell freezes over," he replied sarcastically.

"What?" she demanded.

"Jus' that there ain't gonna be a story, that's all. *Comprende, mi amiga*?"

"No story? Of course there is! The biggest story the *Post* has ever had," she quoted.

"I thought so too," he said wearily, hitting his head with his hand in a vain attempt to sober up. "But as much as a few of the guys in the editorial gang want to run with it, the answer from on top was 'no way.' Seems that our story lacks substantiation," he explained, trying with only partial success to keep from slurring his words. "Whatever the fuck they mean by that. Told 'em it was pretty fuckin' hard with all the parties dead."

"That's crazy," she shouted. "What about the murders—Lionel, and Victoria and George Willard?"

"Very interesting, but they rudely point out that from the sound of things we can't prove nothin'. The cops have found no evidence linking Howard to the murders. Different guns used on Lionel and Victoria, not that it matters if ya can't find the guns. Bet one of 'em was the same one used so expertly out there taking pot shots at MachCopt. Only problem is, that little piece of metal appears to have melted away in that hellish inferno. Ain't gonna be any tracing of that weapon."

"What about the *Tribune* fire?"

"What about it? Oh, the authorities know it was arson. Very professional. So professional that essentially all evidence that might give some clue to the perpetrators was completely obliterated. That includes whatever incendiary devices were used."

"But…" she interrupted.

"No buts," he replied. "As for the culprits, let's see, there's a fair amount of speculation it's a paramilitary group, retaliating for the *Tribune's* Pulitzer prize winning series by a reporter who had gone undercover and infiltrated the bizarre world of these crackpot would-be soldiers. Seems he concluded that they have real links to the international arms merchants, and real capabilities to get their hands on seriously dangerous shit, like some bad ass incendiaries. Then again, there's another account that the powers-that-be really suspect a Mexican drug cartel. The *Tribune's* editorial pages have recently been full of unwavering support for a joint state and federal drug enforcement task force to cross the Mexican border and go on offense."

"Unbelievable!" Samantha exclaimed.

"No," Daniel said, laughing. "Unbelievable is exactly the word the *Tribune* is calling our story. Ya see, darlin', my *Post* editors have talked directly to their counterparts at the *Dallas Tribune*. Let me emphasize the word *Dallas*. It seems the last theory the *Dallas* newspaper is going to buy into is that this had something to do with their fair city's most infamous crime. No, they're hot on every other available explanation. Can't blame 'em, I guess. Seems they've found one paid informant inside the Mexican mafia claiming he's got the evidence. So, the guys at the *Tribune* are running with that scenario. By the time they find out it's bullshit, if they ever do…Well, cutting right to the bottom line, Sam, it ain't enough for the *Post*. My editors kindly suggest that I could sure as shit get my story in the tabloids, but then again, that would be in-fucking-consistent with being a real reporter."

Samantha shook her head. "Daniel, they have to run it!"

"Funny," he replied. "That is exactly what I told 'em. But they wouldn't buy it. Said they decided way back that as a 're-sponsible *newspaper*—get it? They emphasize the *'news'*—they don't run with every new theory or speculation or wacko story about the crime of the 20th Century. No hard evidence, no forensic evidence, no multiple corroborations, no story." Daniel laughed. "All they said was, do what all the other jerks with Kennedy assassination theories do, write a book, and don't put on the jacket that I'm with the *Post*."

Samantha sat down. "That's just what I am going to do. I'm going to write down this entire story, starting in the morning."

"Great idea," he replied. "And who the hell is gonna publish it?"

"I'll find somebody, or I'll publish it myself—put it out over the Internet. One way or the other, this story is getting out." She paused and thought again. It would be a major undertaking. She looked at Daniel. "And if you sober up, and grow up, you might get a chance to help."

CHAPTER EIGHTEEN

Samantha's fingers raced across the keyboard of the her old Sony VAIO, trying to keep up with the rapid pace of her thoughts and memories. She had not been able to sleep. She gave up at 4:00 a.m., and for the next hour reviewed Daniel's handwritten notes and the first draft of the article he'd written, assuming that it would be published by the *Post*. At first Daniel had been reluctant to turn over the materials to her, hoping the *Post* decision would change. But when one final, pleading meeting with the editors confirmed that the editorial policy would stand, he delivered his work product with his promise to help. "I'm not throwing away my credibility by signing on with the tabloids."

Daniel's draft article was a good start, but incomplete. She could do more. She would particularly place the events of the last few days into the historical context of the Vietnam War and the Pentagon's expenditures on armaments.

At 5:00 a.m. she prepared a cup of tea and started on a detailed outline. She did not care how good her memory was, she knew it was crucial to write down verbatim the confessional statements of J. Kingston Wittlefield and Colonel Howard and Frank Mullen. She needed to be certain that the story was precise and complete.

Six hours later Samantha had stopped only once for a trip to the bathroom and to grab a Diet Coke from the refrigerator. When the telephone rang, she ignored it. But when she heard the message being left on her answering machine, she leaped for the phone. "Hello, yes, this is Samantha Wright."

"Ms. Wright. Good, you are there." The woman's voice was not unpleasant, but it was crisp and all business. "I'm the scheduling secretary for the President. He would like to see you today.

Five o'clock. A car will pick you up at four-thirty. It's a short window in an extremely tight schedule."

"The President? At the White House?"

"Of course."

"It's Inauguration Day!"

"Trust me, Ms. Wright, I'm well aware of that fact. The appointment is important enough to be squeezed in between the end of the parade and the start of the balls."

"What's it about?"

"That is for the President to tell you, Ms. Wright. We will see you at five."

Samantha sat back down at the dinette table and stared at the computer screen. Her thoughts were scrambled, the free flow of events from her brain to her fingers to the laptop's screen stopped, replaced by new thoughts. She sat there for half an hour, making no more progress on the manuscript. Then she gave up, and took a shower.

She had not planned on watching it, but given her sudden scheduled meeting at the White House, she decided that she had to do it. At five minutes to noon, she turned on the television to witness the swearing in of President Michael Prescott.

Consistent with his reputation for always running behind schedule, it was ten minutes after noon before the President-Elect's six-year old daughter gleefully came forward. She opened the Bible, while directly behind her mother sat with her squirming two-year old brother in her lap. Michael Prescott smiled down at his daughter and placed his left hand firmly on the Bible at twelve minutes after twelve. He raised his right hand, and in a powerful, clear voice repeated the words of the oath of office as administered by the Chief Justice of the United States. In seconds, he became the new President of the United States. Samantha stared at the images on the screen—images of a strong, confident man and his young and beautiful wife, and their two small children. She thought of the president years before whose life was cut so short. She watched and tried to listen, but she could not focus on what was being said. At the end of the fifty-five minute speech, all she could recall were the repetitive challenges for a break from the past. His campaign slogan of "new politics" had given way to a challenge for "new governance" with a "new beginning," and a "new commitment."

She waited inside the main door to the lobby of her apartment building, expecting a nondescript government sedan. When the black Suburban favored by the Secret Service pulled into the porte-cochere followed by a black stretch Lincoln limousine, Samantha remained where she was, assuming a VIP was being picked up for the Inaugural festivities. Two Secret Service agents with the telltale radio earpieces came through the front doorway and approached her. "Ms. Wright?" one said.

Her feeling of being a very important person intensified as the two car caravan was waved quickly through crowded intersections along Constitution Avenue, and without stopping was waved through the west gate on Pennsylvania Avenue onto the grounds of the White House. A few moments later Samantha was standing in the reception office of the personal secretary to the President, adjacent to the Oval Office.

At 5:08 p.m. on the day of his Inauguration, President Michael Prescott hurried from the Cabinet Room to the Oval Office. As soon as he saw Samantha, he broke into a broad smile and reached out and smothered her outstretched hand in both of his. "It is so good to see you again, Samantha." He released his hold with one hand and wrapped it around her waist and pressed her toward the door to his office. "We need to have a quick private chat before we're joined by someone I need you to meet."

Before she could finish saying "it's an honor," Samantha was seated on the sofa in the sitting area of the Oval Office across from the President's desk. The President pulled one of the wing chairs close to the sofa, sat down, reached over, took one of her hands in his, and charged into the conversation.

"Tracy Goodrich tells me you have had one hell of an adventure. Now is not the time or place to go into the details, but I want you to know that I have ordered Tracy to get to work as soon as she is sworn in—to get the Justice Department to conduct an immediate and thorough investigation. I've told her I want a complete report on my desk in ninety days. Your full cooperation will be needed, of course."

"Of course," Samantha agreed. "In fact, I've started writing it all down this morning, with the benefit of my friend Daniel Garcia's notes."

"The *Post* reporter?"

"That's right. He can…"

"I'm planning on this being an official, confidential law enforcement investigation. While it's in progress we can't have the press reporting on what's going on—leaking official information."

"Oh, you don't have to worry about that, Mr. President. The *Post* has passed on covering the story. Seems the fact that what we know can't be corroborated because the perpetrators and witnesses are dead, and evidence destroyed, means the *Post* won't run with it."

"I see," President Prescott replied. "Be that as it may, let's see what our sleuths from the Justice Department figure out. They're the pros. Speaking of pros, Samantha, you're a pro when it comes to the Defense Department. Nothing about that has changed. I need you in this administration. More so than ever after this unfortunate episode with Frank Mullen and Colonel Howard."

"And Kingston Wittlefield," she added. "He was a big supporter of yours."

"Yes he was," the President agreed without hesitation. "My campaign benefited from his fund raising, no doubt about it. From everything I've heard, it's a good thing we weren't personally close. But back to the subject at hand, I need you in my administration."

"But Mr. President, I, ah…"

"I'm not interested in hearing any 'buts'. Here's the situation. I can't give the top job to your Senator D'Angelo. We're all agreed on that. And I can't let this Frank Mullen fiasco slow down the momentum of my new administration. My choice is Jeff Jefferson. He's going to be here," the President released his grip on Samantha's hand, rolled his wrist around and looked down at his watch, "in two minutes."

"The congressman?"

"That's right. Solid guy, ideal credentials. He was always on my short list of candidates. He's African-American. That will be a first for Secretary of Defense. He was a Navy pilot, a POW in Vietnam. He's a salt of the earth guy, ambitious, even though he's no spring chicken. With you as one of his deputies, I know I'll have a strong team I can count on." He stared intensely at Samantha. "The deal I cut with him is he stays for eighteen months, and then he goes home to California and runs for the Senate, with my backing. By that time, if things go the way I expect, I'll be in a position to appoint the first woman as Secretary of Defense. History making–the first black followed by the first woman. That sums it up," he said as the intercom on the coffee table buzzed. The President grabbed the phone, listened, then said, "bring him in."

Samantha started to ask a question, but the President held up his hand. "Samantha, you're going to love this guy. Smart, like you, a great sense of humor, and his head's on straight. Hard to believe he's a politician. You'll work well together. I have to be able to count on you getting on board with the program. Now here, take this," he said, handing her a simple white business card with handwritten numbers on it. "It's my direct, private line. No operators. " he smiled. "Call me if there is anything I can ever do for you."

Suddenly Samantha found herself standing and shaking hands with Secretary of Defense-Designate Jeff Jefferson. The slim black man was medium height. He was dressed in a tuxedo, had a warm smile. As she looked into his clear, friendly eyes, she felt the strong hand of the President resting on her shoulder, and saw his other arm around the last of his cabinet selections. "You both will have to excuse me," the President said as he physically pressed the two strangers closer together. "Duty calls. It's a tough job," he smiled, "but the First Lady insists that we make every single Inaugural Ball. Record number this year. Sixteen. I've got one direct assignment for you both. Get on top of the base closure issue immediately."

"It's already in the works, Mr. President," Jefferson replied. "First order of business will be an inspection tour of all the prime targets."

"Great," the President concurred. "Remember, Samantha knows where the fat can be cut. She's your right hand. Take her along."

"Yes, Mr. President," Samantha and her new boss replied in unison.

———— ❦ ————

Samantha spent the next three hours in a White House office with one of the most down to earth, genuinely nice people she had ever met. The President was right. They hit it off immediately. She almost accepted his invitation to join him and his wife at the California congressional delegation's Inaugural Ball, but she already felt comfortable enough with him to be honest and decline saying she had best get a good night's sleep if she was going to be ready to get to work the next morning.

———— ❦ ————

The White House limousine dropped her off at a little past 9:00. Inside her apartment she turned on the television to glimpse the coverage of the quadrennial gala festivities accompanying the Inauguration of a president. She watched just long enough to see the Secretary of Defense-Designate being interviewed on the ballroom floor of the Ritz Carlton hotel. When Samantha saw his lovely, smiling wife standing arm in arm with her husband, she mentally kicked herself. They were obviously an adoring couple. She should have gone to the party and met Mrs. Jefferson. But she was not in a party mood. She turned off the television as the reporter was concluding, "And there you have it folks. Obviously, big changes are ahead for the Pentagon under the management of President Prescott's selection for Secretary of Defense."

She put on her flannel pajamas and poured herself a glass of Chardonnay. She couldn't remember how long the opened bottle had been in the refrigerator, but the wine still tasted good.

She sat down at the dinette table and turned on her laptop. In a few moments she was able to clear the events of the day from her head, and return to the important job of preserving the events of the past. She was writing about Lionel, and the electronic surveillance of their luncheon that had led to his death, when she remembered the listening device hidden in her telephone. "Physical evidence!" she exclaimed to the room. Something, anything tangible to substantiate the story, she thought. Maybe it could be traced.

She raced to the kitchen for the small screwdriver and grabbed the phone. She quickly opened the instrument, and reached for the minute silver disc. The tiny but very real piece of evidence, the tiny bit of corroboration, was gone.

Her whole body trembled, then she called Daniel. He was home, not having been assigned by the *Post* to cover any of the Inaugural.

"Calm down," he reacted. "It's to be expected. These special ops guys—no, it's not special ops, what Howard was trained in they is black ops—these black ops guys clean up after themselves—leave no trace."

"I guess so," she said, but she wasn't convinced.

At 11:45 p.m., the First Lady lifted her six-year old sleeping daughter from her chair, then leaned in close to the President. "Give us both a kiss goodnight, Michael."

The President turned away from his balcony view of the grand ballroom below, gently kissed his daughter on the cheek. Then he pulled his wife closer and tried to make himself heard over the pulsating rock 'n roll roaring from the bandstand. "I thought you said we had to attend all of the balls. This one makes thirteen. Three more to go."

"No," she shook her head. "I said *you* had to. I'm tucking Cynthia in, checking on Michael, Junior, and then hitting it. I trust you can find your way home?" she laughed.

"Somehow, someway," he replied and kissed her warmly on the lips.

The First Lady turned to leave, then passed her daughter to the waiting arms of the petite blonde female Secret Service agent who had been selected for the assignment in part because she so resembled the President's wife. The First Lady returned to her husband, took his hand firmly in hers and stared coldly into his eyes. "Just because you're the most powerful man in the world, don't think you can forget our deal. I want you home immediately after the last ball."

"You've stayed by my side," he replied, "as agreed. I've kept my side of the bargain. I'm not going to screw it up now."

"Nice choice of words," she whispered in his ear, then leaned around and gave him a long passionate kiss on the lips. "That should be a good one for the cameras."

At 12:05 a.m. the President ceased clapping with the beat of the music and signaled to the two Secret Service agents behind him that he was ready to move on to the next ball. The taller of the two agents brought his hand up to his mouth and announced into the microphone concealed in his coat sleeve, "Father Bear is on the prowl." He touched his finger to the earpiece, listened a moment, then bent down toward the President. "The Attorney General is at the stairwell and would like two minutes."

President Prescott stood up and moved toward the back of the balcony. He nodded that he would see her.

As the band finished a yeoman's version of "Johnny Be Goode," substituting the President's first name of Michael for Johnny, Tracy Goodrich strolled through the opening of the protective curtain at the back of the balcony. The President extended one hand as he motioned for the Secret Service agents to back away and allow them privacy. She brushed his hand away and instead leaned in close and kissed him squarely on the lips. "Congratulations, Mr. President. You've made it. You've actually made it."

He noticed the distinctive taste of champagne on her lips and remembered how much she liked the bubbly. "Thank you, Tracy." he said warmly. "Or I guess from now on it's Attorney General. And you've made it. It was close. I had to use a lot of chits, but you've actually made it. Like we talked about years ago."

Tracy Goodrich gave him that sultry smile she had used so effectively with him in years past, and placed her hands on his hips. "Now don't tease me with those references to the good times, Mr. President. It's enough to make an Attorney General swoon all over again."

"No swooning," he laughed, realizing the band had not started to play again. He lowered his voice. "No swooning over a happily married President."

"Married, yes. Happily? I see the First Lady has departed for the evening."

"Don't go reading something into it that isn't there. She was tired, and she wanted to personally tuck Cynthia in on her first night in the White House."

"Tired at her young age? As I recall, Mr. President, you didn't like girls who tire out. You were always much more the Eveready Energizer Bunny type. Experienced, marathon athlete types, that's what you like."

"Tracy! I don't need that kind of talk."

She stared into his adorable, deep blue eyes and shook her head. "No, I suppose *we* don't need anything to interfere with my last step."

The President quickly glanced around. He verified that the agents were outside of whisper range. "Jesus, Tracy, don't even mention it. Concentrate on Justice. The Court vacancy will come in due course."

"The *Chief* Justice vacancy," she corrected him.

"In due course," he repeated. "But first get this goddamn Frank Mullen fiasco behind us. At the moment, it's three dead in an experimental helicopter crash, and Samantha says the *Post* won't run the story."

"For now, maybe, but at any time that damn reporter could..."

"Keep it under wraps," he interrupted. "Make it go away before the fifty-three percent who did vote for me start wondering what the hell they did. The country needs a strong leader, if we're going to accomplish what we have to so. I can't help the country if I've got the press all over me and a goddamn special counsel investigating me from the get-go."

"With whatever it takes?" she asked.

He cupped his hand over his mouth and quietly whispered in her ear. "I've done what I can. Samantha Wright is going to be one busy lady. You handle the rest! I do not," he insisted, "want to know the details."

With that the President of the United States left for the fourteenth Inaugural Ball.

Samantha could not sleep. At 12:30 a.m. she gave up, went back to work on her laptop. She reviewed her extensive outline and set it to a detailed time line. At 1:20 a.m. her memories focused on the discussion between Colonel Howard and J. Kingston Wittlefield in the MachCopt hangar. Howard and Wittlefield had argued—Howard needed to get back to Washington and clean up "the mess" he had left behind. But the deadly crash of MachCopt prevented Howard, Wittlefield and Mullen from returning to Washington to do anything. Moreover, Howard could not have retrieved the listening device earlier—he could not have had the time.

Samantha looked around the apartment. Unlike the first time, this time after Wittlefield and Howard and Mullen were all dead, there was no evidence of anyone entering to recover the device. Samantha felt a sudden chill. The chill kept her awake until exhaustion forced her eyes closed at 3:00 a.m.

CHAPTER NINETEEN

One week after the Inauguration of President Michael Prescott, the new Attorney General of the United States sat in her office in the Department of Justice, glaring at the headlines in the *Post*. "It's not fair," she muttered to herself, throwing the paper down on the desk. The full color photograph on the front page showed the smiling faces of the new Secretary of Defense Jeff Jefferson and his three Deputy Secretaries, standing with the President, following their swearing in ceremonies. The lead story in the *Post* explained that the new team at the Defense Department was celebrating their unanimous, swift approval by the Senate.

Seething, Tracy Goodrich re-lived the rancorous, partisan controversy of her grueling Senate committee hearings and the vote of two weeks ago confirming her nomination by a narrow margin of two. The senators had poked and probed, legitimately testing her every position on the important legal issues of the day, but also challenging her credentials to manage the enormous law enforcement agency. It was all a charade. The rabid opposition masking its true agenda and speculations because even in the era of tabloid excess, the President's enemies did not dare attack a female candidate for such a high office by openly revealing their un-provable suspicions—that she had won the nomination by sleeping with Michael Prescott.

Without proof, they didn't dare go public. Dammit, she had the credentials, had toiled long and hard in this city, going back to the early intoxicating days in Bobby Kennedy's Justice Department. She had worked her way up the torturous ladder, proving herself as a party loyalist in increasingly demanding jobs.

She'd given up having a husband, family, children. She'd stayed in Washington during the long, trying periods when her party was out of the White House. She'd practiced criminal law during the day and taught nights at Georgetown Law School, and had always aggressively networked. Some of her steps up that ladder had been calculated, others were fortuitous, none more so than having Michael Prescott in her Constitutional Law class at Georgetown during those dreadful Nixon years. At first she'd befriended him, then she'd mentored him, in law and in bed.

Tracy Goodrich had seen the mighty and the powerful before. Her lover Lyndon and her first boss Bobby exuded it. Early on, she had perceived that Michael could be in their league. He had it all—he was intelligent, fascinating, manly and handsome certainly—a man's man, and a woman's man too. He was telegenic, more cocky than confident, but ambitious with that desperate single-minded determination essential to reach for the ultimate brass ring.

Any lingering doubts she had that he'd do what it would took to reach the goal had disappeared three years before. He had been firm and unwavering. Their sexual relationship was over. He was going to be faithful to his young wife. It was, as he said, the only smart thing to do. Tracy had laughed, then had taunted him, told him he could never be a one woman man. The look in his eyes told her she'd overstepped her bounds. His expression turned cold as he gave her his ultimatum. "I am going to be president. Everything is in place. With the commitment of Kingston Wittlefield and his resources, the financing is a done deal. Hell, just yesterday Wittlefield's man Colonel Howard delivered five hundred one thousand dollar checks. Neat, tidy, legal under the campaign contribution limits. Here! Now!" he'd demanded, "*you* decide, Tracy. Our relationship changes—long time friends of course, political supporters, but never lovers. Our relationship shifts to become the only way it can be with me under the media microscope. It's that, or we have no relationship."

Recalling then-Governor Prescott's reference to Kingston Wittlefield, Attorney General Tracy Goodrich grimaced. She wiped away the past, looked down at the newspaper, and focused on the tall, attractive, sandy haired woman standing next to the President. She tried to concentrate on how she was going to manage and contain the dangerous information Samantha Wright had learned. The Attorney General could not help but wonder if Michael Prescott's uncharacteristic commitment to sexual fidelity was still in place now that he'd won the election.

She brooded over that idea, and over the story in the *Post* which described Samantha Wright as a rising star in the new administration, the most powerful woman ever to serve in the Department of Defense. Goodrich picked up the phone and called the unlisted private number of one of her most powerful former clients—a client who truly owed her. She had plea-bargained the Justice Department charges down to an admittedly enormous fine but no prison time. She knew the grateful client would be a friend to her, and a friend to the President. A plan began to form. If it worked, when it worked, Samantha Wright's story would not destroy her.

A few hours later, a Navy lieutenant junior grade marched into the large conference room adjacent to the office of the Secretary of Defense and handed a typewritten note to Deputy Secretary Samantha Wright. Samantha waited for a pause in the briefing describing each of the prospects for military base closings, then looked down at the note. Why was Daniel thanking her? He wouldn't have gotten the assignment but for her? What assignment? What was he talking about?

At the scheduled 4:00 p.m. break, Samantha walked briskly to her new office suite adjacent to the Office of the Secretary of Defense, passed through the reception area, and closed the door to the inner office. She was not sure of the telephone system, and assumed her calls were not private. She certainly did not need the appearance on her first full day at the Pentagon that she was providing information to a *Post* reporter. But she needed to know what his message was about. She had to chance it.

Daniel answered, and didn't let Samantha finish saying hello. "I mean it, babe. You're the best—class act all the way. One day on the job and you're putting in the good word for me—getting me inside on the first big Pentagon story. *Mucho, mucho gracias!*"

"Daniel! Shut up! I don't know where you're getting your information these days, but I didn't say or do a thing. I don't know what you're talking about."

"The base closure tour, babe. Headed by the new Secretary of Defense and you. Departure tomorrow, 8:15 a.m. sharp. Excuse me, that's 0815 hours. And your favorite *Post* reporter got one of the three press seats on the Air Force plane, riding right along with you guys."

"Goddammit, Daniel, " Samantha shot back. "I didn't set that up. I wouldn't do that. You traveling with me, that's the last thing I need. Everybody knows about our former relationship."

"Sam! *Former*?"

"We're friends, that's all," she said emphatically. "What I don't need is you along on my first big assignment. It's all business, Daniel, and I don't want any speculation about monkey business."

"Fine. I get the message," he retorted. "But get over it, babe, cuz I'm on the tour. My editor confirmed it—invitation from the Office of the Secretary of Defense. Hell knows why I thought it was you. Obviously I don't need you on this one. Somebody knows a goddamn good reporter when they see one, and wanted that reporter along. So see you tomorrow. I was even gonna offer you a lift out to Andrews in the morning, but I'm sure you're too important for that. You finished with my notes and draft yet? I want 'em back, pronto."

Samantha took a deep breath, consciously trying to control her growing anger. This was all she needed. Daniel under foot for the next seven days.

"Notes and draft?" he repeated.

"I'm almost finished. I'm certainly done with your chicken scratch handwriting on legal pads. I'll make a copy, give your originals back."

"Good idea. Then unless my credentials for the trip somehow get mysteriously pulled, I'll see you tomorrow morning." He hung up.

———— ✠ ————

Samantha used her private bathroom, then started back down the hall to the conference room for the rest of the briefing. Halfway there the Secretary of Defense came up from behind and gently grabbed her by the arm. "This trip is going to be a great start. If my math is right, we're looking at an immediate savings of twelve billion a year with just the obvious choices for closure. After this trip, I'll bet we can safely double that number with no compromises in our defense capabilities."

"Twelve billion, three hundred and twenty million in the Class 1 category," she replied.

Secretary Jefferson broke out into a broad smile. "What a team," he exclaimed. "We're going to shake this place up. With the right press coverage, we can not only sell the budget cuts, we can convince the public of what we already know—we can do this with no down side. We just have to be sure the first media take on our efforts is positive. I'm trusting your friend over at the *Post* will be responsive. He's got a sharp, open mind."

Samantha did not try to conceal her irritation.

"Oh. I didn't get a chance to tell you. I've gave a press credential to your Mr. Garcia."

"I see," Samantha was not enthusiastic. They stopped at the door to the conference room. "He's not my Mr. Garcia. We're friends now, that's all. I want you to know that."

"Sam, whatever your relationship, I don't care. That's between the two of you."

"I'm telling you…"

"The President and I just want to be sure we get a positive take from the press on this trip."

"The President?"

"He suggested it—the Pentagon press office and I agreed it was a terrific idea. The right coverage is important. Just friends or just whatever, try to get him to spin things the right way, okay?"

The briefing ended at 7:00 p.m. Samantha returned to her office to organize her briefcase for the trip. The naval officer who earlier had brought her the message from Daniel reminded her that the flight the next morning departed Andrews promptly at 0815 hours. He proposed that her official car and driver pick her up at her apartment in Rosslyn at 0700. She was about to respond, then thought for a moment about Secretary Jefferson's directive that she try to get Daniel to spin his story the right way. "I won't need a car," Samantha told the officer. "I have a ride lined up."

As soon as the Navy man left, Samantha called Daniel. "It's probably best for us to have a private talk before starting this trip. How about picking me up at seven?"

"*No problemo,*" he replied smugly.

At ten minutes before ten that night, Samantha collapsed at her dinette table and opened her laptop. She glanced at the kitchen clock. "One hour," she said to herself. "Write for one hour and then get some sleep," she tried to convince herself. She knew whatever she wrote that night would be the last words for at least seven days, until after she returned from the base closing trip. She turned the computer on and very quickly tuned out the events of the day and found her fingers flying across the keyboard, recording more of the details of the events of two weeks before.

At midnight she got up from the table and heated some water in the microwave for tea. When she sat back down and took a sip of the comforting drink, her thoughts moved away from the culminating events in the MachCopt hangar outside of Dallas to her mother. In the flurry of activity over the last week, she had telephoned her only once. She made a mental note to call without fail from Georgia, the first stop on the tour, then decided to skip ahead in the story. She started a new file within the folder, and entered every detail of her last visit with her mother. She wrote about her mother's devotion to JFK and how her mother had told her she was proud of her daughter. As she wrote and remembered, Samantha realized how she owed it to her mother to tell the story. She thought about sleep, but she could not—she was driven to keep writing it down.

The story flowed so readily that it was almost three hours later when Samantha finally made it to bed. She did not look out the bedroom window and did not notice the wet snow that was rapidly blanketing the Washington area.

———❀———

At about that same time, two men met in a small private parking garage near the Pentagon. The only light in the dark came from a distant flickering fluorescent fixture. The dark shadows concealed identifying characteristics of the men, except that one man at six foot three towered over the other by at least six inches. The men spoke in a low, brisk cadence.

"The op should stick," the shorter man confirmed.

"No chance for discovery?"

"None that I can see." He looked at his partner. "Why?"

"Why what?"

"Why did he put that dumb nigger in the job? The bastard was a goddamn weak sister at the Hanoi Hilton."

"Prescott can't be trusted, that's all. He's proven that in spades by teaming this broad with Jefferson. He's just another goddamn politician. We've learned our lesson."

"Again."

"Again."

CHAPTER TWENTY

Daniel downshifted from third to second gear for the turn into the semicircle driveway leading to Samantha's apartment building. The GTO at first took the turn well, then the rear snow tires slid left and the car started to spin out of control. Daniel reacted instantly, shifting down to first and holding the steering wheel into the turn. He came to a sliding stop in the middle of the driveway, ten feet from the lobby entrance. He looked around at the snow covered roads, then over at the digital message board on the bank building two blocks away. It was five minutes to seven, and twenty-four degrees. He looked at the deserted streets and doubted that any other fool would be venturing up the drive. He set the parking brake, got out, pulled the collar of his overcoat up around his neck, and slogged his way through the four inches of snow to the building entrance.

He glanced up at the downpour of white dry crystals, shivered, then turned to the building electronic access code box. He was about to punch in her five-digit security code when he remembered Samantha's new rules. "Announce yourself like any other visitor," she'd demanded. He sighed, grabbed the intercom phone and inputted her number. It rang four times. No answer. "Come on, Sam, it's freezing out here," he shouted into the intercom. When the connection disconnected, he pounded on the electronic box and re-entered the number.

At the third ring, she came on the line. "Hello. Daniel?"

"Sam! Of course it's me. Buzz me in. I want out of this goddamn snow."

"Snow? Oh my God!" There was a pause. "What time is it? I overslept. The alarm didn't go off."

"Overslept! Sam, it's a couple of minutes to seven. The plane leaves at eight-fifteen. And it's snowing like hell. We'll need every minute to make it over to Andrews."

"Dammit," was her reply as he heard the telltale sound of the front door buzzer.

At twenty-five minutes after seven Samantha raced from the bedroom pulling a medium-sized suitcase and carrying a navy blue laptop bag and purse. Her hair was only partially blown dry. She wore no makeup. "I'm a wreck," she exclaimed.

"Look great to me," he replied, smiling broadly.

"Yeah, sure, right down to the bags under my eyes. I was working on the story till close to three last night."

"Speaking of which," he responded, walking over to the dinette table and picking up some papers. "I want my notes and draft back. I'll do some polishing on this junket."

"No way! Leave everything where it is. I've finally got your mess organized—pretty obvious you were hitting booze."

"Sam, give me a break!"

Samantha rolled her eyes. "In any event, you'll get your part back soon enough, after I finish my first draft. I can crank it out in a week."

"You're not working on it on this trip?"

"Of course not," she replied abruptly. "This tour is strictly business—concentrate on the base closing issues."

"You don't want your laptop?" he asked, folding the screen down and reaching for the power plug.

"No! The Department issued me a new Thinkpad—strictly for official business, security encoded and protected." She pointed at the computer bag. "I'm not going to mix the two. Now let's go. I can't afford to be late."

"Speaking of which, don't you think you better check in, be sure the flight is still leaving on time. This snowstorm could screw up the schedule."

"From the car," she answered, holding out a miniature flip up cell phone also issued to the new Deputy Secretary of Defense.

The GTO plowed its way south on the George Washington Parkway, aiming for the Fourteenth Street bridge on the route from Northern Virginia over to the Anacostia area of Maryland and Andrews Air Force Base. Samantha called the flight information number for Andrews and identified herself with the code name she had been given for purposes of the VIP flight. At 7:40 the major in charge of flight information advised her that the flight was on schedule. "The weather is marginal," the major reported, "but if the cloud cover doesn't close in, it will still be wheels up at 0815."

They had slowly navigated the on-ramp from the parkway to the bridge when their progress came to a sudden halt. Daniel rolled down his window and stuck his head out, cupping his hand over his eyes to protect from the driving snow. "A bus swerved into the guard rail. The driver is out directing traffic around the mess."

"Great," Samantha replied.

It was five minutes before eight when they passed the scene of the bus accident. Samantha looked down at her watch and muttered, "That damn alarm. I think I busted it the last time I used it."

Daniel shrugged and suggested she call again. This time the major advised her that the decision to fly was in the hands of the flight crew. He understood it was still a "go."

Samantha pulled out her trip itinerary from her purse and found the cellular phone number. She punched in the numbers and held the phone to her ear. "Jefferson, here."

"Mr. Secretary, it's Samantha Wright."

"Samantha? Where are you?"

"In route," she replied. "With Daniel Garcia of the *Post*. We just passed a bus accident on the bridge. We're running late."

"You're driving yourselves? Your official driver should have..."

"Yes, well, it hardly seemed necessary to..."

"Samantha, listen up. You're my Deputy Secretary. Your time, my time, is precious. Sticking to the schedule is an absolute must. This plane has got to take off at exactly quarter past the hour."

"Then the snow isn't..."

"A little snow isn't going to bother the Air Force. And the schedule is tight enough as it is. We've got no room for delay. Marine Corp One, the President's helicopter, is arriving at 8:35— Air Force One is leaving at 8:50. There's no air traffic allowed within fifteen minutes of the President's arrival and departure. Our window for take off is no later than 8:20 or we're delayed an hour. I can't have that. Samantha, if you and I are going to get off on the right foot, you better know I'm a fanatic for sticking to the schedule."

"I understand," Samantha sighed. "I'm normally very prompt myself. But it's this snow that..."

"No buts," the Secretary of Defense ordered. "Are you going to make it or not?"

Samantha glanced over at Daniel straining to see out through the windshield as snow accumulated after every sweep of the windshield wipers. "We're doing our best," she replied.

She heard the exasperation in the voice on the other end of the conversation. "Waiting on you isn't an option," Secretary Jefferson answered. "If you make it, great. If not, check in with flight control and see what flights are available for you to catch up with us. Samantha, I only want you to take an already scheduled Air Force flight. No special planes just for you. I don't want the first story on this trip to be about how we pissed away taxpayers' money just because you couldn't get here on time. You'll undoubtedly miss the first base or two on the tour."

Samantha grimaced with the dressing down she knew was well deserved. Why the hell did she stay up so late? She had taken this job. She was going to have to make it priority number one, and not let the writing of the story get in her way. "I understand," she replied. She tapped the "end" button on her phone and turned to Daniel. "We've got to make it."

"I'm doing the goddamn best I can," he retorted.

⎯⎯⎯ ∞ ⎯⎯⎯

It was sixteen minutes after eight when Daniel gently pumped the brakes and brought the car to a stop at the main entrance to Andrews Air Force Base. The uniformed guard carefully reviewed the identification cards tendered by Samantha and Daniel, then checked them against his list of authorized persons. He asked each for the individual code name they had been assigned for the trip. A minute and a half passed before the security check including an explosive sniffing dog was completed and he waved them through, directing them to the VIP passenger terminal and parking lot.

At the parking lot they jumped out of the car into the swirling snow, grabbed their bags from the trunk, and raced to the terminal entrance. An Air Force sergeant saluted and grabbed Samantha's suitcase and laptop bag and pushed her along toward the gate on the opposite side of the terminal leading to the waiting planes. At the gate he stopped, held up a wireless air phone. "Terminal to Air Force Two-Niner. Come in."

"Air Force Two-Niner, here. We're rolling. Over."

"I've got two of your VIPs here. Deputy Secretary Wright and the *Post* reporter. Over."

The voice on the other end replied, "Hold on."

On board the Air Force KC-135, the military version of the old commercial Boeing 707, the pilot applied the brakes and gently brought the jet to a full stop on the approach path leading to Runway 2 West, then turned to confer with the new Secretary of Defense standing in the back of the cockpit. "Sir, they can drive them out to the plane." The pilot looked at the digital display of the time on the flight control panel. "It would be wheels up at 0825. Marine Corp One would be delayed five minutes. No big deal in the scheme of things, Mr. Secretary. The word around Andrews already is that this President always runs late."

Secretary Jefferson smiled briefly, then shook his head. "Appreciate the thought, Captain, but I'm not starting my first official trip by delaying the President of the United States. Let's get going." The Secretary returned to the passenger compartment, sat down, and fastened his seatbelt. He turned to the Navy commander sitting to his right. "I'll bet Deputy Secretary Wright never misses another flight for the rest of the time we work together."

The naval officer smiled and replied, "Yes sir. I'm sure the lady has learned her lesson."

Samantha and Daniel heard the announcement over the air phone that the flight was going to take off without them. "That's great," Samantha said to no one in particular. "Now what?"

The sergeant motioned for them to take a seat next to the wall of glass affording a sweeping view of the runways. "Make yourselves comfortable," he suggested. "I'll check on the rest of the flights for today. I know you'll miss the first stop in Georgia. But we should be able to get you into Homestead in Florida."

Samantha muttered "thank you," then slumped down onto one of the hardback composite chairs. Daniel came over and sat down next to her. He pointed out to the two massive Blue and White 747s parked a hundred yards down the runway. "The President's planes. Whichever one he uses is Air Force One," he explained. "And there, that plane turning onto the runway at the far end. That was our flight. Welcome to the world of military precision."

"Great first impression," Samantha sighed. "Highest position ever for a woman in the Department of Defense, and I can't be on time for my first official trip. I bet the good ol' boys on the plane are having a hearty laugh at my expense."

"Wouldn't bet against it," Daniel answered.

"Gee, thanks for your support."

"*De nada*," he smiled. He reached for her hand, but she pulled it away, staring out into the snowy landscape.

A few seconds later the Air Force jet hurtled down the runway. At precisely 0819 hours the front wheel of the plane lifted up. The thirty-five year old plane angled toward the sky, and with a massive roar undiminished by modern sound control technology escaped the ground. It turned slightly left as the wheels collapsed and retreated into the fuselage. At one thousand feet and one mile from the airbase, the plane tilted right, paralleling the Anacostia River leading to the Potomac.

Samantha and Daniel followed its flight path until the snow nearly obliterated the view. It was in those last ten seconds of visibility before the jet would enter the dense low lying cloud cover engulfing all of Washington that the plane jolted sharply right. The right wingtip dove ninety degrees, hesitated, then jolted down another ninety degrees, tipping the plane completely on its side.

"That's quite a maneuver," Daniel observed matter-of-factly.

Samantha started to agree, then stood up and strained to see more clearly.

───⟨⟩───

Inside the jetliner, Secretary of Defense Jeff Jefferson desperately grabbed for a hand-hold, unsuccessfully attempting to fight the G forces pressing against him. He screamed as the plane turned completely on its side. Pure terror gripped him as the plane keeled over further, and started the plunge. In the last brief seconds of his life, his thoughts suddenly flashed back to his crashing A-4, over Haiphong Harbor. He had parachuted and survived. Secretary of Defense Jeff Jefferson dreamed of parachuting down again, floating safely down again. The dream ended instantly in the deadly carnage of exploding jet fuel and shattering, splintering metal.

───⟨⟩───

Samantha grabbed hold of Daniel, and pulled him close, her eyes riveted on the surreal scene of the airplane crashing down through the snowy sky. In the final seconds before the impact she turned away and buried her head in Daniel's arms.

The quiet terminal instantly turned into a teeming mad-house of uniformed military officers and enlisted men racing about. Wailing, pulsating sirens cut through the morning air all around Washington. Samantha sat, cradled, shaking in Daniel's arms, unable to move, unable to think.

At the White House, President Prescott was running late as usual. While his helicopter waited, he leaned forward in the rocking chair once used by his hero President Kennedy and furiously scribbled a new sentence in the top margin of one of the typewritten pages he was holding. He turned to the Attorney General sitting next to him on the white sofa and asked, "How's this for the personal touch? 'Although I never used my law degree to officially practice law, I feel a particularly close connection to this august group. Not only are some of my best friends trial lawyers, my very best friend, the nation's First Lady, started as a trial lawyer.'"

Tracy Goodrich winced. "States what everybody already knows, Mr. President, plus a fact you don't want the press playing up. You want to get out of there as quickly as possible, and make no headlines, draw no attention to the fact one of your first speeches as President is to the Trial Lawyers Association. Hardly a popular group. It's just a payback appearance for their support. Keep it short and sweet."

The President paused, then took his pen and scratched out the words he had just written. "Point well taken. Let's go."

As they headed out of the Oval Office, the President's press secretary and an Air Force general rushed in. The general blurted out, "Mr. President, there's been a plane crash at Andrews. A total catastrophe. All aboard certainly killed."

The President looked at the Attorney General, hesitated, as he often did when confronted with startling information, taking time to think. Cautiously he asked, "All aboard? Who? How many?"

The press secretary answered. "It was the base closure committee flight. Secretary Jefferson and the whole…"

"Deputy Secretary Wright?" the Attorney General interjected.

"Yes," the press secretary agreed. "Everyone. No chance of survivors."

"Terrible, tragic," the President muttered.

"Indeed," the press secretary replied. "And a time to be very presidential, sir. I recommend you call off the trip to Atlanta. Can't be giving a speech to a bunch of lawyers at a time like this."

"And we need some time, Mr. President," the Air Force general added, "to evaluate the situation at Andrews, investigate the cause. It's best if you not fly out of there today."

"Of course," the President said more firmly. "I'll need to make a statement, visit wives and relatives, extend my condolences."

"Absolutely," the press secretary eagerly agreed. "Very presidential."

The President turned to the Attorney General. "The work of government must go on, even in tragic times like this. You go ahead to Atlanta, Tracy. Assure the Trial Lawyers I still love 'em. I'm sure the Air Force can arrange transportation flying out of National or Dulles this morning."

"Of course, Mr. President," the Attorney General replied.

"Among other things," the President said to no one in particular, "I've got to find another Secretary of Defense. Might not be so easy. It's beginning to look like my selections are snake bit."

The drive seemed to take an eternity. Daniel first tried to drive south toward Virginia, but that was in the direction of the crash site and traffic was completely gridlocked. After a half hour, he pulled an illegal U-turn, headed in the opposite direction through the Maryland suburbs, finally finding the Beltway. He took the Beltway the long way, through the northern suburbs, then connected with the George Washington Parkway and approached Rosslyn from the north.

She held on to him all the way up in the elevator and the walk down the hall. When she got to her door, she fumbled for her key, pushed it into the lock, then jumped back when she realized the door was slightly ajar. She pushed it in. This time there was no attempt at concealment. Everything in her apartment was ransacked. Cushions and magazines were scattered all about, the two bookshelves tossed over, the books lying on the floor. Her eyes darted to the dinette table. "My laptop! The notes!" She rushed over and inspected the table and the floor around it. "All gone."

Once again, they waited for the Arlington County Sheriff's Department to respond to the 911 call. Once again, Deputy Sheriff Carl Callahan arrived at the door to Samantha's apartment. The deputy surveyed the shambles as he raised his right hand to his cheek and gently tweaked the ends of his handlebar mustache. "Got quite a mess here, lady," he summarized. He kicked a few magazines with his foot, then reached around to his back pocket and pulled out his report book. He started to write, then stopped and looked over at Samantha. "Say, you're that new lady over at the Defense Department. Seen your picture on the front page of the paper the other day."

"That's right," Samantha replied without enthusiasm.

"Trouble seems to follow you around," Callahan reported. "Bad plane crash today too. All over the news. Defense Department big shots. Plane went right down into the river. Lucky you weren't on it."

"Yes," Samantha whispered.

Callahan shook his head again and started to write in his notebook. He stopped, walked over to the table, bent down, and stared at the surface. He took out a handkerchief from his back pocket and reached over for the telephone. He gently picked up the hand instrument and examined it.

"Not sure," the deputy explained, "but it don't look like the same guy as before. This guy was in a hurry, or didn't give a damn. Maybe..." his voice trailed off. He put the notebook back in his pocket and pulled out the two-way radio fastened to his belt. "This here's Callahan. Over."

"Copy, Callahan."

"How ya doing, sweetie? I need some prints here at the Rosslyn burglary. Is Sheila on duty?"

"Copy, Callahan. Affirmative."

"Well, send her on along, will ya?"

"Copy. Affirmative. ETA one-half hour"

"Thank ya"

"You're going for prints this time? When a laptop is stolen that's a big enough case?" Daniel asked sarcastically.

"Not a matter of what's gotten stolen," Callahan replied. "It's just that this one doesn't look like a pro. Trashing the place and all. Sloppy job. Might get lucky."

Samantha turned to Daniel. "Sloppy? Or didn't care because they didn't think I was coming back?"

"Us," Daniel corrected her. "Somebody didn't expect *us* to be coming back."

Samantha was about to agree when the telephone rang. She was not surprised that it was the White House operator, but she was worried that she was not surprised.

At 6:30 that night, it seemed like midnight. Samantha was so weary she felt disconnected from her surroundings. What had struck her with awe a few days before, now had no effect on her at all. She had to make a special effort just to focus on what the President of the United States was saying.

"I cannot let an accident, as terrible as the tragedy is, stand in the way of moving this country forward. And if there is a meaning in it all—the fact you were spared—a miracle really—it must be that you were meant to still serve, and I'm going to see to it that you do." President Prescott pushed his rocking chair back, concentrating on her, seeking that special one-on-one connection he always sought with people. He didn't see the reaction in her and he didn't feel it.

"Samantha," he warmly smiled the smile that always worked. "Of course it's quick, but it makes perfect sense. You'll be my Acting Secretary of Defense, until I bring in one of the old respected war horses to calm everybody down. Give 'em a year, then I can move you into the top slot permanently."

Samantha thought about the challenge, about the public service, about the risks—deadly, real and immediate. "I'm not sure I can...that I want to take on that kind of responsibility," she said.

"Samantha, think—think about it. A few hours ago you were ready to take on the responsibility. Nothing has changed, except some piece of machinery went haywire."

"Killing a lot of people."

"People who were dedicated to changing things here in Washington—smart, committed people. People like you. Now, more than ever, I need the best people to come forward and serve. I need you, Samantha."

Samantha reached for her cup of tea and took a sip. She thought about Jeff Jefferson, and the vision of the airplane jolting over and crashing down to earth. Then she thought about whoever it was who had broken into her apartment. She realized she was scared, but that realization gave way to a stronger feeling, an uncontrollable reaction. She was very angry. She looked up into the waiting eyes of the President. "I'll do the best I can," she finally said. "On one condition."

"Name it," he replied.

"I want to be in charge of the investigation into the crash."

"The crash? Samantha, the military will investigate—the NTSB pros are already on site advising."

"I understand. I'm sure they know what they're doing. But I would be the Acting Secretary of Defense. It was an Air Force plane that went down. I want the investigation to report to me. I want to know what made that plane go down."

"We all want to know that," the President assured her. "So we'll do it your way. The investigation reports to you, and you report to me."

"Agreed."

"On one condition of my own."

"And that is?"

"You keep your eye on your basic job—find me billions of dollars of savings out of the Pentagon. I need the money."

"I'll do my best," she answered quietly.

———— ∞∞ ————

At 7:15, as the Acting Secretary of Defense was about to get into the back seat of her official black Lincoln Town Car, the Attorney General's limousine pulled up to the White House. She did not have an appointment, but a call to an old friend now serving as the appointment secretary to the President had given her the information she needed. The President had a brief window in his schedule between the hurriedly called meeting with Samantha Wright and his first private dinner in the family quarters with only the First Lady. It should be enough time, but Goodrich knew that if she needed more than ten minutes, she would have it. The always behind schedule President made no exception even for his wife.

She waited for the Marine guard to open the door, then gracefully got out. She instantly recognized the woman getting into the car in front. She did not want to delay, but she hurried over to the car and reached for the other woman's arm. "Samantha, it is truly wonderful to see you. You are…we are all so fortunate that you missed that plane."

Samantha straightened up and turned to face the Attorney General. "Thank you, ah…"

"Please, call me Tracy. Now that we'll be serving in the President's cabinet together, it's time we got on a first name basis."

Samantha looked at her quizzically. "How did you…?"

"Honestly, Samantha, you know the ropes around here. News spreads like wildfire. And even if it's just Acting Secretary for now, I'm sure in due course it will all work out. We must get to know one another better," she spit out the words in rapid succession, "but I've got to run. Talk with you in the next day or so."

Tracy Goodrich walked into the Oval Office at 7:18 and went directly to the desk once used by President Kennedy. President Prescott glanced up, failed to offer his usual smile, then returned to his intense reading of the document before him. The Attorney General demanded his attention, "Michael!"

He held up his hand to signal her to wait, then ran his finger across each line in the last paragraph of his reading material. When he was done, he reached for a pen and inked his initials in the bottom right hand corner of the document. Then he looked up. "Seems the Iranians are flooding the Balkans with weapons of every type. My predecessor knew about it during the campaign, chose to ignore it, and conceal it. Either he just wanted to keep things quiet until after the election, or he knew I was going to beat him and decided to leave me with the mess."

"The polling was accurate, Michael, but if you didn't know your four point lead in the polls would hold up through the first Tuesday in November, I doubt he did."

The President smiled, and motioned her to sit down in a captain's chair across the desk. "Fortunately, the women's vote held firm at fifty-six percent for me–more than offset that last minute slide with the southern and mid-western men. And lo' and behold, just a few days into my administration and I'm handed an opportunity to really solidify that base–make yet another bold breakthrough for women's rights".

"So you've gone and named her Acting Secretary of Defense."

"Damn right. The opportunity presented itself, and I grabbed it. Best of all worlds. First I name Mullen—had to, no choice, pay back time, and it calmed the military-industrial complex boys. Then he goes and gets himself killed. So I nominate a black congressman—score big with that crowd. Same result—eerie, but shit happens. Now I get to put another woman at the top of a place where there's never been one before. Quite a combination for my cabinet–you at Justice, our Ms. Wright at Defense."

"But only 'Acting', correct?" the Attorney General insisted.

"Technically, yes. But it will still make the point with women voters. Then I slide one of the old standbys into the position a little while—somebody the Senate will take on a voice vote—but I make her his top deputy, give her some seasoning, get her in the public eye, work on the old geezers in the Senate to prep them for her, and then give her the job in plenty of time for the reelection. And playing the cards I've been dealt the right way, she slides through Senate confirmation, not all battered and bruised like someone I know."

"That I was battered and bruised by the 'old geezers' as you call them is not the worst thing," Goodrich replied. "For my purposes, I rather like the image of a woman battered by the old men's club."

The President shook his head. "Agreed. But don't over do it. I glanced at your speech to the Trial Lawyers. Touched on being a victim. Remember, this town may give sympathy to victims, and make them feel better by throwing money at them. But it doesn't respect them. And if I'm going to pull off this one-two punch for women's rights, and, ah, women's votes, before the reelection—with Ms. Wright at the top of the Pentagon and you as our first female Chief Justice—then you're going to have to earn their respect, or they're going to have to fear you. Both would be the best."

"They will," she replied confidently. "But we will also have to keep Samantha Wright under control."

The President shrugged. "I've done my part. I've brought her into the fold. She's got every reason now to play our game by our rules, and no reason to bring up embarrassments from the past, like our friends Mullen and Wittlefield and Harry Howard."

"Unfortunately, I've learned she might have some reason, some personal crusade…"

"Stop it!" the President ordered. "I don't want to hear it. I told you. I've done my part. She's a politician like everybody else in this goddamn town, and I've brought her into our political family. Like I said to you before, just be sure everything else is under control."

"I've taken the appropriate measures. I've…"

"Good. Now I'm going to dinner."

"You and the missus. What a pretty domestic picture."

The President started to ask how the hell the Attorney General knew that, then realized that would show weakness. Of course she knew. It was her job to know everything.

———— ∞ ————

When the Attorney General returned to her restored eighteenth century Georgetown townhouse, she hurried up the stairs to her third floor master bedroom suite. She closed and locked the door, and went to the desk. She pulled out the thick manila envelope, opened it and reached in for the contents. She took the stack of papers over to her king size bed, kicked off her shoes and wearily plunged into the huge stuffed pillows. Within moments she was engrossed in the draft manuscript. She read until her body cried out for sleep, but her racing thoughts kept her awake and alert.

Most of what she read, she had heard before in her briefing from Samantha. She broke into a cold sweat as she got to the part of the manuscript revealing that a young woman in Bobby Kennedy's Justice Department had provided the information to her lover Lyndon Johnson, which when leaked had led to the motive for the assassination. The Attorney General of the United States convinced herself that if the brilliant Samantha Wright had not yet figured out the identity of that woman, she could, soon, just by tapping into the Washington gossip that resurrected during her confirmation hearings. She then carefully read pages of the manuscript she had only glanced at before. Under the title "Family Ties," she read about Samantha's mother, and her heart felt like it would explode out of her chest. She understood what the President did not. A place in his cabinet would not keep Samantha Wright from telling her story. Nothing would stop her. Tracy Goodrich's calculating legal mind focused on one simple fact—it would have been much better if Samantha Wright had just gone down with the airplane.

She thought about that for a few minutes, then picked up the phone and again called her former client. Secure in the thought that there could be no phone taps without the knowledge and approval of the Attorney General, she spoke freely. The advice she received seemed logical. "You need insurance—insurance that she keeps her mouth shut?"

"That sums it up," the highest law enforcement official in the country confirmed.

"You gotta hit 'er where she's weakest, where she's exposed."

Within a few desperate minutes, as the Attorney General thought only about how much she had to lose if Samantha Wright's story got out, she set up her plan to prevent it. It was extremely risky, but Tracy Goodrich was convinced she had no choice.

The two men sat in the shadows a few feet from the spotlights flooding intense light on the grand frontage of the Custis Lee mansion. They looked down at the row upon row of simple grave while crosses cutting across the nation's most famous cemetery. The taller of the men took a last long drag from his cigarette, then pitched the stub out into the black night sky. He leaned his head back, closed his eyes, then slowly rolled his head from shoulder to shoulder. He repeated the motion several times until he could feel the tense muscles in his neck relaxing. He opened his eyes and stared at the familiar lights of Washington, scanning the skyline until his focus narrowed to the missile-sized obelisk guarding over the Washington Mall. "No matter what we do, it's never enough," he said quietly.

"Perseverance, diligence—it's all part of our duty," his companion replied. "Got to now that we're the last two."

"I know," the tall man sighed. "I'm getting too old for this crap."

"Bullshit! The job on the plane was first class all the way. That nigger never knew what hit him."

"Thanks. But a correction is in order."

"A correction?"

"He had a good ten seconds to kiss his ass goodbye and wish he had never taken the job."

"Face facts. We know what this broad is all about—cut from the same cloth as that traitor D'Angelo. She's dangerous—we can't afford to give her much time."

The tall man let out a course, raspy cough, then leaned over and spit into the grass. He wiped his mouth with the back of his hand, then heaved a heavy sigh. "You're right," he concluded.

CHAPTER TWENTY-ONE

The voice was muffled by a handkerchief placed over the telephone, an amateurish but effective disguise.

As he listened in his cubicle on the third floor of the offices of the *Post*, Daniel could determine only that the anonymous caller was a man, probably young. He guessed the age not from the caller's vocal resonance, but from the fact he addressed him as "Sir." Daniel decided to press him for verification. "You're saying you're positive unauthorized personnel had access to the plane the night before the crash?"

"Yes, I know they could have had access."

"You don't know if they did anything?"

"Don't know. Only that they could have."

"You work security at Andrews?"

"No comment," the anonymous caller replied.

"How many people you talking about?"

"Two."

"How did you find out?"

The caller avoided the question. "Look, you're the *Post* reporter covering the crash investigation. Who knows what they'll find? The way that plane crashed in the shallow river, it splintered into a million pieces. All I'm telling you is that there was a breech of security—someone had opportunity, Sir."

"Has the military investigation come up with the explanation for the breech?"

"No. The brass doesn't know."

"Doesn't know?"

"It's CYA time, Sir."

"Cover your ass?"

"Yes, Sir."

"Why are you telling me?"

"It isn't right, Sir. We're in charge of the President's planes—the President!"

Although the sound of the voice was muffled, Daniel detected a genuine respect, a real concern in the caller's voice. The reporter's response to tips was often based on instinct. It was the only way to prioritize, to avoid wasted efforts chasing dead ends. The dead ends could never be completely avoided, but too many wasted efforts led to too few by-line stories. The caller sounded legitimate, and if he was, and Daniel could get what he needed, the story would be huge. "Where do I start?" Daniel asked.

"That's not for me to say." Daniel heard a noise in the background. Another voice. The caller came back on. "That's all, Sir."

The phone went dead.

———— ✸✸✸ ————

The shiny white exterior of the van blended well with the glistening white snow blanketing the grounds surrounding the institution. Two men stepped out of the vehicle. One reached back in to grab a slim briefcase, then they marched together up the wooden stairs of the converted old house. In a few minutes they were ushered into the office of the executive director. One of the men opened the case and presented the documents. In unison, the men reached into the breast pockets of their uniform coats and retrieved brown leather wallets, held up their identification cards, and smiled.

The woman glanced at the identification, then carefully read the letter and release form she had been given. "Everything seems to be in order," she commented, "except I would have expected some notice—a call from Ms. Wright."

"She's been quite busy," one of the men responded readily. "It's all happened so fast. And when security is involved, we must move just as fast."

"Oh, I'm sure—I understand. Well, let me show you to Mrs. Wright's room. It won't take but a few minutes to pack her personal items." The woman stood up and started for the door. She stopped, thinking, then turned to face the two uniformed men. "I hate to bring this up," she said, "but there is a balance owing on the account. You see, the last check Ms. Wright sent us, well, you see, it was returned by her bank. Some oversight, I'm sure. She's been so busy..."

"How much?" one of the men asked coldly.

"Three thousand eight hundred dollars. And that did not include the last increase, for January and February. Brings the total to four thousand, two hundred."

The man again reached into the case and pulled out an envelope. "Cash is acceptable?" he asked. Before the nurse could reply he pulled a stack of one hundred dollar bills from the envelope and began counting them out onto the top of the desk. When he reached forty-two he returned the rest to the envelope, then handed the money to the woman.

"Ah, yes, well, thank you," the woman replied. "This way," she pointed out the door and down the corridor.

"Just a moment," one of the men responded. "How 'bout a receipt?"

"Oh, yes, of course."

Fifteen minutes later Samantha Wright's mother was rolled down the front wheelchair ramp to the waiting ambulance. The old woman glanced back at the building that had been her home for the last three years. Softly, gently, she asked, "Where? Where am I going?"

"To see your daughter," the nurse replied. "In Washington."

"Oh, that's nice," Mrs. Wright replied. "My daughter?" The old lady pulled on the sleeve of the nurse's coat. "You...you tell me. What is my daughter's name?"

While the men opened the back of the van and pulled on the lever to lower the wheelchair lift, the nurse patted Mrs. Wright's shoulder and replied kindly, "It's Samantha, Mrs. Wright. Your daughter's name is Samantha."

"Good," Mrs. Wright replied. "I like that name."

As Mrs. Wright was transported into the back of the ambulance, she repeated to herself, "Samantha... Samantha... Samantha."

―――― ∞∞∞ ――――

Samantha listened intently to the joint briefing from the Air Force colonel and the Vice Chairman of the National Transportation Safety Board as they detailed the basis for their respective theories on the cause of the crash. It had been difficult to sit quietly for the forty-five minutes, but she had respected their request for an uninterrupted presentation, to be followed by a question and answer period. When the colonel finally invited questions and comments, Samantha jumped in ahead of the many different uniformed high-ranking officers from the various branches of the military at the briefing. "Colonel, Vice Chairman, you've presented two distinct theories—the violent wind shear, weather related hypothesis, or the rudder assembly failure. Let's come back to the issue of why this military version of the 707 did not follow the NTSB's written directive identifying the original 707 rudder assembly as defective and calling for immediate replacement..."

"As I stated," the Colonel interrupted, "the budget for this fiscal year did not provide the funds for a fleet-wide retrofitting–the replacement was scheduled for next year."

"The budget as requested by the Pentagon," Samantha shot back, "the same budget that requested ten billion for MachCopt. The funds for the rudder assembly replacements—three hundred and twenty million. Correct? Those funds weren't cut on Capitol Hill. The Pentagon never asked for them, correct?"

The Colonel looked around the room, then allowed himself a slight smile. "That's correct, Madam Secretary. Some of us in this room argued hard for the immediate retrofitting. We fly in those planes, after all. But the then Secretary was adamant. He wanted to allocate the funds to modern weapons procurement, principally MachCopt."

"Thank you," Samantha responded curtly. "Just wanted to be clear on that. Now my question is, these two theories, are they mutually exclusive? Is it possible both could have contributed to the crash?"

The Vice Chairman of the NTSB answered quickly. "Absolutely. Compound, or even multiple failures, converging at the wrong time—very possible. Weather exacerbating a mechanical weakness."

Samantha was about to continue the interrogation when the door to the conference room opened and an Air Force corporal came in and approached her, holding a folded piece of paper. He leaned over and placed the paper in front of her, then quickly took a step back and came to attention, waiting for further instructions. Reluctantly, Samantha allowed the intrusion to break her train of thought. She reached down, picked up the paper, and read the note. She glanced at her watch and calculated that the briefing was clearly going to run well into a second hour. "Gentlemen, let's take a short break. Reconvene in ten minutes."

She got up, turned to the Air Force man, and ordered, "Bring him to my office, please."

She was rapidly perusing the dozens of messages that had accumulated in the last hour when the crisp knock on the door announced her visitor. A moment later she offered coffee to Arlington County Deputy Sheriff Carl Callahan.

"Mighty nice of you, Ms. Wright, but I know you're a busy lady these days. I'll get to the point of my, ah, visit."

"Thank you," she replied, "and thanks for going to all the trouble to personally come to the Pentagon. I hope they didn't keep you waiting too long."

"No sweat, ma'am. They were reluctant at first to take me seriously. Tried to reach you by phone—no return call."

"I've been in meetings," she explained.

"Oh, I understand," Callahan replied. "So I thought maybe showing up in my uniform would help. They take to uniforms around here. I persuaded a couple of the Marine guards that they didn't want to take a chance on making a wrong decision for the new Secretary of Defense—that they outta at least get the message that I needed to see ya passed up the chain of command."

"Acting Secretary," Samantha corrected him.

"Well, whatever, Ms. Wright. It seems you're the one in charge of this place for the time being, any ways."

"Yes, so what can I do for you?"

"It's really a question of what you can do for yourself. I've done hit a roadblock that I cain't get around, that's for sure."

"A roadblock?"

"Yep. Strange one. Never seen this one before. We got a solid make on one of the fingerprints we took at your apartment. Off the telephone. Perfect index finger."

"Great," Samantha assumed. "And it's not mine, or Daniel's."

"Nope."

"Then who?"

"Cain't say."

"I don't understand."

"We cain't get the identity. Ya see, the computer came back and said the print was a match to a print on file. But the file is classified."

"Classified?"

"Didn't know about this myself. Never seen this problem before. But it don't matter, cuz you're in a position to fix it anyway."

"Me?"

"Seems the identity of this guy got his print on your phone, well, he works for you, or at least worked for the Pentagon sometime."

"Classified by the military?" she asked.

"We know we got a match, we just cain't find out who it is. Somewhere in this here biggest office building in the world," Deputy Callahan said, glancing around the room, "you've got the classified information as to who goes with a fingerprint ID'd as A4379421."

"That's it? I've got to find a classified military fingerprint with that identification number."

"That's right," Callahan replied. "Only I'd be real careful, Ms. Wright. If'n I was a betting man, I'd bet you right now that whoever broke into your apartment and has a fingerprint classified by the military, well, that person might jus' know his way around this place."

"I see what you mean," the Acting Secretary agreed.

After thanking the deputy and directing a waiting Air Force corporal to accompany him to the exit out to the parking lot, Samantha walked behind her desk, sat down, then spun her chair around and stared out the window. It was another gray Washington winter late afternoon. The snow of a few days before had mostly melted, leaving only a few dirty mounds here and there on the vast black top parking lot that spread away from the building toward the edge of the Potomac. "A4379431," she repeated to herself. "Who are you? How do I find you without you finding out I'm looking for you?"

She answered her own questions. "Good old Buddy," she said out loud. He'd found George Willard. She was sure he could find A4379431. She had to find where Buddy's office was in the vast labyrinth called the Pentagon, and do so without anybody knowing why the Acting Secretary of Defense needed to talk to the only person in the building she really trusted.

Daniel had anticipated that the direct approach would get him nowhere, and he was right. "You don't really expect me to comment on our security measures, do you, Mr. Garcia?" the Air Force Lt. Colonel asked.

"Look," Daniel replied, closing up his notebook and tucking his pencil behind his ear, signaling to the officer that he was not going to take down their conversation. "Andrews sees hundreds of VIPs coming and going every year…"

"Thousands," the officer corrected him.

"Right. Access to Andrews means access to the most important people, the most security conscious people on the planet. Our readers need to know these top government officials and foreign dignitaries, and the President himself are safe here."

"They're very safe," the Lt. Colonel replied confidently. "One airplane crash, for whatever reason—mechanical failure, bad weather—doesn't change that, doesn't mean you question everything we do."

"I didn't say it did," Daniel quickly replied. "It's just background. While we wait for more developments from the crash investigation, my editors want a page two story on the base itself."

"Like to help you out," he said without conviction, "but you can consider the security operations here the same as the Secret Service. They don't comment on how they protect the President. We don't comment on how we protect this air base. No sense letting the bad guys know what they're up against if they try to take us on."

"I look at it the other way," Daniel explained. "A little publicity on how the security can't be compromised might just keep the bad guys from trying."

"Could be right," he agreed, "could be wrong. Not for me to make that call. I can end this right here, Mr. Garcia. I'm sticking with my 'no comment' unless I get an order from on high to do otherwise."

Daniel smiled. He assumed an order from the Acting Secretary of Defense would be sufficient.

Samantha found herself over and over again retracing the circle she had drawn on the yellow legal pad, until the pen was tearing through the first page. As the briefing dragged on, she realized that all the talk added up to simply more conjecture and theory. The annihilation of the plane left so few meaningful remnants that a mechanical failure might never be proven. The plane's damaged black box flight recorders provided technical data of marginal value, and the voice recorder only memorialized the last desperate cries of "Mayday" from the pilot followed by the co-pilot's plea of "Oh God! No!" The analysis of the radar patterns at the time of the crash indicated the probable conditions for a wind shear, but failed to confirm an actual wind shear. It all added up to a big fat zero.

Samantha glanced away from the legal pad and checked the time. She wondered if there was any reason for Buddy to be working late that night. She did not want to miss him. She abruptly stood up and interrupted an Air Force colonel in the middle of an answer to a question regarding the metal fatigue calculation records of the KC-135. "Gentlemen, thank you very much. I have to move along to my next appointment. We'll re-convene as soon as developments warrant."

Everyone in the room stood up and watched as the Acting Secretary of Defense walked out, followed by a Navy ensign. As she returned to the reception room outside her office, the naval officer observed, "It's 1750. I don't see any more appointments on the schedule."

"I have an important call to make," she replied and entered her office, and closed the door behind her. She hurried to the computer on her desk and pulled up the directory to Pentagon personnel. She went to the Bureau of Personnel, and found Buddy's number. She entered the number and waited.

At the third ring, a voice answered, "BUPERS, Sergeant Bluhorn here."

"Buddy, it's great to hear a friendly voice."

"Samantha?" He paused, then let out a slight cough. "Excuse me, I mean Madam Secretary. That's right, isn't it?"

"Not for you, Buddy. It's still Samantha. How are you?"

"Doin' fine, just whiling my time away here in purgatory."

"Buddy, I'm sorry. I'm sorry there was nothing we…ah, Senator D'Angelo could do."

"Samantha, we've been over that. There's nothing to be sorry about. You kept me from being canned, short of retirement pay time. That was accomplishing a lot what with all the heavy-weights around here out to get rid of me after I testified before the committee."

"You're too sharp to be exiled to a do-nothing job. We've got to get together to discuss that soon—make some changes."

"Thanks for the thought. I'm sure the brass that sent me into exile are sweating now that you're here. But you've got a thousand things more important on your agenda than rearranging a sergeant's career at this point. I've got six months and seven days 'till the big day. Besides, this billet hasn't been all bad. I've done a hell of a job bringing this personnel operation into the computer age, if I say so myself."

"We'll see about all this soon, Buddy. But it's the personnel business I need to talk about right now."

"Shoot."

"I need the identity of someone in the military, from a fingerprint—a fingerprint that the police say is a match, but the identity of the person is classified."

"Police? What's all this about, Samantha?"

Samantha let out a audible sigh. "It's a long story. It's a print found in my apartment. I'll explain later. But right now, I need the identity of the person from a classified number."

"What's the number?"

"A4379431."

"Hm. That's an old one. When was this print made?"

"It's current—the last week or so. What do you mean the number's an old one?"

"A single letter followed by seven digits. Probably thirty, forty years old. Numbers for the last twenty years have been nine digits."

"Why would it be classified?"

"Top people doing top secret work get their identification markers classified. For fingerprints, it would mean someone in operations where a fingerprint might reveal an identity that someone in this great government of ours decided shouldn't be revealed."

"Can you find this one for me, Buddy?"

"Before serving my penance here, it would have taken weeks of manual searching. Now, with what I've done with personnel cross reference software, I should be able to get back to you shortly."

"How long is shortly?"

"Can you wait fifteen minutes?"

"I'll be in my office. The private line is…"

"I know the private line, Madam Secretary. I entered it into your file the day you became an employee of the Department of Defense."

No sooner had Samantha hung up than a knock on her door was followed by the Navy ensign entering and handing her a printout listing telephone messages. She glanced down the list of requests for appointments, invitations for speeches, and congressional callers. Her eyes stopped at the message from Daniel, annotated with the word "Urgent." He had called five minutes before. She excused the officer and picked up the phone.

Daniel quickly described the anonymous call tipping him off to the unauthorized access to the airplane and the cover up, then asked her to meet him for dinner to discuss how she could clear the way for his investigation of what happened at Andrews the night before the flight. "Daniel, I don't know. I'm the head of the official investigation. This is vital information—I can't just let you…."

"Dammit, Sam. We were supposed to be on that plane! And your official investigation is already compromised. They…. somebody, somebodies are covering their asses. That means that even if your official experts are playing straight with you… and that's a big if, they don't have the right info. You've got to let me work this behind the scenes. If you alert the troops and they go charging in, we're never gonna find out who did what."

Samantha fixed her gaze on the Washington skyline across the river, thinking. "I'll get back to you in a few minutes," she finally replied. "After I've got some important information of my own I'm waiting on."

"What's that?" he asked.

"The identity of whoever broke into my apartment and retrieved the listening device."

"That's huge. How are you…"

"Later," she interrupted. She punched out of the call and picked up on the incoming call on her direct line.

Buddy was a man of his word. "I've found your man," he said triumphantly.

"Who is it?" she demanded.

"It's strange. You better come see me, Samantha."

She did not hesitate. "Where?"

"Where you'd expect BUPERS. In Siberia, as far from your office as you can go in this puzzle palace. It's quite a hike—down four floor flights of stairs. No elevators, your know."

I'm game."

"Then go out your office, go right along the E-ring to Corridor 4, stairwell 16. Take the stairs down to the bottom. I'll meet you there."

"Give me five minutes to play ditch 'em with my entourage—send the Army, Navy, Air Force and Marines off on some errand so I can sneak away unescorted."

"Given who your fingerprint man is, I'd say that's a good idea."

The dodge worked as Samantha dispatched each one of the four military aides on separate assignments to retrieve weapon systems procurement reports from each of the military services. When the junior officers had hurried off on their assignments, Samantha matter-of-factly advised her secretary that she would be back in a minute and slipped out into the wide hallway corridor.

As she came down the stairway, Buddy was waiting. No one else was in sight. He saluted, but she brushed that aside and gave him a long, powerful hug. "It's so good to see you," she said.

"Congratulations," he replied with genuine enthusiasm.

"At the moment, condolences might be more in order." She tried to make it sound lighthearted, but failed. "At least I'm going to be able to do something about your career."

"Later," he interrupted. "Come with me."

She followed him down the corridor, entered an office, then went through the office to another large poorly lit room. He led her past several floor-to-ceiling open shelves jammed with files to an old wooden desk tucked away in a far corner. A computer terminal sat on top of the cluttered desk.

"As I told you on the phone, if I hadn't set up the system for computerizing old personnel records, it would have taken forever to find this, but..." he said, pointing to the screen on the computer, "there's your fingerprint man."

Samantha moved closer to the desk and stared at the screen. Staring back was an image of an old style military identification card. Samantha read the name, then repeated it aloud, "Sergeant Gerald Kanesellers."

"That's your man," Buddy confirmed.

"Weird."

Buddy pointed at the screen. "His record ended abruptly in 1964. A mission—in Vietnam. This sergeant and a Corporal Ray Sawyer didn't return from the mission. According to this, no trace of them was ever found—MIAs. Can't figure out how a MIA from Vietnam turns up in your apartment."

It was at that moment when Samantha remembered the first and only time that she had heard the names—Sergeant Kanesellers and Corporal Sawyer. Wittlefield and Howard, in the hangar, talking—no bragging—about the assassination. The two shooters in Dallas who never came back from Vietnam! Samantha instantly realized that nothing had changed since the Mach-Copt hangar. She was still in the deadly grip of the men who had killed John F. Kennedy.

Buddy looked away from the computer screen and back at Samantha.

He saw her stunned expression, and trembling hands. "Samantha! Are you all right?"

Samantha started to say something, but nothing came out. She tried again. "Are you sure, Buddy? The print is definitely Sergeant Kanesellers'."

"I'm no detective, Samantha, but I've always heard there are no two fingerprints alike. The fingerprint identification number you gave me is this guy and no one else."

"But..."

"But what?"

"This Kanesellers, and other guy, Sawyer...they both were supposedly MIAs in Vietnam. Your records... what I was told... he, he, must have come back."

"Not according to the official records. Officially, they went to Vietnam and officially they didn't come back."

"Officially? What are you saying, Buddy?"

"Only what I told you. I've been working on computerizing the old personnel records—making them accessible, being sure they're accurate. I've found they're not always accurate. You take this time period, end of Vietnam, prisoners of war coming home, big push to declare victory and get the hell out. Not the best conditions for 100 percent accuracy, particularly when it came to accounting for missing persons."

"So somehow Kanesellers, and maybe Sawyer, came back, and the Pentagon records don't show it?"

"It's possible. But there is another way to check this out."

"How?"

"The Vietnam Veterans Memorial."

"The wall?"

"Yes. It was created by and for the vets. They relied on Pentagon records for sure, but they wanted to be absolutely certain that everyone who served in that war and died over there or remained missing, was memorialized on the wall. Tell you the truth, I don't think there was any love lost between many of those vets and the Pentagon. The vets compiled their own records, their own evidence—debriefed prisoners, took testimony, tried to reassemble circumstances of MIAs. Checked and double-checked. If you went to Vietnam and didn't come back, your name is on the veterans' wall. If the vets determined you made it back, you're not on the wall."

"I'm going to the wall," she declared.

CHAPTER TWENTY-TWO

The U.S. Attorney General believed that the timing was critical for her plan to prevent the disclosure of the ruinous information. Samantha Wright was a loose canon that could go off at any minute. She had to act immediately, and so she had to take the chance of receiving communications at her Justice Department office. As long as the conversation was camouflaged, it would be safe. The call came at 6:05.

"The package is safely in storage."

"Excellent," Goodrich responded. She placed the phone back in its cradle and again contemplated the next move. The direct approach was risky. Samantha Wright was smart. The cover story would have to be a good one. But it would come from a position of the highest credibility. In Tracy Goodrich's thinking, it would seem perfectly logical that the country's top law enforcement official would be the one to break the tragic news—that Samantha's mother had been kidnapped and was being held hostage.

In the dimly lit basement of a run down farm house thirty miles outside of Syracuse, New York, Mrs. Mary Anne Wright sat motionless in a wheelchair, staring blankly at the television. When one of the two men guarding her brought a tray with a bowl of chicken noodle soup and a glass of milk and attached it to the front of the wheelchair, Mrs. Wright showed no sign of recognition.

The guard shrugged and asked, "Not hungry?"

Mrs. Wright did not respond.

The guard looked at his watch. It was twenty minutes until the start of the heavyweight title fight. He was not about to let the old woman interfere with his enjoyment of the fight. He grabbed the spoon and filled it with soup, and held it to her lips. "Come on, Grandma, it's time to eat."

As he held the spoonful of liquid up to her mouth, he noticed the old woman was absolutely motionless. He lifted the spoon to her nostrils. The liquid did not move. Slowly he moved his hand to her eyes and closed her eyelids. Then he called to his cohort upstairs and together they called their boss to receive instructions for the handling of the deceased hostage.

Samantha raced back to her office and made her way through the junior officers assembled in the reception area, each holding the information she had sent them to retrieve. She put them off, announcing that important business had come up that she had to attend to immediately. Her secretary agreed. "Yes, Ms. Wright. The Attorney General's office called. She needs to see you right away. I checked your calendar. It was open, so I confirmed she could meet with you this evening."

"The Attorney General?' Samantha exclaimed. "What does she want?"

"Her secretary didn't say—only that it was urgent, and she had to meet with you in person. She should be here in fifteen minutes."

Samantha glanced at her watch, then entered her office and slammed the door behind her. She called Daniel to meet her at the Vietnam Veterans Memorial. She said she would not use her official car—she'd come by cab and would be there in twenty minutes.

She was about to leave when her secretary signaled over the intercom that she had a personal call. Samantha picked up the phone and was surprised to hear the executive director of her mother's nursing home. She started to explain that it was not a good time to discuss her mother's care when the woman calling from White Plains interrupted. "It's not about your mother's care. We of course understand your decision to move your mother."

"Move my mother? What are you talking about?" Samantha demanded.

"Down to Washington—the orderlies, the military ambulance. It's just that when we packed up your mother's things we forgot about the strongbox in the safe, with your mother's valuables. I have it right..."

"What the hell are you talking about?" Samantha yelled, but in that instant the fear that had swelled up in her during her meeting with Buddy turned to pure terror. She slammed the phone down and ran out of her office.

———— ∞ ————

It was easy to spot Samantha as she flailed her hands in the air pleading for a taxi. When the cab driver drove up, he showed no sign of recognizing his passenger, but the two men in the black Lincoln Town Car parked at the Potomac end of the parking lot easily spotted the Acting Secretary of Defense trying to flee the Pentagon. Gerald Kanesellers, formerly a sergeant in the United States Army, pressed on the gas and maneuvered the Lincoln into position to follow the cab. As the Lincoln pulled close, the other man in the car, former Army corporal Ray Sawyer, let out a "heads up" and pointed to an official government limousine that had just pulled up to the curb in front of the north portico, ten yards behind the cab. The bright lights of the parking lot clearly illuminated the passenger of the limousine as the woman got out, started for the entrance to the building, then stopped, and turned in the direction of the cab. The woman waved at the departing cab, then ran back to the limousine. In a moment the limousine followed the cab.

Kansellers turned to Sawyer. "Looks like the Attorney General is trying to meet with Ms. Wright."

"Means Colonel Howard was right. Wright has got to be stopped."

Kanesellers pressed the accelerator to the floor and in less than a minute the Lincoln was behind the limousine and the cab, heading north on the George Washington Parkway to the Arlington Memorial Bridge.

The taxi had not come to a complete stop when Samantha opened the back door and leaped out at the corner of Constitution Avenue and Twenty-third Street. She glanced around to get her bearings, then spied the dull gray granite and gravel walkway leading down into the ravine where the memorial wall rested. As she ran, she searched for Daniel.

Daniel circled twice around the Lincoln Memorial in the GTO, hoping against hope for a rare open parking space. Samantha had sounded desperate when she called. He did not have time to waste. He concluded that Washington's parking monitors would find some excuse to stay inside on a cold January night, so he slipped the GTO into a space reserved for tour buses. In a moment he was running toward the northeast across the brown winter grass of West Potomac Park.

Tracy Goodrich assessed the situation from her limousine as it made an illegal U-turn in the middle of Twenty-third Street and came to a screeching halt against the curb. First she saw Samantha Wright run down the walkway leading to the memorial wall. Two minutes later she observed the *Post* reporter running along the grass toward the same destination, but from the direction of the Lincoln Memorial. She instantly concluded that they were meeting at this predetermined rendezvous site to discuss Samantha's story. If she didn't act, the story could appear in tomorrow's headlines.

The Attorney General got out of the back seat of the limousine and ordered her driver and two man F.B.I. security team to remain with the car. When they objected, she shouted, "Goddammit, I'm not the President. I can meet an old friend without you guys hovering around like nursemaids. Stay put!"

Samantha quickly found the volunteer Vietnam veteran who was safeguarding the master list of all names indelibly blasted into the one hundred and forty polished black granite panels that connect to form the "V" of the memorial wall. The long-haired, bearded veteran was the only other person she could see at the wall on this cold January evening, save for an old man at the far end of one of the panels, kneeling, eyes closed, his hand gently resting on a precious name.

Samantha examined the book with the list and realized that it provided vital cross-reference information on all of the names, organized into categories to make it easier to locate individuals on specific panels. She quizzed the volunteer veteran about the completeness of the records. "It's all here," he assured her. "Everyone who served, everyone who didn't come back."

Samantha checked the master list for Sergeant Kansellers and found no one by that name. She checked under Sawyer. There were a handful—no Rays or Raymonds. She found an "R. Sawyer." The cross-reference showed a year of service in 1971. She concluded that it had to be a different Sawyer. Remembering the confessions in the MachCopt hangar, she checked the lists for 1963 and 1964. The names were not there. In her mind she had just eliminated the chance that there had been a mistake about the identity of Kanesellers' fingerprint.

Daniel came up to her, breathing heavily. When he asked why they were meeting at the memorial, she quickly summarized the visit from Deputy Callahan followed by the meeting with Buddy and the confirmation provided by the veterans' records. At least one of the men who had shot President Kennedy and who was later supposedly lost in Vietnam, was definitely not a MIA, and had recently broken into her apartment.

Daniel was about to start asking questions when Tracy Goodrich ran down the path, rushed up to Samantha and interrupted. "Samantha, I've got to see you—in private. It's about your mother."

"My mother!" Samantha exclaimed. "What do you know about my mother?"

The Attorney General grabbed Samantha's arm and firmly pulled her close, forcing Samantha to within whispering range. Tracy Goodrich leaned in, cupped her hand over Samantha's ear, and pleaded, "It's urgent and extremely confidential. Your mother's life depends on your reaction."

Kanesellers grabbed the steel case from the back seat and led Sawyer through the darkening winter night to the high point on the grassy mound overlooking the memorial. He dropped down to his knees next to an ancient oak tree, opened the case, and quickly retrieved the metal barrel and stock. He expertly fitted the pieces of the classic Plainfield M-1 Carbine together, then fell forward on to his stomach. In this prone position, he inserted a magazine into the side chamber of the gun, then looked up. "Hand me the night scope."

Sawyer fumbled in the gun case, then cursed, "Shit. I've only got the daylight."

"It'll have to do," Kanesellers replied and held out his right hand to take the scope. In two smooth motions, he attached the scope, then swung the rifle stock into position nestled against his right shoulder. He eased down into a comfortable fully prostrate position while lifting the scope to his eye. He surveyed the terrain and analyzed the situation. Keeping his eye fixed on the view through the telescopic scope, Kaneseller reported his findings to Sawyer. "The two broads are talking, and the *Post*

reporter is standing by. This is the last chance to shut her up."
He moved his finger from the outside of the trigger guard to
inside the metal protector, felt the trigger, and slowly, methodically pulled on the trigger as he squinted through the scope.

———∞———

The first shot from the M-1 exploded into the night. The
F.B.I. agents who constituted the security detail for the Attorney
General of the United States instantly recognized the sound of
the high-powered rifle and knew that it had been fired from a
position near their limousine. The driver sprang out of the car,
crouched, and retrieved his Webley Mark IV .32 Smith & Wes-
son from its holster and aimed in the direction of the gunfire.
The other two officers quickly opened the concealed compartment in the floor of the limousine and retrieved an Uzi Submachine Gun 9mm Parabellum and a M-16 5.56 assault rifle. A
moment later they joined the other officer on the outside of the
armor-plated limousine.

Samantha felt the warm liquid splattering into her eyes, momentarily blinding her. She rubbed her hand across her face, and
looked down. Drenched in blood, she screamed. Her focus fixed
on Tracy Goodrich's body crumpled on the walkway at her feet.
Then she felt it. A powerful force, attacking her, knocking her off
her feet, and propelling her backward.

Daniel reacted instantaneously. As he saw the back of the
Attorney General's head explode, he sprang at Samantha, forcing her to the ground.

———∞———

"Shit! Goddammit!"

"What?" Corporal Sawyer demanded.

"I am rusty. The goddamn broad got in the way—I shot the
wrong one," Kansellers answered, then again squinted into the
scope, searching for his target. He saw her, on the path, at first

motionless, crouched low against the wall, and then he saw the two of them move. He aimed again.

Daniel pushed and lifted Samantha, willing her to move. Somehow she got a foothold in the loose gravel bordering the walkway, and pushed off. They were moving, falling, when the second shot hit.

The hardened Bangalore granite dedicated to the memory of those who had valiantly served and died in America's most unpopular war cracked. A jagged chunk of stone shot off the wall along with the ricocheting bullet. The stone caught Daniel on the left side of his head, tearing a deep bloody trench from behind his ear forward to within a millimeter of his left eye. At the same second, the bullet penetrated his right thigh, hit bone, then tore through ligament and sinew before stopping in fatty tissue. Daniel screamed and collapsed.

Samantha grabbed the collar of Daniel's coat and pulled, desperately trying to move him and dodge the incoming shots. She had dragged him a body length when the deafening sound of massive, repetitive gunfire erupted.

The first volley of shots passed barely overhead, but Corporal Sawyer made the mistake of slightly lifting up from his crouched position as he turned to see the location of the incoming fire. The top of Sawyer's head was effectively blown off by a dozen bullets from the Uzi submachine gun. Kanesellers saw his co-conspirator blasted backward into the thick trunk of the oak tree.

Kanesellers glanced down the hill, hunkered down low to the ground and flipped over and over, rolling down, seeking any chance for cover. At the bottom, he smashed hard into the wall and lost his grip on the M-1. The rifle spun wildly around and slid away across the walkway.

Samantha's first instinct was to shield the injured Daniel from the out-of-control rifle spinning and crashing toward them. Then she saw the body ten yards away move, and realized the gunman was struggling to get up. She released her grip on Daniel and leaped for the gun. Her hand grasped the muzzle. She felt the presence of the man. She looked up. He was on his feet and staggering toward her. She turned the gun around and placed her hand securely on the wooden breech, then reached underneath with her other hand. She tried lifting the rifle as she got to her feet, but stumbled back under the weight. She dropped a hand to the granite, pushed up, and made it up. She sensed him getting nearer and lifted, pointing the M-1 at Sergeant Gerald Kanesellers.

"Put that down," Kanesellers demanded as he took a deep breath, "before somebody gets hurt."

"You're Kanesellers!" Samantha shouted as she brought the barrel of the gun up to aim squarely at his chest.

"Guilty," he replied coldly as he took a step toward her.

"Don't move," she ordered.

"Everybody stop right where they are!" Samantha heard the man's voice followed by the sound of running footsteps. "Nobody move, nobody breathe. You are surrounded by F.B.I."

"I'm Samantha Wright," Samantha yelled. "Acting Secretary of Defense. Do not shoot him. He's the only link we have…"

The senior agent in charge of the security detail glanced past Samantha to the motionless body of Tracy Goodrich lying face down in a growing pool of blood. "Oh Jesus," he cried. "Oh Jesus. The A.G.'s down!"

A strange smile crossed Kanesellers' face. "It's over—it's finally over," he said calmly. He reached up into the night sky with his left hand and slowly slipped his right hand behind his jacket. His right arm was in motion forward when one of the F.B.I. agents shouted, "he's going for it!"

As the right hand cleared his jacket, a brief controlled onslaught of bullets tore into Kanesellers' chest and back. He collapsed to the ground. In the final throes of death, his right hand released a white handkerchief.

Samantha stared at the horrific, bloody scene, until one of the F.B.I agents approached and firmly took the rifle from her.

She looked into his eyes. "I told you not to shoot. We needed him—we needed him alive."

The agent shook his head. "We had no choice," he murmured, "if we were going to have only one dead cabinet officer tonight, not two."

EPILOGUE

Samantha lingered at the grave site until the morning's falling snow covered the fresh topsoil. Somehow she felt she could leave her mother at peace once she was lying under nature's comforting blanket of white.

The stop by the nursing home was more painful than she had imagined it would be. That the staff she had entrusted with her mother's final days had released her into the cruel hands of strangers was something she could not understand or forgive. When she learned the executive director had made sure that an invoice was paid in cash before releasing her mother, her anger was beyond words.

She took the metal shoe box-sized container from the executive director and placed it into her overnight bag. All of the entreaties of the woman to open the box in her presence so that there could be no question later that something was missing fell on Samantha's deaf ears. She simply wanted to leave, and she did.

It was not until she was sitting alone in a row of seats on the United Shuttle and the airplane was waiting in line at JFK for takeoff clearance did Samantha open the box. On top was a plain white envelope, and inside a single sheet of stationery. As the jet became airborne, Samantha read her mother's elegant flowing handwriting:

> *My Dearest Samantha,*
>
> *When the time is right, I want you to have these simple things I have always cherished, and know that I love you very much.*
>
> *With all my love,*
> *Mother*
>
> *November 22, 1963*

Samantha's eyes filled with tears. She reached into her purse for a tissue. The soft pack that had been new that morning was now almost empty. She dabbed at her eyes and inspected the remaining contents of the box. There were a dozen photographs, tied together with a simple piece of brown twine. She untied the knot and let the string fall away.

Samantha quickly looked through the photos, realizing she had never seen them before. Then she went back and examined each one closely. There was her mother, when she was young and beautiful, with a skinny, youthful John F. Kennedy. She turned over the first of the photos, and then another. On the back of each one, in her mother's handwriting, was a date and a place. As she turned them over, she saw that they were in chronological order, starting with one dated November 2, 1952. Her mother and five other young women were standing arm-in-arm, laughing, with a smiling John Kennedy in front of a Boston red brick row house, a wide banner heralding "Kennedy for Senate" strung across the front of the house.

When she reached the last photo Samantha immediately noticed something distinguishing it from the others. In this one her mother and Kennedy were sitting alone, on a white wicker couch on the veranda of a white clapboard building. She turned the photo over and discovered that it was taken at Charleston, West Virginia, May 10, 1960.

Samantha started to replace the photographs when she noticed another envelope in the bottom corner of the box. This one was tiny and white, just large enough to hold the simple standard size business card inside. The printing on the card stated simply:

Senator John F. Kennedy
Washington, D.C.

Samantha cradled the card in the palm of her hand for several minutes, until her thoughts were interrupted. The plane was on its final approach. Samantha glanced out the window and down at the capital in the distance. She looked back at the box on her lap and started to replace the card when she turned the card over, and in handwriting she did not recognize read:

For Mary Anne,
My thanks for making me a winner in
West Virginia,
                    Love, Jack

Samantha stared at the note. She thought about what was in the box, and what was not—no mention of her father—nothing from him, nothing about him. Everything her mother had left her was about John F. Kennedy.

—◦◦◦—

Samantha did not want to go, but she found it impossible to say no. The taxi dropped her at the west gate on Pennsylvania Avenue, and she entered the West Wing of the White House at 3:30. She waited for twenty minutes until the President's personal secretary escorted her into the private study adjacent to the kitchen and the Oval Office. As she entered the room the President came to her. She reached out to shake hands, but as he had done before, he grabbed both of her hands and smothered them in the grasp of his own large warm hands.

"This whole affair is so tragic, so unbelievable." His voice was a model of sincerity. He moved one arm to around her waist and guided her to the nearby couch. They sat down together and he turned to her. "It's a miracle you weren't harmed," he said. His eyes moistened as he placed a hand on her knee. "At least you were spared, for a reason I am certain—and that reason, Samantha, must be that you are meant to continue to serve your country."

She felt a chill engulf her whole body. She started to speak, but the words would not come out.

He studied her reaction and was distressed to see no sign that he was connecting. "My enemies are already clamoring for an independent special counsel. Can you imagine what a disaster that would be for the country—for my programs that can get this country moving forward again? Just because some people I knew…"

Samantha's eyes flashed a warning.

He saw it and read the meaning. His years of studying people and their reaction to him told him not to pursue that angle. He changed his argument. "We can't allow the bastards who killed President Kennedy to kill my presidency too. We can't, Samantha!"

Samantha reached down and firmly took his hand off her knee, and pushed him away. She stood up and looked down. "Your presidency will have to get along without me," she said coldly. "I will be staying in Washington for the time being, in case whoever investigates needs me."

"But Samantha, don't you see…"

"Yes, I see clearly," she cut him off. "I see who your friends, your biggest supporters, your closest advisors, have been. Goodbye." She could not bring herself to call him "Mr. President."

She rejected the personal secretary's offer of an official driver. She walked out of the White House grounds and grabbed a taxi two blocks away in front of the Willard Hotel. It was close to 4:30 in the afternoon. She knew she should go see Daniel in the hospital, but she had called and confirmed that his status had been upgraded to good. He would be released in a few days. She would go to him in the morning after some rest.

As the taxi headed west along Constitution Avenue toward the Theodore Roosevelt Bridge and her Rosslyn apartment beyond, Samantha looked up ahead into the fading winter sunlight. As they passed the site of the Vietnam Veterans Memorial she felt something stirring inside, a force compelling her to change course. She called to the driver to turn left at the next street. Soon they passed the Lincoln Memorial and drove onto the Arlington Memorial Bridge. When she saw the sign, she pointed to the right and up the hill.

The guard at the Visitors' Center scowled down at his watch, then told her she only had a few minutes to closing. As the cold darkness descended over the cemetery, she hurried up the winding path, toward the eternal flame that would forever burn brightly on the hallowed hill of Arlington. She kneeled before the grave and did something she had not done in a long time. As she thought about her mother, and a father she had never known, Samantha Wright silently prayed.

She stayed until a gentle tap on her shoulder told her it was time to go. She rose slowly, turned around, and walked down the few steps to the granite amphitheater, then turned left, seeking the way out. Then she felt it again—a force guiding her thoughts, directing her vision, focusing her eyes on the far left panel, and words spoken in the Inaugural Address so many years before, but now carved in the stone for all time to come:

LET THE WORD GO FORTH
FROM THIS TIME AND PLACE
TO FRIEND AND FOE ALIKE
THAT THE TORCH HAS BEEN PASSED
TO A NEW GENERATION OF AMERICANS

CPSIA information can be obtained at www.ICGtesting.com
Printed in the USA
LVOW111249200412

278410LV00002B/7/P